DEATH BY BLUEPRINT

Terry Ambrose

BOOKS BY TERRY AMBROSE

Seaside Cove Bed & Breakfast Mysteries

A Treasure to Die For
Clues in the Sand
The Killer Christmas Sweater Club
Secrets of the Treasure King
Treasure Most Deadly
Lies, Spies, and the Baker's Surprise
Dead Men Need No Reservations
The Secret Ingredient to Murder

McKenna Mysteries

Photo Finish
Kauai Temptations
Big Island Blues
Mystery of the Lei Palaoa
Honolulu Hottie
North Shore Nanny
A Damsel for Santa
Maui Magic
The Scent of Waikiki
Mystery of the Eight Islands

License to Lie Series

License to Lie
Con Game
The Scent of Waikiki

Anthologies with Stories

Paradise, Passion, Murder: 10 Tales of Mystery from Hawai'i
Happy Homicides 3: Summertime Crimes
Happy Homicides 4: Fall into Crime
Happy Homicides 5: The Purr-fect Crime

DEATH BY BLUEPRINT

A Seaside Cove
Bed & Breakfast Mystery
Book 9

Terry Ambrose

COPYRIGHT

DEATH BY BLUEPRINT

ISBN: 979-8-9900457-2-9

This book is a work of fiction. Names, characters, places, and incidents are either products of the author's imagination or are used fictitiously. Any resemblance to actual events, locals, business, or persons, living or dead, is entirely coincidental.

Cover design by Dar Albert

ABOUT THE AUTHOR

Once upon a time, in a life he'd rather forget, Terry Ambrose tracked down deadbeats for a living. He also hired big guys with tow trucks to steal cars—but only when negotiations failed. Those years of chasing deadbeats taught him many valuable life lessons such as—always keep your car in the garage.

These days, Terry channels his knack for unraveling problems into storytelling. He's the award-winning author of over two dozen books, including "Con Game", which snagged the 2014 San Diego Book Award for Best Action-Thriller. Readers love his *Beachtown Detective Agency* mysteries, *License to Lie* thrillers, *Seaside Cove Bed & Breakfast* mysteries, and the tropical adventures of the *Trouble in Paradise McKenna* mysteries.

When not writing, Terry is probably plotting new mischief or reliving his repo days—in fiction, of course. Visit terryambrose.com to step into the world of a reformed repo man turned ace storyteller! Or something like that.

1

Alex

11 Nov

Hey Journal,

I'm really starting to hate cranky old Walt Copley. He's a total jerk, and I've gotta vent about him or I'm gonna explode. Ever since Mom dropped the bomb that she wanted a home with some private space, it's been the biggest topic at the dinner table, right? And once we got the plans and Mom and Dad showed me where my room is gonna be (so much bigger than the little one I have here in the B&B!), I was hooked. I've been going over there almost every day. If it wasn't for Grumpy Walt, everything would all totally awesome news.

Robbie and Sasha say I've been obsessed with watching them build the house. It's awesome watching piles of wood and stuff turn into a whole actual home! How cool is that? Anyway, I was hanging out near the edge of the site, just watching the guys work and minding my own business when I heard one of them complaining about "corners being cut." At first, I thought he was talking about the boards. (Which are all kind of a mess 'cause these guys leave everything laying around! Yikes!) But then Big Boss Tommy showed up and literally said, "If you don't like doing things the way I tell you to, pack up your tools and leave."

And that's when the Grump showed up. He's gotta have the award for meanest old man in all of Seaside Cove. If he's not the winner, he totally deserves honorable mention. What makes everything worse is that he's the town's building inspector AND the head of the historical preservation society. Can you believe that, Journal? Anyway, he started stomping around, looking like someone stole his cane (or maybe his joy?). He was walking through the house with some guy who was driving a Greer Construction truck and talking about "tons of money."

Tons of money? For what? If they're talking about ripping us off or ruining the house, they're gonna regret it because I. Will. Find. Out.

I've never seen a Greer Construction truck in town before. I'm gonna ask Mom and Dad if they hired him to do something. And what was he doing with Grumpy Walt?

We might have to have the Grump do all the inspections, but there's no way he's gonna push us around. I went up to him and asked him what he was doing here at our house if he didn't have an inspection, and he just gave me his grouchy old-man look and told me to mind my own business. Um, hello, this is my business. My name's going to be on that freaking mailbox. Well, not my full name, but like my last name. Not his!

Seriously, Journal, what is it with adults and "mind your own business"? Like, maybe if they weren't so sketchy, I wouldn't have to Sherlock Holmes my way into these things. For sure, something's up, and I'm totally keeping an eye on Grumpy Walt and Greer and will find out what they're up to. They can try to blow me off all they want, but I'm not giving up.

Alright, that's probably enough drama for one day. I'm pretty sure even you're rolling your eyes at me by now. But come on, it's hard not to get concerned when it's your house and your family. You know me, Journal, I'm like Nancy Drew, but with better hair.

xoxo,

Alex

2

Rick

RICK ATWOOD OPENED THE DINING room of the Seaside Cove B&B for breakfast at 6:00 AM. As had become the norm over the course of their stay, William and Edith Aldridge were waiting patiently outside the velvet ropes next to the sign with the dining room's hours and the day's specials. The two were quite the pair—lively, incredibly sharp, and friendly. Other than their gray hair and a few lines on their faces, Rick would never have guessed them to be in their seventies.

"Good morning, Mr. and Mrs. Aldridge," Rick said as he adjusted the baby carrier on his chest. At the sight of the couple, his little boy began happily flailing his arms. "It appears Baby Jack would also like to say hi."

Edith was the first to break into a warm smile. She shifted her sudoku puzzle book and a novel to her left hand and took Baby Jack's little fingers in hers for a baby-style handshake. "Good morning, Little Man. Are you happy to see Auntie Edith this morning?"

"Your son has more uncles and aunties than any kid I know," William said with a smile. But then, about two seconds later, he joined his wife in greeting Baby Jack and referring to himself as the little boy's uncle.

Rick beamed at Baby Jack. Over the past couple of weeks, the little guy had become, in many ways, a true charmer with the guests. This morning Rick had decided to try carrying him on his chest while working the breakfast service. It allowed him to spend a little more time with his son and, if he were being truthful, allowed him to demonstrate that he was a 'cool dad.'

"Let's get you two seated." Rick gently loosened Baby Jack's grip on William's fingers and grabbed two menus.

"Do you think we could get our usual table?" William looked past Rick at one of the window tables that looked out on the rose garden. Sun streamed into the room, making the spot feel cozy and warm.

"Well, would you look at that? It just happens to be open, and we have ordered a little extra sun for you this morning."

Edith, apparently unable to resist, gave Baby Jack's hand a final tug. "The early bird gets the worm, remember that, Little Man." At the table, she sat and took the menu Rick handed her.

"You know, Mrs. Aldridge, I was once a journalist. As such, I have a great deal of respect for librarians. How long ago did you retire?"

"I'm actually still involved. I now run the volunteer program at our local library. Thank goodness for the volunteers, otherwise nothing would happen."

William snorted and looked at his wife. "Edith is being modest, Rick. She's been a driving force in that library for nearly fifty years.

That's even longer than I taught math to uninterested teenagers. Now, your daughter, it seems like you've raised her right."

"Thank you, but she's not a big fan of math. She does have other interests, though."

Rick stopped and turned when he caught a movement from the corner of his eye. It was Norm Butterfield. Rick excused himself and went to meet the man that Marquetta said had arrived at the B&B with a travel alarm clock and pre-planned daily itineraries. In fact, each day Norm appeared for breakfast at exactly 6:07 AM—not a minute sooner and not one later. The B&B had a laid-back vibe, but Norm, as he liked to be called, was not averse to critiquing the efficiency of the inn, something that did not always sit well with Marquetta.

"Good morning, Norm," Rick said cheerfully. "Ready for breakfast?"

Norm flicked his wrist, tapped the face of his watch, and barked, "Have to keep to the schedule, Rick."

In his mind, Rick silently parroted what he expected to be Norm's next words, "Places to go. Things to see." It had been the same response since the day of his arrival. But this time, Norm didn't say those words. Instead, he gaped at Rick and his passenger.

"What's that?"

"You mean the baby? That's my son. Norm, meet Baby Jack. Uh oh. My apologies, Norm. I think we have a Code Brown situation going on here."

Norm didn't crack a smile. Rick, on the other hand, felt like he was fifty shades of red. He stammered, "Um, this is truly a case of inappropriate timing. Let me get you seated so I can…" Rick made a face and blew out a breath. "Oh, Jack. Really? Ex…excuse me. I'll be right back."

Bursting through the butler door, Rick lifted Baby Jack from the chest carrier. Marquetta covered her mouth with her hand in a weak attempt to hide her snickers. Lydia, who was standing next to Marquetta, widened her eyes and smiled, but she then made a zipping motion across her lips.

Marquetta put down the spatula she'd been holding and made a face. "I told you that was a bad idea, Rick."

As Marquetta took Baby Jack from Rick, he hung his head. "I called it a Code Brown situation in front of Norm Butterfield."

"Oh. I'll bet Mr. Efficiency was taking notes."

Lydia's eyes widened further, and she repeated the zipping motion even though she looked like she was about to burst out laughing..

"Alright, buddy, you win. You can stay with your mom. I have guests to deal with."

Marquetta kissed Rick on the cheek and went to their makeshift changing table. "Did you teach daddy a lesson, Sweetheart?" She laid the baby on the table. While she began changing Baby Jack, she laughed over her shoulder. "You might be a land baron, Mr. Atwood, but even you need two hands to change a baby. And babies do their thing whenever they feel like it."

"Give the poor guy a break, Marquetta. He's trying."

"Thanks, Lydia." It wasn't like Rick didn't know how to change a diaper—he done it more times than he could count. In fact, he and Marquetta shared parenting duties, just like they did the B&B duties. But Marquetta was right. There was no way he could wait tables with a baby on his chest—oh, no. He'd rushed off and left Norm standing there alone. With that man's desire for schedule adherence, who knows what his response might be.

"I've got to go take care of Norm Butterfield. Baby Jack…"

Marquetta laughed and shooed Rick away with one hand. "Go. I've got this."

"Oh, my," Lydia said. "Looks like this one might take you a few minutes, Marquetta. I'll keep prepping while you take care of Jack." Lydia went to the center island and the assortment of onions, bell peppers of various colors, and garlic. She sniffled as she cut into one of the onions. "I don't know who's getting the better end of this deal. Maybe I should have volunteered to change the baby."

Spinning on his heel, Rick rushed through the butler door and went straight to the dining room. To his surprise, rather than a scowl from Norm Butterfield, Rick got a broad smile and a wave. Norm sat at one of the tables for two with a steaming mug of coffee on the table in front of him; Alex stood at his side, waiting patiently. Rick felt a flush of satisfaction as he eavesdropped on Alex's conversation with Norm.

"That's right, Mr. Butterfield. When I was little, my dad would let me sit on his knee late at night while he worked. He won several big journalism awards."

Norm stroked his chin and pursed his lips. "And now he's running this B&B. That's quite a change."

"He inherited the B&B and thought this would be a better place for me to grow up than in New York." Alex snuck in a quick thumbs-up when Norm wasn't looking, then she acted like she was sharing a big secret and cupped her fingers around one side of her mouth. She lowered her voice only slightly. "My dad's pretty cool, but he's no match for Baby Jack. My little brother has psychic powers and totally knows the worst possible time to make a mess."

After slapping the table lightly, Norm nodded. "You're right, Alex. I'll cut your dad some slack. He does have a lot on his plate."

"Thanks, Mr. Butterfield. You're awesome. I gotta run. School today." Alex returned the coffee pot to the burner on the coffee bar and smirked as she walked by. She whispered playfully, "You're welcome."

Rick caught her eye as she was backing through the butler door. He mouthed a silent, "Thank you," then turned back to the next set of guests who had shown up. After seating them, he doubled back to the Aldridges' table to take their order and, hopefully, get his morning back on track.

At 6:45, the Aldridges were still lingering over the last of their breakfasts, but Norm Butterfield looked ready to go. He stood, laid down his napkin, and chuckled as he passed Rick. "Another good meal, Innkeeper. Time to go. I've got things to do."

And with that, he was off. The man ate with what could only be called military precision. While many of the other guests were still enjoying chatting or just getting ready to order, Norm Butterfield was off like a storm. He'd been at the B&B for three days, and Rick still didn't know how he spent his time because each time Rick asked, he said something equivalent to 'seeing the sights'.

Across the dining room, Lydia delivered an order to a newlywed couple who were staying for two nights before they headed north to San Francisco. As usual, Lydia was splitting her time between the dining room and helping Marquetta in the kitchen. Every time Rick tried to recall how they'd gotten along before hiring her, he couldn't. All he could do was hope they never lost her. When Lydia looked at him after taking another order, he hoisted the regular and decaf coffee pots and said he had the dining room under control.

"Just refills. That's all."

"Great. I'll go help Marquetta. If you need me, give me a holler."

Rick flashed her a thumbs-up and began making his rounds. When he got to the Aldridges' table, they again complimented him on the food.

"Edith and I have been talking, and we've decided we'd love to permanently take up residence here."

It wasn't the first time Rick had heard the compliment, so he gave William his standard reply. "Sorry, but if you do, I'm going to have to put you to work."

William laughed while Edith rolled her eyes."Don't listen to him, Rick. On a math teacher's and a librarian's pensions, we would never be able to afford it. And I'm perfectly happy to be a bookworm."

"As usual, my wife is correct. Neither of us have any desire to hold down a job again. But I do have a question for you. What's going on next door?"

"We're actually building a house on the lot. I inherited this place from my grandfather along with the B&B. At the time, I never thought about the adjoining land. The town's historical preservationist always insisted everything up to the lighthouse was owned by the town. It wasn't until I had our attorney research how we could buy the land that we did a title search. To our surprise, we discovered the B&B actually sits on ten acres of land." Rick chuckled. "That's why Marquetta has started calling me a land baron. We own the largest tract of land in Seaside Cove."

"You never knew?"

"Nope. I always took the town's historical preservationist at his word. If you ask me, I think he just didn't want us to know how much land we owned. To be honest, when I inherited this place, learning to run a bed-and-breakfast filled my plate to overflowing. The problem is now we're getting hit with delays, and it's costing us a lot more than we ever expected."

Rick's phone signaled an incoming call. He took a look at the display, saw it was his attorney, and his stomach plummeted. Why would Jordan Lane be calling him this early in the morning? More bad news? Answering as he hurried out of the dining room, he tried to sound positive. "Hey, Jordan. It's pretty early for you to be calling me, isn't it?"

"Yes, it is. But it's important, Rick. Can you be here at nine?"

"What's this about?"

"I can't say quite yet, but I think you should be here at nine. On the dot."

On the dot? Appointments with Jordan had always be of the 'ish' variety. "Can you be more specific? Why the big rush?"

"I'm sorry, but I don't have anything concrete yet. And, even if I did, I wouldn't be at liberty to say. Whatever you do, don't be late. Okay?"

"Sure. I'll be there."

Rick returned the phone to its holder, took a deep breath, and tried to look upbeat as he returned to his guests despite a sense of impending doom. Why did he feel like the meeting with Jordan was a signal that the axe was going to fall? Among the questions swirling around in his thoughts—what axe, who was wielding it, and why?

3

Rick

RICK STOOD ON THE SIDEWALK in front of Jordan Lane's office, an old Victorian painted teal with white and gray trim. The house was one of the jewels in this upscale neighborhood. The immaculate green lawn stretched to the sidewalk, a lush carpet of perfection punctuated only by a narrow stone walkway leading to a short flight of steps. The edges of the steps had been worn smooth by time and countless footsteps. They rose to a grand entrance framed by intricate woodwork, the kind of craftsmanship that whispered of a bygone era. The whole scene felt almost too pristine to touch.

The faint scent of freshly cut grass lingered in the air while a soft breeze overhead rustled the leaves of a giant old oak and the dappled shadows it cast across the lawn and the front porch. This old house, like so many others in Seaside Cove, seemed almost timeless. In fact, the entire town felt like a relic of history, untouched by the chaos of the modern world. He hoped their new home would blend into the town's persona, but then shook off the thought. Jordan wouldn't have called him unless he'd encountered a problem. It was the question that had dogged Rick all morning. What could that problem possibly be? And how bad was it?

Inside the office, Jordan's assistant, Beth Lee, looked up from her desk as Rick entered. "Morning, Rick. He'll be with you in just a few minutes. He's with Mayor Carter right now."

"I didn't know Francine was one of Jordan's clients."

Beth winced. "Oops. Maybe I shouldn't have said anything. But she should be done any minute."

As if on cue, the elegant oak door to Jordan's office opened a crack, and the mayor's voice drifted out into the reception area. "Honestly, Jordan, I never saw this coming."

The door slipped shut, and Rick heard muffled voices coming from inside. The words were impossible to make out, but Francine's distress was obvious. Less than a minute later, the door opened and Francine stepped into the lobby.

She stood as if frozen, her white-knuckle grip on the doorknob revealing some deep emotion that could have been anger or fear. Her dark hair framed her soft features, which were normally accentuated by a kind, welcoming smile. But this morning, the makeup under her left eye was smudged, and her smile had faded into quiet despair. Her navy blazer gaped slightly, as if she had yanked it on in haste, and the blouse underneath, though silk, bore several wrinkles and the remnants of a coffee stain or something far less mundane.

"Rick? What are you doing here?" Francine's voice cracked with uncharacteristic emotion. She took a hesitant step back, her heel scuffing against the wooden floor as if she might trip.

"Judging by the look on your face, I don't know if I should answer that, Francine. And given everything that Walt Copley has been putting us through lately, I'd like to know what's going on with my house. Why are you letting Copley cause us trouble now that we're halfway through the project?"

Francine swallowed hard and eyed the doorway as if she were considering making an escape. But, instead of running, she said, "Rick, there are things you don't understand. You're going to have to trust me." She hesitated, her hands twisting at her sides, the weight of her words visibly pressing on her shoulders.

"Francine, whenever someone tells me I have to trust them, I get worried. What's happening with my house?"

"There are… discrepancies. But I'm handling them. That's why I came to see Jordan. It's complicated, Rick. Far more complicated than you realize." Francine paused, taking a step closer, her voice softening. "Honestly, the best thing you can do is let me take care of it. I have resources, connections—I know how these things work." She gave a small, strained smile. "Think of me as a buffer, Rick. I'm protecting you from…unnecessary stress."

"Stress, Francine? Stress is having the mayor avoid answering my questions. If you want me to be more relaxed, try being straight with me."

Francine's eyes darted around the room, betraying her nervousness. "Look, I know this isn't what you want to hear, but trust me when I say this is for your own good. Some things are best left undisturbed. Digging into this—it could open a Pandora's Box you don't want to deal with." She reached out and placed a hand on Rick's arm, a pleading look in her eyes. "Please, Rick. Let it go. Let me handle it. You have to trust that I'm doing what's best for you."

"Francine, that's the third time you said I have to trust you. In my experience, when someone is that insistent, it usually means they're doing something behind your back."

Her voice, low and uncertain, was the most tentative Rick had ever heard. "There are discrepancies in the paperwork for your building project. They don't add up. Let me get to the bottom of it."

Rick's jaw tightened, his knuckles whitening. "Everything was fine a week ago. What kinds of 'discrepancies' are we talking about?"

"The Planning Committee has issued a stop-work order. I'm so sorry, Rick. Work has to stop by the end of today."

"Today? Are you kidding me?"

"I don't—we really shouldn't be having this conversation. I never thought it would get to this point."

"You never thought what would get to this point?" Rick demanded.

At first, Francine didn't answer. Instead, she frowned, biting her lower lip so hard that it turned crimson beneath her peach-colored lipstick. Finally, she blurted, "This is a mess, and I don't know what to do. I'm here to see Jordan because I need his advice."

Her words spilled out in a flurry, her tone fluctuating between frustration and vulnerability. She stopped as if she'd realized her words were only making things worse. "I have to go."

Without warning, she sidestepped Rick, her movements jerky and rushed. Clutching her bag like a shield, she murmured, almost to herself, "I shouldn't have said anything. I shouldn't even be here right now." She yanked the door open, paused momentarily as though searching for the courage to turn back, and then darted out with a clipped "I'm sorry" that hung in the air, trailing behind her along with the sound of her footsteps clicking down the stairs.

Rick watched her leave, then turned and stormed into Jordan's office. "What in the world is going on, Jordan? I know you're not on the Planning Committee, but do you know why they are putting a stop-work order on my project?"

"That's why I called you. Isabelle Murdoch contacted me late last night. Close the door and have a seat. I'll explain."

Jordan, who stood a few inches shorter than Rick, had a stocky, but muscular build that belied his daily duties behind a desk. His short, full head of hair was always impeccably styled. Typically, Jordan radiated a sense of calm and control, his poised demeanor making him a reliable figure in any setting. However, this morning, he appeared visibly unsettled, his irritation betraying the composed facade that rarely wavered. Whatever had transpired behind the closed door with Francine, it had clearly irritated him, and the tension was unmistakable in the furrow of his brow and the tight set of his jaw.

"Unfortunately, Rick, there's only so much I know. I can tell you what Isabelle told me. Bear in mind that this is her interpretation of last night's events, but I'm sure there's a healthy dose of truth in this."

"Isabelle is about as honest as they get. Does she think something's not right?"

Jordan's right thumb massaged his left index finger. It was a move Rick recognized, an indication that Jordan was still on edge. "She does. When she called me, she was very angry. She made a comment about Sylvia Archer having a knack for 'double-crossing even her allies.' It seemed cryptic, almost like a warning. But if she's right, it could be a clue."

Rick frowned, his jaw tightening even further. "Sylvia Archer? What's she got to do with any of this? And who are her allies?"

"According to Isabelle, Walt Copley and Tommy Granger."

"Excuse me? Tommy Granger? My contractor?"

"Isabelle also told me that Walt, in his roles as the town's building inspector, head of the historical society, and the Planning Committee, is spearheading this effort to sink your project."

Rick blinked, his jaw tightening as he processed the information. He'd always hated the town's small-town cronyism. It felt like the inbreeding of the European Royals. "You're saying those two are working with her?"

"It would appear so." Jordan scrutinized Rick as if he were gauging his reaction. "Isabelle says she's been digging into this for some time now. It's not just speculation. She's really concerned about Walt's behavior. He's been unusually inconsistent."

Rick tilted his head, suspicion creeping into his thoughts. Did Francine's erratic behavior have something to do with this? "Were these inconsistencies the same thing Francine was talking about? And while I'm on the subject, what the devil is going on with her?"

Jordan sighed as he picked up a folder from his desk. "Sorry, I can't talk about Francine. She's protected by attorney-client privilege, just as you are. What I can tell you is that there have been a couple of building projects Walt initially opposed. He wrote formal objections, cited safety concerns, historical preservation conflicts, zoning issues, you name it. But then, suddenly, he reversed his position on every single one of them."

The dominoes quickly fell into place. Rick had covered this type of corruption several times in his career as a journalist. "Let me guess. Sylvia Archer later developed all these projects."

"According to Isabelle," Jordan said, his face darkening. He handed Rick a folder. "And according to the documentation in that folder, that's happened on at least two of them."

"And did Francine support these projects?"

"That's public record, but she did not oppose them."

Rick flipped through the contents of the folder. Isabelle had provided documents from the town's files as well as news clippings. "Jordan, I'll admit this is all pretty suspicious, but two projects don't exactly indicate a conspiracy."

"Agreed. But Isabelle thinks it's too much of a coincidence. And what you'll see in that file is how Walt's approval was key to getting those projects cleared. Read the documentation and you'll see that Sylvia couldn't have moved forward without Walt's about-face. If Isabelle's right, it stinks."

"It does," Rick said slowly, mulling over his words. Then his expression turned grim. "If Granger's part of this too, and he's been working on my property…" He didn't finish the thought, his hands curling into fists at his sides.

Jordan straightened up, his voice softening slightly but losing none of its urgency. "Rick, Isabelle's worried this runs deeper than just a couple of pet projects. If Sylvia's got influence over the head of building inspections and a contractor like Tommy, we're talking about power that extends way beyond historical preservation."

"Yeah, well, someone's going to need to explain why my contractor's buddying up to Archer," Rick scowled at the door, half expecting Tommy Granger to waltz in without an invitation. "Because starting now, I'm done giving him the benefit of the doubt."

Jordan gave Rick a hard look. "Whatever this is, it's bigger than just you or your house. If Isabelle's right, we're dealing with people who don't care about the rules. Stay sharp, alright?"

A rolling wave of anger built behind Rick's eyes, a growing pressure that made him want to lash out at Sylvia Archer and take her down. "Believe me, Jordan, I will."

4

Rick

ON HIS WAY BACK TO the B&B, Rick gripped the brown paper envelope Jordan had given him. Inside the envelope was evidence of possible corruption and, dare he think it, a conspiracy? Jordan had never admitted to orchestrating the coincidental overlap of his appointment with Francine's, but there was no question in Rick's mind—Jordan had deliberately exposed Francine's involvement. The meaning was clear—Mayor Carter knew what was going on, and Jordan wanted to make sure Rick was aware of her involvement. But what was it that she knew? And why did Jordan deliberately expose his client?

Main Street was still quiet as Rick returned to the B&B. It wasn't yet ten, so the stores, with the exception of Crusty Buns, were still closed. One thing was certain—Crusty Buns was a hotbed of town gossip. Betting that Mary O'Donnell would be willing to share what she knew when he placed his order, Rick slipped in and took his place in line.

As Mary rang up Rick's order, she eyed him suspiciously, seeming to take special note of the envelope he carried. "Are you okay, Rick? Did something happen this morning?"

Mary's Irish brogue lifted Rick's spirits, but the way she'd zeroed in on the envelope put him on guard. "I'm fine, Mary. Just have a few things on my mind." Rick smiled, shifted the envelope in his hands nonchalantly, and stepped aside for the next customer, feeling grateful that they looked like a pair of impatient tourists.

Tempted as he was to ask what Mary knew about the Planning Committee, that would be like stepping into the lion's den. He might have come in hoping to find out what Mary knew, but this was one of the central hubs for gossip in Seaside Cove. Anything he said in this store might soon be telegraphed to the other members of the town's gossip hotline. Although he wanted information, he wasn't willing to give any. At least, not yet.

After gathering his purchase, two chocolate chip, two blueberry, and two banana-pineapple-raisin muffins, Rick started toward the exit. He waved to the table occupied by locals and also spotted one couple he recognized. They were staying at the B&B for two more nights before heading further down the coast. Normally, he'd have been happy to spend a little time talking to his Seaside Cove friends or his guests, but the developments at Jordan's office were making him anxious to get home.

On the street, he shrugged down into his jacket against the mid-November morning chill. Overhead, puffy pale gray and violet clouds drifted across the blue sky. The breeze on his face felt refreshing and helped to clear his thoughts. He was glad that the house would be fully framed and roofed before winter officially set in. Seaside Cove didn't get much rain, but at least once the walls and roof were up, the workers could keep things moving even if it did rain.

He'd just passed Isabelle's Pet Shoppe, which was still dark, when his phone rang with a call from Marquetta.

"Hey, what's up?"

"There's trouble next door, Rick. A couple of the guests told me someone is over there trying to shut down everything. I stuck my head out, and it looks like Walt Copley is being even more obnoxious than usual. Lydia and I are swamped right now. Are you on your way back?"

"I'm approaching the roundabout." He paused, peered down the street, and spotted Copley. "I see him. He's waving his cane around like a madman. I'll deal with him. I've got some muffins from Crusty Buns and an envelope I don't want Walt to see. Can you meet me at the front door?"

"Does this envelope have something to do with your emergency trip to see Jordan?"

"It has everything to do with it."

"I'll meet you out front. The way I feel about Walt right now, he doesn't deserve anything from us. Especially some of Angus's muffins."

"Copley sure makes it difficult to practice the philosophy that you get more flies with honey than vinegar."

"Rick, Walt makes everything difficult. Don't even think about giving him one of those muffins."

"Hanging up now," Rick said as he approached the B&B. Marquetta met him at the front door. As he handed her the bag and the envelope, he said, "The thought of sharing any of these with Walt Copley never crossed my mind."

Rick found Copley standing in the middle of the site wearing his battered flat cap that barely covered his freckled scalp. His thin white hair puffed out on the sides, and his bushy silver mustache, which dominated his face, barely concealed the smirk beneath his perpetually furrowed brows.

Not wanting to start things off on the wrong foot, Rick resolved to greet the old grump with a smile despite the anger he felt simmering inside."Morning, Walt. What's going on?"

"I have papers to shut down this project. This project is done. The Historical Preservation Society has decided it's a blight on Seaside Cove's character."

Gritting his teeth to avoid saying something that would only inflame the situation, Rick snatched the notice from Copley's frail hand and scanned it. So, Isabelle had been right. Most irritating of all was how they'd been through the almost agonizing process of securing the necessary permits, architectural approvals, payment of fees, and more. Architecturally, the new house was a perfect complement to the hundred-year-old B&B it would stand next to.

Copley dared to call the project a blight? The real blight on Seaside Cove stood smirking right in front of him. "This is…" Rick stopped himself, took a breath, and said, "There has to be a mistake."

"No mistake, Atwood."

His fists clenched, the urge to settle this like an old-world duel flared hot, but Rick forced it down. Violence wasn't the answer—not here, not now. Still, Copley was testing the limits of his patience, and every muscle in his body screamed to act. Picking the smaller man up and physically tossing him off his property would be satisfying, but it would only feed the animosity burning in Copley's eyes. Rick needed a smarter move.

Thinking back to Jordan's caution, Rick looked for his contractor, Tommy Granger. He spotted him in the middle of the house, alternately checking the screen of his cell phone and instructing his men to start packing up their tools. Granger—how Rick wished he'd made a different choice. Knowing what he knew now, Rick wanted nothing more than to fire the man, but that would play into Copley's plans. Quite likely, it would put the entire project in peril. With a big enough delay, they might even lose the B&B.

"No," Rick snapped. "I will not accept this. This is a violation of due process." Pushing past Copley, Rick yelled, "Granger. You work for me, not him." Rick jerked his thumb over his shoulder at Copley, who stood behind him, stammering about physical abuse.

"I'm going to have you arrested for assault of a public official!"

Rick spun around and skewered Copley with a look as sharp as a carving knife. "Shut up, Copley. You are not an officer of the law. You have no formal authority to enter my private property. And, if you insist on yammering at me about your two-faced standards, I will do more than escort you off my property. Now, get out of my sight before I forget I was taught to respect my elders."

Copley's jaw moved up and down under his busy mustache. "You don't even own this property!"

"You're a lunatic, Copley. My grandfather bought this land, and I have the title to prove it."

"I have a deed that proves otherwise!"

"Then produce the proof or get out of my sight!"

Turning his back on Copley, Rick faced Tommy Granger. He was primed and ready to give him a dressing down, too, but before he could say anything, Granger, a tall and broad-shouldered bear of a man, raised both hands.

"Sorry, Mr. Atwood, but according to the documents I was handed by Mr. Copley, I need to stop work. I don't have any choice. If I don't follow the rules, I'm done in this town."

"If you leave now, you may be done on this job."

Granger had hands big enough to make a cinderblock look small, and it was obvious that years of labor had etched his skin with scars. He spread his arms, which were mottled with sunspots, wide. "That's a chance I'll have to take. I wish things were different, but this is just one job."

"And you need to appease your…" Rick stopped, thought about the word he'd been about to use, and decided not to say it. After all, 'masters' implied there was an actual conspiracy. And until he had more information, he needed to keep his mouth shut.

"Can I make a suggestion, Mr. Atwood?" Granger's bushy eyebrows framed intense eyes that looked like they could pierce through a lie in seconds. With his ruddy face and crooked nose, he appeared to be as sincere as a man could be.

"What?" Rick asked, his anger softening slightly.

"Don't trust Copley. He really believes he owns this property."

"Have you seen this supposed deed?"

"No. But I can tell you this. Walt Copley is not a man to be trifled with. He's taken a dislike to you and is going to extraordinary measures to ruin you. I can't tell you how I know that, but I do."

During his career as a journalist, Rick had seen plenty of plots and schemes to extract vengeance or retribution. And right now, his instincts were screaming at him about Tommy Granger. The man was way more than a contractor seeking work—he was an active participant in this soap opera they called a building project. "And how do you fit into Copley's little scheme, Tommy?"

Granger put one hand on Rick's shoulder and looked him in the eye. "There's nothing little about it. All I can say is, be careful. This goes all the way to the top."

The memory of Francine Carter's face during this morning's accidental meeting in Jordan's office flashed into Rick's thoughts. Was Granger implying that Francine was behind this land grab? He moved closer to Granger, fully aware of the intensity in his eyes and posture. "What do you mean?"

"I've already said more than I should. But I will say this—you've done a lot of good in this town by solving some tough crimes. That tells me you're a good investigator. Dig, Mr. Atwood. Dig. You'll find what you're looking for if you go down far enough." Granger looked around at his crew, a couple of seasoned carpenters and his young nephew, Jake. To a man, they all avoided looking at Rick as they filed by.

With his anger building again, Rick resolved to do exactly what Tommy Granger had said he should. He'd start digging this afternoon.

5

Alex

UGH. THIS DAY FEELS LIKE it's lasting forever. School is totally dragging because I want to get home and check out our new house. Yesterday, my dad told me the framing should be done this week. That's so awesome. I can't wait until I have my own room in my own house—hey, maybe then I can even have a dog! Talk about super awesome!

When the final bell rings, I tell Sasha and Robbie I'm gonna go check on the house. It sucks that they don't want to go with me, but I get it. They've gone with me almost every day since I started checking it out. Even though it's not gonna be their house, they've been cool about going with me.

I peddle my bike as fast as I can, and when I get to the roundabout, I can see the B&B with the new house going up next to it. The style matches the B&B. It's gonna look like an old Victorian even though it's new. Just like the B&B, it's gonna have two stories plus an attic. The architect said it's going to look like the B&B's little brother. He said they'll be alike, but different. That's cool 'cause Mom and Dad say me and my baby brother are alike but different. I don't know how they know that yet since he's not even a year old. But, hey, they're our parents, so maybe they see things I don't.

What's weird is that when I get closer to the house, there's nobody working. There's no sawing, no nail guns, or hammers. It's just…quiet.

Super quiet. I was gonna put my bike away first and then go next door, but I'm too curious and head straight there. I prop my bike up against one corner of the house. Like I usually do, I go in through what's gonna be the front door and into our new foyer. It's totally cool. How cool! We're gonna have our own foyer, and we don't have to share it with the guests. We'll even have a living room where we can put up a Christmas tree. Awesome!

I almost trip over a loose 2x4 that somebody left in the middle of the room. That's not cool. Once, when I talked to the foreman, Mr. Granger, he told me he was a stickler for safety. Maybe I should take a picture and send it to him? It sure doesn't look like they got much done today. What happened? My dad's so not gonna be happy about this. I wonder if he knows?

Upstairs, I go to my room. It doesn't look like they did anything in here today, either. The more I see—or, maybe I should say, don't see, the madder I get. How are they gonna finish the framing if they don't do any work? After doing a full tour of the upstairs, I head back down to the main floor. The third step from the bottom wobbles when I put my foot on it.

Bending down, I check out the front board of the step. It isn't nailed at all. That's totally unsafe! Even I know that. What's with these guys? Standing up, I put my hand on the railing. A splinter pokes into my skin, and I yank my hand back. This railing isn't finished like it's supposed to be, either. What's with these guys? Now I've got a splinter and my hand stings like the dickens.

I yank at the splinter, but it refuses to budge. I turn sideways to get better light, but before I can do anything, the board tips up and smacks my ankle. Pain shoots through my leg. I stumble and grab for the railing, but pull back because I don't want to get hurt again. I hit the ground with a thud. It kinda hurts, but not too bad. The whole thing is super embarrassing. No way I'm telling Mom and Dad about this. They'll just lecture me about how "construction sites are dangerous," like I don't already know.

This is a super big problem. I want to tell my dad about what I found, but if I tell him what actually happened, I'll be, like, banned from the site. Oh, great. Now what do I do?

* * *

12 Nov

Hey Journal,

My hand is still sore, so I'm gonna keep this short. I found some problems at the construction site today. Then, at dinner, my dad told me why nothing got done today. He says he's looking into it and is gonna get to the bottom of things. Seriously? My dad is good at what he does, but he can be super slow. He doesn't want me doing anything, but you know what? Operation Nail Down is on! If I can solve murders, this should be a piece of cake.

Uh oh. Mom just knocked. I'm gonna bet she figured out that I'm not a hundred percent. Rats.

If anybody's a better sleuth than me or my dad, it's Mom.

Gotta go!

xoxo

Alex

6

Rick

RICK SHUT THE OFFICE DOOR behind him and pressed his back against it. He let out a long, slow breath. The rhythmic crash of waves from Seaside Cove's shoreline echoed in his mind, a small reminder of the calm he desperately sought but couldn't find. He sat in the leather chair at his mahogany desk and opened the file Jordan Lane had given him. By the time he finished reading, he was convinced the file was a ticking time bomb.

On the corner of his desk, Baby Jack's rattle sat partially hidden under a printed menu draft for the B&B. On any other day, the combination of parental chaos and guest management would have been easy enough to juggle. But today wasn't like any other day. Today, his family's future felt like it was slipping through his fingers—not just the house they'd dreamed of, but the safety of everything he'd worked for since arriving in Seaside Cove.

He pressed his palms against the desk and focused on the file. The word "CONFIDENTIAL" was stamped in bold letters across the manila cover like an accusation. The file said it all. The memories of similar stories from his days as a reporter in New York echoed in his thoughts. This ran deeper than a building dispute. If Isabelle's claims were true, his family's new home construction project was awash in shady dealings and deliberate sabotage. How had he not seen it before?

Rick reread the first document in the stack—Isabelle's letter. Her elegant, looping cursive seemed almost too delicate for the weight of the accusations it carried. With each paragraph, his frown deepened. With each line, the problem only became bigger.

Isabelle hadn't pulled any punches. It all started with Tommy Granger, she wrote, a man with a knack—not for accidents, but for cutting corners and bending rules. Then Sylvia Archer and Walt Copley got involved, and what had been a troubling pattern spiraled into what Isabelle called a "perfect storm of negligence and greed."

Rick's grip on the paper tightened. The further he read, the clearer it became—this wasn't just a warning. It was a ticking time bomb, and Isabelle had handed him the fuse.

One particular passage stood out on its own. "During the town hall restoration, there were numerous complaints about faulty wiring and slipshod carpentry. While Walt approved every change order as 'compliant,' Tommy admitted privately to workers that Sylvia had insisted on rushing the timelines. At least one near fire was linked to these decisions."

He pushed back in his chair, the old leather creaking with the movement. His fingers tapped against the edge of the desk. Apparently, none of the three—Archer, Copley, or Granger—were strangers to bending the system. But Isabelle's words painted a starker picture. Sylvia wasn't just the town's ambitious developer; she was ruthless enough to gamble with safety, and Walt seemed all too willing to play enabler.

Rick scanned another memo in the file, this one detailing payments and approvals that Isabelle suspected Walt had rubber-stamped without proper inspections. He hated how easily everything clicked. His aching gut told him these weren't isolated incidents or simple mistakes. There was something bigger playing out beneath the surface of Seaside Cove, and somehow, his family had gotten caught in the middle of it. He ran a hand through his hair, frustration buzzing under his skin. How many loose ends had Jordan handed over, and how was Rick supposed to untangle them alone?

The stop-work order on his house was bad enough, but if Isabelle was right about the concerted efforts to cut corners, then Tommy's work should be checked by an independent contractor. The wiring failures, the hasty timelines, the safety compromises—how far did the problem go? Were Granger and Copley the only pawns in her little game? Did her reach extend to those he trusted?

Turning back to the file, Rick resolved to start where Isabelle had drawn her firmest line. Town hall. The faulty wiring. The rushed approvals. It all led back to Sylvia's orders and Walt's authority.

If Tommy had shared anything about that project, it might have shed light not only on Granger's work but also on why Copley had become so emboldened. And if Isabelle's theory about Walt's involvement was correct, Rick was about to find himself in a much bigger fight with Copley than he'd ever anticipated. He closed the file, drumming his fingers against its cover.

Answers wouldn't come easy, not in this town where everyone had secrets and alliances ran deep. But solving mysteries appeared to be part of the Atwood family DNA, and this one had no chance of staying buried—not if he had anything to do with it. The bigger problem was, who did he trust to help him get to the bottom of this?

7

Alex

My talk with Mom last night didn't go the way I expected. Instead of telling me I needed to stay away from the construction site, she said she understood how accidents could happen and wanted to have my dad talk to our contractor about organizing the site to make it safer.

We're in the middle of the breakfast rush right now, and Mom is busy cooking, but we're still able to talk in between her trips to the fridge, stove, and the island where she does the prep work. In between dicing onions and some red bell peppers, she stops, looks at me, and says, "Sweetie, did your dad talk to you this morning?"

"Kind of. He's acting kinda weird."

Mom stops her prep work. She looks at me, gives me a little smile, and goes back to dicing. "Weird? How so?"

"It was pretty typical at first. He told me the same thing you did last night and how he wanted me to stay away from the new house until after he talked to Mr. Granger. He said he wanted to make sure the construction site was safe before I went there. He said he wants me to check in before I go, but everything should be cool by the time I get home. And that's when he got kinda weird. He got all teary and said he was having trouble dealing with me getting older. He's totally not dealing with me needing more independence."

"Well, you are starting high school next year," Mom says with a smile.

And then I get it. "You talked to him, didn't you?"

"Sweetie, your dad is trying. He really is. You're no longer a child, but as far as he's concerned, you'll always be his little girl." She stops and laughs. "He probably still sees you as the little toddler who sat on his knee while he worked late into the night on his news stories."

I roll my eyes. "I know. He's only told the story to every guest who's ever stayed here."

"Not quite, but close." Mom stops, cocks her head to one side, and says, "Do you hear something? It sounds like a dog barking."

I listen real close. It sounds kinda far away. We don't allow any pets, so it's gotta be. "It sounds like it's coming from outside."

"We might have to call animal control. Take a peek, would you?"

"Okay!" I love dogs, so this could be kinda fun.

I go out the French doors to the back yard and listen. There's still barking. And the dog sounds super upset. It also sounds like he's next door at the new house. There's voices, too. One of them sounds like Chief Cunningham. Oh, no. If he's there, the dog's totally gonna get locked up. I walk along the side of the house and try to peek through the hedge on the property line. All I get are little tiny glimpses, so I've got to go all the way to the street. When I get there, I see two Seaside Cove PD cars parked in front of the construction site.

Why are two cops here for a barking dog? Talk about total overkill—unless they're here for something else.

Chief Cunningham and Deputy Amy Kama are inside the house. I can see them through the open framing. They're at the back, and they're not alone. There's a gigantic black dog. He looks like he's in total guard dog mode.

The Chief and Deputy Kama keep trying to close in on the dog, but each time one of them gets close, the dog turns on them. He's got a deep bark, and he's snarling. The Chief is totally gonna have to call in animal control. No way. I can't let that happen. The dog's too pretty. He's black from his head to his tail. I wonder what they're gonna do to him when they… I can't even think about it. Would they put him down?

I can feel the anger building inside me. Why would such a pretty dog have to die just because he got loose? I bite my upper lip and run toward the front steps. I'm still a room away when I see why the dog's so freaked out. He's standing guard over a body that's spread out on the floor. I swallow hard. What happened? Was there an accident? Something worse than mine?

Deputy Kama's the first one to realize I'm there. She looks at me and holds her hand out. "Alex, go back. This is dangerous."

The dog looks at me, and my breath catches in my throat. His eyes meet mine.

And he stops barking. We just stare at each other.

"Alex, go back!" Chief Cunningham yells. "This is a crime scene. I need you to leave."

What? A murder? Oh, no. Is…was…the dead man the dog's owner? No wonder he's upset. The poor dog will be homeless. He'll be…

I bend over and hold out my hand with my palm facing up. I pull in a breath and take a step forward. And then another. "Hey, boy."

With each step, I keep eye contact with the dog. My heart is pounding a million miles an hour. I can barely breathe—not because there's a dead body on the floor, but because I can't bear the thought of this beautiful dog being put down.

The dog's eyes meet mine, and for what feels like forever, we look at each other. It's getting like super intense, and I think this isn't gonna work, but then he blinks and relaxes just a little.

Chief Cunningham mutters, "What the heck?" He takes a small step forward, but the dog goes nuts again and snarls at him.

"No. It's okay, boy." My voice is soft and soothing. Kind of like when my mom is comforting Baby Jack.

The Chief motions for me to step back. "Alex, keep your distance. This is a dangerous situation. That dog could do anything."

"It's okay, Chief." I take another deep breath, call to the dog again, and step forward, all the while keeping my hand extended in front of me. With each step I take, he watches me, and I watch him back. I remember something one of our guests told me about training dogs. I turn my palm so it's facing down and lower it.

The dog takes another look at the body, but follows the command and lays down.

"What the heck?"

The dog hasn't barked at me since we made eye contact. He stays still while I take one step, then another.

A few seconds later, I'm standing in front of him.

My heart feels like it's gonna burst right through my chest. "That's a good boy."

The Chief and Amy are standing frozen where they were. They look like they don't know what to do.

"I've got him." This is the craziest thing I've ever done. If I get any closer, the dog could tear my hand off. But I can't bear the thought of him suffering. I kneel down and hold my hands out.

"Come here, boy."

The dog seems kinda undecided.

"It's okay. I won't let anything happen to you."

Can I promise that? Really? I can't control what the Chief might do.

The dog takes a last look at the dead man and stands. He takes a couple of steps, and when he's in front of me, I put my arms around him. He lets me pull him close, and even though he probably weighs more than me, he lets me hug him.

Oh, wow. I bury my hands in his black fur and pull him closer. This is a huge problem. My heart is still pounding in my chest. Not because I'm in danger. Oh, no. I'm in love.

8

Rick

RICK'S ATTENTION LANDED ON THE stove first. The burners sat cold and lifeless, a batch of house-fried potatoes slumped in the skillet, abandoned mid-sizzle, their skins blistered, but unfinished. Nearby, a knife lay by the cutting board covered by a scattering of half-chopped vegetables, their vibrant colors looking lonely and neglected. The rich scent of sizzling oil and the savory promise of breakfast hung in the air, but those were only signs of activity. Where was Marquetta?

From the sea foam green walls to the gleaming white granite countertops to the high-end appliances—everything spoke of her. This was her sanctuary, her stage. Yet, she was missing. Something had to be terribly wrong.

"Marquetta?" Rick's voice broke the silence. He winced at his tone. Sharp with unease. It hadn't been how he'd meant it to sound. He turned, and there she was—at the far end of the kitchen, her back to him, framed by the French doors. She stood motionless, staring out at something he couldn't see.

"What's going on?" He called as he started in her direction.

"I made a stupid mistake, Rick. I heard a dog barking outside and sent Alex to check it out. That was almost ten minutes ago, and she hasn't come back. I was thinking I should go looking for her."

Involuntarily, Rick put his hand to his throat. Alex had a penchant for finding trouble. There was nothing inherently wrong with what Marquetta had done, but Alex not returning right away told him his daughter had somehow stumbled into trouble.

"I'll go. Things are quiet in the dining room, and Lydia said she was on her way to help you. I'll take a look around and be right back."

"Okay. Be careful. This isn't like Alex at all."

Rick laid his apron on the nearby table. Actually, this was exactly like Alex. Doing his best to hide his concern, he kissed Marquetta on his way out. "Don't worry. I'll find her."

Outside, Rick heard no barking dogs, but he could hear voices. He hadn't seen anyone in the backyard, so he headed for the front of the house. As he walked along the hedge, he heard Adam Cunningham's voice. What the heck? The construction job had been shut down. What could be going on over there? And what did it have to do with Alex or a barking dog?

When Rick finally got beyond the hedge, he groaned. Alex knelt next to a huge dog he recognized as Tommy Granger's Newfoundland. If he remembered correctly, the dog's name was Shadow. Looking at the two of them, Rick chuckled. Shadow had to weigh well over a hundred pounds. Next to the giant fur ball, Alex looked tiny and frail. Granger had once told him the dog was extremely intuitive and gentle, but he intimidated the other workers. That was why Tommy left Shadow home most of the time. So why was the dog here?

Better yet, why did Alex have her arms wrapped around him? When Granger had bid the job, he'd shown Rick photos and a few short videos of the dog and called him his best friend. So, what the devil was going on?

"Alex, what are you doing with Shadow?"

"Chief Cunningham let me take him. He doesn't like uniforms." Alex pointed past Rick to the house under construction.

"What do you mean he doesn't like uniforms?" Rick asked as he turned to see what Alex was pointing at.

He felt like he'd been body-slammed with a 2x4. There, in the middle of his house that was still nothing but framing, stood Adam and Deputy Kama. Their attention was fixed on a man's body sprawled on the floor. Even from this distance, it wasn't hard to tell the man was no longer alive.

Tommy Granger lay face up on the plywood subfloor, his burly frame unnaturally still. The morning breeze had scattered several large blueprints across the site, and one had settled partially beneath his body, the blue and white paper flapping gently against his outstretched arm like a restless spirit. The crisp architectural lines and measurements on the paper formed a stark contrast to the disarray of death—Tommy's work boots were caked with mud, and his eyes stared vacantly at the open rafters above. Another blueprint had wrapped itself around his leg, the wind occasionally lifting its corner as if trying to pull him back to life. The house plans—once representing a vision for the Atwood family's future home—now served as a macabre backdrop to the contractor's final moments.

Suddenly, everything made sense. Alex had come looking for the barking dog. The dog had been upset over the loss of its owner. The cops had unsuccessfully tried to corral Shadow. And, of course, it was Alex to the rescue. He sighed. Not because Alex had helped, but because he recognized the look on her face. She was getting attached. He had to deal with this. Fast.

Looking closer, Rick knew exactly who it was. Between the lumberjack shirt and the dog, the dead man had to be Tommy Granger, his general contractor. Suddenly, everything made sense. Alex had come looking for the barking dog. The dog had been upset over the loss of its owner. The cops had unsuccessfully tried to corral Shadow. And, of course, it was Alex to the rescue. He sighed. Not because Alex had helped, but because he recognized the look on her face. She was getting attached. He had to deal with. Fast.

"Stay there, Alex."

"I will, Daddy. His name's Shadow?"

Reluctantly, Rick said, "Yes."

"Cool."

At the foot of the stairs to the front porch, Rick called Adam's name. Adam waved to Rick, said something to Amy, then walked over to meet Rick, his face looking more drawn and tired than Rick had seen in a long time.

"What's going on, buddy? You look exhausted. This isn't your first crime scene."

Adam grimaced, took another look over his shoulder and faced Rick. "That's not what's bothering me. As you can probably tell, that's Tommy Granger. He's dead. I found the body on my way to see you, actually. I heard the dog and came over here to see what all the commotion was about."

Something in Adam's tone—a tension he couldn't pinpoint and had only heard a handful of times—put Rick on guard. "What aren't you telling me? Why were you coming to me? And why do you look so upset? You didn't have a fight with Traci, did you?"

"No," Adam said. "If only it were that simple. I was coming to see you on official business."

"Me? Adam, why are you being so evasive?"

Adam rolled his neck in a circle as if trying to release the tension. "Follow me to my vehicle," he muttered, barely loud enough for Rick to hear.

"What are we going to do about him?" Rick asked as they were passing Alex and Shadow.

Alex had her fingers buried in the dog's fur and was letting him lick her face after she had kissed him on the nose. Great. Just what he needed, Alex thinking she was a dog-whisperer or something. Even worse, based on the way she was acting, she was already attached to him. There was no way they could have a dog, especially one so big, at the B&B.

Adam stood off to one side shaking his head. "He almost took my hand off when I tried to get him away from the body."

"He's okay now, Chief Cunningham. He was just upset." Alex scratched Shadow behind the ear. He groaned and pressed closer to her.

"Tommy Granger was Shadow's owner," Rick said.

"So I gathered," Adam said. "I never met the man, so I didn't know."

"He did a lot of work in San Ladron. He's got a nephew, Jake, who was working on the job with him. He can probably take the dog."

"Are you sure he'll take care of him?" Alex asked, her brow furrowing.

"Jake lives with Tommy, Alex. I'm sure he will." He left off the next thought—and don't you even think of volunteering to keep him. But if he knew his daughter, she was already scheming to make it happen.

Adam ran his hand over his mouth, then gestured at his 4x4. "We can put the dog in the back of my vehicle. He may not be happy in there, but at least he'll be safe. But before we do that, I still have something I need to give you." He crooked his head in the direction of his 4x4.

Frustrated with Adam's apparent unwillingness to talk, Rick threw his hands in the air and followed. This was so unlike his friend. They'd worked murder cases together; Adam had been the best man at Rick's wedding; and they saw each other several times a week. Why was he suddenly being shut out?

After opening the door to his vehicle, Adam pulled out an envelope that he'd laid on his front seat. He turned, handed it to Rick, and said, "I'm sorry, buddy. I think this whole thing stinks, but Richard Atwood, you've been served."

Rick stared at the envelope. "With what?"

"A notice of foreclosure."

Adam waited while Rick ripped the envelope open with his finger and read through the document. By the time he was done reading, he was convinced that this had Walt Copley's fingerprints all over it. "This is complete BS, Adam. And you know it."

"I wish there was something I could do about it, but there's not. But there is more."

"For crying out loud, how much more could there be?"

Adam paused to look back at the crime scene. "Rick, I'm afraid that you need to sit this one out. When the mayor heard we had another dead body and where it was, she instructed me to keep you away because you're too close to this."

Rick gritted his teeth. He had mixed emotions about helping Adam—especially after running into Francine at Jordan Lane's office. "I'm not so sure I agree with her, Adam. There's something fishy going on here. I think I should be helping you investigate Granger's murder. You shouldn't have to do it alone."

"I didn't say murder. Right now, this is a suspicious death. That's all."

"Look, Adam. Whatever you call it, my gut is telling me—no, screaming at me— that this is tied to…" Rick stopped. He was right. His gut was screaming at him.

The silence stretched between them, weighted and electric. Adam's body language was telegraphing a message far more potent than words. "What, Rick?"

Rick had seen this scenario far too many times from the other side. He didn't dare say a word about a conspiracy involving Sylvia Archer, Walt Copley, and maybe even Francine. He was not willing to go there. Not yet. "Nothing, Adam. I guess I'm just angry that this is happening to us. Tell Francine I'll stay clear of the investigation."

"Don't shut down, Rick. Talk to me."

"Afraid I can't. Not right now."

"Understood. In your shoes, I might do the same."

Rick looked again at Alex. She still had her arms around Shadow's neck, almost as if she were consoling a person. He felt a pang of sympathy for the poor dog. It had just lost its owner, probably its closest companion, and the one constant it had known. "Alex, why don't you help Chief Cunningham out by putting Shadow in the back of his cruiser?"

Alex's jaw dropped. She tightened her grip on Shadow's neck, and the dog seemed to let himself be pulled closer. Shadow was big and strong and could easily do whatever he wanted, yet here he was letting himself be treated like an oversized stuffed animal. The way he stayed close to Alex, it was almost as if they'd already bonded.

"Kiddo, we can't keep him. By rights, he should go to Tommy Granger's closest relative."

Rick's heart melted as tears brimmed in Alex's eyes. Maybe, after they had their own house—assuming they ever did get their own house now—they could have a dog. Something…smaller. Something that wouldn't eat them out of house and home.

Alex kissed Shadow on the side of his face. He turned his head, made eye contact with her, and gave her a big, slobbery lick. Alex sniffled and gave the dog a final hug before she pulled back. "I'm sorry, Shadow, but you have to go with Chief Cunningham."

When Alex stood, Shadow nudged her with his body. Alex stroked the black fur on his head and scratched him behind the ears. He walked next to her as she led him to the back of the 4x4.

Adam watched, seemingly awestruck, as the dog easily jumped into the back of the 4x4. His jaw hung slack as he scratched the back of his head. "Well, I'll be. Never expected it to be that easy."

"Yeah," Rick said as Alex closed the rear hatch of the vehicle. He thought briefly about telling Adam he'd be getting to the bottom of the foreclosure notice, but decided against it. It was time to go into lockdown mode. And right now, the police were not on the need-to-know list.

9

Alex

ON MY WAY TO SCHOOL, all I can think about is poor Shadow. I should be shocked that we've had another murder in Seaside Cove. But honestly, I can't even think about the murder because all I see is Shadow's sad face as we said goodbye. He looked so lonely. His big, dark eyes were droopy, like he was begging me not to leave. It was the saddest thing I've ever seen.

It broke my heart when I closed the back of the 4x4. Shadow just dropped his head onto his paws, like the weight of the world was too much for him. Even his sigh felt heavy, like he was trying to tell me he needed me.

I wanted to climb in there with him, hold him, and never let go, but I couldn't. Instead, I could only let my dad hug me and cry for poor Shadow. I couldn't even look at Shadow because it hurt too much. My dad tried to make me feel better. He even promised we'd get a dog when we have our own house. But I don't want just any dog. I want Shadow. And deep down, I know he wants to be with me too.

And now, on top of that, there's another murder. Is my dad going to help Chief Cunningham again? Am I supposed to help? Do I even want to? I don't know. What if the person gets away with it? What if Shadow gets sent off to…where? Everything feels so unfair—losing Shadow, the murder…it's all just too much.

When Sasha and Robbie meet me at the school entrance, Sasha knows something's wrong the second she sees my face. And when she asks me, I can't help but tell them how I saw the body and calmed Shadow down and how he's gonna have to go to Tommy's nephew. Robbie, as usual, is sympathetic, but doesn't seem to know what to do. He's like that. I'd call him the strong, silent type, but he's more geek than anything. Maybe in a couple years he'll get some muscles, but for now, heck, we're just kids.

"You found another dead body? You're like a murder magnet, Alex." Robbie's jaw hangs down, like he's in total shock.

Sasha smacks his arm, rolling her eyes with the look you save for a good friend when they've gone a little too far. "Wow, that's harsh."

It's times like this that I wonder why I like Robbie so much. I grumble, "Gee, thanks."

He makes a face. "Sorry. I didn't mean it in a bad way. It's just, like, well, you're not gonna want to solve the murder, are you?"

"I dunno." I realize I'm probably feeling the same way Shadow does. My shoulders feel like they're carrying a huge weight. Another murder. And this time, it happened in what will eventually be our new home.

Sasha gives me a comforting hug, and I can't help but feel grateful for her friendship. "We'll figure it out together, Alex. We always do."

Awesome. Me and Sasha—we're an unbeatable team. But then Robbie chimes in.

"Hey, at least you've got something unusual to add to your college application—I helped the cops solve a bunch of murders."

Me and Sasha look at each other. At first, I think we're both gonna smack Robbie again, but then we all laugh. Robbie's right. This situation sucks. It's moments like these that remind me how important it is to have friends. "Thanks, guys. I know you're here for me."

Sasha hugs me and tells me it's gonna be okay. "I know you totally want that dog, Alex. I could see it on your face when you said his name. Maybe Jake won't take him, and your dad will change his mind."

"What?" Holy cow. If Jake refused to take Shadow, would my dad do that? "Oh, wow, Sash! You're right. I have to get Jake to say he can't take Shadow, and then he'll have to come live with us! You're brilliant!"

Robbie lets himself be pulled into the group hug, but then he blows the mood. "Uh, Alex, how are you gonna get your dad to change his mind about pets in the B&B? Isn't that gonna be kinda hard? And besides, you still haven't told him about Operation Nail Down. Right?"

I roll my eyes. Leave it to Robbie. He might always be there to support me, but he's also always the practical one. "I'll find a way. Besides, my dad doesn't believe in coincidences, so he's gonna be super suspicious 'cause the contractor turned up dead in almost the exact same place as that stupid step. This is so connected. Maybe Operation Nail Down includes me getting Shadow to be my dog."

Sasha is nodding. "You can totally make it happen. And I have an idea about getting intel on how the whole thing might've happened. What about Billy Thornton? Isn't his dad in construction?"

Ewww. Billy Thornton. I'd rather fall down the stairs a hundred times than talk to him. "No way, Sash. You know how I feel about Billy."

"I know, but if you really wanna find out how often that kind of accident happens, maybe you should at least try. Besides, think about Shadow. If asking Billy a few questions could help you get Shadow, wouldn't it be worth it?"

I screw up my face and wonder if Sasha's gone nuts. Why would Billy Thornton, my sworn enemy for life, do anything that would help me? And, if he found out I wanted to adopt Shadow? No. Way. Ever. "Let's get real, Sash. Billy's not gonna help me. Besides, Billy's dad wasn't on the crew, and what would Billy know about construction?"

"Wow. You are one-tracking today." Sasha rolls her eyes and kinda waves her hand in small circles. "Okay, Billy's dad might not have been on your crew, but what if he knows a guy who knows a guy who…"

"Got it, Sasha!" I hate to admit it, but she has a point—even if she is kind of overselling it. "You could be right. And if I can keep from punching him in the face, maybe I'll get something from him. But you've gotta help."

"Me? Why?"

"Because he likes you. He thinks you're pretty." Actually, a lot of the boys think Sasha's pretty. She has dark hair and big brown eyes that Mom says will make any boy's heart melt the minute she smiles at him. Mom's almost always right about all kinds of stuff, so it's totally time to test it out 'cause Billy's gonna walk by us in about ten seconds.

My stomach is churning like somebody made me eat worms. He's got his usual stupid smirk on his face. It's one of the reasons I hate him so much. The other is because he's a total bully to the younger kids. He tried to bully me when we first met, and I punched him. You should've seen the look on his face! Total shock. But he never bothered me again. Of course, now he's getting bigger, and he's got a couple of bully friends.

If I have to be nice to him—that's gonna totally break the stalemate. Oh, man, Shadow had better be worth it."Smile at him and say hi."

Sasha rolls her eyes again and grits her teeth, but then she flashes a smile at Billy and follows it up with a sultry, "Hey, Billy."

He stops dead in his tracks, and he looks like he's lost his ability to think. "Uh…hi…uh…Sasha."

Oh, man, if I could only get a pic of him like this. But I don't care about that as much as I do about seeing if he can help. And maybe with Sasha making nice, we can pull this off. But my hopes go down the tubes when I say hi, and Billy snaps outta the stupid-me trance he's in.

"I heard you took a tumble down the stairs at your new house, Alex. You gotta watch your step on construction sites. It ain't no place for a girl."

I can totally feel the urge to slam my fist into his face rising when Sasha saves me. "Me and Alex were just talking about that. You know, how there's always a million things going on, and it's easy for stuff to get overlooked. Right?"

Billy's gone stupid again 'cause Sasha's actually talking to him. He forgets all about taunting me and swaggers from side to side a little. "For sure. My dad tells me stories about how accidents can happen all the time."

"Oh, that's right! Your dad works in construction. What's he do?" Sasha is twirling a lock of her dark hair around her fingers, and Billy's totally mesmerized.

"Um…he's a plumber for Greer Construction. He works out of San Ladron almost all the time."

"Has he ever said anything about accidents on construction sites?"

Billy gives Sasha a funny look, like maybe he's getting suspicious. Rats. I think he's figured it out—we still hate him, and we're playing him for a fool. He shifts his weight, and the cockiness in the way he stands fades. "Why're you askin' so many questions? You seem awful curious about somethin' that ain't really your business."

Sasha doesn't miss a beat. "Just making conversation," she says and kinda bats her eyes at him. "You know, trying to learn new things like how dangerous a construction site can be. I figured you would know."

Billy's eyes kinda ping pong around, and then he gets it. He's being played. The corner of his mouth twists into a smirk, and that's when I'm sure the game is over. "Construction sites ain't places for every random person to be hanging around. Especially not girls. Nothin' personal, just sayin'. Ain't where you belong."

He turns, stomps off, and leaves me and Sasha behind. "Well, rats," Sasha mutters. "There goes my rep. Alex, we're gonna have to up our game."

"For sure." But as I replay Billy's words and the blank look on his face, I have to wonder how much—or how little—he really knows. Maybe he's just a loser and we should forget about him.

10

Rick

THE LOOK OF GRIEF ON Alex's face from closing Shadow into the back of Adam's 4x4 haunted Rick for most of the morning. He didn't want her anywhere near Granger's murder. But he knew Alex. She was determined and resourceful. He'd bet anything her curiosity already had its claws in this mess, especially if she thought it might help her adopt Shadow. How was he going to keep her out of danger? How was he going to keep her from getting any closer to that dog?

The only answer Rick could come up with was to beat Alex at her own game. He had to move fast and cover his tracks. He'd start with Isabelle Murdoch. He packed up the file, secured it in his desk, and headed downstairs. If he hurried, he could get to Isabelle's Pet Shoppe before lunch.

Before leaving, Rick stopped in the kitchen, where he found Marquetta and Lydia cooing over Baby Jack. He'd hoped to talk to Marquetta alone, but was sure he could trust Lydia, so he did a hurried explanation.

To Rick's surprise, Lydia said, "If you want to get information out of Isabelle, buy her lunch at the Rusty Nail. She loves it there."

Marquetta nodded. "Lydia's right. Isabelle usually has lunch at the shop, so if you really want her to open up, get her out of the store. And, FYI, the last time I saw her, she was raving about Sally's shrimp and avocado salad."

"Got it. Would you do me a favor? Get me a reservation for two."

"I'll do you one better. You go to the Rusty Nail. I'll call Isabelle and ask her to meet you there. Now, go."

He considered running back upstairs to his office and grabbing a small notepad to take notes, but decided to rely on his memory and walked to the restaurant. His spirits sank when he got to the Rusty Nail and saw the line out front. Obviously, he was behind the curve as far as the lunch crowd went and could only hope that Marquetta had gotten him a reservation.

The nostalgic maritime charm enveloped him as he entered the door. Weathered wooden floors and the scent of the ocean wafting through the windows were topped off by antique nautical décor—complete with ship wheels, lobster traps, and marine ropes. In addition to the entire maritime experience, he hoped the aroma of fresh seafood on the grill would loosen Isabelle's tongue.

Sally Costas greeted him with her usual high-energy persona. "Hey, Rick, Marquetta had me reserve a table for you and Isabelle. Follow me."

Rick said a silent thank you and followed Sally. Marquetta had not only come through, but it appeared she'd be correct about Isabelle—she'd wasted no time getting here. Sally stopped suddenly, turned around, and rested a hand on Rick's arm. "I heard about

Tommy Granger. How terrible! Having someone die on your job site. That's awful."

"Thanks, Sally. I guess it's impossible to stay ahead of the rumor mill in this town. But it's not my problem. The investigation is a matter for the police."

Sally nodded and took off again, leading Rick to the table where Isabelle sat. His butt had barely hit the chair when Sally asked him if the rumor was true that he wouldn't be helping on the murder investigation. There were times when Rick truly hated the town's rumor mill. And this was one of those times. It felt like the sharks were circling.

He did his best to brush off the rumors. "The mayor thinks I'm too close to this one because it happened on my property."

"Right. I guess so. What about Shadow? Are you going to adopt him? Is that why you two are meeting like this?"

Rather than correcting Sally's assumption, Rick decided it was the perfect cover for this lunch meeting. "You can't say a word to anyone, Sally."

"Pet adoptions can be very tricky," Isabelle added. "And we don't want Alex to get her hopes up."

"No worries. She won't hear it from me." Sally made a zipping motion across her mouth and pretended to turn a key before she darted away.

"How many people do you think she'll tell?" Rick asked.

"Not Sally. She hears everything, but doesn't like to repeat it. Now, down to the serious business. Marquetta's probably already told you that I have a huge weak spot for their shrimp and avocado salad. Do you mind if I order a glass of wine?"

"Go for it. You're doing me a huge favor by meeting me here. How are you feeling?"

Isabelle gave a careless flick of her wrist. "The brain tumor is slow-growing enough that the docs don't know how long I'll be around. In the meantime, I'm enjoying life's little pleasures—and maybe trying to right a few wrongs."

"I admire your attitude, Isabelle."

"Well, at least now I have an excuse for forgetting where I put my glasses!"

They made small talk until they ordered, Isabelle noting that every detail in the restaurant, from the creaking floors to the maritime memorabilia, told a story of the sea. Rick surveyed the restaurant and nodded.

"You know, Isabelle, in a way, this place makes me wish I'd known my grandfather better."

"I'm sure you've heard plenty of stories from Marquetta and others who knew Captain Jack, but they're no substitute for the real thing."

"So true. You know, I only met him once, so I guess I'll have to settle for the stories. Anyway, did you bring the file?"

Isabelle sipped from her glass. "Yes. What's in there speaks for itself, but there are things that aren't in the file you might find of interest."

"Such as?"

Isabelle set her glass down, her eyes meeting Rick's with a measured intensity. "Such as Tommy's nephew, Jake Morales," she began. "He's a regular at the pet store, always chatting about his uncle. Harmless enough, but every so often, he drops little crumbs of information—things he probably doesn't realize are important."

Rick raised an eyebrow. "Like what?"

"For starters, Tommy and Walt have had disagreements. Jake mentioned it offhand. I guess something happened between those two during the town hall upgrades. Sylvia Archer showed up, and the three of them were going at it. Finally, Sylvia told them both to get over their differences. She said bad behavior was bad for business. Whatever it is, it's probably been simmering under the surface."

"And Jake told you about this out of the blue?" Rick asked, skepticism lacing his words.

"Not intentionally," Isabelle said with a faint smile. "He's a teenager, Rick. He talks because he doesn't know what not to say. And, I may have coaxed him a little."

More like a full-court press, thought Rick. But he smiled, took a sip of his water, and waited for Isabelle to fill the silence.

She didn't disappoint. Biting her lip, she glanced around and lowered her voice. "When you piece together the snippets, it doesn't paint a pretty picture. There's more here than what's in the file. Tommy, Walt, Jake—you add Sylvia Archer into the mix, and there's a tangle of problems nobody's talking about directly, at least not yet."

Rick contemplated Isabelle and what she was telling him. If it was all true, the web was even more tangled than he'd thought. "It sounds messy."

"It was. Is."

"Is there anything else you can pull from those snippets that Jake's been spilling?"

Isabelle looked out the window and watched the surf rolling in for a few seconds. "Well, for one, he mentioned some arguments with Tommy. Jake claims he confronted his uncle when he realized Tommy was being paid to slow your job down. According to Jake, this wasn't just a one-time thing, either—he said it was a deliberate pattern. I didn't press him on it at first, but he complained about the whole situation while he was looking at aquarium supplies."

"Excuse me? Jake likes fish?"

"Yeah," Isabelle said with a small chuckle. "He's been into fish tanks lately. It's his way of zoning out, I think—something calm amidst all the chaos. We were talking about a new tank when it slipped out. He was so frustrated with Tommy that he was thinking of leaving town. He's a good kid, but his uncle, not so much."

Rick rubbed his chin thoughtfully. "Paid sabotage is something I never saw coming. Although maybe I should have, given the way Walt Copley feels about me."

"It's not you, Rick. Walt's wanted the B&B for as long as I can remember. And Sylvia wants the property where you're building your house."

"Wait. Walt wants the B&B, but Sylvia wants the property where our house is going up? Don't tell me she wants to develop it."

"As far as I know, yes. They're quite the pair. Walt's too proud for his own good and won't admit he's wrong about his fantasy of your grandfather swindling his family out of the B&B. And Sylvia, well, she's different. She's shrewd, calculating. A crook if you ask me, though she'd never get her hands dirty. She's the type to smile sweetly while pulling strings from the shadows." Isabelle's finger traced a slow circle at her temple, as if teasing out the words before they came. "And Tommy, he's always had a chip on his shoulder. Always ready to pick a fight, even when there's no reason to. I'll tell you one thing. He was smart as a whip. I always thought he'd get a job as a computer programmer in San Ladron, but I guess he never liked being locked up in an office."

Rick had no way to judge how much of what Isabelle was telling him was true and how much was exaggeration—talk for the sake of talking. But he'd learned long ago to keep a source going and sort out the truth later. "You really know a lot about all of them, Isabelle. I'm impressed."

"Don't be. I've lived here my entire life. I know a lot about everybody, Rick. Including our illustrious mayor."

Rick edged closer, his attention sharpening. He considered mentioning his run-in with Francine at Jordan Lane's office, then decided not to mention the incident. Better to just let Isabelle talk. "What, exactly, do you mean?"

Isabelle lingered on the silence, her eyes sliding from booth to booth. Only when she seemed certain of the room's indifference did she hover nearer and let her words slip out not much louder than a breath."Francine didn't get to where she is on her own, Rick. She needed help—financial help—to get elected."

"Where did she get the money?" Rick asked innocently.

Isabelle took in Rick's expression before she continued. "Sylvia Archer. She's the one who stepped in with the deep pockets. She put Francine's campaign in the black."

"Isabelle, do you think that means Sylvia is the one telling Francine what to do?"

"To be honest, I don't know what's going on in Francine's head. When you think about it, if Francine really wanted to, she could make things pretty uncomfortable for Walt. Maybe even get him to quit. Instead, what is she doing? Sitting around letting him run roughshod over you."

"Because he's Sylvia's henchman?"

Isabelle pushed back in her chair, almost as if she needed a break from the conversation. She crossed her arms over her chest. "Sure looks that way to me. Now, the question is, what can you do about it?"

11

Rick

RICK ROLLED TO A STOP in front of a modest Craftsman-style bungalow, tucked away on a quiet street on the inland side of Seaside Cove. Shocked, he checked the address again. This was the home of Tommy Granger? The weathered exterior suffered from peeling gray paint, and the front porch sagged from years of neglect. A pair of mismatched chairs occupied the porch. One had a broken armrest. An old gray flannel shirt draped over the back concealed the other like a bad slipcover.

The front yard was no better. Wildflowers and weeds competed in a game of one-upmanship. The well-worn path to the front door suggested frequent comings and goings. Rick had a fleeting, snarky thought. He should start asking to see the homes of the people he was going to hire.

The sounds of a large dog howling inside the house grew louder with each step. The deep, mournful tone tugged at Rick's emotions. He hadn't thought about how much Shadow must be missing his owner. "Get it together," he muttered to himself. He couldn't let himself be distracted by a dog's feelings.

Rick rang the bell. He recognized Jake's voice when Jake yelled at the dog to be quiet. Another mournful wail pierced the air. Jake muttered something to himself, then called out, "Who is it?"

"It's Rick Atwood. I wanted to talk to you about coming back to work." Not exactly true, he thought. But it was only a partial lie. If he could get the job moving again, he'd put in a good word with the new contractor for Jake. But until he had a general contractor and the approval of the historical society, he was stuck.

Despite the paint peeling at the edges, the dark gray door opened a crack without a sound. It was the only sign Rick had seen so far that Tommy had ever done any maintenance. Jake eyed Rick from the crack in the open doorway, doing his best to hold Shadow back while he tried to focus on Rick.

"Stupid dog's been crazy since…" Jake stopped, winced, and yelled at Shadow. "Shut up!"

Having seen how Shadow acted with Alex, and now Jake, Rick wondered if this was even the same dog. "Maybe I could come in so we can talk for a few minutes?"

"I gotta…I gotta do something with him first."

Jake tugged on Shadow's collar, but the dog seemed to barely notice. He'd suddenly taken an interest in Rick and had begun sniffing. His large, bushy tail wagged slowly and steadily, a sign Rick recognized from when Alex had been holding onto the dog this morning.

"I think he'll be okay," Rick said hesitantly. But Shadow's behavior reminded him of a couple of the missing person cases he'd covered in New York. Could Shadow be picking up Alex's scent? Is that why he'd suddenly calmed down? Maybe. He hadn't changed clothes since this morning, and he'd hugged Alex at the construction site and again on her way out the door to school.

Rick pushed the door open further and let Shadow sniff his pants. At one particular spot, the dog whimpered slightly. He reached down and scratched Shadow behind the ears, then let the dog lick the back of his hand.

Jake watched in disbelief as Rick and Shadow interacted, then apparently gave up on trying to move the dog. Jake might be taller than Shadow, but he was lanky and wiry—the build of someone still growing into his frame—whereas Shadow was more than a hundred pounds of solid muscle. That contrast made forcing Shadow to go anywhere he didn't want to go an almost impossible task.

"Maybe he wants a little attention, Jake. You know, he did just lose his owner."

"And I lost the last of my family," Jake shot back. "Sorry. Didn't mean to snap at you. You said you want me to come back to work?"

Rick wrestled with the two voices in his head—one told him to use the lie to his advantage; the other told him to not be cruel and lead the kid on. At five feet nine with long limbs and hunched shoulders, Jake was a stark contrast to his uncle's heavier frame that had been toned by a life of construction work. Jake was definitely not ready to take over for his uncle, but if he thought Rick was considering him for the job, he might answer Rick's questions. Rick unconsciously scratched Shadow under his chin as he made up his mind.

"I'm certainly anxious to get the job back on track, but I'm sure you know that until the historical society gives the okay, we're dead in the water."

Jake's brown eyes darted nervously to the side, and his cheek quirked ever so slightly. "Thanks to no-good Walt Copley. Uncle Tommy said he was a professional at nothing other than causing trouble."

"Did your uncle ever say why he didn't like Copley?"

"Nah. He never got into specifics." Jake looked away again and adjusted his faded baseball cap. "Uncle Tommy kept a lot of stuff to himself."

"So I'm discovering. Look, I'm not here to make your day worse. I need to understand what was going on with your uncle. We both know my job wasn't running smoothly. Now, there's a good chance the whole project will be shut down. Surely your uncle said something. Jake, I need to understand what the relationship was between him and Copley. Is there anything at all you can tell me?"

Jake shifted on his feet, his fingers running across the bill of his ball cap. The motion was slow and deliberate, as if tracing the curve of the worn fabric helped him gather his thoughts. The brim, softened and frayed from years of use, bent slightly under the pressure of his touch. It was a small, absent gesture, but it spoke volumes about his unease.

"Mr. Atwood, Uncle Tommy didn't exactly trust a lot of people. You know? Especially anyone sniffing around our work like Walt always was. He didn't say a whole lot. I dunno. You'd hear him mutter things like, 'That old fossil thinks he runs this town.'"

"And when he made those kinds of remarks, did it feel like your uncle was worried? Or maybe was fed up?"

Jake crossed his arms, his shoulders hunching a bit more. "Both, I guess. Uncle Tommy didn't back down from anyone. I mean, like, nobody. He'd stand his ground no matter what. But, yeah, I think all the little inspections and complaints were wearing him down. He hated games. Thought people like Walt were all about tossing their weight around to see who flinched first."

Rick thought about everything Isabelle had told him as he studied Jake's tense expression. The way the kid fidgeted, he felt certain Jake knew much more. Rick kept his voice even. "Did your uncle talk about anything specific Walt might've done? Something that made him feel like this wasn't your typical back-and-forth?"

Jake looked up, his dark eyes scarcely meeting Rick's before they flicked away. "He didn't get into details, but he didn't have to. I could tell it was bad. Uncle Tommy hated the way Walt talked down to people, like he was better than us 'cause he had history backing him up or whatever. My uncle, he was…" Jake hesitated, his voice softening a little as if he were trying out the words. "He said he was giving Copley enough rope to hang himself."

Frustrated at how this conversation was going in circles, Rick said, "It sounds like your Uncle Tommy might have made some enemies. What I don't understand is that he once told me he had a good working relationship with Walt Copley. Do you think maybe Walt double-crossed him?"

"I dunno. But he would mutter stuff sometimes, like, 'You can't trust people, and you gotta have the proof if they ever stab you in the back.' I figured he was just talking about the usual job site drama, you know? But lately… I don't know. He seemed more on edge."

Rick nodded, his journalist instincts kicking in. "Did he ever mention Sylvia Archer?"

Jake's eyes darted to the side, and he shifted uncomfortably. "He didn't like either of them, that's for sure. He said Walt was always poking his nose where it didn't belong, and Sylvia… well, he called her 'slick.' Said she was the kind of person who'd sell you a dream and then charge you for the nightmare."

"Sounds like your uncle had a way with words."

"Yeah, he had a lot of sayings like that. He always told me to CYA, you know? Said it was the only way to make sure you didn't get blamed for something you didn't do. He was big on keeping records and writing stuff down. He even had this old metal box he kept locked up in his bedroom. Said it was his insurance policy."

Rick's breath quickened. An insurance policy in a metal box? What kind of insurance could Granger have possibly had? "Do you know what was in it?"

"No idea. He never let me near it. But he always said, 'If something ever happens to me, you make sure you find that box.' I thought he was just being dramatic, but now, I don't know what to do." His voice trailed off, and he studied the floor, his expression clouded with worry.

"Is the box still in the bedroom?"

"No. The night before he died, he put it in the truck. I didn't think to look right away. When I did, it wasn't there. I don't know if someone took it or if he moved it somewhere else."

Rick's jaw tightened. If Tommy had been keeping records, this missing box could be the key to unraveling the web of secrets that seemed to be growing by the hour. "Jake, if your uncle was worried about being double-crossed, it means he knew something—something big. And if that box is missing, someone else must have known, too."

"Look, Mr. Atwood, I gotta be honest with you. I've already got another job offer. Sam Greer wants to hire me. My uncle must've told him I was a good worker, 'cause he called me just before you got here. I'm thinking of taking the job."

"Sam Greer? Really?" It wasn't the first time he'd heard Greer's name, and not in a good way. The local gossip mill claimed Greer was a bad contractor. Then again, maybe the man was an opportunist —something that might not set well in this small town. "That's interesting timing, don't you think?"

"I guess. I mean, I need the work, and he's offering decent pay. Said he could use someone who knows their way around a site."

"Jake, I don't want to tell you what to do, but you should think about this. Why is he reaching out to you now, right after your uncle's death? Don't you think that's a little convenient? Maybe even calculated?"

Jake's eyes flicked back to Rick, doubt crossing his face. "You think he's up to something?"

"I don't know," Rick admitted. "But I am coming across a lot of people who don't do anything without a reason. If Greer is offering you a job, Is it because he sees some kind of advantage in it? And I mean for him, not necessarily for you."

Jake let out a frustrated huff. "So what am I supposed to do? Turn him down and hope something else comes along?"

"I'm not saying you should turn him down outright. But maybe take a little time to think it over. Ask yourself why he's so eager to hire you now, of all times. And if you do take the job, keep your eyes open. Listen to your uncle's advice, and don't let him pull you into anything that doesn't feel right."

Jake nodded slowly, his expression conflicted. "Yeah, maybe you're right. I'll think about it."

"Good. And if you need anything—anything at all—you know where to find me."

"Thanks, Mr. Atwood. I appreciate it."

Rick gave Shadow a final scratch under the chin, then turned to leave, a knot of unease tightening in his chest. Sam Greer's sudden interest in Jake felt far too convenient, a thread dangling just out of reach. Was this the start of a deeper entanglement in the murder investigation he'd been warned to steer clear of? Or a fresh wrinkle in the already fragile plans for his family's future? Either way, it left him with one thought burning in his mind: What if this wasn't a coincidence at all?

There was one way to find out. Go visit the source, Sylvia Archer.

12

Alex

SHADOW'S COAT IS SO SOFT under my hands. It's like the biggest, fluffiest blanket you could ever imagine. When I picture him, he's bounding across the yard behind the B&B, his huge paws kicking up the freshly cut grass, his tail wagging so hard it could knock over a garden gnome. I toss a ball. It doesn't go very far because, well, I'm terrible at throwing—but Shadow doesn't care. He charges after it, ears flopping, like it's the most exciting thing ever.

I crouch down as he barrels back toward me, and he skids to a stop just in time, dropping the ball at my feet and daring me with those deep, droopy eyes to do it again. It's almost like he's saying, "See, I brought it back for you. Aren't I awesome?"

"Good boy, Shadow!" I say, ruffling his ears before throwing the ball again. This time, maybe I'll manage to get it past the hedge without hitting the bird bath.

A long "rrrrriiiiinnnnnnggg!" jolts me out of the perfect daydream, and I blink at the whiteboard at the front of the room. Oh, great. Mrs. Holbrook's halfway through wiping away whatever science diagram we were supposed to be studying. Did we even get homework?

The classroom erupts into noise as chairs scrape against the floor and kids rush to stuff books into their backpacks. I don't even have time to panic about how much I probably missed because Sasha's already next to me. She's got the biggest grin on her face.

"Daydreaming about Shadow again?" she teases, tossing her dark hair over her shoulder.

"Shhh!" I hiss. I do a fast check around us to make sure no one heard. Not that anyone cares about some random dog… except he's not random. He's Shadow, and he's amazing, and I have to figure out how to make him mine.

Sasha chuckles, completely ignoring my wide-eyed attempt to keep her quiet. "Come on, Alex. I've seen that goofy smile a hundred times today. You were totally picturing him chasing a ball, weren't you?"

I can't help but grin. "Maybe. But it's not goofy." I grab my notebook and jam it into my bag, trying not to blush as Robbie shows up out of nowhere.

"What's not goofy? Your crush on a dog?" Robbie chuckles as he swings his backpack onto one shoulder. "That's, um, unique."

"It's not a crush!" I shoot back, tightening the straps on my bag and standing up so fast I bump my leg on the desktop. "I just… I feel bad for him, okay? He lost his owner. He's lonely. It's sad."

They both stare at me, Sasha with her head slightly tilted like she's trying not to laugh again, and Robbie with his classic Robbie face—half teasing, half 'how do I survive these lunatics?'

Sasha seems to get that I'm embarrassed and smacks Robbie's shoulder. She loops on arm through mine and pulls me toward the door. "Oh, come on, Robbie. Shadow's adorable. Be nice."

"I am nice," Robbie says, following us into the hallway. "I just don't see how you're gonna convince your dad to adopt a dog the size of a small horse when you live in a B&B. You know he's gonna say no. Again."

I grip the straps of my bag tighter, knowing he's right. "I'll think of something. I always do, don't I?"

And just like that, my focus shifts back to Operation Nail Down, my brain already buzzing with ideas to add to the growing list. Because no matter what Robbie or anyone else says, I'm not giving up. Not on Shadow, and definitely not on the mystery of how his owner died.

"Hey, I've got an idea. Sasha, I need to ask Billy Thornton another couple of questions. Will you come with me?"

"Okay, but I'm not pretending to be interested in him again."

"What are you gonna do, Alex? Make him think you're crushing on him?" Robbie teases.

"Ewww. No way. He makes my skin crawl," I say. "But actually, that's not a bad idea. If I'm nice to Billy, maybe he'll actually give me something I can use."

Robbie's jaw tightens up and he makes a grunting noise. He looks kinda miffed about me even talking to Billy Thornton. Me and Robbie have been friends since I moved to Seaside Cove, and I was totally sure I was gonna marry him someday, but he seems to want to stay in the friend zone.

"I gotta go. You two are gonna cause all kinds of trouble." Robbie flips his backpack over his shoulder and storms away.

Wow. I never thought I'd see him angry. Or hurt.

"Earth to Alex. We gonna do this, or what?" Sasha asks as she slants her eyes off to the right.

It's Billy. And he's glaring at me like he hates my guts. Well, I hate his, too, but maybe I can get information from him anyway.

"Hey, Billy," I call out.

The look on his face changes. It's like he doesn't know what to think. Finally, it changes to some kind of 'whatever' thing as he starts towards us. The last time I punched him in the nose, we were about the same height and weight. Now he's a few inches taller and weighs more than me. If I punched him now, I don't think he'd go away crying like he did the last time. "What do ya want now, Alex? You gonna have Sasha pretend to like me again so I answer all your questions?"

"Nah. You fell for it once. It won't work again. I just thought you'd know more about construction sites that you do."

Billy's face turns red. Even his eyes look like they're angry. He sputters, "Who says I don't know nothin' about construction?"

"It seems totally basic. We asked you a question about a loose board on a job, and you didn't seem to know anything about how it would get handled."

"Oh, yeah? I know plenty about what goes on. And what happened to you ain't normal. In fact, it probably got done on purpose. Somebody wanted you dead. That's what I think. And there's only one guy in town who's gonna have the details—the gravedigger. That's who you're gonna be talkin' to next, Crazy Willy Hobbs."

I wasn't gonna get angry, but the thing about the gravedigger did it. I practically spit out the words, "You're stupid, Billy."

He takes a step toward me, and the air in the hallway feels heavier. His jaw is clenched so tight I'm half expecting to hear his teeth crack. His voice is low, sharp, and way too serious. "What did you just call me?"

I freeze, suddenly realizing what I've done. Punching out Billy when we were in grade school was one thing. But now he's taller, heavier, and stronger than me. My brain's yelling at me to say something smart, to find a way out of this, but the words catch in my throat.

"You heard me," I manage to say, though my voice doesn't come out nearly as bold as I want it to. My palms are clammy, and my heart is hammering like crazy.

Billy makes a face. It's not his usual annoying, cocky smirk. This one sends a chill down my back. "You think you're so smart, don't you, Alex? But calling people names? Who's stupid now?"

I look around, hoping someone, anyone, will step in. Sasha's taken a step back. It looks like she's ready to bolt. I don't blame her. The air feels like it's closing in on me. The kids around us are just blurry shapes in the background. Billy takes another step forward. He's close enough for me to smell his anger. The way he towers over me makes my stomach twist, and I can't fight the urge to move back a little.

My dad's voice is shouting at me in my head, warning me about kids like Billy. For once, I think he might be right. Billy looks like he's not bluffing, and for the first time that I've known him, I'm scared.

I don't know whether to run, apologize, or what.

Before I can decide, Robbie's voice cuts through the tension like a whip. "Hey, Billy, back off!"

Billy's head snaps to the side. Robbie's standing there. Just two feet away. Then, he moves in front of me in some kind of ninja move that has me in awe. Where did he come from? How did he learn to move like that?

I thought he was gone. I thought he was angry with me. Robbie's not built like Billy—he's slighter in the shoulders, shorter by a few inches—but the way he set his feet and refused to blink made the difference vanish.

"What's your problem, huh?" Robbie says, his voice firm and steady. "She said something dumb. Big deal. Doesn't mean you get to act like a jerk."

Billy tries to intimidate Robbie by moving a little closer, but Robbie doesn't flinch. Billy's hands are balled into fists at his sides, and his chest is puffed out like he's ready for a fight.

But Robbie doesn't flinch. He totally oozes confidence and looks ready for Billy to throw a punch. "Seriously, Thornton? Walk away. You might be able to scare a girl, but you don't scare me."

I feel my heart lurch, not knowing whether to be terrified for Robbie or if he's somehow turned into a kind of superhero. Someone I don't even recognize.

Billy's jaw is working like he's debating what to do, but finally, he exhales sharply through his nose and backs off. "Whatever," he mutters, sneering at me one last time before he leaves. "Pick your fights better next time, Atwood."

I hold my breath as he storms off, shoving past a group of kids who'd gathered to watch. The second he's out of sight, my knees go weak, and when Robbie looks at me, I think they might buckle.

"You okay?" Robbie's voice is soft, welcoming, like a warm hug on a cool day. My heart beats faster. My throat dry. Somehow, I manage to agree. "Yeah…thanks, Robbie. Really. That was, I mean, thank you."

His cheek scrunches up for a second like it's no big deal, but then the corners of his mouth twitch into a small, sexy smile. "Anytime."

Oh. My. Gawd. What just happened? The way he's looking at me. My knees are totally gonna give out.

I force myself to break eye contact. I've gotta breath. But when Robbie's fingers touch mine, I'm drawn back to him. In his eyes, I see, oh, wow. Something warm and fuzzy fills my chest. This is me, turning into a puddle on the sidewalk.

And it feels so good.

13

Rick

RICK STEERED HIS CAR INTO a narrow gravel driveway, cutting the engine as he took in the sight of Sylvia Archer's office. Once a grand Victorian home, the structure stood like a relic from a bygone era, carefully preserved to exude both charm and authority. The creamy yellow siding glistened in the afternoon sun, its brightness almost unnervingly pristine, as if Sylvia had the entire house repainted at the slightest hint of weathering. Ornate white gingerbread trim framed the roofline and porch, twisting into intricate patterns more ornate than strictly necessary, leaving the impression of a façade designed to dazzle.

A turret on the southeast corner, capped with slate tiles that glinted darkly in the sun, reached toward the sky. The windows were decorated with deep green shutters, but reflections from the sun betrayed nothing of the building's interior. Even the porch seemed staged; its polished oak rocking chairs and small wrought-iron table had been adorned with succulents, all perfectly symmetrical, all arranged with purpose. Below the steps, masses of lavender added a gentle fragrance that masked the meticulous planning behind every detail.

Rick exhaled slowly as he climbed out of the car, the crunching of gravel underfoot breaking the stillness of the driveway. There was nothing casual about this house; Sylvia had claimed it as her statement piece. The brass plaque by the front door confirmed her calculated touch, its elegant script reading "Archer Development & Design." A smaller sign attached below made it clear this was no open-door affair with its prim admonition, "By Appointment Only."

Forget that. He was here and wasn't about to be turned away. Everything about this house felt deeply curated. It gave the impression of someone who wanted to be seen as both a historical preservationist and a modern visionary. But Rick didn't buy it. The lavender in the garden, the sedate colors, the welcoming front porch—none of it could hide the clinical precision behind every choice.

If appearances reflected intentions, then this house contained more secrets than those hinted at by Isabelle Murdoch and Jake Morales. Both had claimed Sylvia wasn't known for her honesty—an opinion Rick found himself inclined to believe. From the fragments he'd been able to assemble, he was rapidly becoming convinced that the rules Sylvia operated by didn't align with those of the rest of Seaside Cove.

Rick stepped toward the stairs, paused at the bottom, and scanned the intricate woodwork. Drawing a deep breath, he climbed the stairs. A small sign to the right of the door indicated he should ring for assistance. His fingers brushed the cool brass of the doorbell as he pressed the button. Chimes reverberated faintly on the other side of the thick green-painted door.

Waiting patiently, Rick contemplated how to approach Sylvia. He'd deal with this the same way he would any source for a news story—try the carrot, and if that didn't work, haul out the stick. Unfortunately, in this case, he didn't have much of a stick to use. Truth be told, he didn't even have much of a carrot, either. Oh well, he'd just have to improvise.

After about thirty seconds, a smallish woman who looked to be in her early twenties opened the door. "May I help you?"

"My name is Rick Atwood. There's an urgent matter I'd like to speak to Ms. Archer about."

"I'm sorry, but Ms. Archer isn't available. Would you like to make an appointment?"

Rick exhaled slowly, forcing a polite smile as the young woman sat expectantly, clearly impatient for his answer. The air between them stretched tight with growing tension, and Rick took a beat to size her up. She exuded professionalism, her blazer crisp and her hair pulled back in a no-nonsense ponytail.

"I understand Ms. Archer's a busy woman," Rick began, adjusting his stance to give off just the right mix of patience and quiet authority. "But the matter I need to discuss with her requires immediate attention. I wouldn't interrupt her otherwise."

The woman's lips pressed into a thin line, her polite demeanor frosted with determination. "Ms. Archer's schedule is carefully managed. If you'd like to leave a message, I can see that she receives it."

Rick flashed another smile, this one edged with just enough charm to knock down a small barrier. "I'd prefer to speak to her myself. This concerns my family's construction project. I'm sure she'll want to address it sooner rather than later. I'd really hate for this to escalate. I'm sure Ms. Archer sees the value in dealing with concerns before they become, shall we say, problematic. You could think of this as a courtesy visit."

For a second, Rick thought he'd hit the mark. The woman's eyes narrowed slightly, her hesitation visible. But then her professional shield snapped back into place, and she folded her hands atop a sleek leather-bound planner. "I'll be happy to deliver your concerns to Ms. Archer, Mr. Atwood, and she will decide how to proceed. However, as I have stated, Ms. Archer is unavailable now."

Rick blew out a quiet breath. No carrot. No stick. Just the gatekeeper standing between him and whatever threads Sylvia Archer held. He took a small step back, letting his smile fade. "I see." The words came clipped, but surprise cut his irritation short when he noticed small black orbs perched in the corners of the ceiling, the watchful eyes of a security system.

There was one to his right, carefully hidden in the corner of the porch. Another was to his left. There was no point in pushing this any further. He was convinced the reason he wasn't being granted entrance wasn't because he didn't have an appointment, but because of who he was.

The woman arched a brow at him. "If you'd like, I can make a note of your name and reason for the visit. If she elects to reach out, she or I will be in touch."

Rick cut her off, a hint of steel slipping into his tone. "I think I have the picture." He inched closer, careful to keep the gesture authoritative rather than aggressive. "I'll just take my concerns up with the Chief of Police."

Her expression faltered, giving Rick hope that he'd cracked her defenses with the magic word, 'police.'. He waited for her decision and was rewarded when she said, “Very well. I’ll tell Ms. Archer you were here.”

Rick inclined his head, taking a small step back. “I think she already knows. Good day.”

Upon returning to his car, Rick contemplated his next move. Clearly, he’d underestimated the power of the gatekeeper. It had been a while, but he knew how to get around them. And, if all else failed, he could always go to Adam and suggest he pay an official visit to Ms. Archer.

Rick left Archer Development more frustrated than when he’d arrived. He folded himself into his car, the door shutting with a sharp thunk, the pristine façade of the converted Victorian mocking his attempt to get information. The scent of lavender still clung to his senses. The knots forming in his stomach screamed at him. Direct avenues will not work. Between Sylvia’s fortress, her gatekeeper, and Sylvia’s brazen attitude, he had to get far more creative. One thing hadn’t changed. He felt more certain than ever that Sylvia’s refusal to even hear him out meant she was hiding something big.

All of that was okay because he had a Plan B. Walt Copley. If anyone had insight into Sylvia’s dealings, it was the historical society’s self-proclaimed moral compass. And if Walt’s fingerprints were on any of Sylvia’s questionable choices, Rick knew it wouldn’t take much to trip him up. Like Sylvia, Walt also fancied himself untouchable, but everyone had their breaking point. And Rick was willing to bet that Walt’s breaking point had a much lower threshold than Sylvia Archer’s.

Before he could overthink it, Rick backed out of the gravel driveway and headed toward Walt’s house. Unlike Sylvia’s pristine

Victorian, Walt lived in a dilapidated Craftsman. The pale green paint had faded into the color of stale mint, its chipped edges exposing bare wood underneath. A makeshift stack of bricks propped up one side of the porch railing, its jaunty angle suggesting Walt's jury-rigged solutions weren't meant to last. The windows were spotted with grime, a few edges taped with plastic that flapped faintly in the breeze.

The garden, or what once might have been one, was now a battlefield of overgrown weeds. There was even a bicycle rusting lazily under a crooked tree. It all made Sylvia's manicured Victorian look like Buckingham Palace.

Somewhere beneath all that neglect were the bones of a charming home. If what he'd heard about Walt believing he should own the B&B was true, this home's state of disrepair was an undeniable reason it should never happen.

Rick stepped onto the porch, and the wood groaned conspicuously, his weight coaxing a protesting crack from the loose boards. He rapped on the door, loud enough to be heard over the faint sound of a radio playing inside.

Nothing.

Rick knocked again, harder this time, his knuckles sending vibrations through the loose frame. "Walt!" he called, deliberately pitching his voice to be heard over the din within. "It's Rick Atwood. We need to talk!"

The radio skipped to an ad for arthritis cream, but there was no sound of shuffling shoes or a door unlocking. Rick tried once more, then squinted through a nearby window. "Walt, I can see the light's on. You want to help me out, or should I go get Adam and come back?"

Still nothing.

He returned to the window and did a closer inspection. Drapes hung unevenly, partially obscuring the view inside, but he could still make out the cluttered expanse of books, papers, and what looked suspiciously like an antique telescope. Whatever Walt was doing in there, it didn't include answering his door.

Rick sighed, stepping down from the porch with one last look at the sagging house. How could anyone whose home was in this condition be considered the town's historical preservationist? No question, Walt was in no position to welcome a run-in with his conscience.

"Fine," Rick muttered under his breath, tugging his car door open. "We'll do it your way—for now."

Rick cursed Walt Copley a dozen times on the way home, but his curses stopped when he walked into the kitchen. There, before him, was a sight he'd never dreamed of finding in Marquetta's kitchen—pure chaos. Marquetta stood at the center island, a tired but determined look on her face as she diced vegetables. Next to her, Baby Jack waved his arms in the baby carrier like an overenthusiastic cheerleader. In one hand, he gripped what appeared to be the remnants of a dinner roll. And there, along the tiled floor, lay a suspicious trail of bread crumbs leading straight to the instigator of the chaos, Baby Jack.

"Tell me you solved the case and caught the killer," she said, rolling her eyes without missing a beat on the cutting board. Her knife's rapid rhythm punctuated her pointed sarcasm nicely.

"Not exactly," Rick admitted, setting his keys down and watching as Baby Jack extended a soggy corner of bread toward him in offering.

Marquetta's eyes flicked up. "And by 'not exactly,' you mean you're about as close to figuring things out as Baby Jack is to starting a college fund?"

"Depends," Rick said, plucking the bread from Jack and holding it aloft in a playfully exaggerated victory. "Does college fund equity include saliva-soaked carbs?"

Marquetta huffed and then laughed. It was light and bright and lifted Rick's spirits.

"Sure, why not?" she said. "I guess anything goes in this three-ring circus. Why don't we say anything bartered from your investigative escapades counts as a contribution? It's a win-win. You get good-guy points, and I get something out of losing your help."

Wincing at Marquetta's gibe, Rick let Baby Jack grab the bread back. Jack let out a triumphant squeal, which, in a way, helped to break any tension between them. "I'm sorry I wasn't here to help. I was doing groundwork. Sylvia's office, Walt's house. Neither was thrilled to see me, technically."

"Technically?"

"Walt just wouldn't answer," Rick clarified, crossing toward her and noticing that the pile of carrots was only half chopped. "Sylvia, on the other hand, has a gatekeeper who all but threw me out. Something tells me they're stalling. Both of them."

Marquetta smirked, "I'd expect nothing less from a power-hungry developer and the town's crankiest retiree. Didn't Adam tell you to stay clear of this?"

"Technically, he told me to stay away from the murder investigation. I'm looking into the slowdowns on our construction project." Rick grinned sheepishly, reaching to block Jack from now swiping an entire measuring cup off the counter. "It's all connected to the site delays. I just need to figure out how deep it goes."

"We? I think you mean you. And, by the way, do you know how much you sound like Alex right now?"

Rick winced. "Ouch. That hurts. Like daughter, like father?"

Marquetta rolled her eyes as she returned her knife to the cutting board. "Before you disappear again, do me a favor and move those baby carrots before Jack tries to stuff another one into his shoes."

Rick looked down, saw Jack's hand hovering over the carrots, and grabbed them. "Caught red-handed, young man." He let out a small laugh as he moved the vegetables out of reach, then regarded the bowl. "Holy cow. They're doing the same thing to me."

"What are you babbling about?" Marquetta paused with the knife in mid-air, looking at him as if he were speaking in tongues.

"Walt and Sylvia. They're moving the evidence out of reach so I can't get to it. I've got to go." He kissed Marquetta on the cheek and rushed out of the kitchen.

14

Alex

I KNOW IT'S JUST STUPID girl stuff, but when Robbie's fingers grazed mine, it so rocked my world. My breath caught. Our eyes met. And, whoa. Then, I did the dumbest thing I've ever done in my life and suggested the three of us go to the cemetery to spy on Willy Hobbs.

Sasha makes a face. "Seriously, Alex? That's, like, morbid."

"Alex," Robbie says, pushing his glasses up his nose and crossing his arms, "This is literally the worst idea you've had. Ever."

Oh, yeah. The deep gaze-into-my-eyes thing we shared is so totally over. Nice job, me. "It's just a cemetery, guys."

"Not that," Robbie says. "Listening to Billy Thornton. He's never exactly screamed 'credible source.'"

"Good point, but how bad could spying on Willy Hobbs be? He's, like, what? Eighty? What's he gonna do? Hobble after us with a shovel?"

"Maybe it won't be so bad. Okay, I'm in." Sasha holds up her hand, and we high-five each other.

Robbie shakes his head like he's being sent to the gallows. "Why do I keep letting you talk me into this stuff?"

"Because deep down, you know I'm always right," I say, flashing him my most charming smile, which, all of a sudden, feels less charming and more awkward, like I practiced it in the mirror too many times. "Now grab your bike, Mr. Reluctant Agent, because this is officially the next step of Operation Nail Down."

The cemetery isn't far, just a few blocks over, but as we get closer, Robbie starts slowing down like we're on a hundred-mile trek through the desert.

I motion for him to pedal faster—I don't want him to chicken out now. "C'mon, Robbie, this place doesn't even have a gate. You can't get locked in or anything. It's just grass and gravestones."

"I'm not worried about being locked in," he mutters. "I'm worried about getting caught! What if Willy calls the cops or something?"

"He's not going to call the cops, Robbie," Sasha says. "He's too busy reorganizing the inventory of dirt or whatever it is he does."

"Exactly. Just think of it this way," I say as we chain up our bikes behind a tall hedge, "Willy's probably too busy trying to perfect his 'efficiency rituals' to even notice us."

Once we're in, the cemetery is quieter than I expected, which makes every crunch of our sneakers on the dirt path sound like a series of cannon blasts going off. Robbie keeps looking over his shoulder, and I swear he's one snapping twig away from bolting. It's weird how he's gone from superhero to Robbie in only a few minutes. Sasha, on the other hand, is fixing her ponytail like she's about to meet a celebrity. Typical Sasha.

"There he is!" I whisper, pointing toward the back of the cemetery. Sure enough, Willy Hobbs is crouched down near a grave marker, armed with a spade and what looks like an ancient tape measure. I wish I had some binoculars, but sure enough, it's one of those super-long tape measures like the contractors use.

"What's he doing?" Sasha whispers.

"It looks like he's checking the gravestones to make sure they're on center," Robbie says as we duck behind a cluster of overgrown hedges that haven't seen a gardener in years. When he plops down next to me, he whispers, "This is so dumb. We're going to get poison ivy."

"Shush, or he'll hear us!"

But Willy isn't paying attention to anything other than stretching the tape measure over what has to be the neatest dirt mound I've ever seen. He steps back, consults a little notebook, and then mutters something we can't hear. Sasha's leaning forward so far, I think she might lose her balance and fall over. I grab the back of her hoodie just in case.

"This is fascinating and disturbing all at once," she murmurs.

We watch in silence for a minute as Willy makes a note, then grabs what looks like a small hand rake and starts raking the dirt. But he's not just raking, it's like he's grooming the dirt. Wow. Sasha's right.

"Why's he doing that?" Robbie whispers, his voice tinged with both disgust and curiosity.

"This is so not what I expected," I whisper back.

Suddenly, Willy stands up and spins around, holding the rake in front of him like a knight with a sword. "Who's there?" he barks.

All three of us hit the dirt like a synchronized Olympic team. My heart's pounding so loud I'm sure the whole cemetery can hear it.

"Probably just squirrels again," Willy mutters after a long pause. Shaking his head, he goes back to his notebook.

Robbie hisses, "I told you this was a bad idea."

Okay, so I'm already wondering if this idea was genius or if Robbie's right when Sasha says, "Uh, Alex? Who's the guy sneaking in from the side?"

I freeze, my heart doing this awkward little skip. Slowly, I turn my head right and see Walt Copley approaching. Oh, great. The mayor of Grumpy-land himself.

Walt's trudging toward Willy with his two-tone cane and his permanent storm cloud of crankiness. His face is twisted into one of his trademark scowls, like walking through the cemetery has somehow personally offended him.

Robbie, who's now crouched behind a gravestone and gripping the edge like it's his lifeline, mutters, "This day officially has a 'worse' now."

"Shush!" I hiss, waving him off as we all drop a little lower to avoid being spotted.

Walt stops a couple of feet from Willy, slamming the base of his cane into the dirt so hard it makes a small puff of dust. "Hobbs, why'd you do it?"

Willy looks up, squinting like he's trying to decide if this is real life or just a particularly grouchy hallucination. "Copley. What brings you to my humble garden of eternal rest?"

That's a more diplomatic greeting than I was expecting. Sasha raises an impressed eyebrow.

Copley, however, is not in the mood for pleasantries. He points a bony finger at Willy. "Don't play dumb with me, Hobbs! I know you told Atwood to come to my house."

What? Why did my dad go to Walt Copley's house?

Willy blinks at Walt like an old-timey cartoon character. Then he does it again. "Atwood? Rick Atwood? What're you babblin' about now?"

"Don't you lie to me!" Walt's eyes are so wide, they look like they're about to fall out and start rolling around. And his mustache? If it gets any bushier, it's gonna start looking like a pet he forgot to feed. "He showed up at my house. Probably sticking his nose into business that doesn't concern him! You sent him. I know you did!"

Willy's confusion is so genuine that even Robbie whispers, "I kinda feel bad for him."

"Copley, I don't have the faintest idea what you're yammering on about," Willy says, throwing his hands in the air, one still clutching his ridiculous rake. "Last time I saw Rick Atwood was at the market. I think. In the vegetable aisle."

Walt doesn't blink. His scowl deepens by a mile. "Don't you lie to me, Hobbs," he growls, low and dangerous. "I know you've been squawking to people about things that ain't their business. And if you think I'm just going to stand by while you drag my name through the mud, you've got another thing coming."

Willy opens his mouth, but Walt steamrolls right over him, his voice climbing in volume. "Don't think for a second I haven't kept an eye on you. Always sticking your nose where it doesn't belong. If you stick your nose out any further, it'll end up in the same place as Granger's!"

The air gets sucked out of the cemetery, like we've all realized how bad that sounded. Sasha's hand is clamped over her mouth, her eyes huge. Robbie looks like his brain is in freeze mode. How did he stand up to Billy Thornton like that?

And Willy, poor Willy, actually takes a step back, his face pale under the dirt smudges. "What do you mean, Copley?" His voice falters just slightly, but enough to give Walt the upper hand.

"What do you think I mean?" Copley takes a step closer, looming over Willy like an old-movie gangster, complete with waving his cane. "Granger thought he could blackmail me, and now where is he? You'll be putting him six feet under, that's where."

Blackmail? Is that what got Tommy Granger killed? There's a pause. The weight of Copley's words hangs in the air, heavy and menacing. I'm literally holding my breath, a thousand thoughts racing through my head. Did he just admit to murder? That would mean this wasn't some small-time shady business deal, but this was "call in the FBI" kind of stuff.

"Are you sayin' you had something to do with Granger's death?" Willy straightens up slightly. Now, he's holding onto his rake like it's a lifeline—or a club. "I don't know about Atwood, but I do know this—I mind my own business. I sure ain't planning on making any enemies here, y'hear?"

"You'd do well to remember that," Walt hisses and spins on his heel. As he stalks off toward his car, he keeps muttering under his breath about "meddling idiots."

We stay frozen for what feels like forever, the air still electric with tension.

"I think we should go," Robbie whispers.

"Yeah," Sasha murmurs. "Before something levels up from bad to worse."

Willy starts to pack up his tools in silence, but his usual muttering is nowhere to be heard. I motion with my head toward the exit. "Come on. Before there are any more creepy shovel threats."

But in the back of my head, one question keeps poking at me like a thorn. Just what did Walt Copley mean about Granger? And is Operation Nail Down now a murder investigation, too?

15

Rick

AFTER APOLOGIZING FOR WHAT FELT like a thousand times to Marquetta for abandoning her earlier, Rick tackled the evening's preparations for the next day's breakfast service. The truth was, he hadn't made any progress in finding a way through the defenses of either Walt Copley or Sylvia Archer. Still, as he worked, he kept running the problem through his head in hopes of somehow finding a solution. He'd just done a final check of the dining room and was headed for the kitchen to help Marquetta and Alex when Norm Butterfield stepped in front of him and blocked his path. Norm had his arms crossed and a determined look on his face. He was, as usual, dressed in plaid.

Rick fought back a chuckle as he said, "Good evening, Norm."

"Evening, Rick." A low rumble escaped Norm's throat, like an engine struggling to start.

That was not a good sign. It meant Norm had suggestions. And Rick had one for him—less plaid, Norm. Less plaid! Alex had called Norm The Plaid Whisperer. Marquetta hadn't helped things by saying every outfit Norm wore looked like it belonged in a log cabin photoshoot.

"We need to talk about breakfast," Norm declared.

Rick knew better than to expect this conversation to go anywhere reasonable. He'd already heard a couple of Norm's suggestions—a DIY pancake breakfast art station and a custom omelet bar with 50 toppings.

What the heck? Why not just do international days? How about a Japanese Kaiseki Breakfast complete with grilled fish, miso soup, pickled vegetables, tamagoyaki, and rice?

"Do we?" Rick countered, weighing the odds of escape. Slim to none, based on Norm's stance.

"Yes, we do. Now, don't get me wrong, I like what your cook does with the eggs. Solid scramble technique. But the toast situation? Rick, it's chaos."

Rick tilted his head, pretending to give this serious consideration. "Chaos? That's a strong word for toast."

"Strong but accurate," Norm said, shaking his head as if truly disappointed in humanity. "You need to streamline the system. For starters, guests should be able to toast their bread at the table. It's insane to have one central toaster in the kitchen. You're bottlenecking the process."

"Table toasters?" Sure. Nothing could go wrong with everyone plugging in their own appliances.

"Oh! And pancakes," Norm continued, completely undeterred. "You people think way too small. One flavor per morning? Amateur hour. What if you set up a pancake buffet? Blueberry, chocolate chip, banana nut, maybe even… bacon-infused. Guests love options, Rick."

"Sounds like the pancake art station you recommended, Norm."

"I admit, it's similar, but a little less complex. I realize an art station could become another bottleneck."

Rick arched a brow, thinking through the logistics. "And where exactly do you propose we would put this pancake smorgasbord, Norm? The lobby?"

Norm waved a hand dismissively. "Details, details. The important thing is variety! Trust me, Rick, I know breakfast. I've done the research."

Rick opened his mouth to suggest that maybe Norm should start a breakfast-themed think tank when the sound of heels clacking on the hardwood floors caught his attention. He looked past Norm to the dining room entrance and froze for just a second when he saw Sylvia Archer.

Sylvia wore a perfectly curated smile and a scarf that probably cost more than all the socks in Rick's drawer combined. She strode into the room like she owned it. Which, in her mind, she probably did.

"Rick. Good evening."

Her voice carried a honeyed quality gooey enough to put him on edge. Although he was tempted to launch into a few accusatory questions about why she wouldn't talk to him at her place of business, he opted for civility —for now.

"Good evening. What brings you to the B&B, Sylvia?"

Sylvia regarded Norm as if she were debating between acknowledging him or dismissing him entirely. Apparently, she decided on the latter. Norm, for his part, looked mildly offended but also intrigued. Rick made a mental note to brace for whatever 'feedback' Norm might glean from this encounter.

"I thought I'd stop by with a little goodwill gesture," Sylvia said as she pulled an envelope from her designer handbag.

Rick took the envelope, angling his body slightly to block Norm, who had started craning his neck to see what it contained. Sylvia's every move was controlled, deliberate. Subtle, she was not.

"Go ahead, open it," she prompted, her eyes sparkling with faux generosity. "I think you'll find it... helpful."

Rick slid the envelope open and pulled out a check made payable to him for an amount that would easily cover all of the unplanned expenses at the construction site. Looking up, he noted her smug expression. Based on what he'd learned about Sylvia's business dealings so far, he wasn't particularly surprised by the gesture. The amount, however, was a different story. Almost an obscene one, at that.

"It's for the construction delay cost," Sylvia explained, her tone dripping with false sincerity. "I heard about the mishap and thought, 'What kind of neighbor would I be if I didn't help out?'"

Rick's instincts screamed at him to tread lightly. He already knew Sylvia Archer didn't do anything out of the kindness of her heart. There was always a string, if not a whole tangled web, attached. He was, however, curious and decided to play along. "That's generous of you. But I imagine there's a catch."

Sylvia laughed lightly as if he'd said something funny. "Not at all. Consider it...a loan. No rush to pay it back. I know how stressful construction setbacks can be."

Rick held the check between his thumb and forefinger, careful not to grip it too tightly. "A loan," he echoed. He watched her carefully, noting the way she tilted her head and the faint quirk at the corner of her mouth. She was enjoying this.

"Yes, you can pay me back when the construction project is finished," Sylvia's voice was soft and melodic, with a gentle lilt that seemed to wrap around each word like a warm blanket. "I'm just trying to help, Rick. Truly. And honestly, it's better for everyone if construction moves forward smoothly, don't you think?"

There it was. She wasn't being magnanimous. Not in the least. She had an angle, and Rick didn't like the edges of it. If he was correct, he'd found the string—and he'd bet that it involved Archer Construction taking over his project. He saw no point in pursuing the matter. Just end it, he thought.

"That's a generous outlook. I'll give this consideration."

"Please do." Sylvia's smile sharpened. "We all have a stake in this town's success."

Rick nodded, tucking the check back into the envelope. "As I said, I'll think about it."

"I wouldn't wait too long," she said lightly, her head inclining slightly. "Life is full of opportunities, but they don't always stick around. Oh, and one more thing. It's about Alex."

Norm grunted. He looked pleased as could be. Why wouldn't he be? Mr. Plaid was still present and had been able to eavesdrop on a very touchy conversation.

"Do you mind?" Sylvia skewered Norm with her words.

But apparently, Norm wasn't to be dismissed so easily. "Not at all. I don't know who you are, lady, but I'm the guest here, and we were having an important conversation when you barged in."

Sylvia huffed her indignation, but Rick wanted to see where this went. Besides, he kind of liked the idea of having a witness present. "Alex? What about her?" he asked.

"You need to keep her away from the construction site. Projects like this are very dangerous for a child."

Alex was hardly a child. She was now a young adult who always seemed to take an overzealous interest in crime. And that probably included Tommy Granger's death. And maybe that was the whole reason for Sylvia being here.

Obviously, Sylvia's 'loan' wasn't just a loan. It was leverage. And while he didn't know for sure what she was angling for yet, he knew she wasn't here to play nice. Before he could respond, he heard Baby Jack's gurgling and footsteps behind him. Marquetta winked at him as she approached. A sense of strength built within him when she and the baby stood next to him.

"Sylvia, how nice of you to come by." Marquetta had Baby Jack balanced on her hip like a tiny, unpredictable wrecking ball. Marquetta's expression was sharp enough to hint she wasn't just here for a leisurely chat.

Sylvia's practiced smile froze in place. "Hello, Marquetta."

Ignoring the greeting, Marquetta turned toward Rick, which put Baby Jack within striking distance of Sylvia. Rick had seen far too often how excited his son got when he was near shiny objects. Should he say something? He decided against it when Marquetta fixed him with a look that said she'd spotted Sylvia long before she entered the room.

"Downstairs is all done, Rick. I'm heading up to the guest rooms."

"Thanks for letting me know."

Sylvia bristled at being ignored, and her eyes flicked toward the baby. Apparently, she dismissed him as unworthy of her attention. But Baby Jack was having none of that. His little hands shot out like heat-seeking missiles, aiming for the shiny chain on Sylvia's handbag,

"Ba!" he squealed, his voice piercing and filled with enthusiasm.

"Whoa, buddy! Easy there," Rick said, stepping forward just as Jack managed to snag the attention magnet on Sylvia's overpriced, undoubtedly Italian leather bag. The baby yanked with surprising determination, giving the strap a solid tug that made Sylvia lurch forward.

Sylvia's gasp sounded like she'd been yanked into an impromptu wrestling match, which, when Rick thought about it, she had. Norm pulled back and planted his hand over his mouth. He didn't say a word, but Rick noticed he was enjoying the show. For that matter, so was he.

"Oh, for heaven's sake," she muttered, fumbling to pull the bag away. But Jack wasn't letting go so easily; he giggled, tightening his grip on his new toy. Rick, caught somewhere between apologetic and wildly amused, reached out to pry the baby's chubby fingers from the strap.

"Jack!" Marquetta scolded, though she didn't seem particularly upset. If anything, there was a hint of enjoyment in her eyes as she shifted her weight slightly, tilting the baby just out of Sylvia's reach. "What is it with you and grabbing things you shouldn't?"

"He's got a strong grip," Rick offered, still struggling with Jack's unexpectedly effective tug-of-war technique.

"Future Olympian, I'd say," Norm offered.

Sylvia straightened, finally managing to pull her handbag free with a decisive yank. She smoothed her scarf and shot daggers at Marquetta. "Quite the handful, isn't he?" she sneered.

"They say babies take after their parents," Marquetta replied smoothly, her smile just a touch too bright.

Sylvia's jaw muscles twitched in a way that suggested she desperately wanted to lash out. And Jack, still riding the high of his victory, babbled nonsense sounds and flailed his arms like he was preparing for round two.

"Well," Sylvia said after a beat, her tone straining under the forced civility. "It's always delightful to see Seaside Cove's next generation growing up."

"And it's always delightful to see how concerned everyone is about our children," Marquetta replied with a sweetness equal to Sylvia's venom. She shifted Jack on her hip and pressed a quick kiss to the top of his head. "Anyway, Rick, I'm heading upstairs. If you need me, let me know."

She turned, pausing only long enough to offer Sylvia a tight, saccharine smile before sauntering away, Jack on her hip, still waving one hand enthusiastically in Sylvia's direction.

Sylvia's expression was frozen somewhere between strained politeness and thinly disguised irritation. A flush of warmth flooded Rick's chest. He was proud of his son's ability to pierce Sylvia's veil of goodwill. "Well, that's life with a baby, Sylvia. Never a dull moment."

From her tight-lipped smile to her rigid posture, Sylvia's angst over the entire encounter with Jack was obvious. She adjusted the strap of her bag, her nostrils flaring as she glared back at Rick."Clearly."

"If that's everything, I still have a lot to do before my day is done." Rick briefly considered returning the check, but decided against it. If nothing else, it was evidence—or, perhaps, a way to secure another chance to get a face-to-face meeting. Either way, it could be a valuable weapon in whatever battle was coming his way.

16

Alex

14 Nov

Hey Journal,

Things were getting kinda weird tonight at dinner. Mom and Dad were sitting at the dinner table when I walked in talking about some sort of insurance policy Tommy Granger had in a metal box. As soon as my dad saw me, he changed the subject and started apologizing for abandoning Mom this afternoon. When I asked what happened, they both said it was nothing. You and me, Journal, we both know that nothing totally means something, and it's probably something big.

I'll bet my dad is investigating what happened to Mr. Granger. Especially 'cause he also said a couple of times how Chief Cunningham won't let him help with the police investigation. My dad also warned me to stay away from the case. But since the warning came from my dad and not Chief Cunningham, it's not exactly official. Right?

Then there was the whole super big drama with Sylvia Archer. Why would she try to pay us off unless she had something to do with the murder? I'm super curious about that connection, too. The thing is, I can't really say anything with my dad around 'cause I'll just get another warning to mind my own business. Well, hello! If people like Sylvia Archer are messing with our house and the B&B, it is my business.

While my dad will for sure refuse to admit there's something going on, I'm totally sure if I ask Mom the right way, she'll be honest with me. That's kind of a problem 'cause once we start talking, she'll know I'm keeping a secret, too, I'll probably have to tell her about the trip to the cemetery. She'll probably say I should not stick my nose in this business between Walt Copley and Willy Hobbs, but the way Old Geezer Copley was talking, he's hiding something, too.

The big question I have, Journal, is if Tommy Granger was blackmailing Old Geezer Copley, where's the proof?

I'm gonna talk to Mom. I'm sure she'll be cool as long as I keep her in the loop. You know what, Journal? I hear a dog barking. I'm gonna go check it out.

xoxo

Alex

It's after nine, and most of the guests are in their rooms, so I tiptoe down the stairs, each step testing how stealthy I can be. It's the kind of quiet where even my breath feels loud. Another muffled bark shatters the silence, and when I get to the bottom of the stairs, Mr. Pennyworth looks up from where he's sitting by the fire and asks if I know whose dog is making so much noise.

"I don't know, Mr. Pennyworth. We don't have dogs, but I'm gonna go check it out."

He nods and returns to the bird book he's reading. He's like totally obsessed with birds. And, I guess, not dogs.

My heartbeat thuds in my ears as I speed-tiptoe toward the back door. The glow of the moon spills through the glass panes, lighting up the kitchen just enough to turn the furniture into shadowy forms. The French door is super quiet when I open it, and outside, the salty tang of ocean breeze fills the cool night air. For a second, the world is still, nothing but the whisper of leaves rustling and the hum of the distant surf. Then, there it is again. A bark that sounds like it's coming from next door.

"Hello?" I whisper-shout, not wanting to wake anyone. My heart's racing now, and I follow the sound of a dog whimpering. The gravel bites into my bare feet, sending sharp stings through my toes if I step too hard.

Why didn't I put on shoes? Duh. I stop short when a big and slow-moving shape comes toward me. A hiccup of fear rises in my throat. I'm out here in the dark, and this isn't any random chihuahua. This dog is huge.

Then he steps into the moonlight, and suddenly my cheeks are wet with happy tears and I'm all blubbery inside.

"Shadow!" My voice cracks as I ignore the sharp stings in my feet and stumble toward him. He tilts his head to one side as he walks toward me. "What are you doing here?" I drop to my knees in front of the giant Newfoundland, my arms outstretched, and that's all the permission he needs. He practically tackles me, his big paws landing squarely on my lap, his droopy, sad eyes staring straight into mine.

"You crazy dog," I murmur, hugging him so tightly my fingers sink into his thick coat. He smells like grass and dirt and a hint of something I don't want to think too hard about. "You're not supposed to be here. You're supposed to be home."

He's wagging his tail like he hasn't seen a soul in years, his big tongue flopping out as he slobbers all over my cheek. "Oh, I love you, too, you crazy dog!" I laugh, pushing at his jowls, but there's no stopping him. His tail sweeps the gravel like a broom on overdrive, and for a few brilliant seconds, it's just us. Me and this enormous, dopey dog whose happiness feels way too big for a single body to hold.

But then it hits me. He's wagging and licking and goofing around, but his eyes. His eyes hold questions he can't ask, no matter how much his tail tries to make up for his confusion. "You're looking for Tommy, aren't you?" I ask softly, my voice catching. He tilts his head at the name, ears pricking slightly. "You miss him, don't you?"

I press my face into his fur, my throat tightening. "I'm sorry, buddy." My words are muffled, but he doesn't seem to mind. He sits down, leaning into me with all one hundred fluffy pounds of him, like if he just presses hard enough, he'll finally feel like everything makes sense again. I stroke his fur, my hands shaking, and try not to cry, because nobody wants to be the girl sobbing into a dog at nine o'clock at night.

Maybe…I could… I stand, tilt my head, and start toward the French doors. "Come on, Shadow."

My dad's gonna kill me. Unless, of course, this works.

17

Rick

RICK SANK INTO HIS LEATHER desk chair, listening to the creaking of the soft fabric as it harmonized with the groans and whispers the old house made as it settled into the darkness of night. Since inheriting the B&B, he hadn't made any significant changes to what had been his grandfather's sanctuary. Although he'd considered the room's decor ostentatious when he arrived, he'd since come to realize that it, like the B&B, was an ode to times long past.

The desk, a fortress of mahogany, was tidy save for his laptop. An old brass clock he'd picked up at Howie's Collectibles occupied the far edge. A mug with the long-cold dregs of hot cocoa sat on a coaster next to his laptop. Around him, the scent of leather and old books filled the air, grounding him in this space. His grandfather had built the room, making sure to spare no expense in creating his refuge from the world. Beyond the tall windows, the ocean shimmered faintly in the moonlight, but that view wasn't why Rick was here so late. He returned his focus to the glowing screen before him.

His earlier conversation with Marquetta played again in his mind. After grumbling about his debacle of a visit to Sylvia Archer's office, Marquetta had mentioned the so-called 'developer war' from a decade ago. She'd described it as 'the time when half the town wanted bulldozers and the other half threatened to chain themselves to trees.' On top of it all, add in Sylvia Archer's attempt to—well, for lack of a better term—bribe him earlier this evening had transformed his suspicions into a full-fledged itch he couldn't ignore.

His old editor had always told him, "If you've got an itch, scratch it." He reached for the keyboard. Scratch, he would. It was time for a deep dive into the digital abyss of online newspaper archives. He began with the national newspaper site he'd used in his days as a reporter, but quickly realized Seaside Cove was way too small to make the national archives.

"Of course not," he muttered, shaking his head. There was only one place likely to have what he was looking for.

Opening a new tab, he navigated to the San Ladron Times' website. He wasn't thrilled about using their archives because the search function was, to say the least, finicky. He typed slowly and deliberately into the bar: 'developer war, Seaside Cove, zoning disputes.'

"Come on, give me something good," he murmured as he pressed the enter key. A few seconds later, the screen loaded with a mix of headlines. Most were tangentially related at best. Grumbling, Rick refined his search, narrowing the results by including key players he remembered Marquetta mentioning. He added quotes around each name and put an OR in between the names to force the search engine's hand. If any articles included the names of Francine Carter, Sylvia Archer, or Walt Copley, he knew they should show up.

One headline finally grabbed his attention: "Zoning Wars Escalate as Developers and Town Clash Over Historical Preservation." He checked the date of the article. December 30, 2013. The muscles in his back and shoulders stiffened. That was just a couple of months before Francine's first election.

"Bingo," Rick whispered, clicking into the article. The text loaded slowly, as though testing his patience. He scanned the story, his fingers still resting lightly on the keyboard. The article recounted a bitter battle between Seaside Cove's previous mayor and two developers—Sylvia Archer and Sam Greer. As Rick read the names, he realized the developer war must have been the beginning of the end for Greer.

Both Walt and Sylvia had wanted to build a resort on the land next to the B&B. As part of that project, the B&B would have been sold and 'integrated' into the master plan. Copley, who couldn't resist dramatic gestures, was quoted as championing "a desire to preserve Seaside Cove's historical integrity." Rick snorted. So much for the B&B being part of his family's legacy. Based on the recent decisions Copley had been making, any sense of integrity had flitted out the window long ago.

Reading on, Rick's brow furrowed as a pattern emerged. The developers had been split into two camps, but it was Sylvia Archer who was quoted as managing to broker compromises between the factions. Her involvement alongside Francine's political maneuvering made it no surprise that Greer had finally lost the war.

Digging deeper, Rick started copying quotes into his notes. Words and phrases leapt out at him—'political clout,' 'untraceable funds,' and 'the incumbent mayor's last-minute withdrawal.' He paused to let the pieces arrange themselves in his head. Part of him felt like he was watching a poorly scripted soap opera, and yet there was a thread of something sinister weaving through it all. He swiveled his chair slightly, staring out the window where the moonlight shimmered on the ocean like a secret just beyond reach.

Theory or not, Rick knew one thing for sure now. Whatever the truth was, it was buried in those years between Sylvia Archer's deals and Francine Carter's rise to power. And he intended to unearth it—right after he dealt with the commotion down on the first floor.

Rick hurried down the stairs, doing his best to remain silent despite the noise coming from the living room. The B&B had quiet hours. Rick's brow furrowed as he tried to comprehend the scene before him. A giant Newfoundland was sprawled in the middle of the living room, looking like it owned the place. Shadow, positively enormous compared to the person scratching his tummy, thumped his tail against the floor with enough vigor to rattle the lamp on the side table.

Rick gaped at Alex, unable to believe what he was seeing. Alex sat cross-legged next to the dog. Her grin was wide and unashamed, her hands vanishing into the dog's thick black fur. Shadow looked at Rick with what he could only describe as a doggy smirk, his wide tongue lolling out as if he were the happiest creature on Earth, and let out a low woof that practically rumbled the table lamps.

"What on Earth is he doing here?" Rick's voice came out sharper than he intended, and Alex looked up, the sparkle in her eyes dimming just slightly.

"I guess he missed me," Alex said, moving her hand to behind Shadow's ear. The dog groaned in apparent bliss, tipping his enormous head to give her better access. "I heard barking and came downstairs. When I went out back, there he was. Isn't that right, boy?"

Shadow answered with a noise somewhere between a bark and a burp, his tail thumping anew against the floor.

Rick pinched the bridge of his nose, sighing. "Alex, we've talked about this. We can't take in a dog. And especially not one the size of a small bear. You know the B&B's rules about pets. How would we explain Shadow to the guests?"

"I don't think they'd mind," Oliver Pennyworth said. "He's a very gentle dog."

He'd been so focused on Alex and Shadow that Rick hadn't even noticed his guest. "Not helping, Mr. Pennyworth."

The man waved his hand. "No worries. This is between you and your daughter."

"You're right. It is. Alex, we have Baby Jack to consider, too."

"Oh, Newfoundlands are extremely good with children. Protective and gentle at the same time. It's almost as if they have a natural instinct to protect and care for them."

"Mr. Pennyworth…"

"Oh, sorry. As the kids say, my bad."

Rick huffed and turned back to Alex. "Besides, we have new guests coming in all the time. What if Shadow took a dislike to one of them?"

"That's unlikely, those dogs are gentle giants. Why they…" Mr. Pennyworth stopped and looked at his watch. "Oh my, would you look at the time? I must be up early to see if I can catch sight of the Seaside Cove Chickadee tomorrow!" He stood and wove his way around the couch and Shadow, nudging Rick's elbow as he passed and whispering, "Good luck."

Alex's expression shifted, her smile fading into something that resembled disappointment but didn't quite tread into outright sadness. Not yet, anyway. Rick's heart broke when she buried her face in Shadow's fur. When she pulled away, she was pouting. "I know what you're gonna say. Shadow isn't our dog. He belongs to Mr. Granger's nephew now."

"Exactly, and I need to call him right now. He's probably worried sick." Rick shoved his hands into his pockets and stepped closer, but stopped short when Shadow raised his head to look at him, one eyebrow quirked in a way Rick swore was deliberate.

The dog blinked slowly, his jowls wobbling a bit as he yawned. It was the kind of yawn that seemed to take all the energy in the world, ending with his lips smacking together in a way that sounded uncomfortably judgmental.

Rick pointed at Shadow. "Don't look at me like that."

The dog huffed and laid his head back down on Alex's lap with the dramatics of an exhausted opera singer.

"See?" Alex said, her voice so soft it nearly broke him. "He ran away from home, Daddy. And you know what happens to dogs without homes." Her bottom lip trembled, but she quickly pressed her face into Shadow's neck.

Rick's chest tightened. He paced in a small circle, shooting glances from the dog to Alex and back again. He hated this. Every single bit of it. The logical part of him warned him about cramming a giant dog into a busy B&B. I would be a disaster, for sure. But the sight of Alex, now scratching Shadow's ears again while whispering to him, hit him below the belt.

He crouched down to Alex's level and lowered his voice. "Kiddo, it's not like I don't get it. I do. He's a good dog."

Shadow seemed to puff himself up at the compliment, his chest rising like he was suddenly the king of the household.

"But," Rick continued, ignoring the wagging tail smacking rhythmically against his shin, "we're in the middle of a hundred things right now. We're building the house, running this place, and…" He sighed. "A dog is a lot of responsibility. Especially one like him. He'd need space, walks, the right care."

"I could do it," Alex said quickly, her blue eyes shining with hope. "I'll wake up earlier to walk him, and I'll clean up after him—we can even give him a bed in the laundry room if you think he's too big for my room."

Her room? How could they even begin to explain that to the guests? Rick opened his mouth to respond, but Shadow cut him off with another massive yawn, rolling onto his side and stretching out so far he looked like he'd taken over half the room. His large, expressive eyes landed on Rick as if to say, 'Your move, pal.'

Rick groaned. "Oh, come on. Do you have to look so pitiful?"

Alex's voice softened to near a whisper. "Shadow doesn't have anyone else."

"No, that's not true. He's got Jake. And he has to go home."

Alex's hand stilled on Shadow's fur. Her eyes brimmed with tears as she looked at Rick. "I know it's not what you want, Daddy, but… maybe we're exactly what Shadow needs."

Rick drew in a sharp breath. He was losing. No, he'd already lost. What choice did he really have? Jake hadn't seemed at all interested in the dog, and if Shadow had escaped once, he could do it again. The thought of sending him away to an uncertain future made Rick sick.

He reached out and gave Shadow a tentative pat on the side. “This… this doesn’t mean its permanent.”

Alex’s squeal of delight was instant, and Shadow woofed once, as if claiming victory. Rick muttered, “What have I done?”

Shadow’s thumping tail was the only answer before Alex threw her arms around Rick’s neck. “Thanks, Daddy. You won’t regret this, promise.”

Oh no, he already did. Rick noticed how the Newfoundland had sprawled out like royalty and sighed. “Alex, listen to me. If Jake wants Shadow back, we have to return him.”

“And if he doesn’t?”

Rather than answer, Rick decided to let Alex and Shadow have their temporary euphoria. Tomorrow, he’d have to deal with the harsh reality. A B&B was no place for a dog. Not one the size of Shadow. “We’ll cross that bridge later if we have to.”

He pulled out his phone, found Jake’s number, and dialed, all the while hoping Jake would answer this late at night. He also hoped Jake would want Shadow back, but based on what he’d seen earlier in the day, he wasn’t so sure.

18

Rick

WHEN THE ALARM WENT OFF the following morning at five, Rick wanted nothing more than to turn it off and grab another hour's worth of sleep. That, however, was impossible when you owned a B&B and had a breakfast service starting in an hour and a half.

He didn't even realize he'd fallen back to sleep until Marquetta shook his shoulder. Through the haze of too little sleep, her bleary image came into focus. "Hey, Sleepyhead. You were up late. What happened?"

"I had to take Shadow back to Jake," Rick muttered. "Alex was devastated, so I was up until midnight trying to console her." He pulled himself to a sitting position and blinked a couple of times. "I'll need a shower and coffee to wake up."

"I can bring you the coffee, but you're on your own for the shower. Baby Jack is still asleep, thank goodness."

Rick told Marquetta he'd get the coffee when he came down to the kitchen, got in the shower, and was downstairs in just over twenty minutes. While they worked on preparations for breakfast, he recapped the previous night's conversation with Jake, how he'd convinced him he needed to try again with the dog, and how he'd finally relented when Alex insisted on going with him. He told her how Alex had cried herself to sleep, after which Rick had needed time to let the adrenaline wash out of his system.

Marquetta blew out a long breath and rested her hip against the counter. She thought for a moment, then said, "I'll talk to Alex this afternoon when she gets home from school. Maybe I can get her to understand why we can't take in a dog."

"Especially one the size of…"

"I know," Marquetta said as she rolled her eyes. "A small bear. Really, Rick. You need to up your game. Anyway, Lydia will be here any minute. She can help me, but I need you to get the coffee bar set up. It's getting late."

"Right."

With that, Rick got to work with his daily innkeeper duties. In only a few minutes, the first guests would arrive. He stood at the coffee bar in the dining room, lining up mugs like little soldiers, while he simultaneously chugged down the hot liquid from his own. The aroma of the fresh coffee mingled with the buttery scent of Marquetta's pancake batter that was now drifting in from the kitchen. At 6:30 on the dot, the first half dozen guests arrived. Rick got them seated, their light chatter and occasional laughter making the room more cheerful. It was the calm before the storm, but he'd take it. Later, the dining room would probably be packed.

Rick had just finished delivering a plate with bacon and eggs to Oliver Pennyworth when Adam Cunningham walked through the front door, his tall frame filling the entryway. Rick raised an eyebrow and smirked at his friend. "My, my, Chief Cunningham.

I'm surprised to see you here. Are you here for breakfast, or did something else bring you by?"

"Could be both," Adam said, tugging his cap off as he gave Rick an embarrassed grin. He gestured at a corner table away from the other guests. "Mind if I sit?"

"Have a seat." Rick wiped his hands on a towel and followed, bringing a mug of coffee as a peace offering. Something in Adam's demeanor told him this wasn't a social call, but he still felt bad about their last conversation. And when Adam slumped into the chair, the muscles in his jaw working overtime, Rick knew something was up.

"You don't usually wear your 'concerned face' when you're here, Adam. What's on your mind?"

Adam sipped the coffee and let his shoulders drop an inch as the warmth settled him. "First off, I owe you an apology." He paused as if he expected Rick to respond, but Rick merely tilted his head, waiting. "I should've looped you in about the Granger case from the start. I should have known something was up when Madame Mayor told me to cut you out."

Rick slid into the chair opposite Adam's, his posture tilted forward in quiet reconciliation. "I could have handled the conversation better myself. I'm sorry, too."

Adam sipped from his mug, then planted his elbows on the table so they wouldn't be overheard. "You need to know that Francine called me this morning and reiterated how much she wanted me to keep you out of this one. She's pushing hard to get this case wrapped up. Wants me to declare it as a cold case, end of story." He ran a hand over his face, looking ten years older in the span of a breath. “And she wasn’t exactly subtle about you, Rick. She said I need to ‘rein you in.’ Whatever that means.”

Rick’s mouth pulled into a wry smile. “Rein me in? Sounds like I’ve ruffled some feathers. Did she tell you why she’s so interested, or is this the part where we guess?”

“She’s keeping her cards close, but it doesn’t take a genius to figure out something’s off. Every time I turn over a rock, she’s tripping over herself to make sure I put it back. And now she’s prodding me to pretend we can’t solve Granger’s murder. Rick, there’s more going on here than she wants anyone to know.”

It felt like the gears in Rick’s head were spinning on overdrive. While he would be happy to work with Adam again, he wanted it to be above board and sanctioned by the mayor. That, however, sounded like a pipe dream—especially if Francine might be involved. “Someone’s nervous. That means we’re getting close to something.”

“Which is why I wanted to talk to you.” Adam tapped a finger on the table. “She wants to keep us in our corners. I say no. We’re better off sharing what we know, keeping each other in the loop.”

Rick crossed his arms and rested his elbows on the table. Why had Adam changed his mind so suddenly? And what would happen if they agreed to collaborate? “That’s not going to win you any points with Francine.”

“You know what? I don’t care about her,” Adam said, his frustration cutting through the morning ambiance. A few guests turned their heads at the sharpness of his tone, causing Adam to lower his voice again. “When I took this job, I knew nothing about being chief of police. You taught me how to investigate. It was on-the-job training. I owe what I know to you. And I’m not going to play politics, Rick. I want to do my job. If there's something dirty about Tommy Granger's death, I'm not sweeping it under the rug."

"I never did think you were the type to cave to pressure."

Adam's face cracked into a small grin. "Good. Then you'll be glad to hear I'm not about to start now."

The two men exchanged a weighted look, one that needed no words to convey the depth of understanding between them. Rick felt a warm glow blossom in his chest. Sorry, Francine, but his shared experiences with Adam had forged an unbreakable bond, one not shaken by the petty politics of this small town. His lips twitched upward in what might have passed for a subtle smile, the corners of his mouth turning up ever so slightly as a quiet sense of satisfaction settled over him.

"Okay," he said, squaring his shoulders with a nod of quiet assurance. "Give me a few minutes to get Lydia. Then, I'll tell you what I know"

Ten minutes later, Rick was recapping the key details he'd uncovered, careful to stick to the facts without overreaching into speculation. Every time he mentioned Sylvia Archer or one of her tangled connections, Adam's brow furrowed further.

When Rick finished, Adam steepled his fingers, thought for a few seconds, then said, "This lines up with things I've heard through the grapevine. Got to admit, it's more than I expected."

Across the room, Lydia was delivering plates to guests. Seeing her at work gave Rick a twinge of guilt. He should be helping her right now. "We've got more to dig into, Adam. I'm not giving up on this, even if it means butting heads with Francine."

Adam raised his coffee mug in mock salute. "Here's to a long day of irritating the people in charge."

Rick snorted and stood. "Look, I've got breakfast to finish serving. Your order should be ready by now. Let me go grab that, and we can reconnect after we close the service at 8:30."

"Sounds good," Adam said.

The rest of the breakfast service went smoothly. Oliver Pennyworth disappeared, presumably in search of the Seaside Cove Chickadee or whatever he was chasing. Adam slipped out after finishing his breakfast—but Rick felt certain his disappearance had nothing to do with birds. Norm Butterfield sat at his table making notes—most likely concocting new schemes on how to improve the efficiency of the breakfast service. And, the Aldridges lingered at their table enjoying a leisurely breakfast, coffee, and apparently, each other's company. Finally, something normal, thought Rick.

At 8:30, Rick closed off the dining room. He and Lydia cleared the tables, set up the coffee bar for the remainder of the day, and then went to the kitchen to help Marquetta. As usual, they'd all then take a break and have breakfast themselves.

Rick's mind was still churning over Adam's revelations about the mayor. Why would Francine want him stay clear of the investigation? The only reason Rick could come up with. There were things she could hide from Adam that she couldn't hide from Rick. Quite honestly, nothing in Francine's behavior made sense.

Marquetta looked up from where she was scrubbing a griddle. "There you are. I was starting to wonder if Adam had recruited you for another case."

"Not exactly," Rick said, grabbing a clean mug. "Though he did have some interesting things to say about our mayor."

"Oh?" Marquetta stopped scrubbing and raised her eyebrows. "The kind of interesting that explains why she's been acting so strange lately?"

"Let's just say Francine seems very invested in having this investigation wrapped up quickly." Rick poured himself coffee, the steam rising between them like the tension in the air. "A little too invested, if you ask me."

Lydia pushed through the butler door and stopped. "This looks serious. Do you two need a minute?"

"No, stay," Rick said. "We're going to need all hands on deck to keep this place running while I figure out what's really going on with our construction project."

Rick settled onto one of the island barstools, his coffee mug warming his hands. "Adam said Francine's been pushing hard to get the Granger case wrapped up. She wants it declared cold and forgotten."

"Sounds like Francine." Marquetta wiped her hands on a dish towel and rested her hip against the counter, her voice distant as if she were musing to herself. "Get it wrapped up fast so it doesn't affect tourism is probably what she's thinking."

"Could be." Rick took a sip of his coffee. "But I don't think that's it. She specifically told Adam to keep me away from the investigation."

Lydia stopped wiping down the counter and gazed at Rick. "Kind of makes sense, I guess. It is your property where Tommy died."

Rick drummed his fingers on the countertop. "True, but the timing's too perfect. First, Walt Copley's threatening me with some fantasy about a deed, then there are these bogus zoning issues, and then Tommy's death. Add on the foreclosure notice and Francine wanting to sweep everything under the rug, and I'm telling you, something stinks in Seaside Cove."

The butler door pushed open again. Adam walked in and added, "I heard what you said, and I couldn't agree more. Someone is trying to control the narrative. The question is, who and why?"

"Welcome back. Where did you disappear to?"

"Can we talk in your office?"

Marquetta placed a load of dishes into the sink and gave Rick a thumbs-up. "We've got this. You two go save the world. Or at least our house."

The two men headed upstairs. Even before they'd settled into their chairs, Rick said, "So, you said you have news?"

Adam ran a hand through his hair and grunted as though he was exasperated. "Guess who got himself kicked out of the Rusty Nail last night? Jake Morales. He got drunk as a skunk and started spouting off about how his uncle would be 'exonerated once he's buried.'"

"Jake was at the Rusty Nail? Adam, Shadow showed up here last night, and I returned him around ten. Jake was sober when I left him."

"Well, about an hour later, he was drunk and getting himself thrown out. Walt Copley was there buying him drinks and egging him on."

"Walt? Our so-called building inspector and the one who's trying to sink my new-home project?"

"The very same. He was egging Jake on, getting him to talk."

Rick's stomach knotted as the pieces clicked together. "Walt's so tied up in this web that I can't tell if he's the spider or the fly.

What the devil does he have to do with Tommy Granger's death? And what's his real reason for wanting to stop our construction project?"

"Listen, buddy." Adam placed both hands firmly on Rick's desk. "Let me handle Walt. You need to focus on keeping your family safe. This goes deeper than we thought."

"Truer words were never spoken, Adam, but I'll tell you this. If trouble comes after us, I won't be running away."

19

Rick

A WISP OF FOG DRIFTED by on its way back out to sea, and Rick burrowed deeper into his jacket, enjoying its warmth and protection against the damp November morning. While Adam had told him to steer clear of Walt Copley, he'd given no such warning about Sylvia. He probably would have if Rick had told him about Sylvia's visit to the B&B, but Rick had left that detail unmentioned. So, Rick stood under an old oak tree a short distance from Archer Development, watching and waiting for Sylvia to arrive.

The old Victorian, with its pale yellow siding and white gingerbread accents, couldn't have been more perfectly coordinated for maximum effect. He was as impressed this time as he had been on his first visit. Every detail screamed money, from the copper downspouts to the period-appropriate stained glass windows in the turret he hadn't noticed on his first visit. Everything in this house had probably cost a small fortune to restore.

To pass the time, he mentally tallied the renovation costs. New slate roof, restored gingerbread trim, period lighting fixtures – the list went on. For someone who claimed the historical commission's requirements were too costly, Sylvia had certainly spared no expense on her own property. The hypocrisy wasn't lost on him.

At 10:15, Sylvia's black BMW pulled into the driveway, its tires crunching on the gravel. Rick waited five minutes, then walked up the driveway, climbed the stairs, and took a deep breath before placing his hand on the polished brass doorknob.

This time, Sylvia's assistant greeted Rick with a smile and guided him along a hallway lined with framed architectural drawings. Her heels clicked against the hardwood floors in perfect rhythm, like a metronome keeping time. The office door swung open to reveal Sylvia's private domain—a study in calculated intimidation.

Mahogany bookshelves stretched floor to ceiling, laden with leather-bound volumes on architecture and law. Late morning sun streamed through the stained glass, casting jewel-toned patterns across an antique Persian rug.

Sylvia rose from behind a massive desk that dominated the room. "Rick, what an unexpected pleasure." Her smile didn't reach her eyes. She gestured to a leather chair positioned slightly lower than her own. "Please, have a seat."

Rick remained standing, hoping to use his height as leverage in this little power game. "I think we both know this isn't a social call, Sylvia."

"Apparently, so. You don't have the baby with you."

She stood, smiled sweetly, and crossed the room, positioning herself so the light from the window was to her back. Rick admired the bold move. Obviously, Sylvia was practiced at power games.

"You know what? Maybe I will sit," Rick said as he turned his back to Sylvia and sat in the chair.

Sylvia let out a small growl, but returned to her desk. "I assume you're here because you've decided to accept my offer?"

He could almost sense the poisoned honey dripping from her voice as she tapped her pen against the desktop. If Rick was right, he'd thrown her off her game, and she was now angry. It was hard to be calculating when you were ticked off. He now had the advantage. "Walt Copley's been causing quite a stir with my construction project. He seems to be particularly invested in the historical preservation of my property."

Sylvia gritted her teeth and tapped the pen again. Rick catalogued the move for future reference. "Walt can be… passionate about preservation. I'm not on the commission, but I'm sure any delays are purely procedural. The historical commission has strict guidelines."

"I'm not so sure about that."

"About what?"

"The strict guidelines. They're a little too convenient. That's okay. I'll get to the bottom of it. Especially after what happened last night at the Rusty Nail." Rick shifted his weight, noting how Sylvia's fingers stilled on her pen. "Jake Morales had quite a lot to say about his Uncle Tommy. Mentioned some interesting connections. How he'd soon be exonerated."

Sylvia's composed mask slipped for just a fraction of a second before she recovered. "Tommy Granger was a scheming, no-good…"

"Go on," Rick said.

"Jake has no idea what he's talking about." She stood and smoothed her skirt. "Now, if you'll excuse me, I have another appointment."

Rick didn't move. "Jake seemed pretty convinced Tommy was mixed up in something bigger. Something illegal that involved permits and inspections." He paused, watching carefully for a change in Sylvia's demeanor, but there was none. "And certain developers."

"That's quite enough! I won't be accused by a grieving boy's drunken ramblings. My reputation in this town speaks for itself."

"Tell me something, Sylvia. How did you know Jake was drunk?"

Her face flamed red, and she jabbed a manicured finger toward the door. "Good day, Mr. Atwood."

Rick held his ground and studied Sylvia's face. The flash of anger was already receding, vanishing almost instantly. He'd seen that kind of control before, back in his reporting days. It was the mark of someone who'd weathered far worse storms than this morning's little attempt at confrontation.

"Never mind," he said. "You don't have to answer that."

"This town has quite the gossip mill. My assistant told me."

Good to know, thought Rick. If her assistant was plugged into the rumor mill, he might be able to use that. He pivoted to a light and casual tone, hoping the switch would throw Sylvia off. "You're right about the rumor mill. But, just so you don't have to rely on gossip, Jake was pretty drunk. He was probably talking nonsense because he is so upset by his uncle's death."

Her shoulders relaxed a fraction, but her eyes remained sharp. Those weren't the eyes of someone who'd been rattled by his accusations. Or by his change in tactics. They were the eyes of someone cataloging his every word, every gesture. The eyes of a hunter.

"Perhaps I overreacted. I appreciate you stopping by, Rick." Sylvia moved toward the door with fluid grace. "I hope you're still considering my offer of financial assistance. After all, I still think we could be friends—despite this little…misunderstanding."

The supposed loan. Of course. She'd known exactly what she was doing with that check, laying groundwork he hadn't fully grasped until now. If he took her money, she'd have leverage. If he refused it publicly, she'd appear the wronged benefactor. Who else might know about the check? Copley? He doubted it. The man was more of a pawn than he was a player.

"I'll discuss it with my attorney." Rick matched Sylvia's practiced smile with one of his own and headed for the front door.

"Of course." Her heels clicked against the hardwood floor as she followed him down the hallway. Each step felt like a checkbox on a list enabling him to escape the suffocating perfection of her Victorian fortress.

Outside, Rick pretended to check his phone while his mind raced. Jordan had tried to warn him about Sylvia's cunning, but he'd underestimated just how many moves ahead she was playing. That carefully orchestrated office, the strategic power game, even the timing of her visit to the B&B—none of it was accidental.

He'd walked in thinking he could rattle her, but instead she'd let him show his hand while revealing nothing of her own. Adam needed to know they weren't dealing with some small-town developer throwing her weight around. This was someone who'd built her empire on knowing exactly how to manipulate people and situations to her advantage.

Rick walked toward the B&B, his earlier confidence replaced by a gnawing certainty that he'd stumbled into something far deeper than a simple zoning dispute or even a single murder. What else could Sylvia Archer be hiding?

Rick strolled along Main Street, the salty breeze tousling his hair. The quaint storefronts of Seaside Cove bustled with life, but his mind swirled with thoughts of espionage and betrayal. If Sylvia's assistant was plugged into the rumor mill, what sort of network did she have? Were any of these people one of Sylvia's spies? Each passerby seemed suspect, their faces morphing into potential informants for what he suspected were underhanded dealings.

As he turned the corner, he almost ran into Bill and Edith Aldridge emerging from Bound to Please, bags in hand. Bill's face radiated joy, a childlike glee that Rick found infectious.

"Rick! You won't believe what I just found!" Bill's excitement crackled in the air.

"Must be pretty good. You seem very excited." Rick's curiosity cut through his unease, allowing him to set aside his thoughts of Sylvia Archer and her plans.

Bill held up a tube Rick recognized. "In Howie's Collectibles, I found a map of the California coastline from the early 1800s! It has incredible detail. I'll have to show you back at the B&B." He carefully slipped the tube back into their oversized shopping bag.

Edith chimed in, her blue eyes sparkling as she pulled a book from the bag and held it up for Rick to see. "And I found a first edition of Agatha Christie's *The Secret Adversary*! Can you imagine? I can't wait to read it again." She clutched the book to her chest as if it were a prized possession.

"I love first editions. I got hooked on them when I inherited the B&B. My grandfather was a collector." Rick smiled at their enthusiasm, taking heart from the idea that all he needed was a map to show him how to solve the mystery. "You two have quite the haul," he added.

As they chatted about their finds, Rick scanned the sidewalks for anyone who might be watching or listening. As he'd learned before, witnesses were everywhere. He hated that Sylvia's influence had him so focused on finding answers, but he'd get answers sooner or later.

"Have you been keeping busy trying to get your construction project back on track?" Edith asked innocently, the warmth in her voice reminding him how much he enjoyed running a B&B.

"Busy enough," Rick said vaguely, not wanting to burden them with details about Tommy's death or the chaos surrounding his home project. "Just dealing with some… complications."

"Oh dear," Edith murmured, her brow furrowing slightly as she studied him. "Complications are never good. Well, I'm sure you'll work everything out."

Bill nodded vigorously. "I agree. You and Marquetta are very savvy about business."

Their support brought a flicker of comfort amid his swirling doubts. Yet as he watched them chat animatedly about their finds and plans for dinner later that evening, Rick couldn't shake the unease creeping back in—was someone out there eavesdropping? Someone aligned with Sylvia? The stakes felt higher than ever as he and the Aldridges said goodbye.

On his way back to the B&B, Rick stopped at the harbor roundabout to watch the sailboats bob in their slips. The salt breeze cleared his head, but did nothing to settle the unease in his gut. Sylvia could crush him without breaking a sweat—his home, the

B&B, his future with Marquetta. Everything he'd built could vanish with one carefully placed chess move he might never see coming.

He pulled out his phone, thumb hovering over Adam's number before sliding it back into his pocket. Adam was already walking a tightrope with Mayor Carter breathing down his neck. Adding more complications would only make things worse.

Actually, Edith's find had given him an idea. This situation called for someone who worked in the shadows of Seaside Cove's underbelly, someone who'd witnessed decades of buried secrets and whispered scandals. Someone who was tied into the town's infamous gossip mill. He needed the kind of person who knew where every skeleton was buried and who'd put them there. Someone to combat Sylvia's network, assuming she had one.

He needed Joe Gray—the unofficial guardian of Seaside Cove's gossip mill, and he hoped, its darkest secrets.

20

Alex

IT'S NOT EVEN LUNCHTIME AND already I'm bored. Mr. Orbison told us we were spending the whole day on water. He started out with the liquid, then spent fifteen minutes talking about its boiling point. Now, he's going on about the structure of a snowflake.

That's Mr. Orbison. A lot of the time, he doesn't even notice how half the class is either texting or asleep. He's kinda quirky, but his loud bowties and glow-in-the-dark socks are kinda fun. Then there's the times he talks to Mr. Bonesworth—he's the class skeleton. When that happens, we can usually do almost anything we want 'cause Mr. Orbison's like so out there. Uh oh, there he goes.

While Mr. Orbison has his conversation with Mr. Bonesworth, I pull out my phone and text Sasha to tell her I wanna go back to the cemetery after school. I think me and her and Robbie ought to make friends with Willy. He doesn't like Walt Copley, so we should get along great. I'm pretty good at getting people to talk, too. Maybe he'll tell us something that will help Operation Nail Down.

Right after I hit the send button, I look up and see Mr. Orbison watching me. And so is the rest of the class.

A second later, Sasha's phone vibrates. She rolls her eyes, makes a face, and mouths, "Seriously?"

I swallow hard, trying to think of what I'll tell Mr. Orbison.

"Well, Alex? What do you have to say for yourself?"

It's hard to come up with something when I'm staring at Mr. Orbison's blue and red and green bowtie.

"Would you care to share the message you just sent?"

Mr. Orbison's hair might look like a science experiment that went wonky, but behind those thick eyeglasses, I see steely blue eyes slicing through me like one of Mr. Orbison's crazy laser experiments.

"It was about someplace I wanted to go after school, Mr. Orbison."

He crosses his arms over his chest, and the blue in his eyes gets a little colder. I've gotta make him realize what's at stake.

"It isn't just for fun, Mr. Orbison. We're building a house next to the B&B, and I was exploring there one day. I kinda like to watch everything come together. And when I was coming down the stairs, one of the stairs hadn't been nailed down, so I fell."

I expect him to ask me what this has to do with science, but instead, his brow furrows. He rests his right elbow on his left hand and taps his chin with his fingers. One of the reasons everyone likes him so much is that he's endlessly curious. And I think I just gave him an idea. His irritation is gone, and it's being replaced by curiosity. He's tapping his lower lip faster and muttering to himself. "I see…why would a carpenter go through the trouble of placing a step, but then forget to nail it down?"

Then, suddenly, he turns and strides back to the whiteboard, waving his right hand in the air, and shaking his head. "Shoddy workmanship! This is like building a rocket and forgetting the launch button! It defies all logic, order, and gravitational courtesy! Honestly, it's a structural betrayal!"

He grabs one of the markers and the eraser and starts wiping off everything he put up there this morning. All the kids are watching. Their jaws, like mine, are hanging open as Mr. Orbison takes a last swipe with the eraser and whirls around to face us.

"This, my young scientists, is how accidents—and spontaneous experiments in falling—begin. Always respect your materials. And your steps. New lecture!"

What have I done? I don't know whether to crawl under my desk or take a bow for getting us off the structure of snowflakes.

Mr. Orbison's eyes light up as if he's also happy to leave snowflakes behind. His voice is excited when he asks, "What about the wiring, Alex? Is it safe?"

"Uh...how would I know, Mr. Orbison?"

"Perfect question!" He throws one hand in the air with his finger pointed toward the sky. "Electricity is one of nature's most thrilling forces, harnessed to make our toast, light our rooms, and power our robots." He stops and looks right at the skeleton. "Or at least the ones we dream of building. Right, Mr. Bonesworth?"

Oh, no, what have I done? I think Mr. Orbison blew a fuse.

He turns back to the class and begins pacing from Mr. Bonesworth, who's in one corner, to the other wall, then back again. All the while, he's rambling at lightning speed.

"But here's the shocker, no pun intended: electricity doesn't care if you meant to wire things correctly. It follows the path of least resistance, whether it's through copper or your unsuspecting fingertips. That's why wiring a house isn't just about getting the lights to turn on—it's about making sure everything flows safely and predictably, like a well-trained lightning bolt in a tuxedo."

I slowly raise my hand. I mean, I am kinda responsible for derailing the whole class. "Mr. Orbison? That's all good, but how would I know if our house is wired correctly? I'm not, like, an electrician or anything."

"Excellent point, Alex! Well class? How would you know?" Mr. Orbison's huge blue eyes scan the classroom.

Nobody moves. Nobody says a word. But for once, they're all watching him.

Mr. Orbison grunts, shakes a finger in the air to make another point. "Never fear. We have answers. So, how do you know if a house is wired correctly? First, check the breaker box. Are the circuits labeled? Neat? No rust or scorch marks? Good sign. Are outlets grounded? Three-pronged and evenly powered? Fantastic. Do light switches operate without sizzling or flickering like a haunted movie set? Even better. But here's the golden rule, dear students: when in doubt, call an electrician—not your cousin Todd with the YouTube degree. Electricity isn't something you guess at. You measure it, test it, and respect it—always."

I start to raise my hand again, but Mr. Orbison hasn't wound down yet. In fact, I think he might just be getting started. Thank goodness there's only a few minutes left in class. But that doesn't seem to bother him.

"For instance, Alex, if you're inspecting, there are a number of incongruities to watch for—overloaded circuits, inadequate grounding, incorrect wire gauge…" Mr. Orbison practically throws his hand at me and points. "Alex, do you know what AWG is?"

I swallow hard and mutter, "Uh, no."

"If you are watching the construction process, you should be aware that it means American Wire Gauge, and you should find it marked on the wire in your house."

Geez. I just fell down a stupid stair. I didn't want to rewire the whole house.

Mr. Orbison turns back to the whiteboard and draws two circles. "If this is 14 gauge at 1.63 millimeters, which is commonly used for lighting circuits, then this…" He stops and points at the larger circle, "This would be 12 gauge."

Whoa. Mr. Orbison is really on a roll. I had no idea he'd get so wound up over wiring. He goes on about what each gauge is used for, then snaps his fingers and looks around the room.

"Class, who would know how to determine if the wiring is safe?"

Robbie raises his hand and says it would be a building inspector.

"Very good, Robbie! You get an A for the day. I'll make it an A plus if you can tell me how a building inspector knows what he must inspect."

Oh, that's easy. My dad was complaining about all the permits. I call it out, and Mr. Orbison smiles.

"Yes, indeed, Alex! Let's talk permits," he bellows. "I know, I know—'permits' sounds about as exciting as a damp sponge, but hear me out! Permits mean someone with real credentials has reviewed the plan, inspected the work, and signed off, saying, 'Yes, this won't burn your house down.' They're not just paperwork—they're a safety net woven by people who know their volts from their amps. Skipping permits is like skipping the parachute check before skydiving. You might land fine… once."

Thank goodness the bell rings. Everybody crams their stuff in their bags and heads for the door. Some of them are glaring at me and making nasty comments as they push by me. I mutter my apologies, but most of them ignore me.

Outside the classroom, Sasha and Robbie are talking and laughing.

"Nice job, Alex," Sasha snickers.

I wince. "Sorry."

"No way!" Robbie says with a laugh. "I thought it was cool. At least you got us off of snowflakes."

But I barely notice Robbie's enthusiasm because outside the entrance to the school, I see a big, black dog. It's Shadow.

21

Rick

RICK WALKED ALONG THE WEATHERED dock toward Gray's Sailing Charters, enjoying the onshore breeze and the sound of creaking boards beneath his feet. The skies were starting to clear, and the air still held a damp chill, but in some odd way, walking here reminded him of his grandfather. He'd never really known the man, but when he was near the docks, he wondered if he might have inherited some of Captain Jack's deep appreciation for the sea. Then again, maybe he was just imagining things.

At the houseboat that served as the office of Gray's Sailing Charters, Joe Gray stood at his usual post, methodically sanding the teak railing. But something was off in his posture—his shoulders were hunched and his movements lacked their typical fluid grace.

"Morning, Joe." Rick planted his feet at the edge of the dock.

Joe's hand froze mid-stroke. He kept his eyes fixed on the railing, the sandpaper gripped too tightly between his fingers. "Rick."

The strained greeting confirmed Rick's suspicions. Joe Gray, the man some might call "The Mayor of the Grapevine" in Seaside

Cove, never missed a chance to chat, but today he couldn't even look Rick in the eye.

"Can we talk about what happened with the Planning Committee?"

Joe's weathered face flushed red. He set down his sandpaper and gripped the railing with both hands, knuckles white. "I was there. It's a complete mess. That's what it is."

"And?"

"Walt Copley had some cockamamie story about archaeological artifacts. Said we had to protect the town's heritage. Load of stale baloney if you ask me."

"But the committee bought it?"

"They didn't have much choice after Sylvia Archer backed him up." Joe finally met Rick's gaze, guilt etched in the creases around his eyes. "I tried speaking up. I even tried appealing to their sense of community and their moral values. Heck, I told them I've known Marquetta since she was running around in diapers, and feel strongly that she deserves her own home."

"I appreciate your support, Joe. But it sounds like you didn't get very far."

"Money talks." Joe grabbed his rag and twisted it between his hands. "Sylvia made a fancy speech about preservation grants and tourism dollars. Next thing I know, they're voting to stop construction." He tossed the rag aside. "I'm sorry, Rick. I should've fought harder."

"It's not your fault, Joe. And I don't know that you could have stopped it."

"Still doesn't sit right." Joe picked up his sandpaper again, but his movements were agitated. "Something fishy going on with Walt and Sylvia. They never agreed on anything in the old days. Now, they can't stop praising each other enough. I knew I couldn't stop it when Francine showed up and chimed in."

"What did she have to say?"

"Huh," Joe huffed, then motioned with his head for Rick to come aboard. "The question is more like, what didn't she say? Why don't you come inside? For your sake, I'd rather make sure nobody knows you were here."

Rick boarded the houseboat and followed Joe into his office. A familiar black-and-white photo of Joe hung on the wall. It was a much younger version of Joe, a man in his early twenties, dressed in a Navy uniform, standing tall on the deck of a destroyer. Softening the maritime atmosphere were touches Rick recognized as belonging to Joe's wife, Angela. Fresh flowers brightened the counter where Joe handled bookings, and a potted fern thrived in the corner.

Joe eased the door shut, his shoulders loosening as the latch clicked into place. "Look, Rick, you need to watch your step. These people—I don't know how far they'll go."

"Who, Joe? And what do you mean? Are you talking about Tommy Granger's murder?"

Joe seemed lost in thought as he slipped behind the counter, his fingers caressing the smooth glass countertop absently. "I'm not referring to Francine or Walt. At least, I don't think I am. But Sylvia? I have no idea what she's capable of. You should know that she and Francine go way back. They graduated together from Seaside Cove, class of '92." Joe rested his elbows on the counter, a subtle smile softening his face. "Those two were always trying to outdo each other. Sylvia was the golden girl—debate team captain, student body president. But Francine? She worked twice as hard just to keep up."

Rick shifted closer to the counter, his eyes meeting Joe's with quiet understanding. "So what changed?"

"Sylvia left town for college, then went to work for some big development firm in Seattle. Meanwhile, Francine stayed here, built Scoops n'Scones from scratch." Joe's weathered fingers drummed against the glass. "Then about six years ago, Francine decided to run for mayor. It looked like she didn't stand a chance. But then, out of nowhere, Sylvia shows up with a fat checkbook and starts campaigning for her old rival."

"Joe, you should understand that I don't believe in coincidence."

"Neither do I." Joe took a deep breath. "Here's something else only the old-timers know. Sylvia donated enough money to run three campaigns. Suddenly, Francine's posters were everywhere. The town paper started running all kinds of negative press about Everett Carmichael, Francine's predecessor. It turned the election around, and she won by a landslide."

Rick felt the pieces clicking together. "And now Francine won't stand up to her."

"I'd say can't is more like it." Joe glanced toward the window. "Whatever Sylvia's got planned for that property of yours, Francine's not going to stop her. She owes her too much. My guess is you'll be getting served with a foreclosure notice any day now."

"Already happened," Rick grumbled. "Do you think Walt had something to do with it?"

"Could be. If he does, it's got to be at Sylvia's direction. Walt Copley's as stubborn as they come, and he's never played nice with developers before. Now, suddenly, he's backing the biggest one in town? Something's not right there, Rick. And I'm sorry to say this, but you're caught in the middle of it."

"Thanks, Joe. You've confirmed what I suspected." Rick reached into his jacket pocket and pulled out Sylvia's check. "Guess who stopped by the B&B the other day to supposedly help me out."

Joe licked his lips, then sighed. "What are you going to do with it?"

"Save it as evidence. I have no intention of cashing it."

"Good man. My advice is to see if you can use it as leverage somehow. Although right now, I have no idea how that might be."

"I hear you. Look, while we're sharing secrets, what can you tell me about Jake Morales?"

Joe's weathered face softened. "Jake's had it rough most of his life. His dad split when he was young, and his mom passed a few years back. Tommy stepped in, tried to fill those shoes."

"Sounds like he needed the guidance."

"Previous chief hauled Jake in once when he was just a kid—caught him vandalizing the pier. Instead of letting him off with a warning, he sent him off to San Ladron and locked him up overnight. Thought it'd scare him straight." Joe's mouth turned down, he blew out a sad breath, and shook his head. "His mom raised Cain about it, threatened to sue the department. That wasn't long before she passed. In a way, Jake takes after Tommy."

Rick traced a finger along the edge of the counter. "Like uncle, like nephew?"

"Tommy never backed down from a fight. He butted heads with everyone—contractors, inspectors, you name it. Jake picked up some of that fire." Joe's attention drifted to the photo of his younger self. "But the kid's different. There's good in him. He just needs someone to believe in him, give him a chance to prove himself."

"And now with Tommy gone…"

"Exactly. Jake's adrift, trying to figure out who he is without Tommy's shadow looming over him. Question is, will he learn from his uncle's mistakes or repeat them?"

"Funny you should say that. What about Shadow? Tommy's dog?"

Joe's eyes crinkled at the corners as he let out a hearty laugh, his face brightening with genuine mirth."That dog. Tommy took him everywhere. They were inseparable, but Jake never really liked him. Jake is more into fish. He's fascinated by his fish tank. Go figure."

"Maybe that's how the dog got away. Thanks, Joe. This has been a huge help."

Joe wagged a finger in the air and said, "There's one more thing all this talk reminded me of."

"Okay, I'll bite. What?"

"A few years ago, Walt was under a lot of pressure. His wife had been sick for months. He was always running her to appointments in San Ladron—doctor's visits, tests. It took a toll emotionally as well as financially."

Rick rubbed the back of his neck. He thought he knew where this was going. He'd heard the story many times before in New York. "Okay. And this has something to do with Sylvia?"

"None of this is confirmed, mind you, but I heard whispers around town. Walt suddenly came into some money—not just a little, either. Enough to pay off his wife's medical bills and his mortgage."

"And you think he got the money from Sylvia."

Joe snapped his fingers and jabbed them as though he were spearing a fish. "Exactly my thought. You know how she is—smooth-talking and charming when she wants something. Ready to dole out money when it suits her purposes."

"You think she might've bribed Walt to back her development plans?" Rick felt an uneasy knot form in his stomach. If Copley was on Sylvia's payroll, it was bad news for him, but also for Walt. Sooner or later, Sylvia's need for Walt Copley would run out. Was that what had happened to Tommy Granger?

Joe tried to feign indifference, but the furrow between his brows betrayed him. "Walt might think he's doing right by helping her out with her project. For all I know, he thinks he's protecting Seaside Cove's history at the same time. But it doesn't sit right with me."

"If you're correct, then Walt's looking at a serious conflict of interest. That's something he won't want anyone to know about. I can't believe this," Rick muttered under his breath. "With all these skeletons in the closet, it's no wonder Francine doesn't want me working Tommy's murder."

Joe nodded knowingly. "Watch yourself out there, Rick. This is Seaside Cove—we may be small, but people can be ruthless here, just like they are in the big city."

"Thanks, Joe. I appreciate your candor." Rick straightened up as determination flickered within him. "I think no matter what the mayor wants, I'm now involved in both a murder and a conspiracy investigation."

"That's not going to make Marquetta happy."

"No, but I'm pretty sure it will delight my daughter."

22

Rick

SUNLIGHT POURED THROUGH THE MULLIONED windows lining the back wall of the kitchen, spilling warmth and light across the room and wrapping everything in a bright, welcoming glow. The soft tint on the walls caught the sunlight, lending a cheerful glow to the kitchen, while the white marble countertops gleamed with quiet elegance. Despite the room's brightness, Rick felt a weight pressing down, a gloom he couldn't shake. At the sink, Marquetta wiped dishes with deliberate care, her movements calm and steady as they usually were. She'd been quiet since he'd told her about his conversations with Joe and Sylvia Archer, but when she looked at him, her gray eyes held a sense of curiosity.

"So, what you're telling me is there's no good news. Right?" She watched him as she dried her hands with a dish towel.

Rick dragged a barstool away from the counter, the legs scraping against the floor with a faint squeal, and dropped onto it with a heavy thud. His laptop landed with a solid smack, the sound echoing in the otherwise quiet room. He slumped forward, elbows resting on the cool, polished surface.

"There's certainly no good news on our construction project, and there's also nothing regarding Granger's death. It all sounds pretty ugly right now."

But there was something. Something gnawing at him. Rick didn't know what, but he felt a sour unease in the pit of his stomach. Fragments of his exchange with Joe, almost like sharp, jagged pieces of a puzzle that refused to fit neatly together, circled his thoughts. Something about it felt wrong, off-kilter, and no matter how he turned the pieces over in his mind, they never formed a complete image.

"Tommy Granger's death is looking more and more like it could be tied to his business connections. He wasn't very honest, not like we thought he was. For that matter, the guy appears to have been corrupt. " His fingers drummed against the counter's surface. "His connections to Walt and Sylvia go way back, according to Joe."

"At least now I understand why Lydia acted the way she did when I told her we'd selected Tommy Granger as our contractor." Marquetta took a quick look at the butler door as though she were expecting them to be interrupted. "We should have talked with her and Matteo more instead of relying on Tommy's references."

Rick nodded. "And don't forget Francine's reference. She said Tommy was the man to get the job done right. I should have listened to Matteo instead. He said Tommy could be hardheaded and stubborn, but he never said anything about him being…well, crooked."

"Maybe we didn't ask the right questions."

"Maybe. Do you want to work on this during lunch?"

"Sure. No problem at all."

As he waited for Marquetta to finish the lunch preparations, Rick's fingers tapped the keyboard of his laptop to bring up his bookmarks. From there, he jumped to the San Ladron Times archives. The archives weren't as organized as the New York Times, but years of experience had taught him how to spot and follow the breadcrumbs.

An article from eight years ago caught his eye. "Local Developer Faces Accusations of Cutting Corners." Tommy's name appeared halfway down. He'd been a foreman on the job and blew the whistle on what he claimed were shortcuts to increase the developer's profit margin. Rick sat up straighter when he read the developer's name—Sylvia Archer.

"Here." Marquetta set a plate and a bowl beside him. "Found anything?"

The scent of grilled cheese and tomato soup wafted up and filled the air. Comfort food at its finest, thought Rick. He then pointed to Tommy's name in the article. "Looks like Joe was right. Tommy and Sylvia had history. He wasn't just some random contractor who crossed her. He had dirt on her." He tapped the screen. "Look at this quote: 'If anyone thinks they can sweep safety violations and cost cutting under the rug, they've got another thing coming. I've got proof that'll bury them.'"

"Bury them?" Marquetta's eyebrows shot up. "Poor choice of words, considering."

"Yeah." Rick pushed the laptop away and picked up his sandwich. "The thing is, it doesn't look like anything ever came of it. I'm looking for a follow-up on the story. With those kinds of accusations, there has to be something. I can't help but wonder how

Tommy went from being a foreman to becoming a General Contractor for our project."

"That's not unusual, Rick. Not if you're set on having your own business."

Rick's senses came alive at the satisfying crunch of the toasted bread and the buttery edges followed by the delight of warm, gooey cheese. The creamy, slightly salty richness spread across his tongue. It was simple yet indulgent, filling him with a small, unexpected comfort.

"True. As a foreman, he was used to managing crews. Getting his license wasn't a stretch. I don't know. It seems ordinary, but playing whistleblower with Sylvia and then dying just as she shows interest in our project? That can't be a coincidence." He set the sandwich down. "What if Tommy knew something about the property? Something Sylvia didn't want others to know?"

"But why would she care about our lot?"

"It's a very large plot of land for Seaside Cove. This would be a multi-million dollar project." Rick pulled the laptop back. "Tommy made that threat eight years ago, so what happened between then and now? I have to find the evidence. It's the only way to tie all of this together."

"Unless, of course, it's buried with him," Marquetta said.

If Rick's fingers hadn't been moist with buttery goodness, he might have smacked himself on the forehead. "Of course, Jake told me Tommy had an old metal box that he kept records in. I wonder if that's it?" His appetite forgotten, Rick typed in another search. He followed one of the links, his eyes widening at the headline. "Town Hall Renovation Faces Scrutiny." The article, dated just two years after Tommy's whistleblowing threat, painted a different picture.

Tommy now worked directly with Sylvia, overseeing the electrical upgrades for Seaside Cove's town hall renovation.

Reading the information on the computer screen, Rick's brow furrowed as he recalled his conversation with Isabelle. An anonymous source had reported serious code violations in Tommy's work. Could the source have been Isabelle? Whoever had blown the whistle this time, the complaints had sparked public outrage, forcing Mayor Carter to demand immediate action.

Rick snickered at Sylvia's quoted response. It smacked of political gamesmanship. "Do you remember the town hall renovation project?"

"Not really. Those were the days when Captain Jack's health was declining. Between keeping the B&B running and taking care of him, I didn't have time for much of anything. Why?"

Rick summarized the article for her, then said, "Sylvia's response sounds like pure BS to me. She said, I will personally ensure every issue is addressed, no matter the cost. The safety of our historic town hall is paramount."

"In her defense, they did do a nice job on the town hall. But that does sound like big city talk to me."

"It doesn't add up," Rick muttered, pushing back from the counter. "Tommy goes from threatening to expose Sylvia to working for her? And then suddenly he's making rookie mistakes? Tommy switched sides for some reason—was it money? Or something else? The question is, who was the cat and who was the mouse?"

"Eat your lunch, Sherlock. I'll bet if anyone can dig up the truth, it's you."

Rick picked up his sandwich, eyed it, and smiled. "This might be the perfect lunch." He gave Marquetta a kiss and added, "There is something that bothers me about this whole investigation. What about Jake? What's this going to do to his memory of his uncle?"

Marquetta gazed out the window for a few seconds, then nodded to herself. "You know, Rick. I have an idea. Why don't you talk to Cecelia Martin about Jake. They were in the same class, and I'll bet you anything she knows him better than anyone. I think they were good friends at one point."

"That's a great idea. I'll call her right after I talk to Adam. I want to see if he can confirm something Joe told me about Jake being arrested when he was a minor."

"What? Wait. Jake was arrested? When?"

"Chief Jackson busted him when he was a kid. Claimed he was vandalizing the pier."

"I never did like that man."

"Fortunately, I never had the pleasure," Rick said as he dialed Adam's number.

He kept the phone pressed against his ear as he watched Marquetta clear away the lunch dishes. The line clicked after two rings. After a quick hi-how-are-you, he launched into the reason for the call. "Joe Gray told me something interesting about Jake Morales. Apparently, Chief Jackson arrested him when he was a kid. Think you could find out anything about the arrest?"

Adam snorted, then let out an exasperated chuckle. "To be honest, Joe's probably a better source than my predecessor's files. Did Joe tell you what Jake was arrested for? And I don't suppose he gave you a date?

"He said it was for vandalizing the pier. And no, he didn't say when. Only that Jake was a kid."

"Sounds like a fool's errand, Rick. Since Jake was a minor, even if there are records, they're sealed. And that's assuming Chief Jackson even pressed charges. From what I've learned about Jackson, he wasn't above tossing someone in jail just to scare them and then accidentally misplacing the paperwork."

"In other words, his town, his way, screw the rules?"

"Exactly. Jackson wasn't meticulous about paperwork. Half the time he'd handle things off the books, especially with kids."

Rick's fingers traced the edge of his laptop. "Not a problem. I just wanted a little more insight into Jake's background. Especially after what I learned about his uncle."

"Is this more from the Joe Gray gossip archives?"

"No. I did a deep dive into Tommy Granger's and Sylvia Archer's backgrounds. Turns out the two have a strong connection." Rick described what he'd learned, then asked, "What about Walt Copley? How do you think he figures into this?"

"He could be another connection." Adam paused, and Rick heard papers shuffling. "The guy was born and raised in Seaside Cove and knew all the traditions as well as everyone in town. He was a decent contractor until a degenerative disk forced him to stop working. Madame Mayor's predecessor decided to hire Walt as the town's building inspector out of a combination of compassion and respect. The timing was…convenient."

"Joe mentioned that Walt came into some money—enough to pay off his wife's medical bills and then some. Do you think it had anything to do with his support of Francine?"

A vein throbbed at Adam's temple, the subtle pulsing betraying the pressure bubbling beneath the surface. "I have no idea, but before Francine took office, Walt had become the poster boy for historic preservation. He was a real stickler and would hold up permits, claim code violations when they weren't there, and drag his feet on inspections until the applicants met his demands. The previous mayor wanted there to be more development, but Walt was adamant about keeping the status quo. Rumors are that he was about to get fired."

"Based on my experience with him, he should have been fired years ago. What changed?"

"Francine campaigned on the platform of preserving local values and protecting the town's character. Walt became one of her supporters, so once she was elected, his job was pretty secure. Between you and me, some folks think there's more to it. I tend to agree with them. Walt's employment, his support of Francine, and his ability to pay off his wife's medical bills are all just a little too coincidental."

Oh, how Rick hated that word. "You know I don't believe in coincidence, Adam."

"I might have once, but not anymore."

The weight of their conversation was beginning to sink deep into Rick's shoulders. "Which means all of these events are tied together. And if we start pulling at the right string, the whole thing will unravel."

"Feels more like we're chasing shadows through a rabbit warren."

Rick snorted, his tone dry. "Does it ever. When this started, I was just fighting Walt's harassment, and you were dealing with a murder. Now?" He ran a hand through his hair, trying to sort out all of the questions rushing through his thoughts. "Now it's bribery, blackmail, murder… who knows what else. Every step forward feels like tripping into another hole, deeper and darker than the last. And here we are, still trying to figure out which questions we're even supposed to be asking." His fingers drummed once against the table. "Answers feel like a distant dream right now."

"I hear you, buddy. You know what, though? We should go with the advice you've given me in the past—follow the money."

"That's exactly what I've been trying to do, but Sylvia seems to be a master at covering her tracks. The problem is, to properly follow the money, we need a warrant. To get a warrant you need time. And time is the one thing we don't have."

"Agreed. As you know, even if I got a warrant today, who knows how long it would take us to find the trail."

Rick closed his eyes and pinched the bridge of his nose, his knuckles turning a sharp, waxy white. When he let go the breath he'd been holding, he said, "Somebody, probably Sylvia, wants to keep the truth hidden. The question is, how far will she go to keep it buried?"

23

Alex

Shadow sees me and practically flies across the school lawn, his tongue lolling and ears flapping like he's been searching for me all day. My heart flips as he barrels toward me.

I squeal his name and drop to my knees just as he crashes into me. His whole body wiggles with excitement, nearly knocking me over as he licks my face. I bury my fingers in his thick coat, breathing in his familiar doggy smell.

"What are you doing here?" I ask, pulling back and trying to look stern, though my face refuses to stop smiling. "You can't just run away from Jake's house and come to school. You're gonna get in trouble!"

Shadow tilts his head, his deep brown eyes locking on mine like he understands every word.

"You big goofball," I whisper, wrapping my arms around his neck. "You're supposed to stay home where it's safe."

He nudges his nose against my cheek, and warmth spreads through my chest.

"I love you too, but seriously," I say, scratching behind his ears, "you can't keep running away. What if something happens to you?"

Shadow wags his tail harder, completely unbothered. Robbie has to do a little sidestep to avoid getting hit, and Sasha is laughing at the spectacle.

"Come on, boy. We need to get you back home." I stand and look down at him, but my resolve melts instantly. Rats. He's giving me those sad eyes.

Behind me, Sasha laughs again. "Watch out, Robbie. You're about to get…"

"Ow!" Robbie jumps away and grabs his leg where Shadow's talk connected. "That hurt. How'd he get here, Alex?"

"I dunno. He just showed up." I wrap my arms around his neck again to try and settle him. "Calm down, boy. You're hurting my friends."

"He probably smelled you," Robbie says as he rubs his leg again.

His comment makes me wanna smack him, but Sasha beats me to it. She punches him in the shoulder. It's not a hard hit, but it sends the message.

"Hey!" Robbie yelps, now alternating between his leg and his arm. "What I meant was that Newfoundlands are, like, really good at tracking scents over land and water. They're used in search and rescue and stuff."

Sasha and I just gawk at him, saying nothing.

"What? So I got curious. I looked them up," Robbie mutters.

"He could really do that? Follow my scent all over?" I ask.

"I dunno. He's here, isn't he?"

An idea explodes in my head like one of those huge fireworks on the Fourth of July. "Maybe Shadow can help us with Operation Nail Down. Would you like be on the team, boy?"

Shadow looks up at me, and I swear he smiles. Okay, maybe he doesn't actually smile, but it totally feels like he does because his tail is doing big sweeps through the air. Robbie and Sasha back up to stay in the clear.

"You guys thinking what I'm thinking?" I ask, glancing between Robbie and Sasha. "We should take Shadow to the cemetery."

"Uh…no. Not what I was thinking," Robbie says. "Are you crazy? If you don't take him back, aren't you, like, dognapping?"

Sasha shoots Robbie a nasty look. "Don't be a stick-in-the-mud, Robbie. Shadow came here all on his own. Do you want to do this like right now, Alex?"

"Totally." I scratch under Shadow's chin. "School's over, and he tracked me all the way here. Maybe he can help us figure out what Walt and Willy were arguing about."

Robbie shifts his backpack. "What about Jake? Shouldn't we return Shadow to him? He is his owner now, right?"

I roll my eyes. "I don't think Jake even cares about him. If he did, he wouldn't be letting him get away all the time."

"True," Sasha nods. "And we did want to check out the shed where Willy and Walt were fighting."

Robbie wrinkles his nose like he's smelling something nasty. "We?"

I brush long, black dog hairs from my pants. "My dad was telling my mom about Tommy Granger and how he had some kind of insurance. He said it was in a metal box. What if it's at the cemetery?"

Robbie hesitates. He doesn't sound happy about the idea of going back there. "Okay, I'm in. But if we get caught—"

"We won't. Come on. Let's take our bikes. I bet Shadow can keep up, no problem."

Sure enough. Shadow trots alongside me as we pedal toward the cemetery, his massive paws eating up the ground effortlessly. All the way there, he looks up at me like he's checking to make sure I'm still there.

"He totally thinks you're his person now," Sasha calls from behind me.

The thought makes my heart squeeze. I've always wanted a dog, but my dad says the B&B isn't the right place. He did say things could change with the new house.

When we reach the cemetery gates, I slow down. "Let's leave our bikes here and walk in. Less obvious that way."

Shadow stays close to my side, but it's like his nose is in overdrive as we wind through the gravestones. The place feels different this time—less creepy, but still quiet in some weird way that makes me want to whisper.

"There's the shed," Robbie points at an old metal building with a rusted roof and banged up sides. It's not even as big as my bedroom.

My stomach does a little flip when I spot Willy Hobbs in his grave-digging gear, walking from a freshly dug grave to the shed. But what really catches my eye is the small gray metal box he's carrying. He'd holding it really tight, like it's important.

"Did you see that?" I whisper. "He's got something locked up in there."

"Could be. We need to get a closer look," Sasha murmurs.

In the background, I hear Robbie moan. But then, as usual, he says, "Okay."

I look down at Shadow, then back at my friends. "I have an idea. You two sneak over to the shed while I take Shadow to distract Willy."

I take a deep breath and step into the open where Willy can see me. "Come on, boy," I whisper.

Shadow pads alongside me, his massive paws silent on the grass. I can't believe how glad I am that he's here with me. He makes me feel braver somehow, like I've got my own furry bodyguard.

"Excuse me, Mr. Hobbs?" I call, using my best B&B voice—the one Mom and Dad taught me for greeting guests.

Willy's eyes go wide, but I can tell he's not looking at me. He's staring at Shadow.

"Well, I'll be…" Willy's mouth hangs open. "That's Tommy's dog!"

Shadow's tail wags slowly. Maybe 'cause he recognizes Willy?

"Um, yessir. I'm Alexandra Atwood. My dad owns the Seaside Cove B&B?" I stick out my hand like I always do when I'm meeting new guests.

Willy shakes it absently, still staring at Shadow. "I know who you are, young lady. What I don't know is why you've got Tommy Granger's dog with you."

I pat Shadow's head. "I think he's kind of adopted me. He keeps running away from Jake's house to find me."

Out of the corner of my eye, I spot Robbie and Sasha creeping toward the shed. I need to keep Willy talking now.

"It's a crime what happened to Tommy," Willy says, shaking his head. "A real crime. That man had secrets worth keeping, that's for sure." He starts to turn in the direction of the shed, but I distract him by clearing my throat.

"Mr. Hobbs? What do you mean, secrets?"

His face gets all tight and wrinkly. “Got ‘em in my treasure chest. It ain’t none of your business.”

“What kind of treasure chest?” Like maybe that box he was carrying?

“I told you. It doesn’t concern you. Just a figure of speech, that’s all,” he snaps.

Shadow woofs. Not like he’s angry or anything, but like it’s a friendly greeting. It seems to throw Mr. Hobbs off.

“You really take good care of the cemetery, Mr. Hobbs.”

“Well, thanks, young lady. Say, you interested in cemeteries? Is that why you’re hear? Not many kids your age appreciate the artistry of a well-designed burial plot.”

“Um, sure?” I say, trying to keep him from looking around and seeing Robbie and Sasha.

Willy’s face lights up. “Well then! You’re in for a treat! I’ve been perfecting my grave arrangement techniques for years. It’s all about efficiency, you see.” He grabs my arm and starts walking me away from the shed. Shadow follows, like he’s glued to my side.

“Did you know that the angle of the shovel determines digging speed? Forty-five degrees is optimal for clay-based soil, but sandy loam requires a more vertical approach for maximum dirt displacement.”

“That’s…fascinating,” I manage, desperately wanting to let Willie blather on while I go to the shed where Robbie and Sasha are now peeking inside.

“And that’s just the beginning! I’ve invented a revolutionary new grave packing method. It reduces settling by thirty-two percent! I call it the Hobbs Honeycomb Technique.”

While he goes on, I wonder how much longer it’s going to take Robbie and Sasha. They’d better hurry. Finally, I can’t take it any more.

“Actually, Mr. Hobbs. I was hoping to ask about something else. I, uh, happened to be here the other day when you were talking to Mr. Copley.”

Willy’s enthusiasm vanishes like someone has flipped a switch. “You were eavesdropping?”

“Not on purpose! We were just walking by and heard you guys arguing about Tommy.”

“We?” His eyes narrow.

"Me and…my friends." I wince. Oops.

Willy sweeps the cemetery like he's on guard for zombies or something worse, but when he, lands on the shed where Robbie is now clearly visible through the doorway, he shouts, "Hey!"

Robbie ducks down, but it's too late.

Willy turns back to me, his face stern. "Listen here, young lady. Whatever you think you heard, whatever you're looking for—this isn't a game. Tommy Granger's business is dangerous business."

"But—"

"No buts. You need to leave. Now." He points toward the cemetery gates. "And take your friends with you before I call the cops."

Shadow presses against my leg, sensing my disappointment.

"Come on, Shadow. Let's go."

We might be leaving for now, but we're coming back—secrets, a treasure chest, and an insurance policy. I'm totally onto something. But what?

24

Rick

THE CROOKED MAST'S NAUTICAL THEME enveloped Rick as he stepped through the door, the soft lighting and maritime decor creating an atmosphere far removed from thoughts of construction projects, conspiracies, or murder. Cecelia Martin stood behind the host stand, straightening menus. Her chestnut hair was tied back in a practical ponytail, just like it had been every other time Rick had seen her working.

Cecelia gave Rick a warm smile when he approached, then cocked her head to one side and frowned. "Mr. Atwood? You're alone today?" Her eyes widened. "Oh, no. What happened?"

Rick winced at the reality. The only time he came to the Crooked Mast during the day was when there'd been a murder. It felt like a grim pattern, one he wished he could break. "I know. Sad, right? To be truthful, I'm not here on police business."

"Sorry. You and Chief Cunningham…oh, sorry." Cecelia clamped her hand over her mouth, and her cheeks colored slightly. She looked like she might be trying to do a mental reset. "Let's try that again. How can I help you?"

"No worries, Cecelia. Actually, I'm here because I need to pick your brain and maybe ask for a favor. Marquetta mentioned you might know Jake Morales pretty well."

"We were in the same class." She bent down and picked up a couple of the menus from the bottom part of the stand and clutched them to her chest. "He doesn't have many people looking out for him."

"He seems to be very lonely now that his uncle is gone, and that's why I'm here." Rick caught the subtle tightening at the corners of Cecelia's eyes and how she now avoided looking at him. "I spoke to Jake about Tommy's death, but I think he was holding back."

Cecelia grimaced and lowered her voice. "Jake doesn't trust easily. Especially not authority figures. His uncle was his only real family, and, to be honest, he wasn't a great role model."

"So I've learned. Please, all I want to do is help Jake. The last thing I want to do is cause him more pain or trouble. If I can get him to open up, I may also be able to find out who killed his uncle."

Rather than answering, Cecelia's brow furrowed and she hugged the menus closer to her chest. "Mr. Atwood, I don't understand why you're asking me all these questions. If you're not working with the police—then why are you here?"

Rick mentally cursed himself, wishing he could rewind the last five minutes. "I'm so sorry, Cecelia. I went about this all wrong. I believe whoever killed Tommy Granger was involved in a conspiracy that could potentially stop our building project and even force us to sell the land. Worst case is they're successful and force us into bankruptcy."

Cecelia's brow creased with a concern he hadn't seen before. "Oh, wow. I had no idea. I get it now. Mr. Atwood, you've got a lot at stake. I'm sorry."

"Thanks. We do have a lot at stake, but I think Jake does, too. I'm worried he's becoming a pawn in whatever game someone is playing."

"Mr. Atwood, I'd really hate to see that happen to Jake. And you and Marquetta are too nice to have to be dealing with this kind of stuff. What can I do to help? Do you need me to talk to Jake? Maybe put in a good word for you?"

"Would you? Let him know I'm just trying to help."

Cecelia took a deep breath and looked away, seemingly lost in thought for a few seconds. "Sure. I can try. But you have to understand something. Mr. Atwood, I think that whatever Jake's uncle was mixed up in, it's got Jake looking over his shoulder."

Not sure of how much he should share, Rick decided it was better to remain the investigator rather than the informer. "Do you think Tommy Granger was doing something illegal?"

"I don't know for sure. But Jake's isolated himself lately. Nobody I know has heard from him. As far as I can tell, his Uncle Tommy is the only one he was talking to."

"Have you heard anything about him getting a job offer from Sam Greer?"

"No, but working for Mr. Greer could be good for him. Jake's only known construction work—he's never done any other kind of work. His uncle always encouraged him to follow in his footsteps. He doesn't have other skills."

Rick heard footsteps approaching and looked to his right. Ken Grayson, the owner of the Crooked Mast, waved and said hello.

Ken's prematurely gray-brown hair caught the light; his green eyes remained sharp behind wire-rimmed glasses.

"Ken, good to see you."

"You, too. Haven't seen you in here since the baby was born."

Rick ran his fingers through his hair and laughed. "Yeah, the little guy has really disrupted our routine. Everything revolves around his schedule."

"I hear you. How's Marquetta holding up? She's got a lot on her plate."

"She's doing good. Thank goodness for Lydia. How are Abby and Maxie?"

"Abby's doing great. Maxie, however, she's a teenage girl. You know how that goes."

Cecelia, who'd been watching the humdrum conversation about kids and family with wide eyes, said, "Just be patient with her, Ken. She'll come out the other end okay."

"I'm sure she will," Ken snickered. "The question is, will I?"

"Guess I got lucky," Rick said. "Alex seems to be on a steady path."

"Except when it comes to solving murders." Ken laughed again, then cocked his head, and his tone turned serious. "Heard you asking Cecelia questions about Tommy Granger and his nephew."

"I hope you don't mind."

"Not at all," Ken said. "If it were my family, I'd probably be doing the same thing."

"Thanks for understanding, Ken. I'm trying to understand what happened to Tommy. It might help me figure out why someone's trying to stop my construction project."

“I’ll tell you this. Tommy had a knack for making enemies. And, from what I’ve seen, Walt Copley doesn’t seem too broken up about his death.”

“You’ve talked to Walt about it?”

Ken’s green eyes narrowed slightly. “Good grief, no. But Walt came in about three months ago, all smiles. Said he’d finally paid off his wife’s medical bills. He was celebrating being ‘free from debt,’ as he put it.”

Rick’s spine straightened, the hairs on his neck feeling as if they were standing at attention.”That’s a pretty specific thing to remember.”

“Not really. It’s so unusual to see Walt happy about anything that the good stuff sticks out.” Ken lowered his voice. “And there’s something else. I’ve already told Adam this, but about a week before Tommy died, both he and Walt were in here at the same time. Not together, mind you, but they still managed to disrupt my business with a heated argument. Tommy nearly took a swing at Walt.”

Cecelia’s head bobbed up and down as she watched he boss. “Oh, yeah. It was bad.”

“Three months ago, you say? What were they arguing about?”

“Couldn’t hear everything, but Tommy kept saying Walt owed him. Walt denied it, said Tommy was the one who’d be paying.” Ken rubbed his throat and took a deep breath. “I ended up throwing Tommy out. He was drunk and getting belligerent.”

“Ken, other sources have also told me Copley was able to pay off his medical debts, but I had no idea he’d decided to celebrate.”

“To be fair, Walt became pretty isolated around the time his wife died. He had no money, and he wanted nothing to do with anyone.

My guess is he decided he owed himself a night out after he got rid of the medical bills."

"I was working that night, Mr. Atwood," Cecelia said. "He came in and said he only wanted to have a drink at the bar and was sitting there all alone when Mr. Granger showed up."

"And then, three months later, Tommy winds up dead on my construction site. Thanks, you two. This has been helpful. Say, do you think Tommy was blackmailing Copley?"

"I have no idea," Ken said.

Cecelia tilted her head, her eyes narrowing as if the pieces of a puzzle didn't quite fit. "Me, either."

"Ken, have you seen Copley since then? Has he mentioned anything about my construction project?"

"Not to me." Ken pulled in a deep breath and watched the floor for a few seconds. "If I were you, Rick, I'd be careful around him. Walt's always been the type to hold grudges."

"What did I ever do to him?" Rick snapped. His shoulders tensed immediately, and he quickly regretted his reaction. "Sorry. I didn't mean to bark at you."

"No worries. I'm not completely sure, but I think Walt's animosity has more to do with your grandfather than with you. Walt thinks the house should be his, not yours."

Rick let out a slow breath. "So he's said."

Cecelia craned her neck and furrowed her brow. "Why?"

"He claims to have a deed to the B&B. I told him to show me the proof or leave me alone."

"Ouch," Ken said. "Walt's made noises off and on since before you inherited the B&B about how his father was cheated out of owning the place by Captain Jack. It could be that's the grudge he can't let go of."

"The man's a lunatic. Jordan reviewed all of the paperwork with me when I inherited the B&B."

"I'm not disagreeing with you, Rick. All I'm saying is, be careful. After all the murders you've investigated. I think you should understand better than anyone how dangerous emotions can be."

25

Rick

AFTER CECELIA CALLED JAKE, RICK drove straight to Tommy's house. He approached, immediately noticing something different from his last visit. Jake was sitting on the front porch, still looking dejected—his lanky frame slouched in one of the mismatched chairs. He looked like a man defeated. Nothing had changed there, but there was one huge difference—no dog barking. Quiet. So quiet he could hear a bird chirp in a tree across the street. Had Shadow settled down? Gotten used to his owner's death? Or was he as depressed as Jake?

Rick winced at the thought. A dog with depression? Was that a thing? He supposed so. Jake certainly looked like he was in the depths of it.

"Hey, Jake," Rick called out, trying to gauge the young man's mood.

Jake looked up, his brown eyes clouded with a mix of confusion and guilt. "Mr. Atwood," he replied, his voice barely rising above a whisper.

Rick already knew the answer, but decided to go with a reminder as a precaution. “Cecelia called you?”

“Yeah.”

“Can we talk?”

“I guess.”

Rick scanned the yard searching for signs of Shadow’s presence. The grass lay undisturbed, and there were no tufts of black fur on the porch or even on Jake’s pants. His stomach twisted ever so slightly. The young man hadn’t gotten rid of his uncle’s dog, had he?

“What’s going on? Where’s Shadow?”

Jake shifted, scuffing the toe of his boot against the wood of the porch. A flicker of embarrassment crossed his face. “He, uh… ran off again. Slipped out at lunch.”

Rick frowned at the thought of a dog the size of Shadow roaming alone in Seaside Cove. Not only might the police be inundated with all sorts of complaints, but the dog might even be picked up and taken to San Ladron. Rick shuddered at the thought—and of what Alex would say when she found out.

“Jake…”

“I know, I know. He’ll come back.”

“Jake, I’m not so sure about that.”

Jake let out a nervous laugh, but it sounded hollow. “He came back the last couple of times, right?”

“Chief Cunningham brought him back the first time, and I brought him back the last one.”

“Oh, yeah. Well, I’m not too worried about him. He’s gotta know his way around town.” He shifted in the chair and switched his focus to a fingernail that he began picking.

“What’s wrong, Jake? You don’t seem yourself,” Rick said softly.

“Just…everything.” Jake’s shoulders slumped further as he rubbed a hand over his hair, which was looking like it hadn’t been washed in days. “Uncle Tommy is gone… And now I lost his dog. Uncle Tommy loved that stupid dog.”

“You don’t like Shadow?”

“I guess he’s okay. He’s just…so big. So much work.”

Jake went on for nearly another minute about all the tasks involved with a big dog, but by the time he finished, the complaints sounded hollow.

“Sorry, Jake, but there’s no such thing as the poop fairy.”

Finally, Jake almost laughed. “If only. It would be a big job.”

“This isn’t really about Shadow. Is it?” Rick said.

“I don’t know what to do, Mr. Atwood.” He ran his hands through his grimy hair and groaned. He kept looking over his shoulder at the front door, almost as if expecting something—or someone—to emerge.

“I’m sure you have options.” Following a hunch, Rick continued, “I’m sure Sam Greer would hire you.”

Jake peered at Rick, a wild, almost fearful look in his eyes. “I dunno if I’d wanna work for him. Maybe I should leave town.”

“Why would you want to leave?”

“Something my Uncle Tommy said just before…” His voice trailed off again.

“He passed away?” Rick suggested, choosing his words with deliberate care.

“Yeah.”

Rick watched Jake closely, noticing the red rimming his eyes and his puffy cheeks. The kid was a mess. Rick stepped closer and put a gentle hand on Jake's shoulder. Then, he waited.

Jake took a deep breath, as if he were searching for the courage to go on. Deep down, Rick saw vulnerability, but he also saw something else—fear, perhaps? He waited patiently, drawing on his old reporter trick of staying silent to force the other person to fill the void.

"He always told me to watch my back—especially around people like Walt Copley or Sylvia Archer." He looked away again, biting his lip nervously.

Rick raised an eyebrow. He'd been right. Jake had been holding back during his first visit. If Tommy had talked about Walt and Sylvia, Jake might have drawn a whole different view of them. It was important that he get the facts, but at the same time, he didn't want to put Jake in a precarious position. Perhaps, even danger. And, he had to find a way to get Jake to open up completely. Rick felt like he was walking on eggshells in a room full of shadows.

"Why do you think your uncle felt that way?" Rick asked carefully.

"He… he never really explained it." Jake gave the fingernail a final tug, winced, then gripped his knees tightly, as if they were lifelines holding him steady in a storm of memories.

Rick sat in the chair next to Jake, testing it as he sat to make sure it wasn't as rickety as it looked. He kept his voice soft and reassuring. "I hope you understand how important this could be."

"Yeah," Jake exhaled, and it sounded like a balloon deflating slowly.

"Are you scared, Jake?"

"I ain't…" He stopped, closed his eyes, and nodded. "Who am I kidding? Yeah, I'm scared."

"Of what?"

"I dunno. Uncle Tommy…he had…secrets."

"That's what you told me the last time we talked. You said he had an old metal box with insurance just in case something happened to him. Have you had any luck in finding it?"

"Nah. It's like I told you before. He put it in his truck the night before he died, and when I checked, it wasn't there."

"So you saw him put it in the truck yourself?"

"Yeah. Right after he added some papers to it." Jake seemed lost in thought, as if he were reliving the memories of that night. "He caught me watching and said something weird. Told me, 'If anything happens to me, it'll be your leverage.'"

"Leverage? He called it leverage, not insurance?"

"Yeah, I guess. I think maybe. I'm not totally sure, Mr. Atwood."

Did it really matter? Leverage or insurance, they both could mean the same thing. "Do you know what for?"

"I dunno."

"The box must contain something important, Jake. We have to find it."

"I dunno where it is, Mr. Atwood. It's gone. I can't find it anywhere."

"Has anyone broken in?"

"Nope. Up until today, Shadow was here."

"Right. And you said your Uncle Tommy moved the box to the truck. So, if it's not there, maybe he gave it to someone else."

Jake blew out another breath and let go of his knees. "Mr. Atwood, there's something else I didn't tell you. The morning Uncle

Tommy died, he fired me just before he left for work. He said it was for my own good."

"And how did that make you feel?" Rick asked, trying to keep the suspicion from entering his voice.

Jake closed his eyes and buried his face in his hands. "I was mad at him. I said some awful things. I would've moved out, but I didn't have nowhere to go."

Rick wondered if Jake had told any of this to Adam—probably not. He hoped he hadn't because that alone could be a motive for murder. It might be weak, but people had killed for less.

"Jake, I think we need to take this one step at a time. For now, let's keep this information between you and me. I'm confident you didn't kill your uncle, so I think it had to be whoever stole that metal box. Did Tommy ever say anything to you about Walt Copley?"

Jake's eyes widened, and he lowered his voice as if the house itself might be listening. "Yeah, actually. About a month ago, I overheard Uncle Tommy on the phone with him. Uncle Tommy was really heated, man. Saying something about how he knew Walt was taking payments under the table."

There it was, another possible motive for murder. "Did you get anything specific?"

"Nah. Not then. It was later, after he got off the call. Uncle Tommy saw me and told me I had to keep everything I heard quiet."

Rick rested his elbows on his knees, trying to make himself less imposing as he watched Jake. The poor kid was so over his head. He felt sorry for him, but he needed to push a little further. "Sounds like your uncle had way more secrets than I ever realized. But there's not much I can do without some sort of proof."

Jake screwed up his face and gazed at the sky. "I don't know what to do, Mr. Atwood. I wanna do the right thing, but what does that mean? Everybody always says, do the right thing. But I kind of feel like I should just let Uncle Tommy rest in peace. You know?"

"I can't tell you what to do, but I can tell you this. Do you really think your uncle would want you living with all this guilt? I think your uncle was a fighter, and he was keeping things in line the best way he knew how. Jake, if you don't tell me everything you know, these people may get away with whatever your uncle was trying to stop."

After a few seconds of seeming to ponder Rick's argument, Jake's jaw tightened. "Okay, I get it. I can finish what my uncle started."

"Exactly."

"So, um, Uncle Tommy told me he had paperwork—actual proof—that Walt had been doing illegal stuff. But he told me to keep quiet."

"Was this paperwork part of what was in the metal box?"

"I dunno. But after Uncle Tommy got off the phone call with Copley, I asked him to level with me. I told him we were all either of us had, so we had to trust each other."

Rick waited, letting the silence fill the void. Jake's comment to his uncle had shown a much deeper maturity than Rick would have expected from the kid, but it was good to know he had it in him.

"At first, Uncle Tommy said what he knew was too dangerous for me to know. But a couple weeks later, Walt started showing up at our construction sites, like, all the time. He'd show up out of nowhere. He'd have that stupid clipboard of his, and he'd start asking a whole bunch of questions that didn't make sense." Jake's voice grew more animated as he spoke. "After that, Uncle Tommy told me Copley was retaliating. He said it was 'cause he'd threatened to blow the whistle on him. Then, he told me Copley had approved dangerous shortcuts at Town Hall for some developer. Said it was all documented and time-stamped."

"No wonder your uncle didn't want you to know about this," Rick said, his eyes widening as he processed Jake's words. "What else did he tell you?"

"The last thing he ever said to me about Walt was..." he swallowed hard, "he told me to watch my back around 'that old snake.' He said Walt wasn't the harmless history buff everyone thought he was." His fingers drummed anxiously against his knee. "That's gotta be connected to what happened to my uncle, right?"

"I agree, but I think there's more to all of this. I'm sure the developer who handled the Town Hall restoration was Sylvia Archer. Could she be the one who was paying off Copley?"

"He never said who they were talking about, but she did show up here at the house one night."

Rick blinked back his surprise. While Jake had said before that his uncle never told him much about business, he'd actually shared a lot. And Rick wanted to know how much. "Did she come here often?"

"No way. It was a one-time thing. They got into a huge argument about keeping promises."

"Any idea what these promises were?"

"Yeah." Jake nodded, then made a face before he said, "It had to do with slowing down your house project. She was saying she needed more time, and Uncle Tommy told her he'd already given her more than he should have. If she couldn't work with his terms, it was too bad."

If there was ever a time Rick wanted to make his own accusations, it was now. He held back. Jake wasn't the reason for the delays—that had all been on Tommy…and Sylvia. "I'm listening," Rick said with carefully controlled restraint.

Jake kept his attention fixed on some invisible point across the street as he spoke. "Uncle Tommy told me everything that night. After she left, I found him in the living room. He couldn't stop pacing. I think it even made Shadow nervous 'cause he kept watching."

"What exactly did he tell you?" Rick asked, his tone now more insistent.

Jake swallowed hard. "That Sylvia was paying him to mess with your construction site. Said it started with little stuff—you know, 'accidentally' getting orders wrong, scheduling mix-ups. But then it got bigger."

"I see," Rick gritted his teeth. Thought about all those 'little problems,' as Tommy had called them. What a fool he'd been to trust and ignore the rumors.

"You should've seen his face, Mr. Atwood. All crumpled up with shame. He told me the money seemed too good to walk away from at first, but…" Jake's voice cracked. "He was watching you try to build something real for your family, and it was eating him up inside. He said he felt stuck between what Sylvia wanted and what he knew was right."

Rick sat silent, knowing he should do something, but just like Jake when they'd first spoken, he had no idea what it should be. Then, he thought about Alex and what he might do with her. He reached out and put his arm around Jake's shoulders. Jake slumped into him, his shoulders shuddering ever so slightly.

"You did good, Jake. You've given me a lot to work with."

"There's more, Mr. Atwood. The night before Uncle Tommy died, he made me memorize a bunch of numbers. The thing is, he wouldn't tell me what they were for."

Rick sighed. How many secrets did Tommy Granger have?

26

Alex

I LOOK AROUND THE CEMETERY as I walk away from Mr. Hobbs. Shadow is at my side, kinda like he knows we're getting kicked out. I hate that Mr. Hobbs won't help us. Especially 'cause he seems like the kind of person who's organized and could maybe be helpful. I mean, he's done an awesome job of making the cemetery look nice. The grass looks like it's been manicured. The headstones are arranged in such neat rows. The place is super peaceful. The afternoon sun makes everything look kinda pretty, with shadows from the oak trees stretching across the graves like long fingers. And then I realize Shadow isn't beside me. He's stopped at a gravestone and…uh oh. He's…

"Stop that dog! Stop that dog!" Mr. Hobbs yells. He picks up his shovel and runs towards us, his baggy forest green coveralls with about a million pockets, flapping in the breeze, and his glasses about ready to fall off his nose.

Shadow doesn't seem to mind. He continues doing his business right there in front of Mr. Hobbs. Then, just when Mr. Hobbs is like five feet away, he trots over to me. His massive paws make almost no sound on the soft grass, which is kind of impressive when you think about it.

Mr. Hobbs is standing there staring down at the wet headstone. He's holding his old-time shovel with the polished blade at his side. "He… he…"

Robbie and Sasha are about twenty feet away. They've got their hands cupped over their mouths. I totally want to give Shadow a high-five—or maybe that would be a high-four with a dog. Instead, I see my opening.

"Bad dog. Bad dog." Somehow, I keep myself from laughing as I say the words, and Shadow seems to get the message—this is all show for Mr. Hobbs.

Shadow barks. A super deep woof that's enough to wake all the dead people here.

"This is totally not how I pictured spending my afternoon," I mutter.

Robbie and Sasha are whispering to each other. Probably about how crazy I am for coming back here. I don't blame them. After what happened with Mean Old Walt Copley and Crazy Willy Hobbs, most normal people would stay away. But I'm not most people, and besides, we need answers. And Shadow has just opened the door for me.

"I'm super sorry about that, Mr. Hobbs."

The poor man looks like he's about to cry. "I've got to wash this off. This is a travesty!"

"Do you want me to do it for you?"

Mr. Hobbs looks at me like he's super suspicious. "What do you want?"

Maybe he's not so crazy after all. I flash my best innocent smile—the one I use on Dad when I want extra dessert or I'm in super-deep trouble. "I should've told you before. I'm doing a school project." I tuck a strand of hair behind my ear, trying to look studious. "We're learning about, um, efficient grave-digging techniques throughout history. My teacher says you're the expert."

He stands a little taller and puffs out his chest like I just told him he won the lottery. "A school project, you say? About efficient grave-digging?" He clutches his shovel like it's suddenly precious. "Well, why didn't you say so? I've been perfecting the art for decades!"

Out of the corner of my eye, I see Robbie and Sasha slowly inching back toward the shed. If I keep Mr. Hobbs talking, maybe they can get a look inside. "I bet your shed contains some fascinating historical tools worth documenting. For my project, you know." Gosh, I almost sound like an adult, or at least an interested and mature teenager.

"Oh, you have no idea!" His eyes light up and he taps the side of his nose with one dirt-stained finger. "The implements I have in there could revolutionize the industry! Self-designed, of course."

"Really?" I widen my eyes, like this is the most interesting thing I've ever heard. "Like what?"

"Like my patented Dirt Dispatcher!" He nearly knocks his glasses off when he makes a careless, sweeping motion with his arms. "Reduces digging time by thirty-two percent! I calculated it myself."

"Whoa. That's, like, really efficient."

He wags a finger at me. "Efficiency is no accident, young lady. It's a science! A philosophy! A way of life!" Each word gets louder than the last until he's practically shouting.

Shadow woofs like he's agreeing.

"I think maybe Shadow is super interested in grave-digging, too."

"Is he now? Well, Tommy always said that dog was smarter than most people." He eyes Shadow, and his face softens, but he still looks super tense. "Guess I shouldn't be too upset about the…" He trails off, clearing his throat a couple of times before muttering, "Business. Given which headstone he picked."

I take a closer look at where Shadow did his business. It's bigger than most of the others. Its polished surface shines in the afternoon sun. Then, I read the last name, and I can't help but smile. Copley. "Is that Mean Mr. Copley's father?"

He chuckles. "Mean Mr. Copley? I like that. You got a good sense of humor, young lady. You can call me Willy."

"Thanks. What about Mr. Granger? Is he gonna be buried here?" I ask, trying to keep my tone casual.

Any hint of a smile on Willy's face disappears. His hands tighten on the shovel, and his knuckles get all white. "Poor Tommy," he says, his voice quieter now. "Always checking around him, jumping at sounds those last few weeks. Wasn't like him at all."

Shadow, who had been sniffing around the headstone, suddenly grows still, his ears pricking forward. The air feels heavier, the faint rustle of leaves in the distance suddenly too loud. My pulse quickens, but I force myself to stay calm. Still, when I speak, my voice is barely above a whisper. "Why was that?"

"It's not something you should be concerned about, young lady."

"Mr. Hobbs, I'm not so sure you're right. Copley wants to take away our house. And you said Mr. Granger had secrets. I think there's a connection."

Willy hesitates and looks at the ground. He starts to say something, then stops himself and shakes his head. When he looks back at me, there's a deep sadness in his eyes. "Some secrets are better left buried, young lady. Tommy learned that the hard way."

My heart skips a beat. This is exactly what I came for. "C'mon. What do you mean? What secrets?"

Willy's jaw tightens, and I think he's going to shut down completely, but then he makes a sound like a hissing balloon and goes on. "Tommy… he knew too much. Always said he had an insurance policy, just in case. But knowing things like that…it changes a man. Makes him see danger where there might not be any. Or maybe there was." He seems super nervous 'cause he keeps looking around like he's expecting trouble.

What's he so worried about? We're alone in the middle of a cemetery. But when the breeze rustles again, I wonder if we really are alone. Should I push harder? There's something about the way Willy's shoulders hunch and the way his grip on the shovel tightens that makes me hesitate. He's protecting something—Tommy's memory, maybe? Or could it be something bigger? Something darker? "Were you and Tommy close?" I ask, testing the waters.

Willy's expression softens, a flicker of something—pride, maybe—crosses his face. Then, his voice drops, and he looks at me with a mix of warning and regret. "I told you. Some things are better left alone, you hear me? Dig too deep, and you might not like what you find."

Shadow lets out a low growl. This is getting super creepy. "I understand," I say, but I don't. Not really.

Willy studies me for a couple seconds longer, then nods. "Well, in that case, I suppose I could show you my collection. For educational purposes."

He starts to turn around, but he's moving slow and stiff, like he's still on edge. Uh oh. Robbie and Sasha are standing right outside the shed. My stomach drops. If I don't do something, they'll get caught. I raise my voice to catch Willy's attention.

"Mr. Hobbs! Before we go in, could you tell me more about your… um…soil aeration techniques? You said you have a special method. Don't you?"

Willy's face lights up again. "The Hobbs Honeycomb Method! It's revolutionary!" He launches into a detailed explanation involving something about dirt molecules and optimal decomposition rates that makes me wish I'd paid more attention in science class. Or maybe less.

While he's distracted, I signal frantically to Robbie and Sasha to move away from the shed. They hide behind a nearby oak tree just as Willy finishes his lecture.

"…and that's why I always say, 'A good grave is like a good soufflé—it's all in the preparation!'" He chuckles at his own joke, slapping his knee.

I force a laugh. "That's…hilarious."

"Come on then. Let me show you my tools. I got enough to start my own museum of cemetery history!" He chuckles and starts toward the shed.

As we approach the old shed, which looks like it's ready to fall down in a stiff breeze, my stomach does a nervous flip. This could be it—our chance to find out what Willy was arguing with Walt about and maybe even discover what Tommy knew that got him killed.

Willy steps inside and motions at the floor. "Watch your step now. I organize by efficiency, not aesthetics."

The shed is packed with tools of all shapes and sizes, some looking ancient enough to be in a museum. But what catches my eye is a small metal box sitting on a workbench in the corner—exactly like the one I saw Willy carrying earlier.

"Is that your treasure chest?" I ask, trying to sound casual while pointing at the box.

Willy looks where I'm pointing and frowns. "That's just—"

Before he can finish, there's a bloodcurdling scream from behind us. I whirl around to see Sasha standing in the doorway, her face pale as she points at something hanging from the ceiling.

"Skeleton!" she shrieks, backing away so fast that she trips over her own feet and almost takes Robbie down with her.

I look up and, sure enough, there's a plastic skeleton dangling from a hook, wearing what looks like a tiny green hard hat. But Sasha's scream has spooked Willy. He hustles me out of the shed, locking it quickly behind him. "I think that's enough education for one day," he says firmly. "You kids should be heading home now."

"But my project!"

"Will have to wait for another time." Willy's tone makes it clear the discussion is over.

As we trudge back toward the cemetery gates, Shadow pads along beside me. I can't help feel like we just missed something important. This mysterious box had to contain something valuable—maybe even proof about what happened to Tommy.

"Well, that was a total bust," I mutter.

"Sorry about the skeleton thing," Sasha says, looking embarrassed. "It looked so real."

"It's okay." I give her shoulder a little squeeze to show her I'm not mad at her.

"We'll figure out another way," Robbie says enthusiastically.

"What?" I gape at Robbie. "Are you on board now?"

"Totally! Did you see all the cool stuff in there?"

"Yeah. We have to find a way to get back in." Robbie might be hooked on Willy's inventions, but as long as I get to see what's in the box, I don't care how or why we get in. All I know is, I'm totally sure it could have answered my questions.

Shadow looks up at me with those big brown eyes like he understands exactly how I feel, and that's when I know I need to get him home. "I need to take Shadow back to Jake's house before we both get in trouble."

As we leave the cemetery, I can't shake the feeling that we were so close to finding answers. But at least now I know one thing for sure—

Willy Hobbs is definitely hiding something in that treasure chest of his, and somehow, I'm going to find out what it is.

27

Rick

RICK HAD HANDLED HIS SHARE of family secrets—his own, and plenty belonging to others—but he'd never heard of anyone making someone memorize numbers and not giving them a reason. Like everything else in this case, this secret of Tommy Granger's unsettled him in a way he didn't care to admit.

"Your Uncle Tommy made you memorize numbers? What kind?"

"I dunno, Mr. Atwood." Jake rubbed the back of his neck with a calloused hand. "He made me repeat them like twenty times because he said they were important—that I might need them someday."

"Do you still remember them?" Rick tried to keep the eagerness from his voice, but the reporter in him sensed they were onto something significant.

Jake scratched his chin. "Of course, I do. Uncle Tommy was real serious about it. Made me say them over and over until I got them right." He straightened his hunched shoulders briefly. "3-7-4-8-2-9-1-5-4."

Rick quickly pulled out his phone and typed the sequence. He repeated the numbers and studied them. There was no pattern he could make out. "And you have no idea what these numbers might be for?"

"No clue." Jake's frame collapses into itself, reminding Rick of a puppet with its strings cut. "I figured it was maybe a combination or something. But it's too long for a padlock, and we don't have a safe."

Rick read the numbers on his screen over and over, his mind racing through possibilities. "Could be a phone number with an area code," he mused, "but it's one digit short."

"Maybe an account number?" Jake offered, picking at his fingernail again. "Uncle Tommy had that box he said was important…"

"Possibly." Rick restructured the digits in his mind, trying to come up with different options. "What about coordinates? Or a date combined with something else?"

"I dunno, Mr. Atwood. Uncle Tommy never explained. Just kept saying, 'Remember these numbers, Jake. They could save you someday.'" He imitated his uncle's gruffer voice before deflating again. "Fat lot of good they're doing now."

Rick drummed his fingers against the weathered porch railing. "When exactly did he make you memorize these? What triggered him to do this?"

"It was after Sylvia left. He was all worked up, pacing around." Jake's eyes narrowed. "He went to his room for a while, came back with the box and started going through it. Then he closed it up, called me over, and made me memorize the numbers. He also said not to write them down anywhere."

Rick nodded slowly, filing away each detail. The timing couldn't be coincidental—Tommy sharing this cryptic sequence right after an argument with Sylvia, the night before his death. Maybe he'd known, or at least suspected, what was coming.

"Jake, what did he have in the box? Papers? Documents? Would you recognize any of them if you saw them again?"

"Maybe? They looked official. Lots of small print." Jake made a vague gesture with his hands. "One had a town seal on it, I think."

"Are you sure about that?"

"No, but I think maybe."

Rick read the number sequence again. Nothing jumped out at him—no pattern, no obvious meaning. If it was a code or combination, what did it unlock? And if Tommy thought it was important enough for Jake to memorize, why hadn't he told him what it was for?

"These numbers could be anything. A bank account, a safety deposit box, coordinates, dates… We need more context."

Jake slumped further. "I know. I've been racking my brain trying to figure it out. Uncle Tommy wasn't exactly the most organized guy, but he wouldn't make me memorize something for no reason."

Rick's phone vibrated in his pocket. He checked the display and saw that the caller was his mother-in-law. Rising from the porch steps, he said, "I need to take this. But Jake, don't worry. These numbers mean something, and we're going to figure out what."

Jake nodded, his expression a mix of hope and doubt. "You think so, Mr. Atwood?"

"I do," Rick said as he stepped away from the porch and answered the call. "Madeline, this is a surprise."

"Rick!" Madeline's voice crackled through the speaker. "Marquetta mentioned your construction troubles. I think I might know something that could help."

"Really? What is it?" Rick motioned with a raised finger to Jake that he'd keep the call short.

"Well, it's something I just thought of when I was talking to Marquetta. It concerns Walt's father. I really shouldn't say anymore over the phone. Can you come by?"

Typical Madeline. Everything was sensitive. Needed to be handled in person. On the other hand, Madeline was plugged into the gossip mill and had no qualms about speaking her mind. It was possible that whatever she knew might help expose the tangled web of motivations behind the delays plaguing his family's future home. It was also possible it was another Madeline-induced wild goose chase. Back on the porch, Jake still sat dejectedly. Under other circumstances, he might have tried to get the information out of Madeline over the phone, but he wanted to spend a few more minutes with Jake.

"I'll be there in fifteen minutes, Madeline."

Rick returned to the porch and sat next to Jake. "Listen, Jake, I'm concerned about you. You've been through a terrible shock, and I want you to know that if you need someone to talk to, I'm available. I have an idea. Why don't you come to dinner at the B&B tonight? Marquetta's cooking is the best."

Jake rubbed the back of his neck and let out another heavy sigh. "I don't know, Mr. Atwood…"

"Okay. If not tonight, perhaps another time. Remember, the invitation stands." Rick placed a hand on Jake's shoulder. "And if you need to talk—about anything—I'm here."

After reassuring Jake that talking with him wouldn't be a burden, Rick finally convinced him to think about the offer. Jake even agreed to come to dinner at the B&B 'soon.' Convinced the vague promise was the best he would get, he left for Howie's Collectibles. He arrived right on time and found Madeline talking to a customer.

Meandering through the small shop filled with antiques while he waited, his eyes drifted over the eclectic collections lining every available surface. Glass display cases housed delicate porcelain figurines and vintage jewelry that caught the light. The distinct aroma of furniture polish filled the air, a reminder of the effort that went into maintaining the inviting atmosphere of this small shop.

In one corner, a grandfather clock ticked away solemnly, its brass pendulum swinging in hypnotic rhythm. Nearby, a small collection of vintage cameras sat frozen in time, their lenses staring back at him like curious eyes from another era. Each item in this store had a story—a past life before ending up here among fellow relics, waiting for someone new to appreciate its history.

From the corner of his eye, Rick caught sight of a wheelchair rolling toward him. Howie Dockham raised his hand in a small wave and said, "They're pretty amazing, aren't they?"

"Howie, as usual, you have excellent taste. I've seen these cameras before and always wondered if you sell many of them."

"I got those a few years ago when one of the town's residents was liquidating his collection because he needed some cash. Madeline knew the man from way back, and he gave me a great price, so I couldn't refuse. A few days ago, I sold one to a collector from San Ladron. I guess it turns out that the collectors like the mechanical simplicity and how those cameras remind them of a time when things were built to last."

Madeline bustled out from behind the counter, her bleached blonde hair perfectly coiffed despite the day's humidity. "Rick! So good to see you. Has Howie told you about the cameras?"

It seemed an odd question, but then, Madeline never did like diving straight into a conversation. "Only that he bought them from a resident."

"Did he tell you why he decided to carry them?"

What was this, twenty questions? "Why do I have the feeling these cameras have something to do with why you called me?"

"It's true," Howie said. "Originally, I bought them as kind of a favor, but over time, I've gotten attached to them."

"They're quite impressive," Rick said, turning his attention from the cameras to Madeline. "Is there something special about them?"

"Originally, those belonged to Powell Finnegan," Madeline said, adjusting her glasses. "The poor man needed the money. It's such a shame what happened to him."

Rick didn't quite know what to say. Seaside Cove was a small town, but there were plenty of people he'd never met. "Powell Finnegan? I don't think I know him."

"Oh, he's been around for years. Well, he was, anyway. He moved away after that nasty business with his house. Nobody's heard from him since."

"Sounds like he landed on hard times." Rick felt certain this was going somewhere, so he asked, "What happened to him?" Rick knew all the gossip—and the history, and these cameras seemed to have something to do with her call. But what did any of this have to do with Walt Copley?

Madeline's eyes lit up at the invitation to share 'local knowledge.' "Well, Powell Finnegan lost his home when he tried to renovate it a few years ago. You probably don't know who he hired to do the job."

Obviously, no. He hadn't even heard of the man until a few minutes ago. "Who was that?"

"Sylvia Archer."

Heat flashed up Rick's neck, quick and uninvited. Sylvia Archer? Again? "Oh, I see. You have my attention, Madeline."

"I thought I might. You probably never realized how much real estate drama Seaside Cove has seen in the past."

"So I'm learning." Fortunately, the last of the customers had left the shop, so they had the place to themselves. At least while the store was empty, he felt like he could talk freely, but he knew another tourist could wander in at any minutes. "You said Powell Finnegan lost his home. How did it happen?"

"Very sad case. He had a beautiful property he was remodeling. Sylvia handled the project, and when a fire nearly burned the place down, Powell lost everything."

"I never knew the man well," Howie added, "but he showed up one day and said he was liquidating his prized possessions. I heard he was never the same after that. Started ranting about corruption and conspiracies.

"He went around town claiming Sylvia had swindled him," Madeline said.

Rick rubbed his chin, thinking about the gravity of the accusations—and the process they would have triggered. "If he claimed there was arson, there should have been an investigation. Was there one? What happened?"

"Oh, there was an investigation, alright. That's the curious part," Madeline said. "The investigator determined that it was an electrical fire caused by faulty wiring. Unfortunately, since he had done the wiring himself, he couldn't prove it wasn't his mistake. You see, Powell was an experienced electrician, and he insisted the electrical work had been sabotaged."

If he hadn't been dealing with the same problem himself, Rick thought he might have been on the side of those who believed Powell was trying to foist the blame on someone else. "Sabotage would be almost impossible to prove. How did Sylvia respond to his accusations?"

A glimmer of self-satisfaction danced in Madeline's eyes as the edges of her mouth curved upward. "Oh, that woman is clever. Instead of fighting back directly, she waged a campaign to elevate herself above the charges. She showed up at town meetings talking about using quality work to protect Seaside Cove's authenticity. She talked about preserving our town's character. She even got a reporter from San Ladron to write a piece about her dedication to responsible development. The louder Powell Finnegan complained, the more like a lunatic he looked."

"You're right, Madeline. She is clever. By positioning herself as a champion of preservation, she made herself the victim of Finnegan's charges."

"Exactly! She makes these grand statements about overdevelopment and shoddy workmanship erasing our town's identity, all while quietly acquiring properties and exploiting preservation laws for her own benefit."

Howie chuckled dryly. “The irony is that she’s built her entire business on the very thing she claims to protect against. She’s made connections with everyone who matters in this town.”

“And that’s where Walt Copley comes in? Madeline, didn’t you say you wanted to talk about him when you called me?”

“Yes, indeed. Did you know Walt’s father tried to buy the B&B decades ago? Captain Jack outbid him at the last minute. The Copleys never forgave him.”

“I’ve heard about this, yes. Walt claims his family lost the opportunity to buy the B&B because Captain Jack did something underhanded. Walt believes his family was cheated out of ownership, and now I’ve discovered why he’s been so determined to block our construction. His father losing the B&B was just the trigger. Walt wants it so Sylvia can gain access to the rest of the property. She wants to develop it.”

Madeline nodded gravely. “Walt’s always been proud to a fault. I suspect Sylvia found a way to exploit that pride, along with his family’s history with yours.”

Finally, the pieces were falling into place. “And I’m guessing Walt was the one who did the investigation into Powell Finnegan’s claims?”

“Absolutely. The records should be in the Town Hall archives.”

“Madeline, this has been more help than you know. Thank you.”

“I’m glad to help.” A pleased-with-herself hum rumbled in Madeline’s throat.

“I have one more question,” Rick said. “Given the ties between Sylvia and Walt, do you think Tommy might have had evidence that could expose Sylvia’s schemes?”

Madeline made a face and nodded. “From what I’ve heard about Tommy Granger, I wouldn’t be surprised.”

28

Rick

ON THE DRIVE BACK TO the B&B, Rick replayed the revelations about Powell Finnegan and how his plight might be related to Sylvia Archer's schemes, Walt Copley's anger, and Tommy Granger's death. He was so caught up in the drama, as Howie and Madeline had called it, that he nearly collided with Bill and Edith Aldridge on the front steps.

"Oh, Rick! Thank goodness!" Edith clutched at his arm, her normally cheerful face drawn. Her fingers trembled slightly against his sleeve, and he couldn't tell if her tremor was acting up or if she was afraid. "Is it true? There's been a murder at your construction site?"

Bill stood beside her, his wire-rimmed glasses askew, his weathered face slightly pale. "We heard about it from another guest. People are saying all sorts of things."

Great. They were scared. Just what he needed. Rumors running rampant through the B&B. Rick guided them gently away from the door. "Let's move over here." He didn't want this conversation happening where another guest might hear it, and he also wanted to calm these two down.

"Yes, there was an incident." Rick kept his voice steady and reassuring. "But there's absolutely no danger to anyone at the B&B."

"But a murder!" Edith's voice rose slightly before Bill placed a calming hand on her shoulder. "Right next to where we're staying! Aren't you worried? You have Alex and that precious baby to think about!"

If only they knew. He'd been through this far too many times. And, as for Alex, she was becoming a seasoned pro—which was a thought he truly hated. "The police believe it was targeted," Rick explained, choosing his words carefully. "Tommy Granger, the victim, was involved in some complicated situations."

Rick could almost see the little gears turning in Bill's analytical mind as he nodded thoughtfully. "So you're saying this wasn't random violence?"

"Exactly. Chief Cunningham is handling the investigation personally, and there's no reason to believe anyone else is at risk. I wouldn't let my family stay if I thought there was any danger." Well, that wasn't exactly true, but he would take steps to protect them.

Edith's breathing slowed as she clutched a cozy mystery novel to her chest. Rick recognized the author's name and nearly cautioned her to avoid doing any sleuthing.

"Well, if you're certain… We were just about to cancel our remaining days."

Oh. So much for being an amateur sleuth. "Please don't," Rick said. "We'd miss you during breakfast. You two are such a delight to have as our guests. And Alex would be heartbroken if you left early."

Bill chuckled, some color returning to his face. "Edith does enjoy those breakfast muffins too much to leave, I suspect."

"William!" Edith swatted his arm playfully, the familiar gesture breaking the tension. "Though he's not wrong about the muffins."

Rick felt his shoulders relax slightly. "So you'll stay?"

The elderly couple exchanged a look of understanding before Bill nodded. "We trust your judgment, Rick. Just promise you'll let us know if anything changes."

"Absolutely."

As the Aldridges continued on their way, Rick watched them go, wondering how many more conversations like this awaited him inside. Keeping the guests calm was part of running a B&B. Unfortunately, a small-town murder added a whole extra layer to his already complicated situation.

Rick entered the house and was relieved to find the common areas mercifully empty of anxious guests. He moved quietly through the living room, the late-afternoon sunlight casting long shadows across the furniture and polished hardwood floors. The weight of the Aldridges' concerns still pressed on his shoulders as he passed the dining room, mentally preparing for what tomorrow might bring—a day filled with reassuring nervous visitors.

As he approached the kitchen, he heard giggles and babbling. Rick pushed through the butler door, its hinges giving a familiar squeak as it announced his arrival. The scene that greeted him instantly lightened his mood: Marquetta stood at the island counter with Baby Jack sitting proudly in his high chair, both of them covered in white dust—most likely, flour. The baby's chubby face was streaked white, his dark eyes sparkling with delight as he slapped his hands against the countertop, sending small puffs up into the air with each enthusiastic smack.

Marquetta wasn't faring much better—a white dusting covered her hair and cheeks, making her look like she'd aged thirty years in the last few hours. She was laughing, attempting to wipe Jack's face with a kitchen towel while the baby squirmed and giggled, clearly enjoying their impromptu baking disaster far more than any actual baking.

"What happened in here? Did the flour explode?" Rick held back, making sure to keep well away from the flour-covered duo.

"Your son decided flour is more fun to wear than bake with," Marquetta laughed, trying to wipe Baby Jack's face as he squirmed again. "Hold still, Sweetie!"

"Ba-ba-ba!" Jack slapped the counter again, sending another cloud of white powder into the air.

"I was only gone a couple of hours, and you two look like ghosts."

"We were making cookies," Marquetta said, blowing a flour-covered strand of hair from her face. "Then someone—" she tickled Jack's tummy, "—grabbed the measuring cup."

"Dada!" Jack reached for Rick with flour-coated hands.

"Oh no. I don't think so, buddy," Rick backed away playfully. "I don't need to change my shirt, thank you."

"Coward," Marquetta teased, her eyes sparkling. "Come help me contain Hurricane Jack."

"And get covered in flour? My dear, I think I'll just stand here and enjoy the show."

"Traitor!" She tossed a kitchen towel at him as Jack giggled uncontrollably.

"Alright, let's get this mess cleaned up," Rick said, finally stepping into the flour-war zone.

Marquetta reached for a damp cloth. "Grab Jack while I wipe down the counters."

"Come here, little troublemaker." Rick lifted his son, who patted his cheeks with powdery hands.

Twenty minutes later, with Jack settled in his playpen, the kitchen restored to some semblance of order, and Marquetta looking more like her normal self, Rick's expression turned serious.

"I learned a few things today."

Marquetta's smile faded, and she winced. "From the sound of your voice and the look on your face, it must not be good."

Rick described the number sequence Jake had given him and then repeated his conversation with Marquetta's mother and Howie.

"Whew! You're right. You've had a day. I don't want to add to what you've been through, but there's something else you need to know. Alex hasn't come home from school yet."

Rick frowned. It wasn't unheard of for Alex to be this late, but given the circumstances, he figured he knew the reason. "Terrific. Another complication. Ten bucks says she's off playing detective again."

"There's no way I'm taking that bet," Marquetta laughed. "But seriously, Rick, I think we should talk to her when she gets home."

"Agreed. When she walks through the door, we're definitely going to have some questions for our junior sleuth."

Less than ten minutes later, Alex came through the French doors at the back of the kitchen. The knees of her jeans had grass stains, and black dog hair clung to her legs. Rick knew exactly where she'd been and where Shadow had gone. He was about to say something when she said, "What's Mr. Greer doing next door?"

"What? I have no idea. I'll go find out, but your mom and I want to talk to you when I get back."

Rick hurried out and along the side of the house until he could cut over into the adjoining lot. Sure enough, Sam Greer's truck was parked on the street.

"Hey, Mr. Atwood," Greer called out when he saw Rick. "I heard about what happened and was curious about what kind of mess Tommy left you."

Not sure what to say, Rick went with a simple, "Sam."

"Guess you're wondering what I'm doing here. Well, sir, I'm looking for collectibles. You know how these kids are these days. They'll throw away anything if it even looks broken."

"Why would you think anyone would leave their tools behind?"

"Because I've had the same thing happen. You'd be surprised what my crews have 'lost.'" He made finger quotes in the air. "Yessir, I've seen it all in my time. I found a perfectly good drill one time. The cord got frayed, so they tossed it away. Then, there was the…"

"So, you find discarded tools and fix them up?" Rick was having trouble buying Sam's explanation, but it was just crazy enough to be true.

"Yeah. Got a few more things I found today in the back of the truck if you want to see them. Tools, old clocks—you name it. That's my passion," Sam nodded, then lowered his voice. "Business hasn't been the same since Sylvia started blackballing me. So, I've been doing a little scavenging."

Rick studied the man, noted his heavy five o'clock shadow, and the dirt on his hands. It looked like he'd put in a solid day's work already, and Rick wondered if he was trying to rebuild his reputation in town. Then there was the fact that he'd offered Jake a job. If business was so slow, why did he need the help? "You're still a licensed general contractor?"

"Sure enough. And, to be honest, once I heard Tommy was dead, I thought you might need someone to step in. I, uh, have already talked to Jake about hiring him on. I could get the rest of the crew, too, if you wanted."

"Jake told me you'd spoken to him. So you'd be interested in picking up where Tommy left off?"

"Of course," Sam replied, scratching his chin. "Very interested, actually."

"Let me get back to you, Sam." Right after he checked with the local gossips to see if they had any dirt on his possible replacement contractor.

29

Alex

Nov 14

Hey, Journal,

Today was epic! I never knew I could have so much fun. Shadow is so big and goofy and awesome all at the same time. The way he got Crazy Willy all worked up was totally cool. Now, I just gotta figure out a way to get into the shed where Willy's got that locked box. So, what do you think is in the box, Journal? Do you think it really is a treasure chest? Maybe it's got to do with Walt Copley.

The bad news is I almost got grounded by Mom and Dad. They're sure I'm investigating, which I kinda am, but I'm not really looking into the murder. Well, I guess I am, but I told them I'm not. Confusing, right?

I did tell them about Shadow and how I returned him to Jake. It was the only way I could cover for how late I was getting home—and all the dog hair. Oh, wow. I just had an idea! What if I had Shadow distract Willy? I could sneak into the shed and see what's in the box. I don't have to steal it. All I have to do is peek inside. It might help me finish up Operation Nail Down.

Uh oh. I heard a knock on the door. It sounds like Mom.

Gotta go!

xoxo,

Alex

* * *

Mom sits on the edge of my bed. I can see how concerned she is by the look on her face. She doesn't even have to say a word, and I know.

"Sweetie, I know you've been investigating on your own," she says gently.

My eyes widen. "I'm not—"

"Alex." Mom's voice is firm but kind. "Your dad is in his office tracking down a lead, and I thought this might be a good time for us to be honest with each other. Okay?"

My journal sits over on my little white desk. It's the desk Mom arranged for me to have when she heard me and my dad were moving here. It's probably about my fifth or sixth journal, but she's the one who gave me my first one. The truth is, she's the one who knows me best 'cause she says we're soulmates. I can't lie to her. She'll know. "Am I in trouble?"

"No, but I'm worried." Mom reaches out to tuck a strand of hair behind my ear. "This situation is becoming dangerous. Tommy Granger is dead. And there are other problems. Your dad didn't want to say anything to you, but I'm sure you'll hear sooner or later. Walt Copley is making threats, suggesting he can take away the B&B. And, we suspect Sylvia Archer is interested in the rest of the property so she can develop it. These aren't games, Alex.

My shoulders slump. Wow. It's way worse than I thought. Now I really have to get into Willy's box. There's gotta be something in there. There has to be. "Are we gonna lose everything?"

"Your dad was a top-notch crime reporter. Hopefully, he can get Adam to help him. I'm sure that between the two of them, they can get to the bottom of this."

"But Chief Cunningham isn't working with Daddy."

"They've agreed to share information, but, to be honest, unless the two of them decide to work together, we could be in trouble. Your dad needs Adam's help. And Adam needs him. Right now, Mayor Carter is preventing them from working together for some reason." Mom takes my hands in hers. "Just because the two of them aren't working as a team doesn't mean we can't. I need you to work with me, not keep everything to yourself."

I bite my lip, clearly wrestling with whether to share what I know. "I can't tell you everything," I finally say. "But I promise I won't do anything dangerous."

"That's not good enough, Alex." Mom's voice cracks slightly. "We're talking about people who might have committed murder."

"I know, but…" My eyes fill with tears. "There's so much money in the house now. What if we lose it all? What if we can't finish building?"

Mom's expression softens. "Is that what you're worried about? The house?"

"It's our home," I whisper. "Our real home, where we can be a family without guests around all the time."

Mom pulls me into a hug. "Oh, Sweetie. We're a family, no matter where we live."

"But you've wanted this for so long," I mumble against her shoulder.

There's a heat rising in my chest. I don't wanna cry, but if we lose this house, it might be my fault 'cause I didn't find out what was in Willy's treasure chest. And if I tell Mom what I'm doing, she'll want me to stop and if I don't, she'll be really hurt.

"Yes, I have wanted a home of our own for a long time," Mom says, pulling back. There are tears in her eyes. "But not at the cost of your safety. Nothing is worth that."

We sit in silence, and she waits for me to say something. "I can tell you what I know, but there's something I have to do. It could change everything. I can't tell you what it is. Not yet."

"Alex…"

"Mom, I promise I'll be safe. Shadow's gonna help me. He'll keep me safe."

Mom lets out a long, slow breath. "Is this thing you have to do illegal?"

"I need to look at some papers, that's all."

"You're not breaking into someone's home, are you?"

"Nothing like that. They're in an…open space." That's kinda, sorta true. At least, when Willy has the shed open it is.

"You didn't answer my question about this being illegal."

"Nuh-uh. It's just a quick peek."

"Where are these papers located?"

"Can't say. But Shadow will be with me."

"You're going to do this no matter what I say, aren't you?"

I feel the weight on my shoulders as the question hangs in the air. My eyes dart away, fingers twisting nervously in my lap. I can't bring myself to make a promise I won't keep, so my silence becomes my answer.

"You're putting me in a terrible position, Alex." After another long breath, Mom sighs, "Okay. I must be insane to agree with this. You promise me you're not doing anything dangerous?"

"Promise," I say, relief washing through me. "So… do we tell Daddy?"

"Let's start with us," Mom smiles. "Your dad has enough on his plate right now. We'll be his secret weapon."

30

Rick

THE CONVERSATION WITH MADELINE HAD thrown a new light on Sylvia Archer's actions, and Powell Finnegan's unfortunate history had added yet another layer to the web of deceit. If he could talk to Finnegan directly, though, he might get some valuable information. He smiled at a sound he recognized all too well. It was Marquetta, knocking softly on Alex's door. That was one advantage to having his daughter's room next to his office—he could almost always tell when the door opened or closed.

After Alex had gone up to her room, he and Marquetta had decided it was time for a mother-daughter heart-to-heart while he tracked down Powell Finnegan. Rick reclined in his chair and planted his hand under his chin, remembering how things had once been. Before moving to Seaside Cove, he had been Alex's world—her mentor, her confidante, and her closest friend. But his relationship with Alex had begun changing from almost the minute she and Marquetta had met. It wasn't a bad change. In fact, he was happy Alex now had a mother who cherished her.

Returning to the property records for Powell Finnegan's home, he recognized the grim routine of someone about to lose everything —foreclosure notices, court battles, and finally, eviction. The foreclosure had moved suspiciously fast, pushing through the system with none of the usual delays. Interestingly enough, all of the inspection reports and the documented statements about faulty electrical work bore Walt Copley's signature.

"How convenient," Rick muttered, clicking through more files. A news clipping from the San Ladron Times caught his eye—"Local Man Claims Developer Conspiracy in House Fire." The article was buried on page six, barely a paragraph long. No follow-up stories appeared. Rick recognized that pattern, too, having had his editors in New York telling him to drop a story. Despite the egregious loss Finnegan had suffered, he'd become irrelevant as a news item.

Rick returned to scanning through the property records he'd pulled up, but found himself straining to hear the muffled conversation in Alex's room. The faint laughter and chatter brought a fleeting smile to his face, yet an unease nestled in his stomach.

Letting out a long sigh of resignation, Rick pushed back from his desk. Marquetta was right—they needed to focus on keeping Alex safe. And the best way for him to do that was to solve the murder and stop Sylvia before Alex became involved—assuming she wasn't already.

Rick began pacing the room, his mind racing through all the angles. If Powell Finnegan's troubles were connected to Sylvia's shady dealings, finding him could provide some critical background. It was time to broaden the search.

A soft whoosh filled the air when he sat again in his leather chair. The serene atmosphere in this office was a stark contrast to the whirlwind in his mind. He had to focus and avoid becoming overwhelmed. He wished he was working with Adam because they balanced each other out.

He paused before beginning his next public records search, an attempt to find out what other projects Sylvia Archer or her company had been involved in. "Well, well," he muttered as the screen filled with more results than he'd anticipated.

After fifteen minutes of skimming through documents, he came across an office complex in San Ladron. Sylvia's company had purchased it after the owner declared bankruptcy. It took another twenty minutes to surface the stories of two more homeowners who had lost their homes to mechanics' liens.

He searched the public records for nearly an hour, and by the time he'd finished, he'd discovered a dozen deals spanning a decade, several marked by disputes, legal fights, and zoning issues. Some cases settled quietly; others had gone to court. What was most amazing was that unless someone did extensive research, they'd miss the trail of disgruntled homeowners and ethical questions.

No more, thought Rick. No more.

"How do you keep getting away with this?" he muttered as he turned his attention back to the news archives. If the local governments had failed to protect the people, surely the news reporters wouldn't have let those stories go. At least, that's what he hoped.

He tapped his pen against the desk, eyes drifting over to his grandfather's collection of first-edition, leather-bound books. Captain Jack had loved stories—something Rick appreciated now more than ever. He said a silent thank you to his grandfather for starting the collection. He'd never known how much Captain Jack loved old books until he'd taken over this office. But, he got it. Stories, whether they were news or fiction, had a beginning, a middle, and an end. So far, he only knew part of Powell Finnegan's story. What parts was he missing?

Rick reclined in his chair, the soft creak of the wood breaking the silence of the room. Years of chasing down sources and information had taught him that the devil was always in the details, and tonight, he was determined to find them. Opening a browser tab, he navigated to try a more complex search. It was a technique he'd used countless times during his journalism days. This wasn't a flashy way to do things. In fact, it could get quite tedious. However, it was reliable, and Rick trusted it like an old friend because it filtered out all of the garbage that typically filled online searches.

He typed his first keyword phrase, Powell Finnegan, in quotes, then added an AND to link it with his next keyword, arson, which he also put in quotes. His fingers hovered over the keyboard before hitting enter. The search churned for a few seconds before spitting out a list of results. Rick's eyes scanned the headlines with a practiced focus that filtered out the noise and zeroed in on only the most relevant.

Most of the articles painted a grim picture of Powell's downfall—financial ruin, a failed project, and whispers of sabotage. But nothing directly tied Sylvia Archer to the arson. Having just been through the process himself for their own home construction, Rick knew right where to look next.

Rick navigated to the San Ladron Building Department's online portal. He keyed in the address he'd found for Powell Finnegan. Years of investigative work had taught him an important lesson about construction permits—they sometimes revealed more than people intended. In this case, the permits would disclose exactly what work Archer Development had been hired to do.

The search results loaded, and Rick scanned the list. There it was —a permit issued six years ago for a home renovation project. The applicant? Archer Development. Rick clicked on the record, his pulse quickening as the details appeared. The project had been approved several months before Powell's fire. In the electrical inspection report, there was a suspicious note stating that the electrical work had been performed by the homeowner. The note had been written by Walt Copley at the request of none other than Tommy Granger.

A satisfied smile tugged at the corners of Rick's mouth. The pieces were starting to fall into place. Granger had been setting up Finnegan but the poor man hadn't known it. Rick jotted down the permit number, his mind already racing with the next steps.

Rick went back to his notes to add questions. Was this how Granger had gone from worker to general contractor so quickly? Could his business startup have been funded by Sylvia after he made sure Finnegan failed? His gut told him this wasn't a coincidence. One thing was certain—now that he knew Granger was involved, it made finding Powell Finnegan even more critical.

Switching gears, Rick focused on the neighboring town of San Ladron. If Powell Finnegan had left Seaside Cove after losing everything, San Ladron made sense—close enough to keep an eye on his enemies, but far enough away to avoid the whispers of his disgrace. Rick dove into property records, utility accounts, and business registrations, following the digital breadcrumbs. He wasn't about to stop now.

"Where are you hiding, Powell?" he murmured, his voice low and steady as he scanned line after line of data. The glow of the screen illuminated his face as the time slipped by. His shoulders ached, and his coffee had gone cold, but he barely noticed. He was in the zone, the familiar thrill of the chase driving him forward.

Just as frustration began to creep in, something caught his eye—a residential listing on the outskirts of San Ladron for a P. Finnegan. Rick's pulse quickened. It wasn't much, but it was a lead. The address was in what he'd heard was a rough part of town, the kind of place where someone might go to disappear.

"Gotcha," he whispered, a sense of satisfaction washing through him and easing the tension in his shoulders. He reached for his phone and punched in the numbers. Each key press felt deliberate, each digit another step in the right direction. He checked the time. It was late. He should wait until tomorrow, but this felt too important. He pressed the button to dial and hoped he wasn't wrong.

"Hello?" The craggy voice sounded both guarded and wary.

"Mr. Finnegan? Powell Finnegan?"

"Yes."

"My name is Rick Atwood. I run the Seaside Cove Bed & Breakfast. My grandfather was Captain Jack Atwood."

After a long pause, Finnegan said, "I knew your grandfather. Good man. Helped me out a couple of times when we were young."

"I'd love to hear that story sometime, Mr. Finnegan. But, for now, I'm digging into what happened with your home."

"Why?" Finnegan demanded.

"Because I think you were swindled. And the same thing is about to happen to me."

Finnegan's voice warmed ever so slightly. "I'm listening. How'd you find me?"

"Let's just say it wasn't easy." Rick skipped past the question and described what had happened on the construction project. "Quite honestly, Mr. Finnegan, I'd like to hear your side of the story."

Finnegan uttered a cynical laugh. "I got involved with Sylvia on what was supposed to be my retirement dream home. I had a small place, nothing fancy, but I wanted to fix it up. Since I was an electrician my whole life, I insisted on doing the wiring myself."

"And then the fire happened," Rick prompted.

"That's right. But I did not—I repeat, did not—make any mistakes and my work was all up to code. It had to be Granger. He was on the job everyday, and he was hungry to start his own business." Finnegan's voice hardened, and Rick could almost hear the man grip the phone tighter. "The electrical inspections were tampered with."

"Are you sure? How would that happen?" Rick asked.

"Of course, I'm sure. I know my work, Mr. Atwood—had been doing it for forty years. Somebody doctored those permits. I don't know how they did it, but they did."

"What about your copy of the permit. Don't you have a copy from the day of the inspection?"

"Burned up in the fire."

Rick's jaw tightened as memories of his own construction delays and suspicious permit issues surfaced. Under other circumstances, he might be skeptical, but with what had been happening to him, he was inclined to believe Finnegan. "Why didn't this come out at trial? Didn't your lawyer fight for you?"

Finnegan laughed. "Didn't use a lawyer. Couldn't afford one. Didn't trust them. Guess the joke's on me."

"Still, didn't the judge catch…well, the fraud?"

"The judge had already made up his mind, and I was left holding the bag while Archer and Granger walked away clean." Finnegan drew a ragged breath, and his next words came out rough and unsteady through the phone line. "Let me tell you something, Mr. Atwood. Fighting city hall when you've lost everything is impossible. When you don't have any resources, you can't even get your foot in the door."

31

Alex

JAKE OPENS THE DOOR A crack, and when he sees it's me, he opens it all the way. He looks kinda cranky, like he just rolled out of bed—or didn't sleep at all. He starts to rub the sleep from his eyes, but Shadow pushes him aside and slips through the opening into my arms.

"Sorry if I woke you up, Jake."

"What are you doing here? Shouldn't you be at school or something?"

"I'm getting a late start today," I say as I rub my fingers under Shadow's chin. He slumps against me like he's in doggy heaven, and I have to brace myself to avoid falling over.

"You mean you're ditching class. Whatever."

"Like you never did." I'm not supposed to talk back to grown-ups, but Jake hasn't been acting like one since his Uncle Tommy died.

"Look, I don't want to get in no trouble. Okay?" Jake's voice drops. "Uncle Tommy's dog mean that much to you?"

"I need to borrow him for a little while. I'll bring him back before anyone notices." I give Shadow's ears a scratch, 'cause I know he likes that about as much as he does under the chin. The way he's closing his eyes, it's like he's telling me, "Oh, yeah, you found the spot."

Jake blinks a few times, but he finally looks like he's awake. "I don't know. Your dad ain't gonna be happy with me if you and that dog get in trouble."

"Don't worry. He's my partner in crime, and we've got something we need to do."

Jake shakes his head. "What?"

"See ya!"

Shadow and I take off. We stick to the smaller streets as we head to the cemetery. I've already lied to Mom and Dad and told them I was going to school early for a project. And now my stomach's doing backflips—partly from guilt, partly from excitement.

But the box in Willy's shed has to hold a lot of answers. I'm one-hundred-percent, totally sure of it. I've never been so sure of anything in my life. And with Shadow helping me, seeing what's inside the box is gonna be a piece of cake.

Shadow and I reach the cemetery entrance. Inside, moss-covered headstones stretch out before us like a garden of secrets. Willy's busy arranging flowers near the entrance, his back turned to us.

"Perfect," I whisper, unclipping Shadow's leash. "Go be your awesome self, boy."

Shadow takes off like a furry missile, zigzagging between gravestones. Willy's head snaps up at the sound of paws on grass.

"Hey! You mangy mutt!" Willy waves his arms. "Those are prize-winning petunias you're heading for!"

As Willy chases after Shadow, I run toward his shed. My hands shake as I pull the door open, wincing at every creak. The musty air hits my nose —a mix of old wood and something metallic.

"Come on, come on," I mutter, scanning the cluttered shelves. Tools, more tools, that totally creepy plastic skeleton, and—there! The box sits on a high shelf, like it's been left there to be forgotten.

I stretch up on my tiptoes, fingers brushing the cool metal. "Got it!"

Outside, I hear Willy's voice growing closer. "Shadow, you rascal! Those flowers aren't fetch toys!"

My stomach twists as I pull the box down. It's locked, but I'll figure out how to get it open later. Right now, I need to—

"Almost caught you now!" Willy calls out.

I clutch the box to my chest. This is so wrong. Like, epic levels of wrong. I told Mom I wouldn't steal anything. I said I just wanted a look, and here I am—I could go to jail for this. But if this helps Dad save our new house? If it proves what really happened to Tommy?

"Sorry, Willy," I whisper, slipping out the door. "I'll return it. Promise."

I duck behind a tall headstone as Willy and Shadow race past. Shadow catches my eye and—I swear—smiles at me before leading Willy on another chase.

That dog totally deserves all the treats in the world.

I tuck the box behind my bike, feeling a rush of triumph mixed with nerves. This could be it—the key to solving the mystery of Tommy Granger and maybe even keeping our new house safe.

Shadow zips back and forth across the lawn, barking like he's on the dog equivalent of catnip. I can't help but laugh. The way he flops around makes it impossible to stay serious. "You're such a goof!" I call out as he zigzags between gravestones.

But then reality crashes back in. My stomach flips—school! If I ditch the whole day, I'll never hear the end of it from Mom and Dad. My heart races; there's no time to waste.

"Shadow!" I call, waving my arms frantically. "Come here, boy!"

He slides to a stop a couple of rows away on the grass and looks at me, his pink tongue flopping sideways with each panting breath. Those deep brown eyes lock onto mine, radiating pure joy that makes my chest warm with love.

Just then, Willy's voice echoes through the cemetery as he chases after Shadow. "You mangy mutt! Get out of my cemetery!"

I can't help but giggle at the mental image of Shadow's antics and Willy trying to catch him. But school is my priority right now. We've gotta get out of here.

"Sorry, Mr. Hobbs!" I shout back, not wanting him to think I'm ignoring him completely. "I'm really sorry about Shadow getting away from me!"

At the sound of my voice, Shadow makes a U-turn and races toward me. Willy's still trying to keep up. I take one last look at the box hidden behind my bike before I step out to meet them. The ticking clock in my head reminds me that class has already started.

Willy stops and stands bent over, panting like he's just run a marathon. I feel bad for him, but I needed to keep him busy. "Young lady, you need to keep that dog away from my cemetery, or I'm going to call the police and have him arrested!"

Somehow, I think if Shadow wanted to get away, even Chief Cunningham couldn't catch him. "I promise, Mr. Hobbs. I'm so sorry! C'mon, boy!"

Shadow barks like he doesn't have a care in the world and charges towards me. Willy gives up and heads the other direction. Now all I have to do is get Shadow home, hide the box, and get to school—all without being caught by Mom or Dad. No problem. Right.

I race back to Jake's house with Shadow loping beside me, the metal box clutched against my chest. Jake seems kinda disappointed that I'm back so soon, but he smiles again when I say I'll be back after school.

The ride to the B&B feels so lonely without Shadow, but all the way, I can't help but feel I'm being watched. I had the same creepy-crawly feeling at the cemetery, but I just kinda figured it was only 'cause of what I was doing.

At the house, there's nobody around, so I wheel my bike back to the shed and slip inside. All I have to do is stash the box, then I'm off to school. After I tell a little white lie to my math teacher, I'm home free.

"And what exactly do you think you're doing?"

The deep voice makes me jump, and my stomach feels like it's dropped down to my ankles. My scream echoes in the shed, but then I realize the voice belongs to our handyman, Matteo.

I turn slowly, trying to hide the box behind my back. "Oh! Hey, Matteo. I was just, um, checking out the gardening stuff."

Matteo crosses his arms and shakes his head. "I don't think so. Not unless this 'gardening stuff' has anything to do with why Willy Hobbs was chasing a certain big black dog that was causing chaos in his cemetery while you snuck away with a gray metal box." He points what I'm holding in my hands.

"I can explain."

"Inside," Matteo says, pointing toward the kitchen door. "Now."

My feet feel like they're made of cement as I walk toward the house. Through the kitchen windows, I can see Mom at the stove and Dad at the island, both looking way too serious.

"Found something that belongs to you," Matteo announces as we enter.

Mom turns, spatula in hand, her eyes going straight to the box I'm failing to hide. "Alexandra Atwood."

Oh snap. Full name. I'm so dead.

"Would you care to explain?" Dad asks, his voice doing this kind of scary-calm thing that probably means I'm grounded until I'm thirty. Maybe longer.

32

Rick

"THANKS, MATTEO," RICK SAID AS Alex shuffled into the room, metal box in hand, with Matteo's firm hand on her shoulder. He marched her to the center island.

"No problem. Repairs are done, so I'm going to start on the painting in the Jib Room."

A heavy silence, broken only by the hum of the dishwasher and the swish of the butler door as Matteo left, hung in the air. Rick propped himself against the granite countertop as he studied his daughter's defiant stance. She still clutched the gray box to her chest like it was a prized possession.

"A spy? You had Matteo spy on me?" Alex's voice cracked with indignation.

Rick pulled out his phone and hit play on the video Matteo had sent him. Alex closed her eyes and groaned at the image of her visit to the cemetery.

"I wouldn't call it spying. We asked him to keep an eye out after you acted strange at breakfast."

"Same thing!" Alex's cheeks flushed red.

Marquetta sat next to Alex and looked her in the eye. "Sweetie, you're the one who lied about going to school. The video Matteo took is proof that you caused Mr. Hobbs a lot of grief after you told me you wouldn't do anything to cause trouble."

"I said I wouldn't do anything dangerous, Mom!"

"Really, Alex? I'm disappointed in you." Marquetta's lower lip trembled and her eyes glistened.

Rick sat on the stool next to Marquetta and looked her in the eye, father-mode fully engaged. "You rode your bike out to Jake's to pick up Shadow, took him to the cemetery, and had him run around wreaking havoc while you stole something from him."

"Daddy, you don't understand! This box could have evidence about Tommy's death. About Walt and Sylvia and everything!"

Rick's stomach clenched as his daughter's words echoed his own investigative path—the same one that would probably have Adam issuing him stern warnings. His eyes met Marquetta's, catching the worry in her expression.

"That's exactly what concerns us. What you did could have been dangerous. Tommy Granger is already dead, and we don't know if the killer will strike again."

"But you're investigating too! I saw you talking to Chief Cunningham at breakfast."

"That's different."

"How?" Alex's blue eyes blazed. "Because you're a grown-up?"

Rick fought back a smile at her logic. They'd had this discussion far too many times and it always seemed to end up the same. "Actually, yes. And because I'm not stealing evidence."

"Daddy!"

"The box belongs to Willy Hobbs. It wasn't yours to take."

Alex's shoulders slumped. "What if it helps solve the case?"

Rick hesitated, his investigator's instincts warring with his parental responsibility. The box might contain crucial information, but encouraging his daughter's dangerous behavior? Was he willing to condone her illegal activities?

"Rick, I feel somewhat responsible for this. I told Alex we could work together. She told me she had something she needed to do. However, she also told me it wasn't dangerous."

"It wasn't!" Alex blurted.

"I'd say that's a matter of opinion, kiddo. It could have been extremely dangerous."

Marquetta nodded slowly, the disappointment clearly painted on her face. "I agree." After a few seconds, she faced Alex and said, "Sweetie, I didn't expect you to go rogue on me. You could have gotten hurt."

"Shadow was there to protect me."

"That may be, but you know what you did was wrong, don't you?"

Alex's shoulders drooped, and her eyes glistened with unshed tears. "I'm sorry."

Rick closed his eyes to shut out the reality. Alex was right. At this point, he and his small family had everything riding on…what? Solving Tommy's murder? Getting to the bottom of Walt Copley's threats? Avoiding Sylvia Archer's treachery? The real problem was, he didn't know which of those were critical and which were distractions.

Rick shot Marquetta a grateful look. "I think we all need some time to think about this. We'll talk again after school."

"But I already missed—"

"No. You're going to school." Rick pointed toward the door. "Right now. We'll discuss this later."

Alex stood, her entire body seeming to be frozen in place. Rick's heart broke when a tear dribbled down her cheek. She reached up and swiped the tear away with her fingers, but it was soon replaced by another. Her voice, barely audible, shook as she asked, "We're gonna lose the B&B and the house and everything. Aren't we?"

Rick stood and pulled Alex into a warm embrace. The truth hurt too much to even consider, so he lied. "No, kiddo. It's not that bad. We'll work through this. Now, go to school and we'll talk when you get home."

As Alex trudged out, shoulders slumped in defeat, Rick contemplated the mysterious box on his counter. His fingers itched to open it. He knew it was wrong. Blatantly illegal. But as a reporter, he'd learned one thing—sometimes, you had to take a chance to get to the bottom of a story.

"Alex is right, isn't she?" Marquetta asked.

"The truth is, I don't even know what I need to fix. Is it solving Granger's murder? Proving Walt Copley's deliberately obstructing our project and exposing his claims to the B&B as bogus? Or should I focus on Sylvia Archer? I'm at a loss." He blew out a long breath. "I really want to open that box."

Marquetta planted a firm hand on top of the box. "You can't. And you know it. Besides, if you do, it will only make things worse."

"I know, but what else can I do?"

"Call Adam."

"I don't think that's going to work. How's he going to do anything but return the box or arrest me?"

"Don't underestimate the power of your friendship, Rick. I've known Adam since grade school. He's always been very loyal to his friends. And don't forget, he's not happy with Francine right now."

Rick's shoes scuffed against the floor as he paced the kitchen. Alex had backed him into a corner he didn't want to be in. He ran his hand through his hair and gazed out the back windows. "You're right. I at least need to give him a chance."

He dialed Adam's number, his heart thumping in his chest as the phone rang. On the fourth ring, the line clicked.

"Rick, I was just getting ready to call you."

Rick's stomach dropped. "About what?"

"I think you already know. Willy Hobbs is in my office right now, ranting about some girl with red-blonde hair who unleashed Tommy's dog in his cemetery."

"Sounds like Willy's had a harrowing experience."

"You might say that. Look, buddy, Willy wants to press charges for theft and trespassing."

"Adam, hypothetically speaking, what would you want me to do if I came across this box?"

"Box, huh? You know what was taken?"

"Lucky guess."

"Okay, I'll play along. Hypothetically speaking, we can't have civilians, especially minors, tampering with potential evidence. And, I don't think you need me to remind you what the penalties for that kind of thing are."

Rick began pacing again, holding the phone to his ear as he eyed the box resting on his kitchen counter. It was a harbinger of trouble if ever there was one. "Did Willy give any indication as to what's in this box?"

"Nope. All he told me was he'd been given instructions to bury the box."

"Bury it? What? Who gave him those instructions?"

"He didn't want to say. My guess would be Tommy Granger since his is the only funeral coming up anytime soon."

"Adam, I believe the box contains information vital to solving Granger's murder."

"I'm aware of that. Which is why I asked Willy to give me twenty-four hours to find the box and return it to him."

"Twenty-four hours isn't much time."

"He wanted to walk down the street and talk to the mayor until I told him I had an idea where to find his box." Adam's voice carried a warning note. "I've talked Willy down from filing charges for now, but I'm going to need that box."

Marquetta mouthed 'speaker' from across the kitchen. Rick nodded.

"Adam, I'm putting you on speaker. Marquetta's got something to she wants to say."

After exchanging hellos, Marquetta said, "Adam, you should be aware of something Alex told me in confidence. Apparently, Walt Copley was at the cemetery the other day and threatened Willy. Alex said she overheard Walt saying Willy would end up like Tommy if he didn't keep quiet."

Silence crackled over the line.

"That's interesting." Adam cleared his throat. "Markie, does the munchkin have any ideas on how I might prove this, since I don't think Willy's any too keen to go public?"

"Not yet."

"This isn't giving me much to go on."

"I'm feeling the same way," Rick said as he ended the call. He placed his phone on the island and looked at Marquetta. "Got any ideas as to what our next move might be?"

"Mine is to relieve Lydia from babysitting duty because somebody around here has to start cleaning rooms. Yours is to convince Willy to let us open the box," Marquetta said.

Rick snickered. "Your next step sounds a lot easier than mine. I've got, what, a few hours at most? If I don't figure this out by the time Alex gets home from school, I might have to give in and open it no matter what the consequences."

"I have a better idea." Marquetta's eyes lit up. "Those numbers Jake gave you? Maybe you should check Town Hall, see if they match anything in their records."

"You're a genius, babe," Rick grinned at Marquetta. "I think you should have been a reporter instead of working here."

"The problem is that I'm the one who would have won all those awards you're so proud of, and we would have never met. Now, get going. You're running out of time."

33

Rick

THE TOWN HALL'S HONEY-COLORED wood paneling glowed in the afternoon light as Rick stepped into the lobby. A familiar scent of lemon furniture polish and old paper tickled his nose. His footsteps echoed on the hardwood floor as he approached the clerk's desk, where an elderly gentleman in a crisp button-down shirt organized files.

"Excuse me, I'm Rick Atwood from the B&B."

The man's steel-rimmed glasses caught the light as he looked up, revealing piercing blue eyes with crinkles at the corners. "Ah, the infamous Mr. Atwood. I'm Everett Carmichael." He extended a weathered hand. "Former mayor, current town clerk, and professional paper-pusher."

Rick's shoulders relaxed at the warmth in Everett's voice. "Former mayor? Was it difficult back in those days?"

"Twenty years of herding cats, as my wife used to say." Everett adjusted his glasses with a practiced motion. "Now I'm just counting down to retirement. Though between you and me, I think Duke here would miss our daily walks to work too much."

A massive mastiff Rick hadn't noticed lifted its head from behind the desk and gave a sleepy woof.

"Duke's not much for conversation," Everett confided, "but he's the best listener in town. How's your wife and baby?"

"They're both doing great. I'll tell Marquetta that you asked about them. Was it Mayor Carter who beat you in the election?"

"Francine? Yes," Everett sighed, patting Duke's head. "I'd gotten too comfortable, assumed the seat was mine. My own fault, really. Though I have to hand it to her—she ran quite the campaign. Blitzed right through my defenses."

"With Sylvia Archer's help?" Rick asked.

"Sore subject. How can I help you, Mr. Atwood?"

"I spoke with Powell Finnegan," Rick said. "He mentioned something interesting about Walt Copley and Sylvia Archer working together. I'm curious about their relationship and wondered what might be in the archives for his project. I've also got a number Tommy Granger gave to his nephew. I'd like to look it up. It could belong to one of your old files."

"Ah," Everett gently nudged Duke with a sideways push of his heel. "What do you think about that, old friend?"

The mastiff's tail thumped once against the floor.

"My thoughts exactly. Mr. Atwood, I'm simply trying to finish out my days, so I have no desire to spread rumors. However, I am here to serve the public, so I'll be happy to guide you to any records we have. You said you have the number?"

Rick pulled out the note he'd made while talking to Jake and handed it to Carmichael. "That's the number Jake gave me."

"Oh, I don't recall seeing this before. In fact, that's not even one of our numbers. But, I can show you Powell Finnegan's file. Come with me." Carmichael stood, looked down at the mastiff, and said, "Guard the door, Duke. Don't let anyone steal anything."

The mastiff rolled over to his side, stretched out, and closed his eyes.

"Only looks like he's sleeping," Carmichael said as he led Rick into a back room lined with rows of shelves. The room reminded Rick of a library, except that where there would normally be books, there were file folders.

Everett moved with practiced efficiency between the towering shelves, his fingers trailing along labeled tabs as he muttered file numbers under his breath. His other hand gripped a wooden cane, which he used to tap rhythmically against the floor while scanning each row. The fluorescent lights cast long shadows across his face, highlighting the concentrated furrow of his brows as he searched.

"The numbering system takes some getting used to," he explained, pausing at an intersection of shelves to orient himself. His steel-rimmed glasses caught the light as he tilted his head back to examine the higher shelves.

"Looks complicated," Rick said as he followed down another aisle.

"We changed it three times during my tenure as mayor, but I insisted on keeping the old systems accessible. Never know when you might need to dig up something from the past. In fact..." He paused, took another look at Rick's note, and said, "You know, this could be one of our old file numbers. Follow me."

He turned abruptly at the next aisle and ran his finger down a row of identical manila folders. The shelves here were dustier than the others, suggesting these records weren't frequently accessed. Everett's movements became more deliberate, his weathered hands moving with the precision of someone who had spent decades navigating these archives.

His finger paused between two file folders, and he let out a frustrated huff. The empty space spoke volumes. "Well, this is peculiar," he muttered, tapping his cane with heightened agitation. "Powell Finnegan's file should be right here. Someone's been poking around where they shouldn't."

"Any idea who it might have been?"

Everett inched closer until Rick could catch a whiff of his aftershave. "Walt's been haunting these archives lately. Claims it's for historical society duties, but he's been acting peculiar. Matter of fact, he was the last one here. No, wait, Tommy Granger would have been the last one. He was here just a few days ago."

"Was that unusual?" Rick raised an eyebrow, his interest piqued by Everett's conspiratorial tone.

"They were both regulars here. Tommy usually dropped in once or twice during the life of a project to double-check paperwork or gather information. He's usually pretty quick."

"What about Walt?"

"He's a different story. He comes in whenever the Planning Commission is considering a project. The last time he was here I overheard him on his cell phone right between these very shelves," Everett whispered, his voice suddenly reduced to a hushed murmur. "The man was beside himself—muttering about guilt eating away at him, about not being able to sleep because of someone's construction project."

Rick's pulse quickened. Had he found the smoking gun? "Did he say whose project?"

"Didn't mention any names, but he didn't have to. I'm pretty sure it was yours."

"Everett, can we look for my file? I'm curious to see if it's missing, too."

"Certainly. Give me a sec to look up the number." He went to a nearby computer, tapped the keys, and muttered to himself. "Of course, that's what I thought it was."

With his cane tapping in time to his footsteps, Everett took off down the aisle, made a right, then another. He stopped about halfway down the aisle and stood there tapping his cane faster.

"What's wrong, Everett?"

"Your file is missing, too. I suspect this is Walt's doing."

"What makes you say that?"

Everett's eyes darted around the dimly lit archives before he pressed on. "First off, Walt's been pretty vocal lately about how your grandfather stole the B&B from his father. Walt's not exactly subtle, so he's probably mentioned it to you."

"He has, so I confronted him about it directly," Rick said. His jaw tightened at the memory. "I demanded he either show concrete proof or stop spreading baseless accusations around town."

"Word of advice, Mr. Atwood?"

"Of course. I'll take any help I can get."

Carmichael checked his watch for the second time since they'd been talking. "Walt's not in this alone. And I'll tell you why. He was talking to Sylvia Archer on that phone call I told you about. He was getting himself all worked up about her plans for some big project. You should've seen him—his hands were shaking so bad I thought he might drop the phone."

"Do you think he was angry with her?"

Carmichael seemed to prop himself up on his cane and nodded. "Could be. It did sound like trouble in paradise. 'This is non-negotiable,' he kept saying over and over," Everett imitated Walt's gravelly tone, punctuating each word with a tap of his cane against the floor. The sharp sound reverberated throughout the silent room, bouncing off the metal shelves.

"So, whatever deal they've made, it sounds like Sylvia could be planning a double-cross. Throwing people under the bus seems to be her speciality. She hasn't been here, has she?"

"No, she's never been here herself. But I will tell you this, Mr. Atwood—I've known Walt Copley for thirty years. Never once heard him sound so desperate. Like a man trapped in a corner with no way out. Made the hair on the back of my neck stand up."

"What about Powell Finnegan's renovation?" Rick asked, shifting his weight. "You were mayor then, weren't you?"

Everett's eyes sparked with recognition, his fingers absently stroking his silver stubble. "Ah yes, the Finnegan mess. Walt signed off on every inspection, but something felt wrong."

"In what way?" Rick asked.

"I always thought the timeline was rushed. Walt claimed it was all normal and told me to keep my nose out of things I didn't understand."

"Pretty blunt for a town employee to speak to the mayor that way."

Everett started to wave away the comment, but then seemed to collapse like a tent folding in when the breeze died. "I had my suspicions about Walt's involvement even then, but without concrete evidence, what could I do? And, as for his attitude, Walt wasn't always crabby. But after the problems with his wife, I felt like he needed a break."

"What investigations were there when Powell's case went to court?" Rick watched Everett's weathered face for any subtle reaction to the question—a darting of the eyes, a tightening of the muscles, or even a quickening of his breath—and saw none of those. He thought he knew the answer, but just like he'd done in the old days, he wanted to double or triple-check his facts.

"Walt oversaw all the inspections himself. Made sure everything went through his office directly."

"He investigated a fire at one of his own inspections? Talk about a huge conflict of interest." His jaw clenched as he stayed laser-focused on the former mayor.

"Now that you mention it…" Everett shifted uncomfortably. "We probably should have brought in someone from outside. Hindsight and all that."

Rick's chest tightened as he absorbed Everett's words. The weight of the town's tangled history and its present deceptions pressed heavily on him. He felt a simmering anger rising, not just at Sylvia and Walt but at himself for not seeing through their schemes sooner. The stakes had always been high, but now the threat to his family's future felt palpable.

"Thank you, Everett," Rick said, his voice steady despite the turmoil within. "You've given me a lot to think about."

Everett nodded solemnly. "Just be careful, Rick. This town has its secrets, and not all of them want to be uncovered."

"I'll agree with you there." It was no wonder Archer and Copley had been able to run roughshod over the town for so long. This town had far too many secrets.

"Now, I hate to be rude, but I'm late for my break."

And Rick wanted time to do more than get a cursory tour of these archives. He needed help. And he knew exactly where to get it.

34

Rick

RICK SAT ON THE WEATHERED bench outside Town Hall, waiting for Marquetta to arrive with Baby Jack. Though it was mid-morning, the air was still crisp enough to tingle his cheeks. The skies, a bright, powdery blue, seemed to stretch endlessly overhead toward the horizon. The streets were growing busier with tourists, but this little spot felt almost serene despite the people walking about. Finally, he spotted Marquetta walking towards him with Baby Jack's stroller. Her hair was pulled back in a neat ponytail secured by a red scrunchie, and her look of determination made Rick smile despite everything.

"I'm not sure about this," she said as she brought the stroller to a stop. "I've never been good at deception."

Rick squeezed her hand. "You're not deceiving anyone. All you're doing is creating a distraction."

"With our baby." Marquetta raised a skeptical eyebrow.

"With the world's cutest baby," Rick corrected, looking into the stroller where Jack was chewing contentedly on a teething ring. "Nobody can resist him, especially not grandparent types."

Marquetta gazed at Baby Jack for a few seconds, shook her head, and snickered. "The things I do for you, Mr. Atwood."

"For us," he reminded her. "Our home is at stake here."

"Fine. But what if Everett asks me directly about why we're really here?"

"You'll improvise brilliantly." Rick kissed her cheek. "Just keep him occupied while I do a little snooping."

"And if he catches you?"

Rick grinned. "Then I'll blame it all on sleep deprivation from our adorable little alarm clock here."

Baby Jack squealed with delight and threw his teething ring, hitting Rick squarely in the forehead.

"See?" Marquetta laughed. "Even he thinks this plan is ridiculous."

"Ridiculous or not, it's the only plan we've got. Let's go."

As they stepped into Town Hall, Marquetta smiled brightly at Everett Carmichael, who sat behind his desk, his steel-rimmed glasses perched low on his nose.

"Everett!" Marquetta called out, her voice bubbling with enthusiasm. "Look who I brought!"

Duke perked up at the sound of Marquetta's voice. He lumbered up to stand, and then moseyed toward the stroller with a curious wag of his tail. At the sight of the giant mastiff's face, Baby Jack burst into a fit of giggles.

"Marquetta! Is this Baby Jack?" Everett bent down and was greeted with a flurry of noises ranging from babbling to giggles. "He's adorable!"

"Thank you, Everett. He's quite the chatterbox today." She lifted the baby from the stroller and held him. The baby's laughter rang out like tinkling bells, making even Duke nudge closer.

Everett chuckled as he reached out to ruffle Jack's tuft of hair. "Ah, yes! Quite the little charmer." He turned to Duke. "What do you think of this new fellow?"

Duke sniffed curiously at one of Baby Jack's feet, then sat as if guarding his new friend.

"I'm just going to use the restroom if you don't mind," Rick said as Marquetta handed Baby Jack off to Everett. Slipping away toward the records room, Rick couldn't help but smile at Marquetta's effortless way with people; it was one of her many talents, and in this case, it was exactly the distraction he needed.

A rush of urgency flooded Rick's veins. He had maybe ten or fifteen minutes before Everett would come looking for him. Rows of shelves loomed over him, filled with boxes labeled in fading ink. He scanned any kind of clue about Walt or Sylvia's dealings—something to help him piece together their motivations.

Meanwhile, he could hear snippets of Marquetta's conversation echoing from outside.

"Did you see this photo?" Marquetta asked Everett excitedly. "That building is where my dad got his first job!"

"Oh yes! I remember. He was a hard worker, your dad…"

Rick chuckled softly to himself as he rummaged through an open box labeled "Zoning Applications." The images of their banter floated through his mind: Marquetta weaving stories while keeping Jack entertained and Duke watching protectively over them all. The box contained plenty of paperwork to be filed, but none of it was for his project.

He pulled the paper he'd gotten from Jake and checked the number against the documents in the box. No matches. Moving on to the lower shelves, Rick winced as his knees popped in protest. The dust patterns told their own story—most files hadn't been touched in months, maybe years. But several spots showed clear disruption, fingerprints smudging the otherwise uniform layer of gray.

Once again, he did the same search in the areas that looked to have been handled, but came up empty. He ran his fingers along the edge of a shelf, searching for anything out of place. Nothing. The distant sound of Baby Jack's laughter filtered through from the main office, followed by Everett's booming voice.

"I tell you, Duke and I were walking by the harbor last Tuesday when Mayor Carter came out of Joe Gray's houseboat. She saw us and acted like she'd seen a ghost!"

"Really? What do you think happened?" Marquetta's voice rang with perfect theatrical curiosity.

Rick smiled. She was buying him time beautifully.

He moved to a filing cabinet labeled "Historical Preservation Appeals" and yanked it open. The metal drawer squealed in protest, making him wince.

"Come on. You guys aren't creative enough to hide things well," Rick whispered, flipping through the neatly labeled folders. "You're the type who puts things just one place over from where they belong."

The drawer yielded nothing unusual. Rick closed it with a sigh and looked around, then pressed his hand to his forehead. Maybe Tommy was more creative than he'd given him credit for. Everett had said the number wasn't a valid file number. But what if it was a file number, just not one that was official?

He again pulled out the paper, held it out, and began searching through the stacks, following the numbering sequences until he came to an aisle where the numbers were similar.

"Darn," he muttered. The town's files only had eight numbers, and the one Jake had given him had nine. That wasn't insurmountable. What if Tommy had added the last number as some kind of suffix? A fine-tuning, so to speak. He followed the file numbers until he found what he was looking for in the middle of the aisle on the bottom shelf.

The folder was much larger than the surrounding ones. It also looked to be much newer. Even though its size and newness made it stand out physically, its location on the bottom shelf made it unnoticeable to anyone who didn't know where to look.

He pulled the folder from the shelf and was shocked to see there were smaller folders inside. In looking at the file number, Rick realized he might have been correct—the last number was a four, and there were four folders inside. The largest of the files was for the Town Renovation project. There was also a file for Powell Finnegan and one for his project. The fourth file was for Sylvia Archer's office renovation.

Rick knew he was running out of time, so with his pulse quickening, he examined what he had. The tabs had been deliberately turned inward, making them nearly invisible unless someone was specifically looking for the number Tommy Granger had given to Jake.

"Gotcha," Rick whispered as he flipped open Finnegan's file.

The inspection reports bore Walt's signature. But it was the additional notes on the building plans that had been signed and dated by Walt after the plans had been approved that caught Rick's attention. Sylvia had requested structural changes after permits were approved. And tucked in the back of the file was a memo with Sylvia's letterhead, authorizing Tommy Granger to "proceed as discussed despite the regulatory concerns."

Back outside, Baby Jack squealed again, drowning out any chance Rick had of hearing what was happening in the main hall—but he was too engrossed now to care about anything except what lay before him.

This was exactly what he needed—proof of the connection between Walt, Sylvia, and Tommy. He couldn't believe that note still existed. Rick swallowed hard. Tommy had made sure the evidence survived, even if he didn't.

The sound of Duke's nails clicking on the floor outside made Rick freeze.

"Rick?" Everett called. "You still in there? Your little man is asking for his daddy!"

"Be there in just a minute or two, Everett!"

"Oh, Everett! Look at this! Isn't he cute?"

"Thank you, Marquetta," Rick whispered and began taking photographs.

Rick's fingers trembled as he flipped through the pages. So many of the documents told the same story—corruption hiding in plain sight.

"Come on, come on," he muttered, his phone camera clicking rapidly.

The handwritten notes in the margins immediately caught his eye. The blocky, all-caps style on a separate note was unmistakable. It was Tommy's handwriting. Rick had seen enough of it on construction plans to recognize it anywhere.

"TOLD W THIS WIRING NOT UP TO CODE. HE SAID PROCEED ANYWAY."

Another note, dated three months later: "S KNOWS ABOUT THE SHORTCUTS. SAYS KEEP IT QUIET OR ELSE."

Rick's heart hammered against his ribs. Tommy hadn't just been a worker—he'd been a knowing participant in the fraud, but he'd also documented everything. For what reason? To protect himself? Or to blackmail his bosses? From what he'd heard about the man, he wasn't sure.

"What in the world are you doing, Rick?"

Rick nearly dropped his phone as he spun around to see Everett standing in the doorway, Duke's massive head peeking around his legs.

"Everett! I was just—"

"Taking pictures of town documents without a warrant or the proper approvals?" Everett crossed his arms over his chest and pulled in a deep breath. "You know, when your lovely wife brought that adorable baby in, I never dreamt you'd take advantage of my good nature."

"I can explain."

"I certainly hope so." Everett crossed his arms. "Because Duke here is very disappointed in you. Aren't you, Duke?"

The mastiff tilted his head, looking more confused than disappointed.

"Look," Rick said, holding up the folder. "Tommy Granger was documenting everything about a conspiracy between Walt Copley and Sylvia Archer. This proves they were cutting corners, falsifying inspections, and more. Tommy knew it all."

Everett's stern expression softened slightly. "And got himself killed for it, I'd wager."

"You knew?"

"Suspected." Everett stepped closer, lowering his voice. "This town's been my home for seventy years, Rick. You think I don't notice when something smells fishier than the harbor at low tide?"

"Then why didn't you say anything?"

"Same reason Tommy wrote notes instead of filing reports." Everett tapped the folder. "No proof. Just an old man's suspicions."

Baby Jack's wail echoed from the front office.

"Sounds like your cover's been blown," Everett said with a wry smile.

"What are you going to do?"

Everett took a final look at the files and tapped his temple. "Funny thing about my memory these days. Sometimes I walk into a room and completely forget why I came in." He turned toward the door. "Take whatever photos you need, then put everything back exactly where you found it. Duke and I need to go spend more time with that handsome boy of yours."

Everett's footsteps faded down the hall, leaving Rick alone with a heavy decision. The files sat on the desk, whispering secrets he could hardly believe. If he returned them to their original spot, there was a good chance Walt would find them—or worse, get rid of them. And Everett? He might get curious, himself.

"Great," he muttered, pacing the small space. "Just what I need—an old politician snooping through files I shouldn't even have touched."

He stood next to the desk, staring at the open folder filled with incriminating notes. What if someone altered them before they could be used? Sylvia had already shown her willingness to manipulate facts for her gain.

"Time to play it smart," he said aloud, as if the empty room might offer counsel. "I can't just shove these back and hope for the best."

Rick pulled out his phone and opened the note with Jake's number sequence. Reversing the numbers might be a good solution, he thought. After all, if you knew the numbers, the files would be easy to find. Otherwise, not so much. It felt silly but also oddly fitting.

"3-7-4-8-2-9-1-5-4," he recited quietly to himself as if invoking magic. He took a deep breath and made his decision—he'd reverse Jake's number sequence. Yup, best to follow the old KISS principle.

He wandered the aisles until he found the spot where he could safely hide the files, pushed them in into their new home, and returned to the lobby, where Baby Jack and Marquetta were entertaining Everett.

"All done?" Everett asked as he turned his attention from Baby Jack to Rick.

"Actually, I think I'm just getting started."

35

Alex

THE CLOCK ABOVE THE WHITEBOARD says there's only three more minutes until freedom. Mr. Orbison has been droning on about electrical currents for, like, the entire class. I doodle question marks in the margins of my notebook. I hate the idea that I'm to blame for today's subject, but I did get him started on electricity last time. Still, the questions I've scribbled for Jake are way more interesting than anything about volts and amps.

Mr. Orbison adjusts his glasses and looks around the room. "And remember, class, your circuit diagrams are due tomorrow. No exceptions."

I tap my pencil against my desk, thinking about the metal box I stole from Willy's shed. Mom and Dad were super upset when they found out I took it, but they haven't returned it. Not yet, anyway. There has to be something important inside.

"Alexandra?" Mr. Orbison's voice snaps me back to reality. "Perhaps you'd like to explain the difference between parallel and series circuits to the class?"

"Um..." My face heats up. "In parallel circuits, electricity has multiple paths, and in series, there's only one path?"

"Correct. Although I suspect that was a lucky guess, given your attention level today."

A few of the kids snicker, but they stop the second Mr. Orbison turns on them. Even Billy Thornton seems to get the point—Mr. Orbison might be making an example of me right now, but he won't hesitate to do it to them, too.

The bell rings, and everyone jumps up and scrambles out of the room while I'm still packing up my stuff. Robbie and Sasha join me. They're both kinda shifting from one foot to the other.

Robbie whispers, "Hurry up, Alex, before Mr. Orbison gives us more homework."

I stuff my notebook into my backpack and make up my mind. "I'm going to see Shadow. You guys want to come?"

Sasha bites her lip. "I can't. My mom's got me starting a new dance class."

"And I promised my dad I'd help out with some chores at home," Robbie adds, not quite meeting my eyes.

Wow. Robbie would rather do chores than…no, I get it. I've pushed their friendship too far. I try not to let my disappointment show. "It's cool. I can go alone."

"We could hang out tomorrow?" Robbie offers. "Maybe do something fun?"

"Yeah, totally." I force a smile. They're making excuses. Ever since I found Shadow and started paying more attention to him than them, they've been acting weird. Like I'm choosing a dog over them. I guess, in a way, I am.

I wave goodbye and head to Jake's house. I don't even have to think about peddling. I haven't since I was six, but today seems different 'cause I'm practicing my questions for Jake in my head. He has to know something about Tommy that could help.

When I reach his house, I knock twice.

"C'mon in. It's open."

The door creaks when I push on it. Inside, Jake is sitting on the couch, a half-finished bag of potato chips and a couple of cans of one of those weird new soft drinks for grown-ups on the coffee table. He looks like he hasn't slept in days. His hair is sticking up in all directions, and there are dark circles under his eyes. And, he kinda smells like he needs a shower.

"Oh. It's you." He reaches for the bag of chips, but instead of taking one, he quirks his cheek and takes a sip from one of the cans.

The living room is a mess—more empty cans, crumpled papers, and a couple of Shadow's toys scattered about. Jake goes back to watching the blank TV screen.

"Where's Shadow?" I ask, looking around.

"Backyard, I guess."

I sit on the edge of an armchair. "So… how are you doing?"

Nothing, at first. Then, he snaps, "How do you think?"

Wow. He's like, really down. "I didn't realize you were so close to your uncle."

Jake shrugs, his eyes are glassy and tired. "He raised me after my mom died."

"Why? Did something happen to your dad, too?"

"He ran out on my mom and me when I was five."

"Wow. I'm sorry."

"Why do you care?" His voice isn't mean, just tired.

"Because I think you need a friend," I say quietly. "And I want to help figure out who killed your uncle."

Jake laughs, but it sounds hollow. "You're, what, twelve?"

"Thirteen," I correct him. "And Chief Cunningham says I'm smarter than most adults in this town."

"That's not saying much. Uncle Tommy always said the same thing about himself."

For a second, I see a flash of the real Jake, and I wonder if he'll tell me more. "What else did he say? Like, was he scared of anyone? Did he ever mention Walt Copley or Sylvia Archer?"

Jake's eyes narrow. "Why those names?"

"Because they're like, totally suspicious. And I think they both want my dad's property."

Jake picks at a loose thread on his jeans. "Tommy kept stuff from me. Said it was safer that way." His voice drops to almost a whisper. "But the night before he died, he was different. Scared. He said he finally had the proof he needed to 'bring them all down.'"

My heart races. "Proof of what?"

Jake's face flushes red. "I already told your dad everything I know!" He jumps up from the couch, sending potato chips scattering across the floor. "Why can't you people leave me alone?"

"Whoa, sorry." I hold up my hands. "I didn't know my dad already talked to you."

Jake paces across the room, picking at a fingernail as he walks. "Yeah, well, he did. Yesterday. Asked a whole bunch of questions. Just like you're doing to me right now."

Rats. My dad already questioned Jake, but my dad's super thorough, so I shouldn't be surprised. I feel kind of stupid for not thinking about that. The living room suddenly feels smaller, like the walls are closing in on the mess and secrets. A photo of Jake and his uncle sits crooked on a dusty side table. They're both grinning in front of what looks like a half-built wall.

I point at it and try to sound casual. "That's a nice photo."

Jake stops and looks at it sideways. His breath comes out in a slow, tragic rush.. "Yeah. Those were better days."

"Looks like it. Hey, when you talked to my dad, did you tell him anything about this proof your uncle had?"

Jake whirls around and skewers me with the same look Mr. Orbison used on the class. "Seriously? You're, like, tag-teaming me now? Your dad asks questions one day, and you show up the next to see if I change my story?"

"No! It's not like that." I feel my cheeks getting hot again. "My dad doesn't even know I'm here. He'd totally freak if he found out."

That seems to calm Jake down a little. He collapses back onto the couch. There's a big whoosh as he settles in.

"Look, I told your dad about this metal box my Uncle Tommy had. He kept important papers and stuff in it. He called it my 'insurance policy' if anything happened to him." Jake rubs his eyes. "But it disappeared after he died. I looked everywhere."

My heart skips a beat. A metal box? Like the one I took from Willy's shed? "What color was it?"

"I dunno, gray, I guess. Yeah, that was it."

OMG. "Did you tell my dad about what was inside?" I ask, trying to keep from sounding too excited.

"How could I? I never saw what was in it." Jake grabs another chip. "Uncle Tommy made me memorize all these random numbers. Wouldn't tell me why."

"What kind of numbers?"

"A string of them. Tommy made me repeat them like fifty times that night."

"That's super weird. And you don't know what the numbers mean?" I hear a dog howling outside the house. It sounds like Shadow. He sounds lonesome and sad, and it makes my heart twist.

"No," Jake says.

"Did your uncle ever mention anything about Willy Hobbs?"

Jake frowns. "The cemetery guy? Not that I remember."

"What about arguments? Did you ever hear him fighting with Walt Copley?"

"Yeah, I told your dad about that, too. Uncle Tommy caught Walt taking bribes from Sylvia to approve sketchy work at Town Hall." Jake's eyes darken. "And, you know what, I didn't tell your dad this, but since I talked to him, I got to thinking the reason Uncle Tommy decided to expose Walt and Sylvia is because he started feeling bad about helping to ruin your family's home."

Whoa! My dad doesn't know about this? I need to tell him. Oh, wait. That would mean I'd have to tell him why I'm really here. Shadow's crying again. It feels desperate, like he's calling out for someone who isn't coming back. My feet practically itch with the urge to go to him, to run my fingers through his thick black coat and tell him everything will be okay. But I can't. Not yet.

"Did your Uncle Tommy ever mention if the construction site was unsafe? Like, if someone messed with the wiring? Or maybe didn't nail down some of the stairs?"

Jake locks eyes with me, and I can see I'm pushing him pretty far. "You're really not gonna let this go, are you?"

"Nope. Your Uncle Tommy was killed because he knew too much. Don't you want to find out who did it?"

"Look, all I know is what I already told you. I don't want to talk about this anymore. He's dead, okay? Just let it go."

"And don't you want to know why somebody killed him?"

Shadow howls again, and Jake stands. "I gotta shut that dog up."

The way he says it, I'm scared he's gonna shoot Shadow or something. I jump up and move in front of Jake. "Lemme try. You saw how we got along. You said I could come back to see him, right? Well, here I am."

Jake plops back onto the sofa. "Fine. I got things to think about anyway."

I race through the kitchen to the back door. When I open it, Shadow's sitting there with his head tilted, like he's been waiting for me all day.

"Hey, boy!" I drop to my knees and wrap my arms around his thick neck. His fur feels like the softest blanket ever, and he smells like dirt and grass and something uniquely Shadow. He licks my face with his giant tongue, making me giggle.

"Did you miss me? I missed you!" I scratch behind his ears, and he kind of rubs his ear against my hand, his eyes half-closed in doggy bliss.

The backyard is pretty sad—just a patch of yellow grass and a tree that looks like it went wild years ago. I see a couple of tennis balls. They're covered in teeth marks and dried slobber. Shadow must get super bored out here all alone.

"Wanna play?" I grab one of the tennis balls and don't even care if it feels really gross. I toss it across the yard, and Shadow charges after it. His massive paws tear up chunks of the yellow grass as he runs. He retrieves the ball in about two seconds flat and drops it at my feet. His tail is wagging so hard his whole back end is swinging.

I throw it again, and again, and each time Shadow seems more excited than the last. It's like he's been waiting for someone to play with him forever.

"You're the best dog in the whole world, you know that?" I tell him as he flops down next to me, panting happily. I run my fingers through his coat, working out some of the tangles. "Jake doesn't deserve you," I whisper.

Shadow rests his big head on my lap, looking up at me with those soulful brown eyes. They're so deep and filled with emotion. I almost feel like he understands everything I'm saying.

"I promise I'll figure out what happened to Tommy," I bend down close to his ear and whisper, "And I won't let anything bad happen to you, ever. I love you too much."

36

Rick

RICK HUNCHED OVER ADAM'S DESK, exhaustion finally taking hold. Hours of combing through photocopied documents, first at home, and now here, had left him stiff and sore. He hadn't come here to rest. No, he'd come because the weight of what he'd uncovered was too heavy to carry alone. Call it a confession. Call it unburdening. Whatever it was, and whatever Adam might say, he couldn't sit on it any longer.

"I've been through these with a fine-tooth comb," Rick said, sweeping a hand toward the pile of documents. "You wouldn't believe what Walt and Sylvia have been scheming."

He tapped one page near the corner of the desk, right beside the photo of Adam and his wife, Traci—as well as Baby Jack's pacifier, which Rick had absentmindedly stuck in his pocket when they'd left Town Hall. "Every one of these ties them deeper into it—doctored inspections, shady approvals. And here—Tommy's handwriting all over the margins. It's a trail of corruption in black and white."

Adam said nothing. Anger flickered across his face, and beneath it, something else Rick couldn't quite pin down—disappointment? Maybe. Distrust? He hoped not.

Rick stretched, rolling his aching shoulders. His neck felt like it was shot from hunching over a desk for too long. "It's all there, Adam. You can see it for yourself. The corruption. The greed."

Adam finally drew in a slow breath, his expression hardening. "You said you got these from the records room? How? I went through it myself—there was nothing there on your project."

Rick hesitated, knowing that the next few moments could change the course of his life. "I had to get creative. They were hidden. Somebody didn't want these found."

"That's a heavy accusation. Who do you think was responsible?"

"According to Everett Carmichael, Tommy was the last one in the records room."

"And so today, Everett distracted him. Marquetta brought Baby Jack for a visit."

"While you snuck in and stole these."

"It wasn't stealing. These are all copies. The originals are still there. All I did was put them in a different place."

"Do you realize you might have compromised my entire investigation? How do I know you didn't doctor the originals while you were there?" Adam stood and began to pace. "A good defense attorney will say this was evidence tampering, Rick. I should arrest you for this."

"Come on, buddy. I was only working on my construction site case when I stumbled across this evidence. The files I found prove Walt and Sylvia were cutting corners on multiple projects, including the Town Hall renovation."

"And you just happened to stumble across them while sneaking around without supervision?" Adam's stern expression suddenly cracked, and he burst into laughter. "You know who you sound like right now?"

"Who?"

"Your daughter." Adam clapped his hand and laughed again. "That's exactly what Alex would say—'I was only looking for my homework when I accidentally found evidence of a major conspiracy.'"

Rick felt his face flush. "I'm nothing like—" He stopped mid-sentence, realizing Adam was right. "Fine. Maybe the apple doesn't fall far from the tree."

"Maybe?" Adam raised an eyebrow. "I'm not sure if the munchkin learned from the master, or if it was the other way around."

Rick gestured at the documents scattered across Adam's desk. "Look, unauthorized search or not, what I found connects everything. Tommy was documenting every shortcut they took. And look at this." He pointed to a page written and signed by Tommy Granger. "This note corresponds to this inspection report. Walt approved the electrical work that wasn't up to code and resulted in Powell Finnegan's fire. And, according to Granger, Sylvia knew about it."

Adam's expression grew more serious as he studied the documents. "This would explain why Jake mentioned his uncle being 'exonerated once he's buried.' Tommy must have been keeping evidence as insurance."

"Exactly!" Rick tapped another document. "And look at this – Walt's signature on a previous inspection report for Powell

Finnegan's property, dated the same day he was supposedly out of town."

"Falsified documents. That's a serious offense."

"And a motive for murder If Tommy threatened to expose them."

Adam straightened up and crossed his arms. "I'm still furious with you for interfering in my case."

"But you're not going to arrest me," Rick said with a knowing smile.

"No, I'm not," Adam admitted. "Because you've just handed me the connection I needed. The problem is, I can't use any of it in court. These are all copies. Besides, they weren't obtained with a warrant, so they're inadmissible."

"I know. That's why I hid the originals in the records room. They're still there, just waiting for you to get a warrant and retrieve them."

"If I get a warrant, Walt and Sylvia will hear about it. And the mayor will also go on high alert. These connections go deeper than simple record tampering or code violations. This goes to murder. We need to move carefully."

"We?" Rick asked, hopefully.

Adam sighed. "Yes, we. I have to assume Francine might somehow be involved."

Rick nodded, sobering at the reminder of what was at stake. "What do you want to do next?"

Adam's jaw tightened, and his back went rigid. He looked past Rick in the direction of the front door. "I want to confront the mayor."

"What?" Rick's voice pitched higher than he intended. "Are you sure that's a good idea? She's already made it clear she doesn't want me involved."

The click-clacking of a woman's heels was all the announcement Rick needed. He turned, saw Francine Carter watching him, her face flushed with anger, and one hand clutching her purse like a weapon.

"Well, isn't this cozy?" Her eyes darted between them, landing on the scattered documents. "Chief Cunningham, I believe I gave you explicit instructions about keeping Mr. Atwood out of this investigation."

Adam rose slowly from his chair. "Madame Mayor, with all due respect—"

"Respect? Is that what you call deliberately ignoring a direct order from your superior?" Francine squeezed her eyes shut and pulled in a long breath, pinning Rick with a look that offered no escape. "I told you I was handling this, Rick. You need to stay out of it for your own good."

With a firm shake of his head, Rick shot back a terse, "Sorry, Francine. But I'm not letting go now. I spent too many years as an investigative reporter to back away from this kind of intimidation."

"This will not end well for you if you persist," she shot back.

Adam's voice came through, steady and firm. "Madame Mayor, the police department serves the citizens of Seaside Cove. And right now, those citizens deserve the truth."

"And they shall get it, Chief Cunningham."

Rick watched the exchange with growing unease. Francine's hands were shaking. She looked like she was on the verge of firing Adam, and it was his fault. He stood, bumping the desk in the process. "I've heard enough, Francine. You were the one who coerced me into helping Adam solve a murder case when he had no formal training. As a journalist—or a consultant to the police—I can assure you these documents—" he gestured to the papers spread across Adam's desk "—tell a compelling story about corruption, falsified inspections, and why Tommy Granger ended up dead."

Francine's eyes widened. "Where did you get those?"

"From the Town Hall records room," Rick said, watching her reaction carefully. "Walt Copley tried to hide these documents, and I found them. The records show how he approved substandard electrical work for Powell Finnegan's house—work that caused a fire and ruined a man's life."

"And the ones that show Sylvia Archer knew about it," Adam added quietly.

"Who was, I might add, your major campaign donor," Rick said.

"You had no right to access those files," Francine whispered, but the fight was draining from her voice.

Rick sidestepped his way from between the chair and Adam's desk so he could stand face-to-face with her. "They're public records, Francine. You know I have every right to inspect them. I also think you know what's in them. I've trusted you since I moved to this town. But lately, I'm starting to wonder if my trust was misplaced."

A sudden clunk and the sound of plastic rolling across a hard surface broke the tension. Baby Jack's pacifier rolled to a stop at Francine's feet, its cheerful yellow duck face smiling up at her.

Francine seemed fixated on the yellow duck face, then bent to pick it up. When she straightened, she had tears streaming down her face. "You don't understand. Neither of you understands what's at stake here."

"Then explain it to me, Francine. Tell me what's at stake. Because from where I stand, it looks like everything I own is on the line. So, what have you got to lose? Please, tell me. I'd really like to know."

Instead of answering, she pressed the pacifier into Rick's hand, her fingers lingering before she pulled away. "I'm sorry," she said, her voice breaking. "Some secrets in this town are buried deeper than Tommy Granger will ever be."

"That's what investigative journalists are trained to find, Francine. And once word of this becomes public knowledge, I can guarantee you one thing—I'm the most understanding reporter this town will be dealing with."

Francine clutched her purse to her chest, then turned and fled, her heels clicking rapidly as she hurried toward the door. When Rick looked at Adam, he saw the same stunned reflection on Adam's face that he felt inside.

"Francine running out wasn't exactly what I expected. Was that a confession or a denial?"

"I have no idea," Adam sighed, running a hand through his hair. "But it confirms one thing—Francine's involved, and she's terrified."

"The question is, what exactly is she afraid of? Or who?"

Adam rubbed the back of his neck, his fingers kneading slowly, but the determination on his face said only one thing would take that tension away—resolution. "I'm guessing we're about to find out. And I don't think either of us is going to like the answer."

37

Rick

RICK'S FINGERS TIGHTENED AROUND THE bright yellow pacifier, its cheerful duck face now a cruel mockery of the chaos unraveling around him. He slipped it into his pocket, the plastic cool against his palm, and let out a slow, measured breath as Adam paced like a caged animal.

"We need to secure those files before someone else does. If what you found is truly incriminating, as you say, it's not going to stay hidden for long. They'll find it, and it will disappear. Why didn't you follow protocol and let me handle this instead of playing detective?"

Rick flinched, the words cutting deeper than Adam likely intended. When he'd first moved to Seaside Cove with Alex, he'd been filled with hope for a new beginning, just like when they'd started work on the new house. But now, they were on the verge of losing everything. Rick let out a sigh filled with lost promises. "That's what I thought I was doing, Adam—protecting them. I thought I was doing the right thing."

Adam stopped pacing and rubbed his temples with his fingertips. Closing his eyes, he looked like a man conducting an internal debate. "How well are the files hidden?"

"I hid them by reversing Jake's number sequence. It seemed obscure enough that Walt wouldn't stumble across them."

Silence hung in the air as Adam seemed to contemplate what Rick had done. His jaw muscles tightened, but then he said, "Okay. What's done is done. The fact is, those records are evidence now." Adam grabbed his jacket from the back of his chair. "Let's go secure them."

The half-block walk to Town Hall took less than a minute, but Rick's mind raced through every possibility. "What if Francine already called someone? What if she warned Walt?"

"Then we're too late," Adam replied grimly. "But I don't think she did. Did you see her face? I don't think that was calculation."

The familiar scent of lemon polish greeted them as they entered Town Hall, but this time, it carried a different quality. What once felt warm and homey now seemed cloying and artificial, like a desperate attempt to mask something rotten beneath the town's polished facade.

Everett's desk sat conspicuously empty, and when Rick went to the desk and looked down, Duke's spot behind the counter was vacant, too. "That's odd. I got the impression Everett never left during business hours."

"He doesn't. Not usually. Unless something happened to him," Adam said, his expression darkening. "Come on."

They hurried down the hallway to the records room. The door stood slightly ajar, and Rick felt his stomach drop. Inside, the fluorescent lights flickered overhead as he navigated the familiar shelves. “It should be right over—“ He stopped mid-sentence, staring at the empty space where he’d hidden the files. “They’re gone.”

“Are you sure this is the right spot?” Adam asked, scanning the neighboring shelves.

“Positive. See the numbering for the files on either side? Besides, I wouldn’t forget the location.” Rick ran his hand through his hair. “Someone knew exactly where to look.”

Adam pulled out his phone. “I’m calling in a search warrant for Walt’s house and office.”

“Wait.” Rick held up his hand and looked around. “Why isn’t Everett here? What if he took them?”

“Why would he—“

“Because he knew I was looking at them earlier. He walked in right when I was taking photos of everything. “But he let me go. He said his memory was failing him, and he sometimes forgot why he walked into a room. Maybe it was all bogus—a fabrication to throw me off.”

“So either he’s protecting you, or—“

“Or he’s in on it too.” Rick slammed his palm against a shelf, sending a cloud of dust into the air. “For crying out loud, is everyone in this town corrupt?”

Adam placed a steadying hand on Rick’s shoulder. “Hey, buddy. Take a breath.”

Rick did as Adam suggested, then exhaled slowly, the tension in his shoulders easing slightly. “Sorry. It’s just… this is my family’s future we’re talking about. Our home.”

"I know." Adam's voice softened. "And that's exactly why we need to do this by the book from now on. No more amateur detective work."

Rick couldn't help but laugh. "Says the guy who became police chief with zero experience."

Adam grinned. "What to do you mean, no experience? It turns out reading meters was excellent preparation for becoming police chief. I'd recommend the town make it a regular career path."

"So what now?"

"We follow the advice of a wise old Chinese general."

"Sun Tzu?"

"Yes. Don't be afraid to hit your opponent when they're down."

"Adam, I've studied Sun Tzu, and he never said that. His advice was actually to give your opponent a way out so they don't become desperate."

"Whatever. Let's go see the mayor. I'll bet we can get her to talk."

The bell above the door of Scoops n'Scones jangled as Rick and Adam entered. The familiar scent of fresh-baked waffle cones mingled with the aroma of chocolate syrup and hot fudge, along with other sugary scents. What was missing, though, was the usual warmth from Francine's chatter. Instead, she was behind the counter, her eyes rimmed in red while she mechanically scooped ice cream for a young mother and her toddler.

"Chocolate in a waffle cone," Francine said flatly, her voice flat and mechanical. For the first time, she seemed to realize Rick and Adam were there, and nearly dropped the scoop.

Rick hung back while Adam approached the counter. The mother, a woman Rick didn't recognize, hurried out the door with barely another word.

"We need to talk, Francine," Adam said once they were alone.

"I'm busy, Chief Cunningham." She wiped the already spotless counter and busied herself by rinsing off the ice cream scoops. "Some of us have businesses to run."

Rick stepped forward. "Like the business of hiding public records?"

Francine's hand froze mid-wipe. "You don't know what you're talking about."

"The files are gone, Mayor." Adam hooked his thumbs in his belt and widened his stance. "Someone moved them right after you left my office."

"What? And you think I took them?" She tossed the rag into the sink with unnecessary force. "I haven't even been to Town Hall today. I haven't taken any files. And I certainly haven't done anything wrong."

Rick moved to his left, positioning himself far enough away from Adam that Francine couldn't look at them both at the same time. "Then why did you run out of the police station crying, Francine?"

"Because I'm tired! Because this town is falling apart, and everyone's looking at me to fix it!" Her voice cracked. "And I'm running out of options. I didn't realize being mayor came with a side job as a referee, therapist, and miracle worker—but here we are! Do you have any idea what it's like trying to keep everyone happy? To make this town work?"

Adam crossed his arms. “Is that why you made deals with Sylvia Archer? To make the town work?”

“I never made any deals.” Francine’s eyes darted between them. “Sylvia was a donor, that’s all.”

Rick spotted the framed photo of Francine cutting the ribbon at the Town Hall renovation. “A donor who got special treatment on inspections? Who somehow managed to sabotage my construction project?”

“I’m looking into what’s happening with your project. The timing is…unfortunate.”

“Unfortunate?” A rush of anger surged under Rick’s skin. He snapped, “My family’s home is at stake! And you call it unfortunate?”

The ice cream freezer hummed loudly, breaking the silence engulfing them. Francine looked away, and then her shoulders sagged.

“What I’m doing is for the town,” she whispered finally. “Seaside Cove needs investment and development. Our infrastructure is falling apart.

“That may be, but what cost should we pay for those investments?” Adam pressed. “Need I remind you that a man is dead, Madame Mayor?”

“I’m well aware of what’s happened.” She swallowed hard.

Rick clenched his teeth to keep from making another accusation. He could see the angst on Francine’s face. She was so close to breaking. “Then let me help Adam find Tommy Granger’s killer. Someone in this conspiracy found out he was keeping records he could use as blackmail, and they killed him for it.”

"What do you know, Francine?" Adam asked, his voice soft and encouraging.

The bell jingled again, and another customer entered the store. This time, Rick knew the faces. It was William and Edith Aldridge.

"Ah, Rick!" William said. "Is your sweet tooth acting up, too?"

"Sorry, William, but no. Adam and I are conferring with the mayor about some town business."

"I'm sure you have plenty to confer about."

Edith touched her husband's arm. "William, I think they need a minute."

"Right." William nodded, then held out his arm so Edith could take it. "We'll step outside. Guard the door, so to speak."

When they were once again alone, Adam said, "Francine, we need those files."

She looked up, tears streaming down her face. "Chief Cunningham, I've told you. I don't have them."

"Then who does?" Rick asked.

"I don't know." Her hands trembled as she reached for a tissue. "But whoever took them knows what's in them. And I don't know how they intend to use the information."

"Madame Mayor," Adam's tone grew more insistent. "If you know something, you have an obligation to tell me. If you don't, it will only cause more trouble."

The implication must have been too much for Francine because she slammed her palms on the counter and snapped, "And if you persist in bullying me, Chief Cunningham, I will take steps to have you removed from your position!"

"Okay, let's all just take a little time to let this settle. Adam, if Francine says she doesn't have the files, I believe her. I think our other option is to find Everett Carmichael."

Adam took a long breath. His green eyes held the mayor's, but then he turned away. "You're right. We should continue this discussion at another time."

"What did you mean when you said you had to find Everett?" Francine asked.

"We were just there and he wasn't at his desk," Rick said.

Francine gripped the edge of the counter as if steadying herself. She blinked rapidly, as though the world had tilted. "Oh, no. This is worse than I thought."

38

Rick

RICK PULLED THE DOOR TO Scoops n'Scones shut behind him. Adam, who had answered a call, was dealing with some new crisis. If he got pulled away, so be it, but Francine's behavior was what worried him most. She'd completely shut down after they'd told her about Everett not being at his desk. What did her silence mean? And which side of this battle was Francine on? He still didn't know.

"Be there in a minute. We're only a few doors away." Adam holstered his phone and pointed up the street. "Let's go to Crusty Buns. Apparently, there's a big argument in progress."

They hurried up one block and heard voices from inside the shop. "Good grief. What's happening to this town?" Adam said.

As they approached the front entrance, Rick grumbled, "Maybe you should go in with your gun drawn. That would stop them."

Adam rolled his eyes and cocked his head. "Just follow me."

Inside, the aroma of fresh muffins swirled around Rick like a comforting blanket. But today, the usual comfort felt distant. A tense energy filled the air, prickling his skin. The small cafe was bustling with morning customers, but all eyes in the shop were fixed on the heated argument taking place in the center of the room.

Small groups were forming, some looking uncomfortable and preparing to leave. Others appeared ready to join the fray. Four figures stood at its heart. Their voices grew louder with each barb thrown back and forth. Mary O'Donnell hovered off to one side, clutching a tray piled high with muffins. Madeline's shoulders slumped and her face twisted into an exasperated grimace.

"Howie," Joe Gray shouted, gesturing wildly with his hands. "You think bulldozing our history is progress?"

Howie's voice boomed back, unwavering. "All you're doing is clinging to nostalgia! We need growth!"

Madeline Weiss chimed in next to Joe, her arms flailing wildly as she gestured around her. "And what about our heritage? This town is not just a cash cow, Howie!"

Rick cringed at the tension among his neighbors, and he saw the same dismay on Adam's face. It was like watching a live soap opera —one he didn't want to be part of, but couldn't escape.

"Do we need popcorn for this?" Rick muttered under his breath.

Adam shot him a look that said now wasn't the time. Rick followed Adam when he stepped closer to the argument, at which point Mary waved her free hand in an attempt to regain control. "Everyone! Please! Let's settle down."

"Settle down?" Howie retorted. "I'm tired of tiptoeing around these preservationists!"

Joe stepped closer to Howie, his face flushed with indignation. "It's not about tiptoeing! It's about protecting what makes Seaside Cove special!"

"Special?" Howie rolled his eyes. "What's special about crumbling buildings? My shop needs renovations, and I can't do a thing because of that stupid Walt Copley!"

Mary took a step forward, balancing her tray precariously as she tried to diffuse the situation with food instead of words. "How about some fresh blueberry muffins? Everyone loves those!"

But instead of calming anyone down, Madeline snatched one from the tray and held it up like it was evidence in a trial. "Is this your idea of progress? Muffins while we lose our town?"

This argument was way bigger than baked goods; even bigger than Tommy Granger's murder—this was about hidden alliances and shifting loyalties among people who should know better. It was about a small town fracturing.

"Let's all take a breath," Adam said firmly, stepping into the mix with authority.

The normally cozy atmosphere of Crusty Buns suddenly felt like a pressure cooker. The tension pressed against Rick's temples, and the smell of cinnamon and sugar hung heavy in the air. Afternoon sunlight streamed through the windows, casting dramatic shadows across the faces of his agitated neighbors—his friends—people he'd passed a hundred times on the street now looking like strangers with their contorted expressions and accusatory postures.

"Enough!" Adam's voice cut through the chaos. "Everyone, sit down. Now."

The authority in Adam's tone had an immediate effect. Bodies shifted, chairs scraped against the floor, and the four who had been involved in the argument reluctantly took their seats. Rick did note that even Howie and Madeline were still shooting daggers at each other.

"Chief, they started it," Joe said, pointing at Howie. "Talking about how we need to tear down half the buildings in town to make way for change."

"I never said tear down half the town!" Howie shot back, but then took in a deep breath and lowered his voice. "I said reasonable renovations without having to jump through Walt Copley's impossible hoops."

Rick noticed that Mary's shoulders relaxed as the volume decreased and the tension in the room subsided. She mouthed, "Thank you," just as Angus walked out of the kitchen, flour dusting his forearms and looking perfectly clueless. He started to say something, but Mary shooed him back into the kitchen.

Madeline's voice, suddenly calm and rational, broke the tension. "What I said is that some people in this town seem perfectly happy to sell our heritage to the highest bidder."

Adam held up his hands. "I don't care who said what. Arguments like the one you were having are disturbing the peace. If it happens again, I'll have to—"

But the warning was interrupted by the ringing of his phone, the sharp electronic tone slicing through the tension. His expression shifted when he saw the name on the display. He answered, his voice curt but professional. "Cunningham."

Judging by Adam's reaction to the call, Rick guessed he had more bad news. Great. Just what they needed.

"When? Are you sure? Secure the scene. I'll be right there."

He hung up and turned to Rick. "Town Hall's been vandalized."

"What?" Mary gasped. "Who would do that?"

"The records room?" Rick asked.

Adam nodded. "Deputy Kama says there are records all over the floor."

"Everything was fine yesterday," Howie said, his anger resurfacing. "When I was there checking on my permit application."

Rick resisted the desire to reveal that they'd been fine an hour ago when he'd been there.

"I need to go," Adam said firmly. "And I need all of you to remember you're neighbors, not enemies."

"Adam, this isn't random," Rick said quietly.

"I know. Nothing in this town is random anymore. That's why I think you should come with me."

"Sure. Whatever you need."

"One more thing before we go." Adam went to Mary O'Donnell, quietly said something to her, then returned. He cocked his head, and Rick followed him across the street, all the while hurrying to keep up with his friend's hurried stride.

"What did you say to Mary before we left?"

"I asked her if she'd seen Everett Carmichael. She said she had. He left Town Hall shortly after you and Marquetta were there. She remembered because she was delivering an order and happened to look across the street. Everett was in such a hurry that he nearly got hit by a car."

Rick was still processing the information about Everett Carmichael when they walked through the Town Hall doors and into the records room. He stopped at the entrance, stunned by how quickly town hall had gone from calm to chaos.

The scent of dust and old paper mingled with a new, chemical tang—spray paint. His foot crunched on scattered papers, and he winced, feeling like he'd trampled someone's grave. The once orderly space had been transformed into chaos. Metal shelving units lay sprawled across the floor like fallen dominoes, one after another in a perfect line of destruction.

The mess in the room was overwhelming, like walking into the remains of a town wiped out by a hurricane. Rick ran his fingers through his hair and muttered, “Who would do this?”

“Be careful not to disturb anything,” Deputy Kama said as Rick picked his way through the wreckage.

She stood near the far wall, her stocky frame rigid with tension as she indicated the message sprayed across the pale green paint in dripping black letters: “THIS STOPS NOW!”

“Found it like this twenty minutes ago, Chief.” She stopped, took another look around, and grimaced. “I got a call from a tourist who was walking around and gawking at some of the photos on the walls outside. Said he saw the mess and phoned it in.”

Adam walked to the far end of the room and crouched next to one of the toppled shelves. He examined the base. “Whoever did this knew what they were doing. They used this one to bring down the entire row.”

Rick eyed the fallen shelves. “Someone who knows the room layout? Do you think this could be Everett?”

“I don’t think so. Everett is too dedicated to this town. Maybe this was someone who knew what they wanted to destroy,” Adam said.

Rick gestured toward the spray-painted message. “That’s not subtle, but it’s obscure. Whoever did this wanted to send a message.”

“Yeah, but to whom?” Deputy Kama asked, tucking a strand of dark hair behind her ear. “And what exactly are they trying to stop?”

Rick bent down, lifting a scattered folder. "The investigation? The construction? Walt's corruption? Take your pick."

"Could be Walt himself," Adam suggested. "He's backed into a corner."

"Or Sylvia," Rick countered. "She has the most to lose if those altered inspection reports surface."

Deputy Kama regarded both of them with a narrowed, piercing gaze, her eyes slightly squinted as if she were scrutinizing their conclusions. "Sylvia Archer wouldn't get her hands dirty like this. She'd hire someone."

"What about Francine?" Rick asked, watching Adam's reaction carefully. "Do you think she lied to us?"

Adam's jaw tightened. "The mayor's many things, but I can't see her trashing her own Town Hall. And, to be honest, I can't see her lying to us. She'd know the truth would come out sooner or later."

"People will do anything under the right amount of pressure," Rick said.

"What about Jake Morales?" Deputy Kama asked.

"Because his uncle was murdered? Maybe," Rick said. "But this feels more desperate than angry. More like someone with power who's afraid of losing it."

Adam surveyed the mess, his brow furrowed, his determination obvious. "We're going to need to catalog everything, see what's missing."

"If we can even tell," Rick said, gesturing at the sea of paper. "It'll take days, maybe weeks, to sort through this."

"Maybe that's the point." Deputy Kama crossed her arms. "One thing's for sure—whoever did this isn't playing by the rules anymore."

"Were they ever?" Rick asked as he read the message on the wall again. It wasn't just a threat. And this wasn't mere vandalism. This was a declaration of war.

39

Alex

I SLOUCH AGAINST THE KITCHEN counter, watching Mom knead pizza dough with those magical hands that can fix anything. The kitchen smells like yeast and oregano, and for a second, I almost forget I'm in trouble.

"So you're saying you went to see Shadow after school?" Mom's voice is soft, but I can tell she's not buying it. "Without telling anyone?"

"I know, I should've texted." I trace a pattern in the flour that dusts the countertop. "I just…I miss him. And Jake's not taking care of him right."

Mom wipes her hands on a towel and gives me that look—the one that says she understands but isn't letting me off the hook. "Sweetie, I get it. Shadow stole your heart the minute you saw him. But we've talked about this—you can't just disappear. When I texted you, you should have gotten back to me."

"I wasn't disappearing! I was literally like fifteen minutes away." Talk about a lame excuse. Everything in Seaside Cove is fifteen minutes away. And Mom's right. I never texted her back. So she called. And I got in trouble. Again.

"Fifteen minutes where no one knew where you were." Her fingers trace a line down my cheek. They're soft and warm and filled with love. "What if something had happened to you?"

The kitchen suddenly feels too warm, too small. The room that usually feels so comforting with its white cabinets and soft color scheme seems to be closing in on me.

"Nothing happened," I mumble.

"This time." Mom goes back to the dough, her movements more forceful now. "Alex, with everything going on—Tommy's death, the construction problems—we need to be extra careful."

I pick at a loose thread on my shirt. "I know. I'm sorry."

My phone buzzes in my pocket. I pull it out, grateful for the distraction.

"This conversation isn't over, Alex," Mom reminds me.

I read the message on my screen, and my stomach drops. "It's Sasha. She says she and Robbie want to meet at Marina Park ASAP."

"And?"

"And I think they're going to dump me." The words tumble out before I can stop them. "As a friend, I mean."

Mom gives me her sympathy smile, the one she uses when she's trying to make me feel better. "Why would you think that?"

"Because I've been a total jerk lately! I've barely paid attention to them. Even when we've been together, I've been all about Shadow." I slump against the counter. What I don't tell her is that I started Operation Nail Down with them and then just kinda dropped them.

Mom puts a finger under my chin and forces me to look at her. "Alex…"

I wanna turn away, but I can't stop myself from looking into her eyes. All I want is for her to comfort me. Am I asking too much?

"Real friends don't 'dump' each other over rough patches. If Sasha and Robbie want to meet, it's probably because they miss you."

"You don't know that."

"I do know it." She smiles. "Because that's what real friendship looks like."

My phone buzzes again. This time, it's Robbie telling me it's important.

"Can I go?" I ask, hope rising in my chest. "I promise I'll text you every five minutes."

Mom laughs. "Text me if you leave the park. And be home for dinner."

I throw my arms around her, flour and all. "Thanks, Mom! You're the best!"

As I dash toward the door, she calls after me, "And Alex? Maybe invite them over this weekend. We'll make a big batch of spaghetti, and you kids can hang out without the old folks watching over your shoulders."

"Will do!" I call back, already halfway out the door, my heart lighter than it's been in days. Wow. Old folks. I never thought of Mom and Dad as old before.

I pedal my bike so fast that I'm practically flying down the street to Marina Park. The wind whips my hair back, and I can feel my heart pounding in my chest. I pedal slower when I start to wonder if Mom could be wrong. What if they really are mad at me?

When I reach the park, I spot Robbie and Sasha sitting on a bench overlooking the harbor. Their heads are bent together, and they both look super serious. My stomach does this weird flip-flop thing. It feels like it did when I fell off that stupid loose stair.

"Hey guys," I call out, trying to sound normal as I prop my bike against a tree.

They both look up, and their faces are totally grim. Oh snap. Mom was wrong.

"Alex!" Sasha jumps up. "We've been waiting forever!"

"Yeah, like ten whole minutes," Robbie adds, rolling his eyes but smiling.

I plop down between them, the sea breeze cooling my sweaty face. "So…what's the emergency?"

They exchange this look that makes my insides shrivel.

"We suck," Sasha blurts out.

"Wait, what?" I blink at her.

"As friends," Robbie says. "We've been total losers."

"We should've been happy about you maybe getting Shadow instead of being jealous of him," Sasha says, twisting her dark hair around her finger like she always does when she's nervous.

"Yeah," Robbie nods. "We got all caught up in our own stuff and left you hanging."

Relief washes over me like the waves hitting the shore below us. "So did I." I hang my head and fight back a sniffle. When I look at Sasha, she's kinda blurry. I mumble, "I thought you guys were mad at me."

"Us? Mad at you?" Sasha laughs. She pulls me into a hug. "Like, no way!"

"We're a team," Robbie says, nudging my shoulder. "Mystery-solving dream team, remember?"

I can't help grinning. "So you guys still want to help with the whole Tommy Granger thing?"

"Duh!" they say in unison, and we all burst out laughing.

The harbor sparkles in front of us, and suddenly everything feels right again. Mom was totally right. As usual.

I grab Robbie's arm and squeeze it. "You guys really mean it? Friends forever?"

"Forever and ever," Sasha says, holding up her pinky finger. "Triple swear?"

We link pinkies in a three-way promise, just like we used to do in fifth grade. It feels silly and perfect all at once.

"Okay, so let's get serious about Operation Nail Down," I say, straightening up on the bench. The ocean breeze ruffles my hair, and I can taste salt on my lips. "We need to figure out what was going on with Tommy before he died."

Robbie pulls out his phone. "I made a list of everything we know so far."

"You did?" I'm genuinely surprised. Robbie's usually the one dragging his feet instead of taking initiative.

"Yeah, well, I felt bad about not helping." He scrolls through his notes. "So we know Walt and Sylvia are somehow involved, Tommy had evidence of something in a metal box, and your parents' construction site is being sabotaged."

Sasha gets a faraway look in her eyes and taps her lower lip a couple times before she says, "And Walt threatened Willy at the cemetery about 'ending up like Granger.'"

"Plus, Jake said Tommy made him memorize some random numbers," I add, watching a seagull dive into the water. "It's all connected somehow."

The waves crash against the rocks below us, matching the rhythm of thoughts flailing around in my head. I wish everything could just fall into place like puzzle pieces.

"Too bad nobody was recording the construction site," Robbie says with a laugh.

"That's the dumbest thing I've ever heard," Sasha says, rolling her eyes.

"I know. Right?" Robbie laughs at his own joke. "Like anyone would waste time recording a boring construction site."

I start to giggle along with them, but then stop suddenly. Wait a minute. "Actually," I say, my eyes widening, "that might not be such a stupid idea after all."

Sasha and Robbie look at me like I'm totally off my rocker. Maybe I am.

November 16

Hey Journal,

I'm gonna keep this short 'cause it's been a super stressful day. I was so happy to find out Robbie and Sasha aren't mad at me, but we spent so much time talking about what we were gonna do next that we didn't have time to actually do it! Bummer!

I'll go to the construction project tomorrow and look for the camera like we talked about after Robbie came up with the idea. I hope I find one! If not, there might be nothing to go on at all. I had another idea, too. I'm gonna do a face-to-face with Mayor Carter tomorrow morning. She respects me, so maybe she'll telll me the truth. Fingers crossed! Wish me luck for tomorrow, Journal!

xoxo,

Alex

40

Rick

THE MORNING SUNLIGHT STREAMED THROUGH the dining room windows, casting a golden glow everywhere. Rick moved between guests, refilling coffee cups and exchanging pleasantries, while mentally cataloging the day's tasks ahead. The Aldridges sat at their usual window table, the sun illuminating their silver hair admiring the rose garden as Rick approached to refill Bill's coffee mug.

"I can't believe we're leaving today," Edith said as she set down her teacup. "This place has been such a lovely respite, despite all the excitement."

Bill reached across the table and patted her hand. "We've certainly had more adventure than we bargained for. Though I must say, your muffins alone were worth the trip, Rick."

Rick bent over the table and whispered as he filled Bill's mug. "Don't tell anyone, but the muffins come from Crusty Buns." He stood taller and chuckled. "It's really not that much of a secret. However, the rest of the baking is all Marquetta's domain. We're going to miss having you both here. You've been wonderful guests."

"Even with a murder happening next door, we'll miss this place, too." Edith's blue eyes twinkled as she turned to look out the window.

"We've never had something happen so close to home. I'm just glad everyone didn't check out at the first sign of police tape."

"As you know, we considered it, but I guess a little excitement keeps the blood flowing," Bill said quietly. "Besides, we've spent enough time with you and your family to know we're perfectly safe."

Edith turned away from the window, where the sunlight played hide-and-seek with the roses, which were still in full bloom, and smiled at Rick. "We'll miss this view most of all. Our apartment back home faces another building. No roses, no ocean breeze."

"The B&B has that effect on people." Rick felt a pang at the thought of losing it all to Sylvia's machinations. "Marquetta says my grandfather bought this house because he believed the morning light here was good for the soul."

"Smart man, your grandfather," Bill nodded appreciatively. "Though I suspect he didn't have to deal with historical preservationists and corrupt developers."

"William!" Edith gasped, though her eyes crinkled with amusement.

"What? It's hardly a secret at this point. Rick knows we're on his side in all this nonsense."

Rick was about to respond when Adam appeared in the doorway, his expression grim. Their eyes met, and Rick knew immediately that something had happened.

"Excuse me," Rick said to the Aldridges. "Duty calls."

As he walked toward Adam, Edith called after him, "We'll be here when you get back, dear. Some things are more important than breakfast conversation."

Rick couldn't help but smile. The Aldridges understood more than they let on. That's what made them his favorite guests—they saw the heart of things, not just the surface.

"What's happened?" he asked Adam in a hushed voice. "Any progress at the Town Hall?"

"No. Everett Carmichael is still missing. Deputy Kama and I made a couple of passes by his house last night, but it looked like nobody was home. We also worked through the night with a forensic team from the County Sheriff. We probably won't find anything of substance. The reason I'm here is because I've been abandoned for the entrepreneurial spirit."

"What are you talking about?"

Adam quirked his cheek and said, "Traci has to do inventory this weekend. She's trying to get a jump on it before she has to open the store. I'm hoping we can use the time to brainstorm about the case."

Rick snuck a peek at the dining room, and noticed that the Aldridges were watching him and Adam with undisguised curiosity. His life had seemed so simple once—run the B&B, raise his daughter, build a home. Now everything he cared about was threatened. Life was anything but simple.

"After the night you've had, you deserve a good breakfast. Grab a seat, and I'll let Marquetta know you're here. Your usual?"

"You bet. Thanks, buddy."

Rick went to the kitchen, told Marquetta that Adam was, once again, staying for breakfast, then grabbed new carafes filled with regular coffee and decaf. When he returned to the dining room, he spotted Adam sitting at the Aldridges' table. Oh great. All he needed were a couple of septuagenarian sleuths to complicate things. He truly liked them, but he was glad they were leaving—before they grew more adventurous and started investigating on their own.

Over the course of the next thirty minutes, Rick refreshed coffee mugs, delivered the last of the orders, and bussed tables. As the last of the guests were finishing up, he wolfed down the quick breakfast Marquetta had prepared for him. After he bused his own dishes, he returned to the table where Adam sat alone and sat for a minute to enjoy the quiet.

The B&B had settled into its morning lull, the peaceful interlude between the breakfast service and check-out time. By the time the last of the guests had checked out, the house would practically exhale its own sigh of relief, almost as if it knew it needed a breather before the next round began. For Rick, the quiet should have been comforting, but today it only amplified his anxiety about what lay ahead.

After taking a couple of minutes to unwind, Rick said, "I've got something to show you in my office. Let's go."

Adam followed, his boots making solid thuds against the herringbone wood flooring. As they approached the door to Rick's office, Adam said, "I'm guessing this has something to do with the hypothetical box we were discussing."

Rick slipped the key to the door into the lock. "Something like that."

His office welcomed them with the rich scent of leather and old books. Closing the heavy door behind them instantly muffled any sounds of guests or the work he had Matteo doing outside. The coffered mahogany ceiling and floor-to-ceiling bookshelves gave the room a sense of solidity Rick desperately needed right now.

"Have a seat," Rick gestured toward one of the chairs facing his desk. "As you can see, the box is no longer hypothetical."

Adam settled into the chair, his uniform crisp against the worn leather. "Why do I feel like I'm about to regret coming here?"

"Because you probably will." He lifted Willy's box from his side of the desk. and placed it in front of Adam. He was prepared to confess to evidence tampering when the door burst open.

Alex rushed in, Marquetta close behind her. Alex's face was flushed, her eyes wide with panic.

"Daddy, don't say a word! This is on me. I can explain, Chief Cunningham!"

"Explain what, exactly?" Adam asked, his voice stern.

Rick pinched the bridge of his nose. "Perfect timing, kiddo."

Marquetta's hands settled gently on Alex's shoulders, her thumbs tracing small, soothing circles. "We thought it was better to face this together."

"Face what?" Adam's eyes ping ponged from one to the other and back again. He crossed his arms and huffed. "Are you planning on getting a family rate on a lawyer for breaking and entering? Theft of personal property? Evidence tampering?"

Alex stepped forward, chin raised despite her trembling lip. "I took it from Willy's shed. But I had a good reason!"

"You stole evidence," Adam said flatly.

Rick went and stood next to Alex. He placed his arm around her shoulders, admiring her sense of right and wrong. "Technically, I'm the one who kept it instead of turning it in."

"And I told Alex she could keep it while we figured out what to do," Marquetta said.

"So you're all accomplices." Adam's voice remained remarkably calm. "You realize I should arrest all of you right now?"

"You'll have to take us all in or let it go, buddy. We're in this together," Rick said.

Alex thrust out her arms, her wrists exposed. "That's right! Cuff me if you want."

Adam drummed his fingers on the armrest, his expression unreadable. "I would hate to think of what your guests would do to me if I arrested you all. Besides, after what someone did to the Town Hall, I don't even care how you got this box. What I want to know is what's inside."

"You're not mad?" Alex asked, surprise evident in her voice.

"Oh, I'm furious," Adam said, "but right now, solving Tommy Granger's murder and finding out who ransacked Town Hall takes precedence over your breaking-and-entering career. But we have a problem. I have no authority to open that box."

"We could claim exigent circumstances," Rick said.

Adam made a face. "Big stretch, and you know it."

"Then it should go back to Jake," Rick said. "He's Tommy's next of kin. And, he told me his uncle wanted him to have it—it was supposed to be his insurance policy. That's what Tommy told him."

Adam stood, picked up the box, and placed it under his arm. He wagged his index finger back and forth between Marquetta and Alex. "You two can stand down. You're not getting arrested today. You, on the other hand," he said, looking at Rick. "We need to go see Jake."

"We?" Rick asked.

"Yeah, we. You and me, buddy, we're going to solve this thing together."

"Can I go, too?" Alex asked. "I'd like to make sure Shadow is okay."

"Sorry, kiddo, but this is police business. I'll check on Shadow for you."

"But Daddy!"

Marquetta placed her hands on Alex's shoulders and gave them a gentle shake. "No, Sweetie. Your dad's right. Maybe he can make arrangements for you to visit Shadow later. What do you think, Rick?"

"Jake's not a suspect. Right, Adam?"

"Correct. I see no danger if you want to do that. Just don't steal anything else you think is important. Okay?"

"Okay."

All the way to see Jake, Rick kept remembering the sadness in Alex's eyes. He knew he was going to have to break down and let her have a dog. But Shadow? The dog was massive. Even in the new house, a dog Shadow's size could do some serious damage.

Adam pulled his 4x4 to a stop in front of Tommy's home behind an old, beat-up Datsun pickup. "I recognize that truck. It belongs to Willy Hobbs."

"What the heck is he doing here?" Rick asked.

"Why don't we go in and find out? Let me go first, though. Just as a precaution."

"Gladly. I've got no problem at all with that." Rick stayed a few feet behind Adam as they climbed the stairs. To his surprise, he caught a glimpse of Willy sitting next to Jake, his arm around him, almost as if they knew each other.

41

Rick

THE PORCH CREAKED UNDERFOOT AS Rick and Adam approached the front door. Adam hadn't even knocked when Willy called for them to enter. Inside the dim interior of Tommy Granger's home, dust motes danced in beams of sunlight slicing through the drawn curtains and illuminating the disarray. Empty soda cans and potato chip bags littered the coffee table, alongside scattered papers that hinted at neglect—nothing had been tidied since Rick's last visit.

Willy Hobbs sat on the couch, a peculiar twinkle in his eye, more lucid than usual, but there was still a wild eccentricity about him. He caught sight of the box and leaped up, pointing at it and yelling. "Hey! That's mine! You better not have opened it!"

"Relax, Willy," Adam said, raising a hand to calm him. "It's not actually yours, is it? Tommy Granger only gave it to you for safekeeping. Didn't he?"

Willy scowled at Adam and threw a finger in Rick's direction. "Ain't gonna respond to that, Chief. How come you ain't gonna press charges against his daughter for stealing it?"

Rather than letting Willy continue, Rick cut him off with a wave of his hand. "I think we both know you're not exactly innocent here either. How did you get that box from Tommy Granger?"

Willy's expression shifted. He worked his jaw back and forth for a few seconds like he was mulling over some deep, dark secret. "What if Tommy did give it to me? That ain't no crime."

"And why did he give it to you, Willy?" Adam asked. "Don't lie to me. I know what you've been doing with those graves."

"All I'm doing is trying to make the cemetery more efficient. You can't arrest me for doing my job."

Adam stepped closer to Willy so that he towered over him. His voice became more gruff and determined. "I'm not sure if you understand this, Willy, but your so-called efficiency work might be considered grave tampering."

Jake suddenly jumped up from his seat. His lanky frame seemed to unfold all at once. His hands trembled as he placed them over his ears. "Stop it! Everybody, just stop arguing!"

The air in the small living room crackled with tension as Jake continued.

"Would everybody stop arguing? My uncle is dead, and all anyone cares about is some stupid box! Shouldn't we be trying to find who killed him instead?"

Rick watched Jake's face flush with anger. The young man's jaw clenched tight as he looked at each of them in turn. There was more than frustration there—Rick recognized the look of someone drowning in grief with no idea how to process it.

"Jake, that's what we're trying to do," Rick said quietly, but Jake cut him off with a sharp wave.

"You don't get it! None of you do! My Uncle Tommy kept all kinds of secrets from everybody, including me. He didn't even tell me he had a brother." Jake's eyes darted to Willy.

Willy dropped his head and mumbled, "That's my fault, not his."

The room went silent. Rick's gaze snapped between Jake and Willy, trying to fathom what he'd just heard. The eccentric gravedigger was Tommy's brother?

Adam straightened, then looked directly at Willy. "Is this true? You and Tommy Granger were related?"

Willy's shoulders slumped as he sank back onto the couch. The wild energy normally animating his movements had vanished, replaced by a heaviness that aged him ten years in an instant.

"Wasn't supposed to come out like this, but, yeah…" Willy ran a hand through his thinning hair. "I was adopted. Me, Tommy, and Jake's mom, Sarah were all raised together until the family broke up. I ain't proud of how much pain I caused them."

"Why keep it a secret?" Rick asked. "And why didn't you tell us when we first started investigating Tommy's death?"

Willy's eyes took on a faraway look. "Our family wasn't exactly the Brady Bunch, Mr. Atwood. I was adopted when I was three. Tommy and Sarah were a few years older. My new parents—they thought bringing me in would fix their marriage." He let out a bitter laugh. "Instead, I just broke 'em more."

"What do you mean?" Rick asked, noting how Jake had retreated to the window, his back to them but clearly listening.

"I was a handful. Too much energy, too many ideas. Drove everyone crazy with my 'improvements.'" Willy's fingers sketched quotation marks in the air. "Our mom—couldn't handle it. Finally, got so bad that our parents separated and then divorced. "When I was eight, me and my dad moved to Arizona, where he could get work. He always blamed me for breaking up the family."

Rick watched the pain etching itself across Willy's weathered face. This wasn't the rambling, efficiency-obsessed character he knew from the cemetery. This was a man confronting decades of buried family trauma. "How did you both wind up in Seaside Cove?"

"This town's where our mom was from. I found a couple of letters in my dad's stuff when we were in Arizona. She told him how good my brother and sister were doing and wanted to know how I was. The letter just made me feel worse, so I ran away and never looked back. Spent five years running from place to place. Joined the service. Spent more time moving around, and then eventually, I moved here."

"Did Tommy know who you were?" Rick asked.

"Not for the longest time. I always avoided him 'cause I didn't want to bring him more pain. Then, about six months ago, he showed up at the cemetery. Said he was in trouble and needed someone he could trust to keep something safe. I figured I owed him, so I said okay."

Adam moved closer, his expression softening slightly. "The box?"

Willy nodded. "He made me promise not to tell anyone we were related. Said it would put me and Jake in danger, too."

Jake turned from the window, his face streaked with tears. "Nobody ever told me about you, Uncle Willy. All those years, and nobody said a word. My mom never talked about when she was growing up. I had no idea you even existed."

"I think, in a way, your mom and your uncle were too traumatized by those years when I was around to talk about it."

Rick studied the metal box in Adam's hands, seeing it now in a new light. It wasn't just evidence. Instead, it might be the key to a family's fractured history. "What's in it, Willy?"

"Don't know. Tommy brought it to me the night before he died. Made me swear not to open it. Said if anything happened to him, it should go to Jake." Willy looked up at his nephew. "I should've come to you sooner, but I was afraid whoever killed Tommy would be watching."

Jake wiped his face with the back of his hand. "Mr. Atwood, those numbers he made me memorize—did you ever figure out what they meant?"

"They were the number of a file folder at Town Hall. A file someone wanted to steal when they vandalized the Town Hall records room. You wouldn't know anything about that, would you, Willy?"

"Town Hall? No. I ain't never been in there."

"What about you, Jake?" Adam asked.

Jake blinked a couple of times and shrugged. "I didn't even know we had a records room."

Apparently satisfied, Adam held the box out toward Jake. "It's time we found out what your uncle wanted you to have."

Approaching hesitantly, Jake took the box in his hands like it might shatter. He sat and placed it on his lap, then picked up a key from the nearest end table. "I found this after I talked to Alex, Mr. Atwood. She got me to thinking about how Uncle Tommy might have left me more clues."

He inserted the key and twisted it in the lock, which clicked open with a pop that seemed to echo in the stillness. Jake lifted the lid slowly, revealing a stack of printed emails, neatly organized with paper clips. Without looking at the documents, Jake handed the stack to Adam. Rick looked over his shoulder as Adam unfolded a note on the top.

Adam held out the note and gave it to Jake. "This is for you."

"What's it say?" The young man asked without looking up.

"That he loved you and wished he could have done better by you. It also has instructions on how you can find information in the records room using the numbers he gave you, which he wants you to turn over to the police."

Jake massaged his temples with his fingers and continued watching the floor. He choked out a shaky, "Okay," but never looked up.

Rick cocked his head at the contents of the box, hoping Adam understood that Jake needed a few minutes to deal with his grief.

"Right. Okay, so these are emails between Walt and Sylvia." Adam pointed to the sender's information.

Rick's eyes widened as he skimmed the content. "Look at this one—Sylvia's assuring Walt that Francine is 'on board with all the plans.'"

"And this one." Adam handed Rick another of the documents.

As he scanned the email, Rick muttered, "This says Walt will gain control of the B&B once foreclosure is complete. So they really were in it together." Rick felt his stomach drop. "That explains why Walt's been so determined to stop our construction."

"This is a gold mine," Adam muttered, sorting through more emails. "Sylvia's been playing everyone against each other. Jake, you've done the right thing. And Willy, thank you for keeping these safe."

"Least I could do for my brother since I ruined his childhood."

Jake pulled what looked like an old, faded photograph from his shirt pocket. In the photo, three children stood ramrod straight. Their forced smiles made them look stiff and uncomfortable. "I found that in the same place as the key. Do you recognize it?"

Willy's jaw quivered. The lines on his face deepened as he held the photo in his shaking fingers. "Oh, my God. Your grandma took that on your mom's tenth birthday. I had just joined the family. That's Sarah, your mom—and that's your Uncle Tommy. That's me in the middle, about ready to have a temper tantrum."

Jake's eyes misted over, and he swallowed hard. "Wow."

Willy pulled Jake into a warm embrace. "Thanks, kid. This means a lot."

Rick's insides churned as he watched the tender reunion. It had taken a tragedy to bring these two together—a tragedy that never should have happened.

The living room of Tommy Granger's house felt smaller now, cluttered not just with discarded trash and papers but with the weight of revelations. The same dust particles he'd seen when they entered floated lazily through the sunbeams cutting across the room. Jake might have a new relative, but he still had the same grief.

"This is exactly what we needed," Adam said, shuffling through the emails. "These connect everything—the construction sabotage, Walt's obsession with your property, Sylvia's plans for development."

Rick nodded, his mind racing. What did that mean for his family? "And what about Francine's involvement? Do you think she's implicated, too?"

"It's not as clear, but our mayor definitely has some explaining to do."

Willy's right cheek inched up into a smirk he couldn't hide. "My dad always said you can't trust politicians. Even small-town ones."

"Or maybe especially small-town ones," Rick said. He noticed that Shadow had wandered in from the backyard and now sat beside Jake, his body pressing heavily against the young man's leg.

Jake absently stroked the dog's head, his eyes still red-rimmed. "So what happens now? To Uncle Tommy's house, I mean?"

Adam looked up from the documents. "Well, that will depend on your uncle's will. If he had one."

"He did." Willy reached into his jacket pocket. "Jake, that's the other reason I came here. This is your uncle's will. You inherit the house and everything."

"Me?" Jake's voice cracked. "I don't know nothing about owning a house."

Rick watched as Shadow nudged Jake's hand when he stopped petting him. The massive dog's eyes seemed to hold a world of understanding—perhaps not the world of legal mumbo-jumbo, but certainly the one of emotions.

"Speaking of homes," Rick said, seizing the opportunity, "Alex has really bonded with Shadow. She's been asking if she could visit him sometimes."

Jake looked down at the dog, then back at Rick with a surprising flash of relief. "Honestly, Mr. Atwood, I don't know how to take care of him properly. Uncle Tommy was the one who wanted a dog. I just…I don't think I can give him what he needs."

Willy snorted. "Mr. Atwood, that dog's been following your daughter around like she hung the moon. You should've seen them at the cemetery the other day."

"I'm aware of the incident, Willy." Rick didn't mention that he'd had someone videoing the entire thing.

"Don't worry," Willy waved dismissively. "Dog was protecting her the whole time. It's so sad, he lost his person. Dogs feel that kind of grief deep, you know. Probably deeper than most humans."

Shadow, as if understanding he was the topic of conversation, let out a soft whine and looked up at Rick, his soulful eyes warm and encouraging.

"He deserves better than what I can give him," Jake said quietly. "I'm barely keeping myself together. And now with all this…I need some time to figure it all out." He gestured vaguely around him.

Rick felt a sudden surge of empathy for the young man. For the dog. "What if we took him? Alex would love it."

Adam's head snapped toward Rick. Jake's eyes lit up. And Rick realized what he'd said. How had he let his mouth engage before his brain had fully processed the implications of what those words meant? The B&B had strict pet policies. Marquetta would kill him. And yet, looking at Shadow and thinking about how Alex would feel if he did this, Rick couldn't bring himself to withdraw the offer.

"You'd do that?" Jake stammered.

"Dog loves your girl," Willy nodded sagely. "Saw it myself. Ain't gonna lie to you, Mr. Atwood, that dog's been tracking your daughter all over town, protecting her. Tommy would've wanted it this way."

Adam rested his elbow on one hand, his palm covering his mouth but barely concealing the faint smile tugging at the corners of his mouth. The glint in his eyes further betrayed him. "Yeah, buddy, think how happy you'll make the munchkin."

There was no way out now. The only thing he could hope for was to postpone the inevitable. "I just can't take him yet. Keep him for a few more days. I need time to work out something at the B&B."

As if understanding every word, Shadow's tail began to thump against the floor, his eyes never leaving Rick's face.

"Maybe I should be there when you tell Markie the good news," Adam grinned.

"Good idea. You might prevent another murder."

42

Alex

MY DAD LEFT WITH CHIEF Cunningham about twenty minutes ago, and that's when Mom told me I was done working for the morning. She suggested I text Robbie and Sasha and see if we could meet up to play. I did that, and we're all meeting up at the construction site in about an hour. Since it's already the middle of the morning, I want to go to Scoops n'Scones and have that talk with Mayor Carter. That's something I have to do on my own. After I've talked to her, I should have plenty of time to get to the construction site.

The overhead bell in Scoops n'Scones jingles like it's announcing my arrival to the whole town. Mayor Carter's eyes dart up from behind the counter, and I can practically feel her suspicion crawling across my skin. She looks away to chat with a customer who's debating between Chocolate Chip and Rocky Road. Mayor Carter didn't even greet me, so I know she's tense.

I wander over to Homer the Turtle's tank. Ever since we first got to Seaside Cove and I was little, Herman's been doing the same slow crawl across the fake rocks. My stomach feels like it's doing backflips. Dad would totally freak if he knew I was here trying to get information from the mayor. But sometimes adults just talk around each other instead of saying what they mean.

"Hey there, Homer," I whisper, tapping the glass gently. "At least you don't have to worry about losing your home, huh?"

When the customer finally leaves with a waffle cone and a scoop of each, I take a deep breath and face the mayor. Her smile looks like it's been stapled to her face.

"Alex! How nice to see you. It's early for ice cream, isn't it? Where's your father?" Her eyes dart to the door like she's expecting my dad to burst in.

"Just me today."

"Oh, you are getting older. Your first trip on your own. Congratulations! What can I get you? A double scoop to celebrate your independence?"

Forget the double scoop, how about answers to questions? "I was hoping we could talk." I take another deep breath and step forward. Mom and Dad always tell me to be confident, and people will believe you know what you're doing, so I go with it. "I've always looked up to you because everyone says you're someone who tells the whole truth."

The mayor's hand flies up to pat her hair. It's one of her classic moves. It's the kind of thing my dad calls a tell. "Well, that's very kind of you to say."

"It's weird, though. Mr. Copley seems really interested in our property. Like, obsessed. Do you know why?"

Her eyes widen slightly. "Walt is just concerned about historical preservation. That's all."

That's total BS, and we both know it. "He was at the cemetery the other day. I heard him threaten Willy Hobbs. He said the same thing would happen to him that happened to Tommy Granger if he crossed him." I watch her face carefully. "That doesn't sound like someone who just cares about old buildings."

The mayor's hand freezes mid-hair pat. "Perhaps you misunderstood what you heard."

"I don't think so. And now we might lose our new home because of whatever's going on." I let my voice crack a little. "My mom really wants that house. It was going to be our first real home together."

Mayor Carter looks around the empty shop nervously, her fingers drumming on the glass countertop. "Alexandra, sometimes adults make complicated decisions for reasons that aren't always straightforward. Or easy for a child to understand."

Oh, so now I'm a child? I look her in the eye when I say, "You mean like lying?"

She winces like I've poked her with something sharp. "No, not lying exactly. Just, um, protecting interests."

"Whose interests? Not ours." Over in his tank, Homer has stopped his crawl and seems to be watching us. "You know, Homer reminds me of this town sometimes. Everyone moves super slow, and then they hide in their shells when things get scary."

Mayor Carter gets this weird look on her face like I've said something super profound. I thought it was a pretty good analogy—at least, that's what I think my English teacher calls that kind of thing. It must have been good 'cause it looks like the mayor's getting super nervous.

"It wasn't supposed to get this complicated."

"If you really want this case solved, why won't you let Chief Cunningham work with my dad? Don't you want to solve Tommy Granger's murder?"

Mayor Carter's face goes from nervous to full-on flustered in like two seconds flat. Her cheeks flush pink, and she starts patting her hair again, but faster this time, like she's trying to put out a fire on her head.

"I told you, Alex. It's complicated. Sometimes adults have to make difficult decisions." She looks nervously at the door again. "There are things happening that you don't understand."

Right. The child thing again. I cross my arms and try to stand a little taller. "I'm pretty good at understanding stuff."

The mayor sighs, looking suddenly tired. "This town has relationships. Balances. When one thing shifts, everything can fall apart."

"So Tommy Granger dying was just what? A shift in the balance?" My voice comes out kinda sharp, but I don't think it sounds nasty.

"That's not what I said!" She looks genuinely horrified, which makes me feel a tiny bit bad. But only a tiny bit.

"Then what did you mean?" I press.

Mayor Carter looks like she's putting on armor. She straightens her shoulders and gives me this look that's supposed to intimidate me. Not happening. I'm totally in the zone.

"I'm the mayor. It's my job to make sure things are done properly." Her voice gets all crisp and formal. "The police department has protocols, and your father is a civilian. It wouldn't be appropriate for him to be involved in an official investigation."

"Me and my dad have helped solve plenty of murders, and you were okay with that. You were okay with it when my dad taught Chief Cunningham how to be a better investigator. C'mon. That's not the real reason, is it?" I take a step closer to the counter.

Her eyes dart around the empty shop again. "Alexandra, I think you should go home now. Your parents must be wondering where you are."

"My mom knows exactly where I am." Okay, that's not totally true. Mom thinks I'm meeting up with my friends, not interrogating the mayor. But technically, I'm on my way to meeting them, so it's not a complete lie.

"Please, Alex." Mayor Carter's voice drops to almost a whisper. "Let this go. Chief Cunningham is handling everything."

"Is he? Because it seems like you're not letting him do his job either." I can feel my heart pounding, but I keep going. "Walt Copley threatened someone, and you're gonna ignore it? Why?"

The bell over the door jingles, and we both jump like we've been caught doing something wrong. An elderly couple walks in, arguing about whether butter pecan is better than vanilla.

Mayor Carterface instantly pastes on that smile again. "Welcome to Scoops n'Scones! What can I get for you today?"

While she's distracted, I slip a napkin from the counter and scribble on it: "I know you're hiding something. My dad and Chief Cunningham will figure it out." I slide it across the counter where only she can see it.

Her eyes flick down to the napkin, then back to me, widening slightly.

"I'll be back for that ice cream another time," I say loudly, then head for the door.

As I push it open, the mayor calls after me, "Alex, wait!"

But I'm already outside, the door swinging shut behind me. My hands are shaking as I untie my bike from the rack. That was either the bravest or the dumbest thing I've ever done. Maybe both.

One thing's for sure, though—Mayor Carter is totally hiding something big. And whatever it is, it has to do with Tommy Granger, Walt Copley, and our new house.

I hop on my bike and start pedaling home, my mind racing even faster than my wheels. When my dad gets back from what he's doing with Chief Cunningham, I need to tell him what happened. When I get to the roundabout at Marina Park, I follow the circle all the way around a couple times. If I tell my dad, he's just gonna ground me, and then I won't get to see Shadow. Maybe ever.

That does it. If I'm gonna get grounded, I'm gonna finish Operation Nail Down first. And for that, I need to go to the construction site. Me and my friends are gonna find out if Robbie was right. There could be a camera hidden somewhere on the property. If there is, I'll bet Jake has access to it. He just doesn't know that yet.

43

Rick

A SMALL PLASTIC 'WE'LL BE back' sign hung in the window of Scoops n'Scones. Rick stood beside Adam, trying to see through the glass if the interior was truly empty. A peculiar stillness hung over the ice cream shop.

"That's odd," Rick said, rubbing his chin. "I've never seen Francine close down during the day. Even during winter storms."

Adam nodded, his hand resting on the doorknob. "Francine doesn't close for anything short of a natural disaster. Or a town emergency."

"Think she's avoiding us?"

"After the way she's been behaving today? Absolutely." Adam tried the door handle, which turned easily. "That's strange. Let's check inside."

The brass bell above the door jingled as they entered, its cheerful tone jarring against the eerie quiet. Homer was in his tank, looking peaceful as usual. "Too bad turtles can't talk."

Adam snorted and cast a sideways look at Rick as he went behind the counter and checked the back room. "That would be helpful. Looks like nobody's here. She must have left in a hurry to forget the front door, but at least the cash register's locked up tight."

"I'd say she was pretty upset, too. I can't imagine Francine leaving the door open and the lights on."

"You're right. That's not like her at all. We need to find her. If nothing else, I have to make sure she's safe. I'll have Deputy Kama walk around the block and talk to the shopkeepers while we go to her house."

When Adam parked in front of the mayor's home, the sunlight glinted off a dark compact sedan parked at the curb ahead of them. The car sat innocently beneath a maple tree, its windshield collecting scattered leaves in the afternoon breeze.

"That's Everett Carmichael's car," Adam said as he turned off the engine. "I wonder why he decided to surface."

"Interesting. He disappeared and now he's paying the mayor a visit," Rick said, eyeing the vehicle as he climbed out of Adam's cruiser. The grand staircase leading to the second-floor entrance loomed before them, its ornate wrought iron railing gleaming in the sunlight.

Adam frowned as he eyed the car. "I don't like coincidences."

"That makes two of us."

The climb felt longer than it should have, each step hopefully bringing them closer to answers rather than more questions. The polished brass knocker on the door dared them to announce their arrival. Finally, it was Adam who rapped the knocker three times. The sound echoed through the quiet neighborhood.

Footsteps approached from inside, followed by a long pause. The door cracked open, revealing Francine's face, pale and drawn.

"I knew you'd come," she said flatly. "You might as well join us."

She stepped back, allowing them to enter. Rick immediately noticed her living room was immaculate, as if she'd been stress-cleaning. The floor-to-ceiling mirror reflected their awkward entrance, multiplying the discomfort in the room.

"We need to talk, Francine," Adam said, removing his cap.

"Everett's in the kitchen. We can talk there." She turned and led them through a pristine hallway that was lined with photographs of her time as mayor of Seaside Cove.

Rick's breath caught when they entered the kitchen. Everett Carmichael sat at Francine's kitchen table, Duke sprawled at his feet. The table was covered with papers—the missing files from Town Hall spread out like a massive jigsaw puzzle.

"Seems we're having a party," Rick said, doing what he could to keep his voice level instead of letting his irritation creep in.

Everett's blue eyes looked tired behind his steel-rimmed glasses. Circles under his eyes reinforced the impression. "We were hoping to have more time before you found me."

"Time for what, Everett?" Adam planted his feet apart and hooked his thumbs in his belt buckle.

"To put it all together," Everett gestured at the papers. "The whole sordid mess. I've been sorting through these since yesterday."

"Where were you?"

"I went to stay with my daughter in San Ladron. I spoke to Francine and she agreed it would be best if I disappeared for a short time."

"So it was you who took the files?" Rick stepped closer, scanning the documents, then turned his anger on Francine. "And you knew about it? So you lied to us?"

"Don't blame Francine," Everett said without a hint of remorse. "After you left, I knew you had hidden something. I inspected the shelves, found one that was fuller than normal, and realized you had hidden something there. When I saw what it was, I knew I had to protect it."

Francine pulled out a chair and collapsed into it. "Tell them everything, Everett. I think we're going to need their help."

"It's quite the tale," Everett said, stroking his chin. "Our mayor here has been trying to keep this town out of Sylvia's web for years. Ever since Francine was elected."

"I never wanted any of this," Francine sighed. "The money seemed like a blessing at first. I needed it to win. What I didn't understand was that my becoming mayor was all part of Sylvia's plan."

Adam relaxed his stance, but kept his voice stern. "Right now, this is sounding like you were both involved in this conspiracy, and you let Sylvia and Walt break every rule in the book."

"You don't have all the facts, Chief," Francine's voice cracked. "Yes, in the beginning, there were some expedited permits and minor zoning exceptions. Those were all perfectly legal, but then, Sylvia became more demanding. That's when I told her the town would have nothing to do with her plans for wholesale development. Unfortunately, she has a cadre of lawyers who would have made me out to be the bad guy."

"So you went along with her?" Rick fought the urge to make his question sound like an accusation, despite feeling betrayed.

"Rick, our town's bylaws are written such that the Planning Commission operates independently. And the Historical Society is also independent."

"She's right," Everett said. "Quite honestly, she was powerless to stop what was happening. That's why we teamed up."

Adam did a double-take, first looking at Francine, then Everett, and then Francine again. "Is this true?"

"Yes, Chief. I'm sorry I couldn't tell you, but Everett and I decided we couldn't take any chances on what we were doing getting back to Sylvia."

Rick felt a pressure building in his head, the kind he'd felt so often as a reporter when new facts surfaced in a story. "What about Tommy Granger?" Rick asked, his voice trending toward irritation no matter how much he tried to hold back. None of this changed the truth—a man was dead. "What happened there?"

"Neither of us realized he was trying to blackmail Sylvia and Walt. When I heard about his death, I was horrified. I knew Sylvia would go to any lengths at that point, and I had to get you to back off. Otherwise, Everett and I were afraid we'd be exposed and everything would be for naught."

Everett picked up one of the documents and held it out for Adam to read. "I came across this while I was in San Ladron. Tommy had been collecting evidence against Sylvia and Walt. He also thought he would be able to blackmail Francine. As you can see, what Tommy thought was collusion on Francine's part was actually something she had no control over."

Adam's jaw worked from side to side as he read. When he was done, he handed the document to Rick and zeroed in on the mayor.

"That's why you wanted the investigation shut down. You were afraid we'd leak this to Sylvia or Walt?"

"Chief, it was more like, we didn't think you would want to sit back and wait. The two of you have had great success by dragging suspects in and grilling them."

"That's what you were worried about?" Rick's voice rose. "You were afraid Adam and I would want to charge in and break up Sylvia's scheme? Because you two delayed, a man is dead, Francine!"

Adam held up a hand and motioned for Rick to slow down. "Hang on, Rick. We're all on the same side here. While I don't like the idea of being kept out of the loop on this, I understand their reasoning. Mind you, Madame Mayor, I don't agree with it, but I can see why you did what you did. What we have to do now is find a way to legally determine who killed Tommy Granger."

Everett frowned and muttered to himself as he shuffled through the papers. He extracted two and held one out for Adam to take. "This is what she used to snare Walt in her web, Chief." He handed the second to Rick. "And that's a copy of the Notice of Foreclosure you received. It proves they were trying to take away not only your construction project, but also the B&B."

Rick's jaw tightened as he scanned the copy of the document Adam had served him originally. "I've already got the original. Adam served me with a subpoena the same morning Granger was murdered."

"Walt's obsession with your property goes back decades," Everett said. "These documents are the paper trail you need to prove Sylvia used his obsession to manipulate him. She promised him the B&B if he helped delay your construction long enough to drain your finances. She knew eventually the bank would be forced to foreclose."

"And you knew about this?" Adam asked Francine.

"Not all of it," she insisted. "I knew they wanted to stop the construction, but it wasn't until after you'd been served the Notice of Foreclosure that I realized Everett and I had run out of time."

"What was Sylvia going to do? Level the house we'd been building and develop the entire area once she got her hands on it?"

"Basically, yes. The ultimate irony," Everett said with a wry smile. "Walt thought he was saving the B&B from modernization, but he was actually helping Sylvia set up the biggest development project Seaside Cove has ever seen."

Duke snored softly from under the table, apparently oblivious to the tension in the room.

"Why did you take the files, Everett?" Adam asked, his tone softer now.

"Because I failed this town once. I let Walt operate unchecked for years. I suspected he was taking bribes, but I never had proof. When I saw Rick digging into those records, I knew this might be our only chance to expose the truth."

"And the break-in at Town Hall?" Rick asked.

"Not me. I may have borrowed these files, but I'd never vandalize public property. Someone must have broken in while I was out hiding these in my car. When I got back and saw what had happened, I was glad I'd done it. I suspect it was Walt, but he wouldn't have known where to find these after you moved them."

Everett tapped his lower lip with his finger and mused out loud. "Sylvia must have told Walt to find the records, and when he couldn't, he got desperate and decided to make sure nobody could."

He rested one elbow on the table and regarded Rick. "As I said, the only reason I found them was because I saw a bulge where there hadn't been one before."

"I guess I was in a hurry and got sloppy."

"It's good you did," Everett chuckled. "If you had been fastidious, all of this information could have been lost."

"I agree with Everett. Walt's probably the one who damaged the records room," Francine said. "He has a temper, and if he couldn't find them, he probably became unhinged."

Adam pulled out his phone. "I need to bring in him and Sylvia Archer for questioning."

"Wait," Rick said suddenly. "If we move too quickly, we might lose our chance to get solid evidence against Sylvia that she murdered Tommy. She's too smart to leave a clear trail. And what if it wasn't her? What if it was Walt?"

"What are you suggesting?" Adam asked, his finger hovering over his phone.

Rick skimmed the content of the papers, then scrutinized Francine's face. "I think we need to convince Sylvia she has a new partner."

Everett's eyes lit up. "Ah, a sting operation. I love it. You know, it's been many years, but I did do some community theater in my younger days. And I was quite good."

"We need Sylvia to incriminate herself. Do you think you can make that happen?"

"I think between Francine and me, we can deliver your evidence on a silver platter. Are you in, Francine?"

"One hundred percent."

"It's risky," Adam warned.

"So is letting her get away with murder," Rick countered.

Francine straightened in her chair, a flicker of her old determination returning. "Let's do it. It's time we took her down."

Everett's face broke into a tired smile. "Duke is quite willing to help, also. Whatever you need."

Rick looked at Adam, waiting for his decision. His expression was stern, but Rick could see the wheels turning.

"Fine," Adam said finally. "But we do this by the book. No amateur detective work."

"Wouldn't dream of it," Rick replied with a grin. "After all, we're just concerned citizens helping our local police."

Adam rolled his eyes. "Right. And I'm just a meter reader who accidentally became Chief of Police."

For the first time since he'd met Francine in Jordan Lane's office, laughter bubbled up from the mayor's throat. It wasn't the practiced political chuckle she often deployed at town functions or the forced pleasantry she maintained during difficult council meetings. This was authentic, genuine laughter. The corners of her eyes crinkled, her shoulders relaxed, and for a fleeting instant, Rick caught a glimpse of the woman she might have been without the weight of secrets and compromises bearing down on her.

In a way, the change gave Rick hope that maybe they really could pull this off.

44

Rick

RICK AND ADAM WASTED NO time in transforming Francine's upstairs guest room from a shrine to bygone gentility into something that looked suspiciously like a low-budget police stakeout. The floral wallpaper—pink roses marching in perfect rows—seemed to bristle at the intrusion of Adam's glowing laptop screen. A room once destined for lace doilies, polite whispers, and the occasional cup of chamomile now hummed with quiet purpose.

The massive mahogany dresser dominated the far wall, its carved vines and fluted columns casting long shadows in the lamplight. It looked like the sort of furniture built by a man who believed every drawer should make a statement. And tonight, its grandiose craftsmanship offered an almost comic contrast to the meager collection of gadgets the two men had assembled: a speaker, two laptops, a stack of notes, and a mystery stubborn enough to demand more equipment than the town could afford.

"Testing, testing," Francine's voice crackled through the speaker as she adjusted a tiny microphone hidden beneath the fruit bowl on the kitchen table. "Can you hear me clearly?"

"Crystal clear," Adam said while watching Everett position himself at the kitchen table. The former mayor looked surprisingly at ease in his role as would-be blackmailer. He'd already arranged the papers from the files with theatrical precision. Beneath the table, Duke was stretched out, once again oblivious to what was about to happen around him.

The doorbell chimed, and Rick's pulse quickened as he watched Francine smooth her hair with her right hand before leaving the room to answer the door.

Adam shifted in his seat and watched the monitor anxiously. "Let's hope they get this right. We need Sylvia to explicitly confess to Tommy Granger's murder."

"It's a tall order, but Sylvia's just arrogant enough that she might do it." Rick mimicked Adam's posture, but sat up straight when the microphone captured Francine's voice as she entered the kitchen.

"For the life of me, Sylvia, I'm telling you I don't know what to do."

"Shut up, Francine!" Sylvia appeared on the monitor, her BMW key fob dangling from her manicured fingers as she swept into the kitchen with the confidence of someone who believed they controlled the room. She pushed Francine aside and made a beeline for the kitchen table and Everett.

"Never seen that before," Rick said quietly as he watched the monitor.

"What? Francine letting herself be pushed around?" Adam asked.

"Yeah, exactly."

Sylvia stood at the table, giving Everett and the mass of papers on the table the evil eye. "Ridiculous, conducting business in a kitchen." Her voice came through crisp and cold, but then turned syrupy sweet. "Everett. What an unexpected surprise."

"Sylvia! Looking lovely as always." Everett's folksy charm filled the room. He gestured at the chair next to his. "Please, have a seat."

"No, thank you. I'm sure this won't take long."

"Very well, Francine and I were discussing some fascinating paperwork I borrowed from Town Hall."

Sylvia's smile remained, but her eyes were now fixed on the papers. "Borrowed? That sounds suspiciously like theft, Everett."

Everett chuckled. He adjusted his glasses, which almost immediately slipped back down his nose when he bent over to stroke Duke's head. "Oh, I prefer to think of it as reallocation. After decades in politics, I've learned that information is the most valuable currency in town. Sit here. You can get a nice, close look from there."

Adam nudged Rick. "Good old Everett. He's pretty smooth," Adam said, his voice holding a certain amount of awe.

"No kidding. He should have been on Broadway." Rick pointed at the laptop screen. "Notice how Sylvia's fidgeting with her key fob. She's definitely nervous."

Sylvia still hadn't taken a seat. Most likely, she was trying desperately to keep control. Her voice hardened. "What are you implying, Everett?"

"I'm not implying anything, my dear." Everett lifted a document. "These papers spell everything out quite clearly. Quite the trail you and Walt have left."

Francine picked up her coffee cup and rotated it with her fingers. Her voice came across as nervous, perhaps even desperate. "He knows everything, Sylvia. About the bribes, the falsified inspections—everything."

Sylvia cut her off with a sharp gesture. "Oh, stop blathering, Francine. There were never any bribes! Besides, I'm sure Everett isn't here to make accusations."

"Actually," Everett seemed to unfold himself in his chair, "I'm here to negotiate."

Rick watched Sylvia's face shift from controlled anger to cautious interest. "Negotiate?"

"My dear, I spent twenty years watching others profit while I played by the rules. When you helped Francine get elected, I was devastated. I never thought I could lose. But you taught me what matters—money." Everett's voice dropped to a conspiratorial tone. "Now, it's time I got my piece of the pie."

"You want money?" Sylvia laughed, finally taking a seat. "That's what this is about? You're trying to blackmail me?"

"Blackmail is such an ugly word, my dear. Don't you agree, Duke?" When the dog yawned, Everett looked back at Sylvia. "See, he agrees. Duke and I prefer to think of it as exercising our entrepreneurial spirit."

"You and that ridiculous dog should be committed. I'll see myself out."

"But Sylvia!" Francine stammered.

"Oh, let her go," Everett said. "After I show these to Chief Cunningham, she'll pay ten times as much to make them disappear."

Sylvia's jaw hardened. Even her nostrils flared slightly, then she seemed to settle into negotiation mode. "Okay, Everett, how much do you want?"

"Fifty thousand should be a nice start. We'll call it a down payment."

"That's extortion!"

Everett continued on as if Sylvia hadn't said a word. "I'll also want a consulting position in your development projects. I'm so tired of that tedious town clerk position." He pushed a document toward her. "These papers show quite clearly what happened to poor Tommy."

Rick held his breath. This was what they'd been waiting for. Would Sylvia crumble? Or push back?

"You old fool."

"Now, now, my dear. I'm not that old." He sat up straight, looked Sylvia directly in the eye, and his voice turned cold. "And I am nobody's fool." Apparently satisfied, Everett slouched back in his chair and smiled politely. "I'm sure you understand. This is just business."

Sylvia, who had her hands resting in her lap, clenched her fists. She looked irritated enough to, quite literally, claw Everett's eyes out. "I don't know what you think you know about Tommy Granger, but you're wrong."

Everett brushed aside her protest with a nonchalant wave of his hand. "Now, now. As I said, I'm not judging. I assume you handled the situation with your usual efficiency." His fingers drummed once against the papers.

Sylvia's knuckles whitened as she scowled at Everett. Rick's stomach knotted because he knew Everett was pushing. He had to, but was it too hard? Sylvia was cornered, but being trapped could make her dangerous—like a predator calculating its final, desperate move. He studied Adam's face and saw a tension equal to his own.

"What do you think?" Rick whispered.

Adam rubbed his chin, but never took his eyes from the monitor. "I think you're right. Everett is missing his calling. He should have been an actor."

"Duke needs water," Francine blurted suddenly, her voice pitched higher than normal. She went to one of the cabinets, pulled down a bowl, filled it with water, and called for Duke to come.

"What are you doing, Francine?" Adam hissed. "We had her."

"I don't know, Adam. Look at Sylvia's face. She's angry at Francine for interrupting her—not at Everett for practically calling her a killer. I think she's making a good call."

Duke raised his head, took one sniff, and seemed to understand he wasn't getting fed. He lowered his head and sighed as if bored with this entire charade.

"What I want to know is how you're planning to handle Walt now that he's becoming a liability." Everett gave Sylvia a cunning smile. "If I'm going to be a partner in your little business, I think I should be kept apprised of your intentions. In return, I will make sure you encounter no resistance or outside interference."

"Walt is none of your concern," Sylvia snapped. Her tone could have frosted the room, and the intensity that shone in her eyes could only be classified as subzero.

"No, my dear. I don't think you understand. Everything in this town is now my business." Everett laid one arm on the table and patted the documents with his palm. "I've made copies, of course. Insurance, I'm sure you understand."

Sylvia stiffened, her every muscle seeming to coil with tension as her hands balled into tight fists at her sides. "Fine. How much exactly do you want, Everett?"

"Twenty percent of your next development, plus a monthly consulting fee—in addition to the fifty thousand."

"Or what? You'll go to the police?" Sylvia scoffed. "With what? Some paperwork that shows I'm a shrewd businesswoman?"

"These papers show far more." Everett's voice hardened again. "They show motive."

"For what?"

"Murder."

The word hung in the air for several seconds. During that time, Rick's heart hammered in his chest as he waited for Sylvia's reaction.

"Murder?" Sylvia scoffed. "Everett, you're delusional. I didn't kill Tommy Granger. He was a valuable asset. I'm a businesswoman, not a killer."

Francine took a few steps toward Sylvia. "Oh no, Sylvia. Tommy Granger wasn't blackmailing you, was he?"

Sylvia snorted uncharacteristically before she said, "He tried. He threatened to expose everything—the faulty inspections, the bribes, all of it. When I told Walt we needed to take care of Tommy, he must have panicked. I had nothing to do with Tommy Granger's murder. I intended to turn the tables on him as he did on Sam Greer. Granger was nothing more than a second-rate contractor who had more ambition than talent."

"What do you think, Rick? Is she telling the truth?" Adam turned so he faced Rick.

"Maybe. Tommy was documenting her shady deals with Walt, so he probably did try to blackmail her. But Sylvia's smart. She wouldn't have to kill him herself. All she had to do was make some suggestions to Walt and let him handle it. Or, as she said, just discredit him."

"So then Walt overreacted and arranged for our victim to have an accident at the construction site," Adam added.

On the monitor, Everett stroked Duke's head as he addressed Sylvia. "And you're going to let him take the fall. How convenient."

"Hardly. Walt has cost me a lot of time and money." Sylvia's voice dripped with disdain. "But you are correct about one thing, He has become a liability."

"Perfect," Everett said. "You do need a new partner, see. Do we have a deal? You meet my terms for my silence? I'll assist you with expediting your business needs."

Sylvia's laugh was brittle. "You're more devious than I gave you credit for, Everett. Fine. We have a deal. But if one word of this leaves this room, you'll never see a penny."

"That's good enough for me," Adam said. "If she really didn't kill Granger, then we at least have her on fraud and conspiracy. Let's go."

It took less than a minute for Rick and Adam to go down the stairs to the kitchen entrance. Everett was still in character and was now making suggestions on how Sylvia could make even more money. Rick stood behind Adam in the doorway, admiring how cool Everett was under pressure.

"Oh, dear." Everett put his hand on his chest and pulled in an exaggerated breath. "I do believe there's a problem. The information has already leaked."

45

Alex

As I approach the B&B on my bike, I see what looks like a rusted pickup truck parked in front of the construction site. There's a logo on the door. It's kind of faded and parts of it are scratched out, but it looks like it says "Greer Construction."

Me and Sam Greer didn't get along the last time we met. Maybe it will go better this time since grumpy old Walt Copley isn't here. My dad never mentioned hiring Greer Construction. Like, not even once. And, from what I've heard, Sam Greer isn't exactly on anyone's favorite people list in Seaside Cove.

What's weird is how different the construction site looks today—not the jumbled mess it was before. Lumber is stacked in perfect piles according to size, the floor has been cleared of loose boards and scrap and other stuff that made it hard to walk around, and there's a weird sense of order that wasn't there before. It's like someone with some serious organizational skills decided to make sense of the chaos Tommy left behind. Everything has its place now. It's all so precise. Almost like the site itself is taking a deep breath after weeks of confusion.

I park my bike behind the truck and cross the street to the house. When I get to the dirt lot, my sneakers kick up little puffs of dust with each step. I remember how gruff Sam was when I saw him with Walt. It was like somebody sewed his eyebrows into a permanent frown. My stomach is acting funny again. I've got a fluttery feeling and want to turn back. But curiosity is totally winning out. It's the thing my dad says is the sign of a good reporter.

Sam Greer is coming down the stairs, the same ones I fell on. He's muttering to himself and making notes on a clipboard. He looks up when he hears my footsteps, his weathered face shifting from surprise to recognition.

"You're the Atwood kid," he says, his voice less harsh than I remember.

I correct him, standing my ground despite my nerves. "Alex," I say. After the way things went the last time we met, I asked Mom about him, and she told me how he used to be respected in town before one of his jobs wound up burning to the ground. She said he now works out of San Ladron most of the time because no one in Seaside Cove will hire him.

His face is lined with years of outdoor work. He's got calloused hands that look like they've never seen hand lotion, and he's wrapping twine that's connected to some kind of teardrop-shaped thing into a tight loop. I've never seen a tool like that before. It's maybe four or five inches long. Shiny brass, I think. The bottom is pointed, kinda sharp-looking. It's definitely got some age; little nicks and scratches all over the brass, along with a few dark smudges. It looks like it belongs in a museum, not on a tool belt.

"What's that?" I ask, pointing at it.

Sam's expression softens as he rubs the brass with surprising gentleness. "This? It's a vintage plumb bob. It belonged to my father. Been carrying it with me for twenty years. And he had it for at least as many before me. They don't make 'em like this anymore. I can get a perfectly straight corner as good as any kid with one of those fancy laser levels. Those plastic gizmos won't last beyond one drop."

The way he handles it as he slips it into a case attached to his belt reminds me of how my dad treats Captain Jack's old typewriter—with reverence for something that connects generations. It makes Sam seem more human, less like the mean old grump I thought he was.

"Is this where you took your tumble?" He gestures at the step where I fell.

"Yeah," I say.

"You doing okay?"

I reach for my arm and rub it. "My elbow still hurts a little, but I'm okay. Thanks for asking."

He actually seems like a nice guy. Maybe we just got off wrong 'cause of grumpy old Walt Copley. He's enough to make anybody nasty.

"Good. I nailed it down properly. Been through most everything, and the stairs are all straight and safe now. Follow me." He turns and walks away from me after making sure I'm following him. "Over here, this is where your mom's kitchen is going to be. Let me paint you a picture," he says, spreading his arms wide. "Top-of-the-line stainless steel everywhere, double ovens, and a gorgeous island right here with a marble countertop."

"Wow. That's gonna be awesome. So, is this gonna be the sink?"

"You bet it is. How'd you know?"

"The pipes come up out of the foundation right there."

"You're a smart kid. Come on, I'll show you some more."

"Wait. Did my dad hire you?"

"Not yet, but we've talked, and I'm sure he will. I just wanted to get a head start on a few things. Call it a sign of goodwill."

As he shows me around the house, he brings the whole thing to life. It makes me even more anxious to see it finished. I also find out he wants to hire Jake Morales—he says Jake has potential—but he admits hiring Tommy long ago was a mistake he regrets deeply. "That no-good Tommy Granger cost me everything. He sabotaged Powell Finnegan's wiring job, then blamed it on me when the house burned down. Even worse, the developer Powell had hired turned on me."

"Are you talking about Sylvia Archer?"

"Yeah. Between the two of them, it cost me everything. My reputation. My business in Seaside Cove." He meets my eyes directly. "I was rude when I was here with Walt. Shouldn't have been. Your family deserves better than getting caught up in old grudges."

Huh, maybe this guy's not as bad as I thought. I use manners, like I would with a guest. "Thanks, I appreciate that."

"You want me to continue the tour? I can show you where everything's going to be."

Actually, a real tour would be kinda awesome. Then I can show Robbie and Sasha when they get here. "Okay."

As Sam leads me from room to room, I can see how tired he looks. And he really does seem to regret what happened the last time. We're getting near the end of the tour when he points up. And those, up there? Those are called ceiling joists. They help hold up the ceiling and keep the walls from spreading apart. Think of it like a skeleton, just like you and me have."

Okay, so I act like a bit of a show-off 'cause Mr. Orbison did mention another way they get used. "So they keep the house sturdy, and we can attach things like lights. Right?"

"Excellent," Sam says absently, but he's staring at something attached to one of the joists. "What the devil is that?"

Sam might not know what he's looking at, but I totally recognize it. It's a small black cube with a lens. It's partially hidden in the shadows. Holy cow. Robbie was right. It's a camera. And it's pointing directly at the area where Tommy's body was found.

"That shouldn't be there," Sam says.

"It's a camera," I say, my voice rising with excitement. "Like a surveillance camera. Someone's been watching the construction site!"

Sam squints up at the small black device. "Are you sure?"

"Totally. It's wireless, and it records to the cloud." I point at the tiny red light blinking just above the lens. "See that? It means it's recording right now. It must be motion-activated."

Sam's weathered face wrinkles in confusion. "Well, I'll be. Who would put a camera up there? And how would it even work? Don't those things need internet or something?"

I can't help but roll my eyes a little. Adults can be so clueless about tech sometimes. "It probably connects to a hotspot or someone's phone. Maybe Tommy set it up to keep an eye on the site when he wasn't here."

"You think Tommy was recording his own job site?" Sam strokes his chin thoughtfully. "That would mean whatever happened to him might be on video somewhere."

"For sure. It would be on whatever device he had it connected to! Like his phone, or a laptop, or something, or maybe a repeater so it could record to his house!"

Sam's eyes light up. "Kid, you might be onto something here." He grabs his clipboard and tucks it under his arm. "We should go check out Tommy's place. See if we can find where the video is recording."

"Right now?" I ask, my jaw dropping just a little. Wow, he's actually taking this super serious.

"No time like the present." Sam grins, and for a second, he looks years younger. "I've heard about your sleuthing skills around town. They say you've helped crack cases that stumped even Chief Cunningham. This could be your chance to solve Tommy's murder."

My chest swells with pride, but then reality crashes back in. "Wait, we should tell Chief Cunningham what we found. He needs to know about it."

Sam waves his hand and pooh-poohs the idea. "We will, we will. But let's find the evidence first. What if someone gets to it before we do? Besides, wouldn't it be something if you were the one who cracked the case?"

I bite my lip, torn between the thrill of solving the mystery and the voice in my head that sounds suspiciously like my dad saying this is a terrible idea. "I don't know…"

"Look, we'll just take a quick peek at Tommy's place. Jake will be there, right? He can show us Tommy's laptop or whatever, then we'll go straight to the Chief with what we find. Promise." Sam holds up three fingers like he's making a scout's honor pledge.

"Well…" I hesitate, staring up at the camera. The tiny red light blinks back at me, like it's daring me to uncover its secrets.

"We'll just go find the video, then call Chief Cunningham right away," I say firmly. "No keeping secrets."

"Absolutely," Sam agrees, already heading toward the street. "We'll be heroes for finding the evidence. Your dad will be proud."

As I follow Sam outside, I can't shake this weird feeling in my stomach. Like I'm missing something important. But the chance to solve Tommy's murder and save our house is too big to pass up.

We're at Sam's truck when I decide I need to confirm what we're doing. "Just to be super clear, we find the video, then we call Chief Cunningham. Right away."

"Scout's honor," Sam repeats, opening the passenger door for me. "Now hop in. It's only going to take us a few minutes to get to Tommy's house."

"I need to put my bike away first."

"Don't worry about it. I'll put it in the back for you. You can ride back anytime."

I climb into the truck, my mind racing. I'll get to see Shadow. But, what's super important is that if Tommy was recording the site, then whoever killed him might be on video. We could solve everything today!

Still, as Sam starts the engine, I can't help but wonder why he's so eager to help.

46

Rick

THE SEASIDE COVE POLICE STATION'S interview room smelled of burnt coffee and old takeout. Rick sat opposite the steel table, watching Sylvia Archer perch on her equally uncomfortable metal chair as if it were a throne. Cardboard boxes labeled "Evidence" and "Christmas Decorations" competed for space in the cramped room. A fluorescent light buzzed overhead, casting harsh shadows across Sylvia's composed face.

"So, Ms. Archer," Adam said, placing a manila folder on the table between them. "We have testimony and documentation showing your involvement in both Tommy Granger's death and the sabotage of the Atwood property."

Sylvia smoothed her pencil skirt and tapped her manicured nails rhythmically against her knee. "This is quite the dramatic performance, Chief Cunningham. I'm almost impressed."

Rick caught Adam's eye. They'd agreed to the good cop/bad cop routine, which was more like bad cop/good consultant. After everything Sylvia had put him and this town through, he'd have been happy to play the bad cop. Unfortunately, he didn't have a badge, which made the entire argument seem somewhat academic—he couldn't be a 'bad cop' if he wasn't even a cop. "Sylvia, we have the emails. The ones where you specifically told Walt to find a way to delay my construction project."

"Emails can be fabricated," she replied with a dismissive wave. "And I'm sure my lawyer will point that out when he arrives."

Adam's jaw tightened. "Your lawyer won't be able to explain away the financial records showing payments to Walt, or your conversation with Everett, which we recorded."

"And was obtained without my consent." Sylvia's smile never wavered. "Such evidence tends to be thrown out in court."

Rick had to give Sylvia kudos for being cool under pressure, but he and Adam were only beginning. In his opinion, they needed to get Walt to fold first, then let the courts deal with Sylvia. "What about Tommy Granger? Was he just collateral damage in your development scheme?"

"I had nothing to do with that. Besides, his death occurred on your construction site, Mr. Atwood, not one of mine."

The fluorescent light buzzed, and despite the harsh surroundings, Sylvia's face remained composed as she maintained her façade of innocence.

"That's it, Ms. Archer," Adam said, his voice taking on an edge Rick rarely heard. "I'm tired of your games. Deputy Kama is preparing your transfer to San Ladron for processing right now."

Sylvia's jaw dropped, her mask of perfection suddenly cracking. "San Ladron? That's completely unnecessary. My lawyer is already on his way."

"That's unfortunate." Adam clucked a couple of times and gathered up the documents he and Rick had been referring to. "You might pass each other on the road."

Rick watched Sylvia's fingers tighten almost imperceptibly, and for the first time, a flicker of genuine concern crossed her face before she quickly masked it.

"This is outrageous," she snapped. "I've done nothing wrong."

"Save it for the jury," Adam said, nodding to Rick. "Let's go pick up Walt."

"Walt? Copley?" Sylvia blurted.

Adam left the room with Rick right behind him. As Rick closed the door, he heard Sylvia saying something about wanting to talk. Rick chuckled. It was a nice turn of events to see the master manipulator worried for a change.

As they walked out to Adam's cruiser, Rick felt a small surge of satisfaction. "You think we'll do any better with Walt?"

Adam started the engine. "Oh, yeah. Mark my words—Walt will crack like an egg."

The drive to Walt Copley's house took less than five minutes. The dilapidated Craftsman looked even more neglected in the harsh afternoon light, its peeling paint and sagging porch screaming neglect.

Walt opened the door before they could knock, his face ashen. "I've been expecting you," he said, his voice no more than a whisper on the breeze.

Rick was taken aback by Walt's appearance. The normally combative preservationist looked like he'd aged a decade overnight. His hands trembled as he gestured them inside.

"Sylvia Archer has been arrested," Adam said bluntly as they entered the cluttered living room. "She's already talking about your involvement."

Walt sank into a threadbare armchair, his weathered face crumpling. "I knew this day would come. I just never thought it would end like this."

"Like what, Walt?" Rick asked, remaining standing while Adam took a seat across from him. "With Tommy Granger dead?"

"I had nothing to do with Tommy's death!" Walt's voice rose in panic. "You have to believe me!"

"Then who did?" Adam pressed, his eyes locked on Walt's face. "Because right now, all evidence points to you and Sylvia. Maybe we'll let a jury decide which one of you is guilty."

"Too bad Sylvia can afford better lawyers than you. Right, Adam?"

"That's true. The best legal defense vs.—who will you be able to hire, Walt?"

Copley's attention flitted back and forth like a butterfly. His breaths came fast and shallow. "Sylvia told me we needed to 'deal with Tommy.' Those were her exact words. He was threatening to expose everything—the inspection reports, the bribes, all of it."

"And you took that to mean murder?" Rick snapped.

"No!" Walt's hands shook violently now. "I thought she meant paying him off, or threatening legal action. I never imagined she'd kill him."

Adam's voice hardened. "Unless you cooperate fully, you'll be charged with conspiracy to commit murder, Walt."

"Murder?" Walt's face drained of what little color remained. "No, no, that's impossible. I didn't kill anyone!"

"Walt, you should be aware by now of how this works. Rick and I have built plenty of cases where the killer claimed he was innocent. So, unless you can provide us with something helpful, I'm going to be charging you."

"I don't know!" Walt cried, his voice breaking. "I swear I don't know!"

Rick circled the room slowly, taking in the stacks of historical preservation magazines and the framed photographs of old Seaside Cove buildings. "What about the falsified inspection reports, Adam? The bribes from Sylvia? The plan to foreclose on my property? How long will Walt get for those crimes?"

"For small-scale fraud, we're looking at one to five years." Adam feigned indifference, and, only because they'd worked together so much, was Rick able to tell that his attitude was an act. Rick loved the fact that Walt had no such advantage. Adam shifted his position, resting one shoulder against the wall. "But then, this went on for a number of years, and there were multiple victims. I suspect we'll find more the deeper we dig."

"So, it could be longer." Rick watched Walt's face pale further.

"Sure. Could be five to twenty. And then there are the conspiracy charges. Those alone could get you another one to ten years, depending."

"You'd just better hope there aren't any federal charges," Rick said, crossing his arms. "Wire fraud, mail fraud—you're looking at five to thirty years."

"Please," Walt whispered, his hands trembling.

"Though," Rick said thoughtfully, "cooperation with authorities can sometimes reduce sentences."

Walt looked up, a flicker of hope in his red-rimmed eyes.

"But the deal only works if you actually tell us something useful," Adam said, his voice hardening again.

Walt seemed to shrink further into his chair. "This was all business. Just business."

"Business?" Rick couldn't keep the edge from his voice. "You were trying to steal my family's home!"

"It should have been my family's in the first place!" Walt shot back, a flash of his old defiance returning. "Your grandfather stole it from my father!"

"That's a lie, and you know it," Rick said evenly. "My grandfather bought the property fair and square. And if you had done any due diligence at all, you'd have known that."

Adam pulled out his notepad and pen. He clicked the pen once, then waited far longer than necessary before he said, "Walt, unless you cooperate, you'll never have a chance to set foot in the B&B, no matter who it belongs to. We have Tommy's records. We know about the box he gave to Willy."

At the mention of Willy, Walt's expression changed to one of confusion. "Willy? What does that crazy gravedigger have to do with this?"

"Willy is Tommy's brother," Rick said, watching Walt's reaction carefully. "Tommy trusted him with evidence against you and Sylvia."

Walt's jaw went slack. "Brother? I had no idea."

"You threatened Willy at the cemetery," Adam continued. "Said he'd end up like Tommy if he didn't keep quiet."

"I was angry!" Walt protested. "Tommy had been blackmailing me for months! He said he had proof that would ruin me if I didn't help him get more contracts. When I saw Willy at the cemetery later that day, I thought maybe they were working together."

"Tommy was blackmailing you?" Adam demanded.

"Granger somehow got hold of documents proving I'd falsified inspection reports on multiple properties. He wanted a cut of what Sylvia was paying me, plus referrals so he could build his business."

"And that's why you agreed to sabotage my construction project?" Rick asked.

"I was trapped," Walt whispered, tears forming in his rheumy eyes. "My wife's medical bills, the mortgage—I was buried in debt. Sylvia offered me a way out. All I had to do was find reasons to help her move certain projects along. In your case, she needed the property where you're building for what she called her signature development."

Adam held the pen up, clicked it once, and stared at Walt.

"Am I under arrest?" Walt whimpered.

"Depends. Did you do anything that might have caused Tommy's death at the construction site?"

"No!" Walt's snapped. "I would never! I'm not a killer!"

The man looked genuinely terrified, but was it fear of being caught or fear of being brought to trial? "If not you, then who?" Rick asked.

Walt wiped at his eyes with a trembling hand. "I don't know. Maybe Sylvia hired someone. She has connections I can't even imagine."

Adam stood, his expression grim. "Walt Copley, you're under arrest for conspiracy to commit fraud, accepting bribes, and falsifying public records."

"But not murder?" Walt asked, his voice small.

"That depends on what else we find," Adam said, pulling out his handcuffs.

As Adam read Walt his rights, Rick watched the old man's shoulders slump in defeat. For all his bluster and schemes, Walt Copley was just a desperate old man who'd made terrible choices.

"One more thing, Walt," Rick said as Adam finished. "Did you ransack the records room at Town Hall?"

Walt looked up, genuine confusion in his eyes. "What? No. The file cabinets were already toppled over when I walked in. Looked like a hurricane had come through, so I turned around and high-tailed it out before anyone saw me."

As Adam led Walt to the cruiser, Rick felt his phone vibrate. He checked, saw it was a call from Marquetta, and answered. "What's up?"

"Rick, get home right away! Alex is missing!"

47

Alex

I DEBATE TEXTING MY DAD to tell him where I am, but something stops me. If I tell him I'm with Sam Greer at Tommy Granger's house, he'll totally flip. Besides, we'll be quick—find the video, call Chief Cunningham, be heroes. Simple. And this way, I'll also get to see Shadow.

"You coming?" Sam's already halfway up the cracked walkway.

The front door opens before we even knock. Jake stands there, his hair sticking up like he just rolled out of bed, even though it's afternoon. His eyes are all red and tired-looking, and he's wearing the same wrinkled flannel shirt I saw him in yesterday. He looks super confused. Then his eyes land on me.

"Mr. Greer? Alex? What are you guys doing here?"

"We found something at the construction site," I say, bouncing on my toes with excitement. "A camera! It was recording everything!"

Jake's face does this weird thing where it goes pale and then flushed all at once. "A camera? I don't understand. What do you mean?"

"Can we come in?" Sam asks, already stepping forward.

Jake hesitates, then steps back. "It's kind of a mess."

Talk about the understatement of the century. The room looks like a beer factory that got hit by a wrecking ball in the middle of a renovation. Blueprints cover every surface. Some are rolled up, others are spread out and held down by empty bottles. Tommy's clothes are draped over chairs, and there's a stack of pizza boxes that looks like it might topple any second. And outside, I can hear Shadow howling. He sounds so sad.

"Sorry," Jake mumbles, kicking aside some papers to clear a path. "Haven't really felt like picking up, you know?"

"No worries, kid," Sam says, his eyes scanning the room. "We're looking for a laptop or a phone. That right, Alex?" Without waiting for an answer or asking for permission, Sam pushes past Jake and heads for the bedrooms. "You don't mind, do you?" he asks, but he's already halfway down the hall.

Jake's still looking like he doesn't understand why we're here, so I explain that we think the camera went to a cloud account. "Well, that's not a hundred percent true. I'm the one who thinks it went to the cloud. Sam still doesn't understand where the clouds are."

"Oh," Jake says, still looking overwhelmed at the idea of two people barging into his house. He scratches his head. "So you think Uncle Tommy had what? Like an account on his laptop?"

"Maybe."

"Okay, so why's this important again?"

I step carefully around a pair of work boots that are flopped over on their sides in the middle of the floor. "The camera was pointed right where they found your uncle's body. It's gotta be motion-activated, so it would've recorded what happened to your uncle."

Jake nods his head a couple times and croaks, "We'd see who killed him."

"Exactly." The air in the room suddenly feels heavy, like we're both holding our breath. Through the grimy window, I can see dark clouds gathering. It matches the knot forming in my stomach. "How's Shadow?" I ask, but I know the answer. He's lonely. I can hear him in the backyard.

"Did your uncle have an office, kid?" Sam's standing in the doorway. He doesn't look happy at all.

"Uncle Tommy mostly worked out here. His laptop's over there," Jake says, then moves toward a cluttered desk in the corner. "He was always on it, especially these last few weeks."

Sam doesn't waste a second. He's already at the desk, throwing papers everywhere as he looks for the laptop. When he finds it, he lets out a little yip.

What I don't get is why he wants to find that video so bad. My mouth goes dry because I can only think of one reason he'd want to find it before the cops.

"Let's see what we got here." He holds up the laptop and looks at me. "Come on, Alex, you're the computer whiz, right?"

"You're gonna need a password, Mr. Greer." I need to buy time. And get a message to Chief Cunningham. Out back, Shadow's barking and howling are getting more frantic. He's scratching at the back door.

"Stupid dog," Jake mutters. "I'll be glad when he's gone."

He starts towards the back door, but stops when Mr. Greer asks him if he knows the password for the computer.

"Uh, no. I got no idea what it is." Jake looks down at the floor. "I suppose if Uncle Tommy wrote it down, it might be in those papers you were throwing around."

Mr. Greer looks pretty ticked off as he tells Jake to help him look for the password. While they're doing that, I walk over to a framed photo on the end table. In the photo, Tommy has his arm around a much younger Jake. They're both grinning in front of a half-built house and looking so happy. I pick up the photo and look at the back of it and my breath catches.

Scrawled across the back on a pale blue removable note are two words separated by a dash. *Shadow-Whistle.*

"Could this be it?" Jake holds up a sticky note.

Sam reaches for it. "Let me see that—"

"Wait." I put down the photo and step between them. "We should call Chief Cunningham first. That's evidence."

Sam's smile tightens. "Of course, but let's just make sure the video's actually there before we bother the Chief."

I take the laptop from Sam, my fingers suddenly feeling clumsy and sweaty. Something about the way he's hovering over me reminds me of a vulture circling its prey. The house feels smaller now, like the walls are inching closer with every second.

"I'll try it," I say, typing in the string of letters and numbers from the sticky note. Both of them are watching me super close, so there's no way I can change it. Whatever's on this computer, Sam wants it bad. Too bad. My heart nearly stops when the password actually works.

"Alright. Now, where's this cloud thing you were talking about, kid?"

Shadow's barking gets even more frantic outside, and a crash of thunder makes all three of us jump. Perfect horror movie weather. Just what I need.

"I might know," Jake says, reaching for the laptop.

I clutch it tighter. "Let's wait for Chief Cunningham. He could send it to the sheriff and have, like, tech people who can check it out without erasing stuff."

Sam's face does this weird twitchy thing. "We don't need to waste police resources on something so simple."

"But what if we mess something up?" I look at Jake, silently begging for backup. "Right, Jake?"

Jake shifts uncomfortably. "Nah. I think Mr. Greer's right. I'm finally thinking I might get some closure on this."

"Gimme that thing, kid," Sam says, his voice suddenly honey-sweet, which is totally creepy.

I reluctantly hand over the laptop, but step closer to Jake. "Hey, can I see Shadow while Mr. Greer works on this? I really miss him."

"Uh, sure," Jake says, looking confused but grateful for the distraction.

"Don't go far," Sam warns without looking up from the keyboard. His fingers are pounding the keys like they personally offended him. It's almost like he knows more about computers than he let on.

As Jake leads me toward the back door, I whisper, "Do you have your phone?"

He nods slightly.

"Cool. Mine's dead," I lie. "Can I borrow it to call my dad? He'll freak if he doesn't know where I am."

Jake hands me his phone as we step onto the back porch. Shadow immediately bounds toward me, his whole body wiggling with joy. I kneel down to pet him, and he practically knocks me over. And that's when I see the small metal whistle attached to his collar. The thing is, it's kinda big for a dog whistle—unless it's not.

Shadow-Whistle. It wasn't a password. It was a hiding place!

I quickly type out a text to Chief Cunningham: "At Tommy Granger's house with Sam Greer. He's acting super weird about Tommy's laptop. Come NOW."

As I hit send, I hear Sam cursing from inside. "Kid! Get back in here!"

48

Rick

RICK FROZE WITH ONE HAND on the door handle of Adam's cruiser and the other pressing his phone to his ear. "What do you mean, missing?"

"The Aldridges were checking out and mentioned seeing her bike next door at the construction site," Marquetta's voice wavered. "They wanted me to know that there was an old pickup truck there, too. I thought she might have just forgotten to put it away and was going to chew her out, so I went upstairs, but she wasn't in her room. Then, Robbie and Sasha showed up and said she'd texted them to meet at the new house. I went over there, and her bike and the pickup were gone. Rick, there's something else that's strange. Everything at the new house has been organized."

How many times had he been down this road? Every time Alex went missing, his mind raced through the possibilities. And every time, each option became worse than the last. Adam was already watching him, the stern expression he'd used on Copley now replaced by concern. Rick covered the phone with his hand. "Alex is missing. I need to get back to the B&B."

Adam nodded immediately. "Let's go."

"Marquetta, we're on our way. Ten minutes, tops."

"Hurry," Marquetta whispered.

The drive back felt excruciatingly slow despite Adam's lead foot. Rick drummed his fingers against his knee, staring out the window. In the back of the vehicle, Walt Copley grumbled about being taken on a wild ride.

Rick turned in his seat and snapped, "Shut up, Copley."

"Rick, calm down. She's probably fine," Adam said, his tone reassuring. "Your daughter's got more sense than most adults I know."

Rick didn't miss the fact that Adam had been looking in his rearview mirror when he'd made the comment. "Most of the time, I'd agree with you, but when she's playing detective, all bets are off," Rick muttered. "With everything that's happened—Sylvia, Walt, Tommy's murder—what if she stumbled onto something?"

"Long as she's not trying to blame me for something else," Walt said with a bit of a snicker.

"Shut up, Copley," both Rick and Adam barked at the same time.

Adam's cruiser skidded to a stop in front of the B&B. Marquetta was already waiting on the porch, Baby Jack balanced on her hip.

"Any word?" Rick asked, jogging up the steps.

Apparently happy to see his dad, Baby Jack grabbed Rick's ear with surprising strength.

"Ow! Not now, buddy."

"Sorry," Marquetta said, detaching the baby's grip. "He's been grabby all morning."

The front porch of the B&B felt unusually claustrophobic despite its openness. Rick scanned the property, hoping for any sign of his daughter. A chill ran down his spine, and it had nothing to do with the breeze coming off the ocean.

Adam's footsteps caused Rick to turn around. Adam was carrying his phone in one hand and had a worried look on his face. Rick considered suggesting Adam leave him behind because he had to search for Alex, but was waved off.

"Rick, we need to go." Adam held out his phone. "Read this."

Rick's heart hammered in his chest as he read the message and the number it had come from. "Whose number is that?"

"Jake Morales," Adam said.

"What is she doing sending a message with his phone? And why is she at Granger's place?" He turned to Marquetta. "Did she tell you she was going there?"

Marquetta's voice shook as she spoke. "No. And Rick, based on the description the Aldridges gave me, the pickup might have been Sam Greer's. That would explain why everything next door is so organized. Sam was always a fanatic about job sites being kept tidy."

"Why would Greer have been here?" Adam was already moving toward the cruiser. "Rick, hurry up. We'll sort this out on the way."

Marquetta grabbed Rick's arm, her fingers digging into his sleeve. "Go. I'll call if she comes back."

"She won't," Rick said grimly. "She's found something at Tommy's house. Something important enough to make her text Adam instead of me."

"Which means she knows she's in trouble," Marquetta said, her eyes wide with fear. Baby Jack grabbed fruitlessly for another shot at Rick's ear, but Marquetta kept him away. "Be careful."

"I will," Rick said as he rushed down the steps and hopped into the front seat of Adam's cruiser.

The ten-minute drive to Tommy's house was the longest ten minutes Rick had ever felt. Even though Adam's speedometer showed they were well above the limit, Rick wished Adam could drive faster. If Alex truly was in danger, then every second counted. Somehow, even Walt got the message—this could be a matter of life. For the rest of the trip, he sat sullen in the back seat, handcuffed and, finally, silent.

"You think Greer's involved?" Adam asked, taking a corner so sharply that Rick had to brace himself against the dashboard.

"I talked to him at our construction site and told him I would consider hiring him to finish the job. Marquetta's right. He has to be the one who straightened up over there. What I don't understand is what he has to do with any of this. Unless maybe this all goes back to Powell Finnegan's job?"

"Would make sense if you're right about Granger working for Greer back then."

"Tommy made sure Greer and Finnegan took the fall for the fire," Walt said from the backseat. "Tommy became Greer's biggest competitor. He was always underbidding him. And after Finnegan, nobody would even hire Sam."

Rick twisted in his seat so he could look Copley in the eye. "What else do you know about him?"

"I know those two hated each other after that. If you ask me, Greer might have killed Tommy to get rid of him."

Adam's cruiser screeched to a halt in front of Tommy's house. A battered pickup truck was parked haphazardly in the street.

“That’s Greer’s truck,” Adam said, reaching for his sidearm. “Stay behind me.”

They had barely stepped out of the cruiser when the unmistakable sound of a gunshot shattered the stillness.

Rick shoved Adam aside and ran toward the house.

“Alex!”

49

Alex

I GRIP SHADOW'S FUR TIGHT as my heart pounds against my ribs. Sam's hand is shaking, the gun he's pressing against Jake's back looking way scarier in real life than it does in movies. Next to me, Shadow senses the danger. A low growl coming from deep inside him rumbles in my ear.

"Where'd you get that?" My voice comes out squeaky and thin.

Sam waves the gun in something resembling a circle. "Found it in Tommy's drawer. Convenient, huh?" The muscles in his jaw are flexing like he's super angry or worried. "Now get in here and shut up."

Jake goes ahead of me, and Greer follows us. When we sit on the couch, the springs creak. Outside, Shadow's barking in a full-on frenzy, like he's trying to tear the door down.

"That stupid mutt. Someone's gonna call the cops if he doesn't shut up." Sam turns toward the door like he can't decide whether to deal with Shadow or us, but he seems to be stuck in place—and that's what's got me worried. He's getting desperate and might do something stupid.

"He knows something's wrong," I say, trying to sound braver than I feel. "Dogs can sense that stuff."

Sam snorts. "What they sense is dinner time. Jake, go shut him up."

But Jake doesn't move. His eyes are super wide, and he doesn't look depressed anymore. Now he looks like he's gonna pee his pants. I need to buy us some time. But how?

"So what's your plan here?" I ask, trying to sound casual. "Like, are you gonna hold us hostage forever? And how come you killed Tommy Granger?"

Sam's eyes narrow. "Shut up, kid. I gotta think." He starts pacing the small living room, waving the gun with each step.

"You were a big deal in construction, right?"

"Of course, I was! I had a deal with Sylvia until Tommy Granger came along. I had all the construction contracts in Seaside Cove. And then that old fool Finnegan just had to do his own wiring."

Jake looks sideways at me, and I tell him how Finnegan's house burned down, and how Mr. Greer got blamed for it.

"That's right! Sylvia didn't like Finnegan being so picky about every little thing. Then, he decided he wanted to cut out part of her profit by doing his own wiring, so she had Granger change it. Tommy always said it was only supposed to be so we'd have to fix Finnegan's screwup, but something went wrong. After the fire, she had Walt doctor the inspection reports and testify at the hearing. The way they manipulated everything, I took the fall for something I had nothing to do with."

"So you killed Jake's uncle because of an old grudge?" The words slip out before I can stop them.

Sam's face turns an ugly shade of red. "I didn't mean to! He was supposed to trip, get scared enough to back off. But he hit his head wrong."

The room suddenly feels like it's spinning. I grip the edge of the couch to steady myself.

"That's why you want the video," I say slowly. "You're on it."

"Give the kid a prize." Sam's laugh is hollow. "Once I delete the video, the evidence will be gone."

A crash from outside makes us both jump. Jake yells something I can't make out, followed by more frantic barking.

Sam's face goes red. He's gone over the edge, and he's gonna do anything he can to get out of this. "Enough! Jake! Shut that dog up or I will. And if you do anything stupid, she dies."

He jabs the gun at me a couple times, and each time it makes my skin crawl. Does he even know how to use it? How not to? He might even kill me by accident.

"Okay, okay," Jake stammers. "Just don't do nothing stupid." He stands when Sam motions with the gun for him to move, then reluctantly heads to the back door. I notice the laptop is still sitting open on the coffee table. If I could get to it.

"I already texted Chief Cunningham, Mr. Greer. He's probably, like, two minutes away."

Sam's face goes pale, but he shakes his head. "No. You're lying."

"Am I?" I put on what my dad calls a poker face. The only one who can see through it is Mom. "Why do you think Shadow's going crazy? He hears the sirens."

"Shut up! Shut up!" Sam puts his hands over his ears like he's trying to block out the sirens that aren't even there.

There's another loud crash at the back of the house, followed by Jake screaming. Two seconds later, Shadow bursts in like a black tornado. He's all teeth and fury.

Sam tries to turn toward Shadow, but it's too late. Shadow's already on top of him. The gun goes off as he falls over backwards, screaming like he thinks he's gonna die. Thank goodness Shadow doesn't bite him. He just pins Sam down, his massive paws on Sam's chest, his teeth bared inches from Sam's face.

"Call 911!" I gasp, but then I hear my dad calling my name, and he bursts through the front door.

Jake's face goes through like five emotions at once as he stumbles into the room. He stands there like a statue staring at Shadow, who's got Sam pinned to the floor.

"Get him off me!" Sam yells.

I sink back onto the couch, suddenly exhausted. By then, Chief Cunningham joins us. He's got his gun drawn, but it doesn't look like he knows what to do with it. All the while, Shadow keeps Sam pinned, growling whenever Sam tries to move.

"Good boy," I whisper, tears pricking my eyes. "Best. Boy. Ever."

50

Alex

November 24

Hey Journal,

OMG! Can you believe it's been a week since I figured out who killed Tommy Granger? Crazy, right? Chief Cunningham came by today to thank me again for finding the password to Tommy's video account in Shadow's dog whistle. He said the Sheriff finished reviewing the video, and it showed the accident, just like Sam Greer was afraid it would. Chief Cunningham said they're gonna bring charges, but don't know which ones yet.

Oh, and get this—Sam Greer is also going to get a lighter sentence because he's testifying against Sylvia. Grumpy Walt Copley is, too. Honestly, I don't think Sam Greer will ever work in Seaside Cove again. No one's going to hire him after this.

We also have a new contractor! Yay! Dad hired Matteo to finish the house today. Matteo decided that since there were no other general contractors left in town, he'd restart his business. It's kinda sad news, too. We're gonna be losing Matteo as our handyman. Bummer. But that's okay. I'm happy he gets back to building stuff, cause that's what he loves doing most.

We also finally got all the files back in place at Town Hall! Mr. Carmichael has been running the whole volunteer effort to fix the shelves and organize everything. A bunch of kids from my class helped out for extra credit, and Robbie and Sasha pitched in, too.

But the best news? Shadow is officially MINE now! We got all the paperwork done today. After my dad learned how Shadow saved me from getting shot, he said, "To hell with the no-pet rule. We're keeping that dog." How awesome is that?

Shadow's basically my shadow now (ha ha, see what I did there?). He's my foot warmer, my protector, and my best buddy. I think he still misses Tommy sometimes, but we're pretty much inseparable. Mom keeps him in line most of the time, and he's so sweet with Baby Jack. Shadow has escaped a couple of times to meet me after school, which is kind of adorable. Robbie and Sasha are obsessed with him now, too. But the best part? Billy Thornton hasn't said boo to me since he found out what Shadow did to Mr. Greer.

Life is pretty great right now.

xoxo,

Alex

www.ingramcontent.com/pod-product-compliance
Lightning Source LLC
LaVergne TN
LVHW100513110826
845146LV00002B/623
* 9 7 9 8 9 9 0 0 4 5 7 2 9 *